Dear Reader,

Firstly may I thank you for all your letters and the questionnaires you have returned? If you haven't yet completed a questionnaire, we'd be delighted if you could fill in the form at the back of this book and let us have it back. It is only by hearing from you that we can continue to provide the type of *Scarlet* books you want to read.

Perhaps you'd like to know how we go about finding four new books for you each month? Well, when we decided to launch *Scarlet* we 'advertised' for authors through writers' organizations, magazines, literary agents and so on. As a result, we are delighted to have been inundated with manuscripts – particularly from the UK and North America. Now, of course, some of these books have to be returned to their authors because they just aren't right for *your* list. But others, submitted either by authors who've already had books published or by brand new writers, are exactly what we know readers are looking for. Sometimes, the book is almost perfect when it arrives on my desk, but usually we enjoy working closely with the author to give their book that essential, final polish.

What you'll notice over the coming months are more books from authors who've already appeared in *Scarlet*. Do let me know, won't you, if there's a particular author we've featured who *you'd* like to see again? See you next month and, in the meantime, thank you for continuing to be a *Scarlet* woman.

Best wishes,

Sally Cooper

SALLY COOPER
Editor-in-Chief – S

About the Author

When she was at school, **Julie Garratt** always came top of the class for writing stories! In the early 90s Julie gained a City and Guilds qualification enabling her to teach creative writing and has since often been employed by Derbyshire Council to take courses in the county.

Julie is the author of three published romance novels and claims that her holidays serve a dual purpose: 'holiday *and* research trip!' She is married with two grown up children and lives at the top of a steep hill, which overlooks a valley dividing Nottinghamshire and Derbyshire. Her hobbies include photography, driving, antique book fairs and music. Julie also has a much loved garden where she can 'sit under the trees to write my novels . . . or play with my dog!'

*Other **Scarlet** titles available this month:*

CARIBBEAN FLAME by Maxine Barry
WIVES, FRIENDS AND LOVERS by Jean Saunders
UNDERCOVER LOVER by Sally Steward

JULIE GARRATT

THE MARRIAGE SOLUTION

Enquiries to:
Robinson Publishing Ltd
7 Kensington Church Court
London W8 4SP

First published in the UK by Scarlet, 1996

A copy of the British Library Cataloguing in
Publication data is available from the British Library

ISBN 1-85487-498-5

Printed and bound in the EC

10 9 8 7 6 5 4 3 2 1

CHAPTER 1

The letter from England arrived in Boston exactly twenty-four hours after Paisley Junior's principal had offered Amy the teaching job she'd set her heart on.

'Oh, no!'

'What is it, honey?'

Amy pushed the pale blue notepaper across the breakfast bar to Kate Weldon, the Titian-haired American who twelve years ago had become her adoptive mother. 'Read it, Kate.' Amy almost choked on the words. 'It couldn't have come at a worse time.'

'It's from Lizzie Abercrombie – brother-in-law Gif's housekeeper.' Kate pulled a sour face, then quickly scanned the contents of the letter, sucking in her breath as she came to the end and groaning, 'You bet your sweet life it couldn't have come at a worse time. What're you going to do, kiddo?'

'Lizzie says Uncle Gif's really bad this time.'

'It's only bronchitis, though.' Kate Weldon made a sweeping gesture with one hand. 'Marty says his brother suffers from it every winter. I guess it must be all that cold and damp they get in the Derbyshire hills.'

'All the same, Uncle Gif must be pretty bad for Lizzie to write and tell me.'

3

'*And* to ask you to go all the way across the Atlantic and visit the crusty old devil in his castle.'

'I'd hate to think it was anything serious, though – and he's not really an old devil, Kate, he's just a mite tetchy at times.'

'That's putting it mildly.' Kate gave a bellow of laughter. 'I tell you this for nothin', Amy, "tetchy" wasn't in it thirty-odd years ago when he learned his kid brother was about to throw his life away on little old me! You should have seen the letter he sent Marty. Told him he'd disown and disinherit him if he turned his back on England and his family – meaning *him*, the old miser. Honestly, it'd make your hair curl, sweetie – not that you need it, that blonde mop looks great as it is – but you know what I mean.'

'But he couldn't have been all that bitter about you. He did, after all, send me out to live with you and Marty when my parents died.'

'He did that, I suspect, because he didn't want the hassle of bringing up a kid – and a girl at that – by himself.'

Amy grinned, knowing that despite the thirty years' difference in their ages she and Kate were more like sisters than mother and daughter. Kate was fifty-four but only admitted to being forty-nine. She'd been forty-nine for the past five years, resolutely refusing to age past fifty.

'Well?' Kate reached for her cigarettes. 'Aren't you going to say something? Bite my head off for slagging him off, huh?'

'What're you getting nervous about, Kate?' Amy teased, knowing Kate's utter dependence on cigarettes in a crisis.

Kate lit up, and, tilting her head back so her mass of attractive hair swung to one side and nestled comfortably against one shoulder, blew smoke into the air, watching it

4

spiral away before saying, 'Who says I'm nervous? Just 'cause I fancy my early morning fix of tobacco don't mean I'm nervous.'

'You should cut down on the smokes. Marty will kill you if he finds out you haven't given them up when you gave him your solemn promise that you would.'

'Ain't nothin' solemn about me, honey – not even my promises. And Marty knows that. If he don't, he should. He's been married to me long enough to find out. Anyway, Marty's not here at the minute, and a squirt of wax around the furniture will kill the smell of smoke. If I didn't have a ciggie, I'd be on the candy – then I'd get fat. What Marty don't see, he don't grieve about.'

Amy laughed softly. 'You sound just like Uncle Gif's housekeeper. I remember Lizzie was always saying things like that when I lived at Wydale for a few months before coming to you.'

'*Before* Gif Weldon got rid of you? *Before* he sent you to live with Marty and me in the States, you mean?' Kate asked pointedly.

'You make it sound like Uncle Gif sold me into slavery.'

'He didn't know what *I* was like, did he? He'd never met *me*. Still hasn't! Wouldn't ever invite me to England to see his bleak, cold castle in the Derbyshire Highlands.'

'I think it's called the Derbyshire Peak District – not the Highlands,' Amy said, chuckling. 'The Highlands are in Scotland.'

'It's England, ain't it, honey? And England's just a teeny little squiggle on the map. Highlands, Peaklands – what's the difference?'

Amy gulped down her morning fruit juice then rested her arms and elbows on the wipe-clean kitchen bar-top. 'Did you *never* meet Uncle Gif, then, Kate?' she asked.

5

'Not me, honey. I got to know my Marty when he came to the States on some hospital exchange thing way back in the sixties. He told me his brother went wild at him when he told him he was going to marry this red-headed little gal from the US of A, and make his home here in Boston with her.'

'But Uncle Gif still writes to Marty, doesn't he?'

'Never mentions *me*, though.' Kate Weldon wrinkled her nose in disgust. 'Believe me, hon – Gifford Weldon is one mean old man. I don't like speaking bad of anybody, you know that, but that man just riles me something awful. Maybe it's as well if I don't ever meet him. I'd probably bop him one for the way he treated Marty.'

'He can't hate either of you, though, can he? After all, he did agree to you adopting me.'

'Like we've told you before, sweetie-pie, Gif didn't have the faintest idea of how to bring up a kid. He probably didn't want his castle looking untidy.'

'Wydale Hall isn't really a castle. It's quite big, and it's made of stone, and it was a cold, draughty old place when I was there, but I don't remember it being at all luxurious – not like the Queen's castles at Windsor and Balmoral.'

'You were only there for a few months, though. Just long enough for Gif to sort things out and then parcel you up and send you out to us.'

'I suppose it would have been difficult for Uncle Gif to look after me – him being a surgeon and living most of the time in London.' Amy felt she had to say something in support of her guardian's actions, even though for years past now she'd often wondered why Gif Weldon had rejected her. Her parents had, after all, left her in *his* charge. And, while it was true he was no blood relation, she'd called him Uncle Gif since she'd been a toddler.

6

Gif Weldon and her father had been fellow surgeons, and good friends too. And she supposed it was only natural that when she'd been christened, Uncle Gif – and his then wife Barbara – should have been appointed her godparents. Amy couldn't remember Gif's wife. She only knew from an old Christening card that Barbara Weldon *was* her godmother because her name was on it. When she'd been five or six years old she'd asked her mother about Uncle Gif's wife, but the reply had been vaguely non-committal, she remembered – something about Auntie Barbara having to go back to Scotland from where she'd originated.'

'But why, Mummy?' she'd asked.

'It's not really our business, darling. It's something between Uncle Gif and Auntie Barbara. We don't have to ask too many questions, do we?'

It hadn't been important to Amy; she'd just been curious. She'd never known Barbara Weldon so she hadn't pursued the matter, she'd just forgotten all about her. It was only years later, just after she'd been orphaned, that she'd remembered Barbara Weldon again as she'd stood in front of the huge marble fireplace at Wydale Hall and stared up at the oil painting.

Barbara Weldon's portrait depicted a dark-haired, dark-eyed beauty, dressed in a black velvet gown, against a backdrop of moorland and purple heather. To Amy, at an impressionable age and an ardent reader of the Brontës, the girl in the picture was Heathcliff's Cathy, straight out of *Wuthering Heights* – and yet again, when looked at in a different light, she might have been Rochester's wife, the mad woman, from *Jane Eyre*, she'd decided. Ever afterwards, in the few months she'd spent at Wydale Hall, Amy had lain in bed and listened to every creak and groan of the old house, and had dived under the sheets when the wind

7

moaned around the turrets so that the ghost of Barbara Weldon wouldn't find her.

Wydale had been no more than a stepping-stone for Amy. She'd no sooner settled in than Uncle Gif had told her he was sending her to New England in America to stay 'for a while' with his younger brother Martyn, who was married to an American girl. They had a boy, he'd told her, a lad called Kip, who would be company for her. On arrival in the States, however, Amy had found out that Kip was going on eighteen – almost a man – so she'd figured he'd hardly want to be lumbered with a girl just entering her teens . . .

She was jerked back to the present by Kate saying, 'Gif Weldon saw a way out of a difficult situation, honey. Don't get me wrong, though – you know we loved you from the minute we set eyes on you. And Kip . . .'

Amy saw the tell-tale trembling of Kate's lips. 'Kip adored having a kid sister,' Amy said softly. 'And the kid-sister adored him.'

Kate drew deeply on her cigarette again, then blew the smoke out slowly. She gazed at Amy through half-closed eyes and said in a tight whisper, 'I can't believe he's really gone, you know. I don't think I'll ever take it in.'

'Kate . . . don't . . .' Amy reached out over the breakfast bar and her fingers closed round Kate's thin wrist.

Kate Weldon's head jerked forward. 'Do you think I'm crazy, honey?'

'No . . . No . . . But it's been such a long time . . .'

'Two and a half years since they sent him to England. Two and a half years since I last saw my boy. And now Gif Weldon wants *you* to go back there. Isn't it enough – losing one kid?'

'Nothing will happen to me, Kate.'

8

'Kip never thought anything would happen to him, Sugar-bush!'

Amy felt close to tears. 'It's a long time since you called me that.'

'I'll lose you sure as I lost my boy if you go to that God-forsaken little island, girl.'

Amy's heart twisted inside her. 'No, Kate,' she whispered. 'You won't lose me. I'll come back. I promise I'll come back.'

'Kip should have come back. Kip shouldn't have finished up in some deep, dark river over there. What was the blessed Army doing anyway – letting boys like that go driving in the dead of night? A sixteen-ton transporter! I ask you – do they have roads in England that can carry sixteen-ton transporters at the side of rivers?'

Amy shook her head, trying not to think of what had happened to Kip. 'I don't know, Kate. There just isn't a clear-cut answer, is there? They said it was pure chance that the accident occurred just at the point where the road bridge crossed the river.'

'Pure chance too that it was a lousy English night, with sleety rain and gales and ice on the roads. I blame the US Army for sending them lads out in that lot.'

'But it does rain in England, Kate . . . quite a lot – just as it does here in America. We get dreadful winters in Boston sometimes. It could just as easily have happened here.'

Kate pulled her arm away from Amy and threw her hands in the air, scattering cigarette ash all over the wipe-clean counter. 'England sure must be a lousy country, though, having sleet and gales and ice all at the same time.'

Amy slid down from her high stool and went round to the other side of the breakfast bar.

9

'I don't need no comforting, girl.' Kate dragged on her cigarette again.

'I wasn't going to get all mushy,' Amy replied. 'I was just going to get something to wipe the top over.'

'Houseproud, are we now?' Kate was forcing her way out of a bad bout of depression, Amy realized. She knew it had hit her hard – the accident in which Kip had been flung into that fast-flowing river in Lincolnshire, England. Harder for Amy to bear had been the fact that his body had never been recovered. And Kate and Marty had never realized how much she had loved Kip herself.

Had loved?

As Amy wiped away the cigarette ash she knew with a shock that this was the first time ever since the accident that she had thought of her love for Kip as being in the past tense. Like Kate, she supposed, for two years she had expected him to turn up, or for the US Army to contact them and say there'd been a mistake, that Kip wasn't dead. But two years was a long time to keep on hoping. Too long to go on believing Kip could have survived – somewhere! If there'd been a body, maybe Kate and Marty could have grieved properly for their son. As it was, though . . .

'It wouldn't have been so bad if we could have traced the girl he'd gotten pregnant.' Kate stubbed out her cigarette and took another one from the packet.

Amy sighed as Kate's lighter flared briefly.

'No good sighing, kiddo. If I want to fog up my lungs, I'll do it.'

'You'd be better off with candy and getting fat.' Amy dropped the wad of paper towelling she'd been using into the kitchen trash-can, then stood, hands pushed into the pockets of her jeans, watching the older woman.

10

'We don't even know her real name, so there's no way of tracing her,' Amy said.

'Kitty! What the hell kinda name is that? He was thinking of marrying her, and all we know is her damned name's Kitty.'

Kip and Kitty! Amy still couldn't think about Kip and another girl without a kind of hatred flaring, tearing her apart. And it was so stupid, she reasoned, because neither of them had got him now. He was somewhere down at the bottom of a deep river – either that or he had been washed out to sea when the tide had turned. That was the obvious, of course. Kip's Lieutenant Colonel had written in person and said so. The letter had been brief: '. . . divers called in . . . wreckage of transporter located . . . three bodies recovered . . .' But four men had gone into the river with the transporter . . .

'I don't suppose it's any good me going down on my knees and pleading with you not to go tearing off to England, is it?'

Amy stared across the room at Kate. 'What makes you think I've decided to go?' She lifted her shoulders in a kind of helpless shrug. 'What good can I do for Uncle Gif?'

'That Abercrombie woman reckons he wants to have you there with him for a while. And I know you, my girl, you never let anybody down without good reason. If the old fella wants you, I reckon you'll go to him. Am I right?'

'Kate!' Amy dragged her hands out of her pockets and held them out helplessly. 'Kate – what shall I do? I'm just about to start a job I know I'll love – working with those kids at Paisley Junior – and this happens.' She looked down at the floor, then tossed her head up again and ran

11

the fingers of one hand through her thick fair hair. 'Heck! This is a mess.'

'I'll miss you, honey!'

Amy felt suddenly rebellious. 'I don't *have* to go.'

'Yes, you do.' Kate stubbed her cigarette out with a viciousness not normal for her. She swung off the bar stool and strode across the room to take Amy's shoulders in her hands and shake them thoroughly. 'He's an old man, for God's sake. And I'm a selfish bitch who can't get rid of a thirty-year grudge. I ought to be ashamed of myself, so I did.'

Amy placed her hands on Kate's shoulders too. The two women looked into each other's eyes. Amy saw a trim, slim, truly American mother in front of her. 'I shall come back,' she said softly. 'I told you, Kate – I *shall* come back.'

'It's a crazy world,' Kate said. 'Just when you think you've got it all worked out, it goes mad on you.'

'But I *shall* come back.'

'Yeah. You do that, honey. We'll be waiting – Marty and me. But do something for me, kiddo?'

'Anything, Kate.'

'Try and find that Kitty – and the kid she was expecting, will you?' A tear glistened in Kate's eyes. She dashed it away and grunted, 'Aw! Hark at me. What right have I got to be having these longings? My hormones must be going to pot.'

'Longings, Kate?' Amy asked with a grin.

'Longings! Yeah! I get longings. I'm crazy. But I've lost my son, and somewhere, thousands of miles away, there's a bit of him left. That Kitty was carrying my grandchild, honeybunch, a kid who must be going on for two years old now. And this longing to be a granny just won't go away –

12

so find her for me, kiddo. Promise me you'll do that? Find Kitty, and the baby, and then maybe my Kip will stop haunting me.'

John Graham, Gifford Weldon's chauffeur, recognized the girl instantly. Her pale head was tilted arrogantly, her grey gaze straight and true. Old man Weldon had given him a photograph so he'd know her. The airport foyer was crowded, but she stood out from the rest – elegant, self-assured. The December day was cold and unwelcoming, but he could tell she didn't care about the weather. Her cashmere suit under a three-quarter-length camel jacket was expensive but casual. Brown wasn't a colour he'd been expecting her to wear; in the photo she'd got a blue T-shirt on and so – idiotically, he realized – he'd been looking out for a kid in a blue T-shirt coming off the plane.

She was no kid, though. And as her eyes alighted on him it was as though the cold December day turned to summer for him. She strode towards him.

'Welcome home, Miss Weldon . . .' The words choked him. He was a man who'd always prided himself on not being a hypocrite, so how in the world could he actually fix that smile on his face and greet her in such a manner? he wondered. Welcome home, indeed. If he'd got anything about him, he'd tell her to turn right round and go back to New England. In his heart, though, he knew that even if he did that she wouldn't heed him.

'You're my uncle's chauffeur?' She stuck out her hand.

His lips twitched at the yankee twang she'd brought home with her. She was going to need friends, he realized, so he tried with his handshake to let her know she could rely on him. His heart raged savagely and silently, however, and he cursed old man Weldon for sending for her.

13

If she'd stayed in America she would never have had to learn the truth about her guardian. As it was, how could she remain oblivious to the secrets of Wydale Hall? The secrets of that stark, brooding wreck of a house that had become a scar – no, not merely a scar, but a great, gaping wound on its hillside above the river. The Pennine hills and the wide, sweeping valleys of Derbyshire were places of outstanding natural beauty, but Wydale had lost its grip on all that was pleasant. Wydale had once been a place to be proud of, but Gifford Weldon had let it slide into murky obscurity.

Poor kid! John Graham released her hand. It wouldn't do to let her know at this stage that there was anything amiss, he decided. He tried to sound jovial. 'Funny how we recognized each other on sight, wasn't it?'

She nodded, her face bright. 'Lizzie . . . I mean Mrs Abercrombie – my uncle's housekeeper – she wrote me and described you. I suppose Uncle Gif showed you my photo anyway, didn't he?'

'He did, miss.' Graham's eyes crinkled into a smile.

'Do you know what I have to do now, Mr Graham?'

'I'll get you settled in the car. Then I'll come back and collect your things.

Outside in the visitors' compound, he opened the rear door of the black car for her.

'Do you mind if I come up front with you?' she asked frankly. 'I'll be real lonely in the back seat on my own.'

He grinned and said, 'I don't mind at all, Miss Weldon. It'll be a nice change for me – having somebody to talk to.'

She slid into the passenger seat at the front, after shrugging off her thick jacket, and settled herself comfortably.

* * *

14

Alone while John Graham went off to get her luggage, Amy leaned her head back against the headrest and let go of all the tension that had built up inside her on the plane. She hated take-offs and landings, but had managed to sleep a little on the long flight.

Her mind flew back to Boston, New England, and to Kate and Marty Weldon. She hoped they wouldn't be missing her too much, even though, to tell the truth, she was already missing them! Twelve years was a long time to be part of a family – and a family it had been until Kip had been reported missing.

Thinking again of Kip brought back the pain – *and* the ever-constant regret. 'Kip Weldon,' she muttered impatiently, 'will I never be able to get you out of my system?'

She sighed and turned her attention to her surroundings, and the busy comings and goings all around her. She was surprised that the scene wasn't more familiar. Twelve years ago, though, she'd been little more than a child, she reminded herself. She felt the car give a jolt, and twisted round in the seat to look behind her. John Graham was stowing her belongings in the trunk of the car. Trunk! Was that the right word? she wondered with a little frown of concentration. No! She seemed to remember somebody saying it was something entirely different – but what?

The dark blue uniform blocked the side window as John Graham pulled open the driver's door and levered himself inside. 'All is safely gathered in,' he joked, glancing at her. 'One trunk, one brown suitcase and a tapestry hold-all packed away in the boot.'

'Boot! That's it. I was just trying to remember what you called the baggage compartment of an automobile here in England. I guess I'll have to spend the next six months

15

reading a dictionary to get my pronunciations right, Mr Graham.'

He pulled the door shut, then held up one finger and said, 'Miss Weldon, I'm known just as Graham at Wydale. I'd rather you didn't call me mister.'

Just Graham – that sounds so uppity and unfriendly.' She gave a tiny frown of disapproval, but the chauffeur had already started up the car, and all his attention was taken up with pulling out into a line of traffic.

'How long before we get to Wydale, Mr Graham?'

'We should make it by teatime, miss.'

'How long have you worked for my uncle?' she wanted to know. 'I didn't realize he'd gotten himself a chauffeur. He always used to drive himself around in the old days.'

She saw Graham's eyes flick to the rearview mirror before he replied. 'I've been at Wydale just over five years, miss. Since Mr Weldon's doctor warned him not to drive a car after that spot of bother with his heart.'

'But Uncle Gif's okay now, isn't he?'

'He has to take things easy.' John Graham concentrated on pulling out onto the main road and then negotiating two roundabouts. 'He mustn't get upset,' he went on then.

Amy's head cocked attractively to one side. 'You don't think I'll upset him any, do you?'

'Not if you learn to speak the Queen's English pretty quickly, miss.'

'Hell's bells! Can I do that in an hour and a half, do you think?'

'I wouldn't worry if I were you.' John Graham spoke kindly.

'I can't change in the twinkling of an eye, can I?' She chewed on her bottom lip for a second or two before continuing, 'What I mean is, I've lived with an American

16

family for twelve years, gone through American high school and then graduated to get a job teaching American kids in the junior grade. I've left American friends behind in New England. Shucks! It's only natural, surely, that I've gotten into the American way of talking?.'

'I'm sure your uncle will understand, miss.'

Amy wasn't so sure. Until now, she'd never had an inkling she would suddenly find herself scared at the thought of returning to Wydale Hall.

'We *did* have American GIs over here during the war, miss.'

'Yeah! But the war's been over for fifty years, Mr Graham, and I bet my Uncle Gif steered clear of the Yanks anyway.' She stared out of the window. They were on a motorway now, and travelling at speed. She grimaced. 'I'm going to stick out like a sore thumb at Wydale, aren't I?'

'You're going to be a welcome breath of fresh air, miss, unless I'm very much mistaken.'

She recognized the sincerity in his voice, and her spirits lifted.

Traffic was heavy. She hadn't realized English roads could be so congested. She was quiet for some time, and John Graham switched on the radio for traffic news and a weather forecast. An intersection was coming up. Graham turned the radio off and indicated left.

'Don't we stay on the main highway?' she asked.

'No, miss. This is where we go across country – and we call these kind of roads motorways in England, not highways.' His eyes twinkled.

'I'll have to hire you as my interpreter, Mr Graham.'

'Not *mister*, please, Miss Weldon. Look – we're nearly into Derbyshire. I'd rather you didn't call me mister once we get to Wydale.'

'What do I call you, then? Can I call you John?'

'No, miss. Plain Graham will do. Your uncle wouldn't like it if you called me anything but Graham – plain Graham.'

Her eyebrows rose expressively. 'Nobody should have a handle like that, Mr Graham. Nobody should be labelled "plain".'

'Chauffeurs *are* plain beings, miss. Chauffeurs are merely functional.'

'Guess plainness doesn't only apply to chauffeurs.' She pulled a face. 'How about me with my gawkiness, and yellow hair all of a tangle – not to mention a hawk-nose that's gotten me into no end of scrapes when I've poked it where it wasn't wanted.'

'Scrapes, miss?' He gave her a sideways teasing look, and asked, 'What on earth are *scrapes*?'

'Now you're kidding me, Plain-Graham!' she drawled. 'Everybody knows what scrapes are.'

'Yes, miss, I am kidding! I go to the cinema, and I've seen hundreds of American films, but if you expect your uncle to understand your accent, well, I think you're asking a bit too much.'

'Gee!' She looked thoughtful. 'Is it that bad? My accent, I mean?'

'I didn't say it was *bad*, miss.' Graham suddenly seemed disinclined to talk about her uncle any more, and sat up straight in his seat to manoeuvre the car along the narrow main street of a small village.

'Oh, heck,' she stormed softly. 'What have I come back to?'

'You've come back to people who care for you,' he replied sharply. 'Don't ever doubt that, Miss Weldon. Mrs Abercrombie for one – she thinks the world of you.'

18

'I've sure missed Lizzie.' Her eyes softened. 'She's written me, you know. On and off for twelve years. That's some going.'

'Wydale would collapse without Mrs Abercrombie.'

'She's a dragon, Plain-Graham! Surely you've discovered that by now?'

John Graham's mouth twitched, but he said nothing.

'But an adorable dragon.'

He laughed outright.

'Uncle Gif hasn't turned into a killjoy, has he?'

Cautiously, Graham said, 'I don't know what you mean, miss.'

'You've told me indirectly that Uncle Gif would have your guts for garters if he knew I'd been calling you mister! That's what I'm getting at,' she remarked with candour.

Again he didn't answer, but she could feel the atmosphere tensing, and knew instinctively that John Graham didn't like her Uncle Gif. She felt uneasy, hazily remembering Uncle Gif as a dear old thing. Maybe a bit distant, she recalled, and rather formal and old-fashioned in his outlook. But what she didn't remember, however, was Gif Weldon being a tyrant of an employer who could so easily strike a chord of fear into the heart of a servant.

'Uncle Gif's a good man,' she insisted.

'Yes, miss.' Graham gave all his attention to changing down a gear for a steep hill. For a while she kept silent, staring out of the window at the drab splendour of frosted hedgerows and little houses nestling under smoky chimneys. On the horizon she could see distant peaks, with mist swirling round their summits.

She drew in a deep breath to steady her heart, which had started hammering away inside her as she recognized the far-off familiar skyline.

'There it is, Mr Graham. The Peak District.' She pointed excitedly at the windscreen, and the joy inside her escalated to a new high.

'There's still quite a way to go, miss. First we have to get over Blackthorn Pass – and that can be tricky when there's mist and frost like we've got today.'

She shivered, but it was with anticipation and not fear. 'I remember the first time Uncle Gif took me driving over the pass in his little open-top car. It felt like I was going to the top of the world.'

He seemed to ignore the mention of her uncle. 'It's going down that worries me, miss.' He glanced back at her and grinned. 'There are some nasty bends – *and* a couple of hundred foot drop down an almost sheer wall of rock.'

'But it's a great feeling, Mr Graham, seeing the whole of Derbyshire spread out below you.'

'Yes, miss.' Graham sounded anything but thrilled by the thought of the experience. 'But coming up and over the pass this morning was no piece of cake. The fog was as thick as rice pudding.'

She settled herself back in her seat. Her heart had stopped its thunderous pounding with joy. She yawned. She'd been awake since before daybreak, she realized, but she didn't want to close her eyes and maybe miss out on all the splendour of the peaks. Her mind wandered back to the conversation she'd been having with John Graham a few minutes before she'd been distracted by the Derbyshire hills. And inwardly she had the niggling feeling that things had changed at Wydale while she'd been away. John Graham seemed particularly reticent to talk about her uncle. She felt she had to put the record straight. Uncle Gif, she knew, had been her saviour,

'He's not really my uncle, you know.'

20

'I know, miss.'

He sounded distant. She wanted the old John Graham back. She felt she had to explain things more fully.

'My parents died. Uncle Gif was my godfather.'

'Really, miss?' He sounded bored. His tone discouraged any more talk that might centre on Gifford Weldon.

'My father was a doctor.'

Graham changed gear again and the car picked up speed.

'He and Uncle Gif were colleagues. They worked in the same hospital. Uncle Gif was a surgeon.'

Graham remained silent.

'Don't you want to know any more about me?' Amy was feeling decidedly impatient with him.

'It isn't my place to know anything about you, Miss.'

Blackthorn Pass thrilled her again as it had done when she was a child. And it wasn't long before the black car turned off the valley road and onto the winding private road that led up to Wydale. The house itself was as always hidden by trees. It wasn't till they got to the last bend, where the flat stone pack-horse bridge crossed over the River Eston, that the house could be seen.

Amy remembered it all, and her excitement increased. She leaned forward in her seat expectantly. The river was high, and gleaming darkly in the late afternoon half-light.

John Graham laughed softly beside her. 'You're glad to be back?'

She nodded, unable to speak. There was a lump in her throat. She hadn't expected it to take her like this. Memory was a strange thing, though. And Wydale had welcomed her when her world had crashed around her all those years ago.

The house looked just the same as she remembered it –

all squat, square turrets, and deeply recessed windows with leaded diamond panes. Its high chimneys were ornate. From the bridge over the Eston, Wydale looked like a medieval stronghold set solidly on that Derbyshire hillside.

The black car purred up the hill and through the weathered open gateway into a slabbed and ancient walled courtyard. John Graham brought it to a smooth halt in front of the main door, where a tangle of summer's rambling roses and honeysuckle had died and now clung pathetically to the great arched porch that shrouded the entrance to the house itself.

Amy unclipped her seat belt and took in a deep gulp of air to steady herself, for in the shadows of the porch the figure of a man was moving towards her – towards what was left of the daylight.

CHAPTER 2

At first she didn't recognize him. Gif Weldon had changed; he was an old man now. John Graham was out of the car and walking round the front of it to open the door for her. She hated him doing that. She was perfectly capable of opening the door for herself. But even as she put her hand on the catch he beat her to it, standing almost to attention as he pulled it open, and giving her only the shadow of a smile as she got out and stood alongside him.

Uncle Gif was still some way off, but he was walking slowly towards her. The sight of him appalled her. Twelve years ago there hadn't been the slightest stoop to Gif Weldon's tall, willowy body. Now he was huddled and bent, and enveloped in a thick tweed overcoat that did little to disguise the fact that weight had dropped off him alarmingly. He'd never carried a lot of flesh, but his features had once been benign and chubby. Now they were haggard, grey and drawn, and his always sparse fair hair had practically disappeared, leaving blue veins criss-crossing his scalp and forehead and brown age spots embedded in the pallor of his skin.

Only his voice remained the same, though even that had a slight waver.

23

'Amy! My dear, dear Amy! How you've grown! But I would have known you anywhere.'

He held out his arms to her, but she found she couldn't rush to him and be enfolded into them. It had been too long an absence, and Gif Weldon had never been a demonstrative man. A pat on the head now and then had been the only touch she'd ever received from him.

As he came up to her, however, she made an effort and reached out to place both her hands in his, she tried not to flinch at the cold, grasping fingers that closed round hers. The skin of his hands was paper-thin; she could feel his bones. It was like shaking hands with a skeleton.

'Uncle Gif . . .' Words wouldn't come. What could she say to him? He looked so old, so ill – almost a stranger now he was up close, she realized.

'I'm glad you decided to come, Amy.'

'I was worried. Lizzie said in her letter that you'd been ill.' To her own ears the words were stilted – a conventional pleasantry, that was all.

'The illness will pass. Everything passes.'

She shivered. He released her hands and she was glad. In New England with Kate and Marty Weldon it had been easy to cast aside the British reserve she'd grown up with. Back in England now, though – it was different. The years melted away. As a child, before her parents had died, she'd once scrambled spontaneously onto Gif Weldon's knee to thank him for a birthday present, she remembered. He'd been embarrassed, and had gently set on her feet again and held her at arm's length . . .

'I've been down at the river bridge this afternoon, watching for you coming. I'd expected you earlier than this.'

24

She realized he was talking not to her but to John Graham behind her. His tone was petulant.

'The flight was delayed, Uncle Gif,' she said gently. 'We couldn't help being late.'

Again he spoke directly to the chauffeur. 'You could have telephoned and let me know.'

'I tried, sir. The telephone was engaged.'

'Nonsense!' The old man was panting, and out of breath with the effort of arguing.

Graham obviously recognized the signs and didn't want to upset his employer further. He just said, 'I'm sorry, Sir.'

'I should think so too.'

It irked Amy to hear the chauffeur being spoken to so patronizingly. In her New England high school she'd taken up arms against rank, and had become passionately involved in debates about the classless society. She found herself comparing the life she'd led in New England to the one she'd come back to now. The difference between the easygoing Weldons in Boston and her Uncle Gif was becoming more and more apparent. Martyn Weldon bore no resemblance to his elder brother, and she thanked providence for that.

She turned her back on him. Dear as her uncle was to her, she knew she couldn't dismiss John Graham without thanking him properly. She moved over to the chauffeur and, whipping out one hand to him, she grasped his leather-gloved one firmly. 'Thanks for looking after me.' She grinned. 'It was much appreciated.'

'It was a pleasure, Miss Weldon.'

She went back to her uncle and felt sorry for him. He was thin and frail – and unloved. Silently he moved aside and indicated that she should precede him into the house.

25

'It's much too cold to stand around out here. This dratted frost hasn't let up for four days, child.' He panted as he followed her inside, then, turning to close the door, he went on, 'There was no need for you to thank Graham, Amy, my dear. The man was only doing the job he's paid to do.'

'The man?' She'd caught the sharp note in his voice that had never been there before. She glanced quickly at him. 'Is that how you regard John Graham? Just as *the man*?'

He looked keenly at her. 'I hope those Americans haven't been filling your head with nonsense.'

'It depends what you mean by nonsense,' she replied, forcing a brightness she didn't exactly feel into the words.

'Murmurings of dissent – liberty, equality – all that mumbo jumbo that Americans love to go on about.'

'But the United States was founded on the principles of liberty and equality, Uncle Gif . . .'

He pushed open another door that led into a huge almost empty room, and she felt a chill envelop her.

'There's liberty and *liberty*,' he said, in a none too patient tone. 'And there's equality and *equality*, Amy.' With a dry little laugh – designed, she thought, to soften his words – he continued, 'It has been said, my dear, that all men are equal. But some are more equal than others – if you get my point.'

Not wanting to appear rude, but with her temper running dangerously high, Amy flung back at him, 'Mr Thomas Jefferson stated that *all* people were entitled to life, liberty and the pursuit of happiness . . .'

Gif Weldon's sallow complexion took on a hint of dull colour as he snapped, 'Would you share all that *you* possess, then, with tramps and vagabonds, child? Would you welcome the destitute, the thief and the prostitute into your home?'

26

She was shocked that he should speak to her in such a way. As far back as she could remember, her beloved Uncle Gif had never before raised his voice to her. She lowered her gaze to the stone-flagged floor of the great hall. The dimly lit wainscotted room was gloomy. On the bare stone walls iron cressets held small, flickering oil lamps. Her homecoming was turning into a nightmare!

Even as that thought assailed her she realised that perhaps she had been too outspoken – and too soon. Miserably she lifted her head and looked at the bowed yet stern figure before her. 'I'm sorry,' she said. 'Uncle Gif – I'd so looked forward to coming home. I never meant us to start off like this.'

His face softened immediately. 'Child! You don't know what it's been like for me these last few years.'

There was no reply she could make. He was the one who had sent her away, but now he was talking as if she'd deserted him of her own accord.

He walked past her, giving her a pat on her arm as he did so, and she buried both her hands in the pockets of her jacket and followed him across the room to the huge marble fireplace where a low fire crackled. He stood looking down into the leaping flames, holding out both his hands towards the heat.

Amy was captivated once more by the picture of Barbara Weldon, but her uncle seemed not to notice the dust-laden reminder of his wife any more. In the light from the fire she was shocked to see how shabbily Gif Weldon was dressed. Oh, the garments he wore were clean enough, but his coat had been darned on one sleeve and his shirt collar was frayed. Glancing down, she saw boots that were down at heel, with deep scuff marks showing beneath the polished surface. At one time Uncle Gif would never have worn scuffed boots; he'd have thrown them on the kitchen garden bonfire.

A sense of misgiving came over her. She looked up at the oil lamps and said, 'The lamps are quaint.'

'Electricity is only laid on in the main rooms, my dear.' He turned slowly to face her and seemed to have forgotten her former outburst. 'It's the generator, you see. It was installed originally in the forties and has never been big enough to run power for the whole house. It's enough, though.'

The bitterness in his voice worried her. He'd always been so patriotic and proud in the old days. And she'd been away so long she'd forgotten how basic the electricity had been. Gently she said, 'I guess I'll get used to it again. It's easy to take things for granted in the States.'

'That's the trouble with people,' he grumbled. 'Once you give them an inch, they want a mile. Nowadays they don't seem able to exist without television receivers and bottled music twenty-four hours a day.'

'Such things are necessary in the nineties, Uncle Gif.'

'Television? Necessary?' He fixed her with a hard stare.

'I thought you would love it – isolated as you are here.'

'Wouldn't give it house room,' he snapped.

'You don't have a TV set?' she asked in disbelief.

He waved a hand dismissively at her. 'Lizzie Abercrombie's got a portable black and white model. No doubt she'll let you watch it if you must.'

'Hell's bells!'

She saw him cringe at her last words and realized that John Graham had been trying to warn her about this. She really would have to try and curb her tongue and cut out the slang. Remembering John Graham, she frowned and half turned towards the door, wondering where her luggage had got to.

Gif Weldon could read her mind, it seemed. 'Graham will have taken your luggage up the back stairs, I expect.'

Before she could bite back the words they were out. 'The back stairs? But they're right around the other side of the house. Surely he won't have walked all that way with such heavy baggage – ' She stopped abruptly and bit down on her bottom lip. *Baggage*! Why, oh, why hadn't she stopped and thought and said *luggage*, like a nice English girl would have done?

Gif Weldon waved a hand impatiently again and said, 'Servants do not come in at the front door, Amy. Servants use the back stairs. And for heaven's sake try and speak plain English, girl. "Baggage" is hardly the kind of word any lady would use.'

If hearts could really break, Amy knew hers was in danger of cracking in that moment. But a clattering in a long passage to one side of the great hall distracted her, and she was glad of that. A woman came striding purposefully towards them. Amy's heart leapt.

'Lizzie!' she cried joyfully, and her hands flew to her lips as Amazonian strides brought Lizzie Abercrombie within two feet of her. She hadn't changed a bit! Lizzie's six feet tall frame was as reassuring as it had always been. Frizzed grey hair stuck out round her long face at all angles. Bony wrists shot out at the ends of red woollen sleeves of a jumper that was too short, too skin-tight and generally too small in all directions. The hands fastened on Amy's shoulders and dragged her into an all-enveloping embrace where Lizzie's bosom – flat as it was – threatened to suffocate the girl.

Amy broke down then, and sobbed uncontrollably as

29

she clung to the red jumper as if it were a life-saving raft bobbing about in fast-flowing rapids.

'Oh, Lizzie . . .' Whiskery fibres of wool tickled her nose and stuck fast to the tears that were a match for those pouring down the housekeeper's face.

How long the two women stood locked together, Amy never knew. They both just held onto each other and fired questions and answers back and forth, until Lizzie was convinced that no harm had come to her one-time charge and Amy could finally believe that one thing had stayed constant while she'd been away – Lizzie's undying affection for her.

At last Lizzie held her away and said, sniffing, 'The old man's gone. Gone to his study, I expect.'

Amy dragged a hand across her eyes and looked round the room. 'Oh, heck! He'll think I don't care about him.'

'Serves him right. I heard how he was talking to you. Giving you a lecture on talking properly, and you not home five minutes. He ought to be ashamed of himself. T'would have been a different matter, I suppose, if he'd sent you to France instead of the US of A, and you'd come back with a fancy, lah-di-dah Parisian accent.'

Amy gave a strangled little laugh. 'He didn't have a convenient brother in France, Lizzie.'

'We – ell,' Lizzie said grudgingly, 'I suppose he *did* have your welfare at heart when he sent you off to Yankee-land.'

'I want to love him, Lizzie. I don't mean to hurt him.'

'I know, sweetie. He's just funny about some things. Can't stand any show of affection and such. And everything's got to be so bloomin' right and proper for him.'

'You should know him, Lizzie. You've been with him a long time.'

30

'Yeah! I'm used to his pernickity ways. I often give him a good talking to.'

Amy said, 'He should marry you. You'd make him more human.'

Lizzie gave her a strange look, and a guarded expression came into her eyes. She abruptly changed the subject by saying, 'You must be ready for a meal, girl. Come and look at your room first, though. It's still the same one you had next to my quarters when you were a little girl.'

'I wasn't so little, Lizzie.'

'You was little to me, lovey.'

'I loved that room. I could look out over the hills beyond the copse to where the old chapel stands.'

'The old chapel's in a right mess now, Miss Amy. It got struck by lightning a couple of years ago and was burned out.'

'The chapel? You never told me in your letters about that, Lizzie.'

'Didn't want you to get all upset about it.' Lizzie started moving towards the staircase that led out of the vast hall. When Amy didn't follow, she halted at the bottom of the stairs, her hand on the carved newel post and turned and said, 'What are we waiting for, then, missy?'

'The chapel. I want to know all about it.'

Lizzie shrugged her bony shoulders. 'Nothing much to tell. It was a real bad storm. Some of the trees around the chapel had to be felled afterwards — it was too dangerous to leave them. The place looks dreadful now. Real spooky.'

'Oh, Lizzie . . .' Amy followed the older woman up the stairs.

They reached the landing. 'Hey! No more tears!' Lizzie ordered.

Amy managed a smile. 'I'm not bawling. Honest, Lizzie, I'm not.'

They walked along the corridor. 'I persuaded his lordship that you'd want to have the old nursery suite next to me again. I'll be right there if you get lonely.'

'Great! And I hear you've got a television set.'

'After a lot of argument and me threatening to leave if I couldn't have one, yes.' Lizzie sighed. 'He won't move with the times. Not that one.' She pushed a door open and clicked a light switch on the wall beside it. 'Remember the old place?'

The harsh electric lightbulb was glaringly bright. It was suspended from a high beam that crossed the ceiling and had a utilitarian pink shade round it that cast a warm glow round the top of the walls. A fire was blazing in the fireplace. The room felt aired and cosy despite its size. Amy stood in the doorway and gazed around. 'You've worked wonders with it, Lizzie.'

The room's generous proportions were diminished slightly by the cabbage-rose wallpaper that was definitely new. Amy guessed that the polished floorboards also owed a debt of gratitude to Lizzie Abercrombie for giving them a sheen they hadn't known in years. Lizzie, too, must have pegged away for hours making the two thick wool rugs that added their bright colours to those of the roses. She remembered the old double-size bed, and hoped its mattress had been replaced. It had always been lumpy, and she and Lizzie had been forced to shake its flock filling vigorously every week in order to make it bearable.

She walked over to it to test its springiness – or otherwise – and Lizzie laughed as she bounced on the edge of it, and said, 'The mattress is new. Almost cost me my soul in begging and pleading with the old miser,

32

though. Spring interior this one. You should be comfortable on it.'

Amy's laughter pealed out.

'That's what this old place needs – laughter and plenty of it,' Lizzie said.

Amy gazed round at the heavy walnut wardrobe and chest of drawers, and at the fat cushioned armchair beside the window. There was a small writing desk there too, which she hadn't seen before. She walked over to it, ran her fingers over its shiny surface. 'This is different. It's nice.' She glanced up at Lizzie.

'It was rotting away up in the attics. I thought you might want something of the sort. Well, you'll be wanting to write home to America, won't you? And there's a lock on it, see? The key's inside in a little drawer. Thought you might have things you want to keep private like, now you're grown up.'

'Oh, Lizzie. You're lovely.'

Lizzie's face went crimson. She flipped a hand at Amy in embarrassment. 'Go on with you,' she muttered, and then, 'First time anybody ever called me lovely in all my life, child.'

'Oh, Lizzie! I've missed you.' Amy turned her back on the window. 'And Gif's brother and his wife'll be missing *you*, girl,' Lizzie said. 'It must have been awful for them, losing their lad.'

Hearing Lizzie speaking of Kip so unexpectedly brought back memories Amy would rather have forgotten.

'Hey! What have I said? You've gone pale as a ghost, girl.'

Amy pushed her hands into her coat pockets again, so Lizzie wouldn't see them shaking. 'It's nothing! I'm okay!'

Lizzie stood and stared at her, then, slowly, understanding dawned in her eyes. Gently she walked over to her and took hold of her arm. 'Ah! I didn't know you felt like that about him. You never let on in your letters.'

Trembling, Amy said, 'I don't know what you mean . . .'

'You were in love with the lad. It's plain enough for anybody to see.'

A knife turned in Amy's heart. She bowed her head.

'Do you want to talk about it?'

'What's there to talk about?' Slowly Amy brought her eyes round to look Lizzie full in the face. 'What good will it do now to admit I'd been in love with Kip since the first moment I met him? It won't bring him back. And if he did come back, he wouldn't want *me*.'

'Don't run yourself down, Miss Amy.'

Amy hunched her shoulders. 'It's true. He didn't know how I felt about him. Nobody knew.'

'Your uncle showed me a picture the Weldons once sent him. It was of you and their lad on a beach somewhere. You had a great stripy ball in your arms.'

Amy remembered the time with clarity. 'It was on the island. We used to go there every summer. Marty and Kate had this beach house – built on wooden legs. Real old-fashioned, it was – just like something out of an old fifties film.' She swallowed and her voice tailed off, then she continued huskily, 'There was nothing but sea and sand. Coarse green grass grew in tufts all round it. Kip and I spent a whole vacation once, painting the inside and outside of that little house . . .' She shook her head, as if to clear it of memories that were too painful to remember, and pulled a rueful face. 'It sure took a whole lot of paint.'

'He sounds like a really nice boy.'

34

Nice! 'Nice' didn't start to describe him. And 'boy'? 'He was a good bit older than me, Lizzie.'

'He looked on you as a kid sister, huh?'

There was a void inside her that couldn't be filled. 'That's about it, Lizzie.'

Lizzie's voice was soft. 'So what happened?'

'He joined the United States Army. He was sent over here to England. And he met a girl . . .' She couldn't go on. She bowed her head again, and her hands inside her pockets were clenched tightly into fists.

'And?'

'She got pregnant. And Kip was killed.' She stared across the room at the brightly glowing fire. 'Kate and Marty don't know anything about her except her name was Kitty. They've moved heaven and earth to try and locate her in the years since Kip died, but with no luck.'

Lizzie frowned. 'Maybe she's dead too. Seems funny she never tried to get in touch with Kip's folks.'

'No. I don't think she's dead.'

'You sound sure of yourself?' Lizzie let her hand fall away from Amy's arm.

'I – I have this feeling that won't go away.'

'But there's nothing you can do, surely.' Lizzie looked at her earnestly. 'Miss Amy, it's not your problem.'

Too quickly, Amy said, 'I'd wondered about putting an advertisement in an English newspaper . . .'

'D'you know where she lived?'

'It must have been somewhere near where Kip was stationed – and that was Lincolnshire.'

'And you think you can succeed where the Weldons didn't?'

'Maybe.' She was unsure of herself, however.

'Are you doing this for the Weldons?' Lizzie asked shrewdly.

'Of course . . .' Amy felt guilty even as she answered.

'So what's in it for you, girl?'

Amy swung away, hunching her shoulders as she looked out of the window into the darkness outside.

'I said . . .' Lizzie began.

She spun round, agitated. 'I heard what you said.'

'You're nervous about something.'

'Lizzie – what ulterior motive could I possibly have?'

Lizzie's eyes narrowed. 'Maybe you want the baby for yourself, Miss Amy.'

Amy flung up her hands. 'That's crazy . . .'

'You lost the man, so now you want anything that's left of him. Am I getting near the mark?' Lizzie walked away from her abruptly, and only stopped when she reached the door.

Amy turned back to the window. 'I just want to know the baby's okay.'

Lizzie sighed. 'D'you think I was born yesterday?'

Amy's eyes were tortured as she almost pleaded with the woman. 'Lizzie – you don't know what it's like. There's a baby somewhere – something that's part of Kip . . .'

'Not exactly a babe in arms, though, is it? The kid must be two or three years old by now.'

'Oh, don't split hairs, Lizzie. You know what I mean.'

'Yeah! I can see right through you, girl. You're aiming to get that child for yourself, aren't you?'

Amy's head shot up defensively. 'I could give it a good home.'

'And its own mother can't? You've admitted yourself you know nothing about the girl.'

Amy began to pace restlessly. 'She wasn't married to

36

Kip. What kind of girl can she be not to have worried about the consequences?'

'And what kind of man ditto,' Lizzie said in a calm voice.

Amy pressed her hands to her ears. 'I won't listen to you,' she declared. 'Kip wasn't like that . . .'

Lizzie Abercrombie stormed across the room to her and without ceremony pulled her hands down to her sides again. Then she shook her – hard. 'An immaculate conception, was it?' She thrust her face forward and Amy looked stunned. 'That's better,' Lizzie went on. 'You're listening, aren't you? Because I intend getting some sense into that head of yours about this affair.'

Amy suddenly sagged. 'I know, Lizzie! You don't have to go on at me. I know I'm being stupid and pig-headed . . .'

'And you've convinced yourself this Kitty was no good, haven't you?'

Amy hung her head, suddenly ashamed of herself. She muttered, 'But what if she didn't want the baby? What if the kid's unhappy? Maybe ill-treated?'

'You're not God. You don't have to go putting the world to rights.'

Amy felt tired and angry. She wished now that she hadn't confided in Lizzie. Forlornly she looked up at the housekeeper and said in a weary voice, 'Can't I be forgiven for wanting to put one little corner of the world to rights, Lizzie?' She shrugged herself out the woman's grasp and walked back to the bed. There she slowly unbuttoned her coat and slipped out of it. Then she ran her fingers through her thick fair hair, which after so long a journey, needed a good raking through with a hairbrush. 'God! I've got a headache,' she muttered.

Lizzie watched her for some minutes, then asked, 'If you find the kid, what then? Imagine for a minute that the mother will give him up to you. How are you going to look after him?'

Amy picked up her coat and walked over to the wardrobe. It wouldn't be a problem, having the child – she knew. Wydale would be hers one day. Kate and Marty had told her that Gif Weldon had made a will leaving her everything he possessed. She'd argued with them, saying that Marty, as Gif's brother, should have Wydale, but Marty had laughingly told her he'd long since been disinherited and didn't care. What would *he* do with a place like Wydale? he'd asked her.

'That isn't a problem,' she told Lizzie. 'I'm going to inherit Wydale, and what better place could there be than a lovely house like this, with woodland and grounds extending to several acres . . . We could have a pony for him and he could learn to ride. You could help me with him, Lizzie.'

'Oh, no!' Lizzie shook her head vigorously. 'Don't include me in your little game, girl. I've had enough of play-acting.'

'But – I thought I could rely on you.'

Lizzie railed, 'Oh, yes! Everybody relies on Lizzie Abercrombie to aid and abet them in their little games – even *him* . . .' She walked over to the door again, then stopped, held onto it with both hands and wearily leaned her head against the scarred and ancient wood. 'Oh, hell,' she muttered. 'Forget it! Forget I spoke!'

'I don't know what you're getting at, Lizzie. What do you mean by play-acting! And *games*! What games? Is there something I should know?'

Slowly, as if she were an old woman and not one just into her fifties, Lizzie pushed herself away from the door.

38

She took one or two calming breaths, then said, 'Forget I mentioned them things, Miss Amy.'

'How can I forget?' Amy was perplexed. 'You've been talking in riddles.'

'There are more pressing things. Things I wasn't going to tell you till you'd settled back in.'

'Uncle Gif . . .' Amy's eyes flew wide. 'Lizzie! He isn't going to die, is he?'

Wearily, Lizzie said, 'We're all going to die one day, girl. It's living that concerns me most at the moment.'

'Living? Lizzie, if you've got something to say, then come on out with it.'

Lizzie closed the door quietly then stood with her back to it. Her head almost reached the top frame, she was so tall. 'There's no money left,' she said.

'No money?'

'That's why he wanted you back in England, girl.'

'Uncle Gif?' Amy felt her legs buckling as she faced Lizzie across the room.

'No money! And the house is practically tumbling down around us.'

'It looks okay to me.'

'Take a closer look – when the light is good. The western tower's not safe any more. All the walls are crumbling. The chapel's burnt out.' Lizzie looked up at the high old beams above them. 'There's rot in the woodwork. The plaster's all crazy. And *he* thinks *you* are going to save it for him.'

'Me?'

'Yes! Little old you.'

'But how?'

'That's for him and you to work out, girl. I'm having nothing more to do with it. I'm just the hired help.'

39

'Lizzie . . .'

But Lizzie had pulled open the door again and was already starting down the stairs.

'Lizzie!' she yelled, leaping for the door and crashing through it to race after the housekeeper.

Lizzie looked back from halfway down the stairs. 'Ask him what he's got in mind,' she suggested. 'Go on, girl. You just set to and ask him.'

Amy stood stock-still on the top stair, fear holding her back.

Lizzie held her gaze for a few more seconds then said softly, 'My God, girl. What Gif Weldon has in mind for you will leave you no time for your romantic dream of finding and bringing up Kip Weldon's kid, I can tell you.'

CHAPTER 3

The road leading to the village of Hawkwood sparkled with early-morning frost as Richard Boden cycled unhurriedly towards Wydale Hall. Fastened securely across the back of his bike seat was a large canvas bag. Twin leather straps kept it in place, though the weight of it, Boden knew, could easily slew him into the gutter at any sudden increase in speed.

He was a heavy man and knew it. 'Raw-boned!' That had always been his mother's description of him, and, as always, the thought of Mam brought a smile to his lips.

A line of black cars came into view, soberly crawling towards him. He slowed the bike, allowed one foot to drift along the ground, then stopped altogether and dismounted, to stand respectfully as the cortège passed him.

There were wreaths of flowers on the roof of the hearse, which was one of the old-fashioned kind that had been much in favour fifty years ago. Funerals, Richard thought, were fast following the fashion of weddings nowadays, and looking to the past for their mode of transport. It wouldn't surprise him if black horses and plumes didn't make a comeback soon, and why not? A carriage and pair of greys was just as popular for a present-day wedding as it had been a hundred years ago.

41

The scent of chrysanthemums was heavy on the air as the leading car passed him, and he was glad when the stately procession was out of sight. It had served to remind him that he was all alone in the world now, having lost first Mam and Dad, and then Grace. But of late he'd made a determined effort not to dwell on the past. There was work to be done, and that was something he'd never shirked – even though today he knew he ought to be up at the quarry, overseeing the men, instead of cycling to Wydale in the hope of seeing old man Weldon's visitor.

He swung his leg over the crossbar of the bike again, knowing full well he had no need to feel guilty about taking a day off from the quarry. They'd manage well enough without him for one day. George Shipstone was a good foreman, who could handle the men as well as anything untoward that might crop up. Before remounting, Richard ran his hand over the back pocket of his brown cords, assuring himself that he'd brought the mobile phone along. He seldom went anywhere without it; quarry business was always uppermost in his mind.

He slowed down before the turning from the main road onto the narrow drive that led up to the Hall. Smoke was spiralling up from the chimney of the custodian's stone cottage, whose garden adjoined the road. Yellow buds of winter jasmine clustered round the cottage gate and dipped over the wall; it was flowering early, and he hoped the sudden frost wouldn't blight it.

Flowers weren't his thing, though. Limestone *was*. Limestone didn't wilt and die at the end of its season. It endured. And alabaster . . . Well, that was an altogether different matter. He started to think about the angel and became lost in his contemplation of silver-green veins running through marbled wings. It was surely a miracle that the damage had been so slight, considering that Gabriel had fallen from such a great height when lightning had struck Wydale's chapel.

From force of habit he mentally ticked off the tools he had in the canvas bag as he cycled up the incline towards Wydale. Chisel, point, claw, wire brush, callipers, various rifflers, pumice . . . Today he'd make a start on that broken wing, and maybe take a turn up to the Hall around midday. Lizzie Abercrombie would always find time to make him a cup of tea.

He became aware of a familiar figure walking towards him from the direction of the Hall, and, not keeping his mind on the road, Richard hit a rut with the front wheel and almost lost his balance. The bicycle wasn't fitted with gears. It was a cumbersome old thing – almost a collector's item now – but, never one to welcome change merely for the sake of change, Richard wouldn't have dreamt of replacing the second-hand Raleigh that Mam and Dad had given him on his fifteenth birthday. Grace had laughed at him for his affection for the monstrosity; she'd always been able to out-ride him on the lightweight model he'd bought her after their marriage . . .

Gifford Weldon was well wrapped up against the cold, his tweed coat flapping round his knees. Richard dismounted again as he drew near the old man. Weldon's rasping breath was steaming on the cold air; his lips were blue. His eyes brightened, however, at the sight of the man blocking his path. 'No prizes for guessing where *you're* off to, Richard.'

Boden's smile was lazy. 'That damned angel gets under my skin.'

'You're working wonders at the chapel – considering the amount of damage that was done. I'm grateful to you . . .'

43

A spate of coughing brought Gif Weldon's words to an abrupt halt. He smothered it with a clean white handkerchief, and was finally able to continue, 'Damned weather! I'll be glad when it gets warmer.'

'Looks like the snow might hold off till after Christmas.' Richard wasn't really interested in the weather; he was just being polite. What concerned him was what had happened the previous day. He was impatient for news of her. He had to ask. 'What about the little lady? Did Amy arrive safely yesterday?'

Gif Weldon nodded, and he even managed a smile of sorts. 'Safe and sound! Lizzie Abercrombie whisked her away from under my nose the minute she got inside the Hall, though, so I didn't get time to sound her out about our plan.'

'There'll be plenty of time for that.' Richard felt a pang of guilt at the old man's words.

'Not getting cold feet, are you?' Weldon's gaze was wary.

'It's not to my liking. Arranged marriages went out of fashion with the Victorians, Gif.'

The laugh that greeted his words was harsh. 'It's hardly that, is it? An arranged marriage? The girl hasn't even clapped eyes on you yet.'

'And when she does, do you think she's going to swoon at my feet? I'm no spring chicken, you know.'

'You're thirty-seven. Thirty-seven's no age. And you don't look it. There's barely a hint of grey in that hair of yours, man.'

'So a hefty bank balance coupled with a head of brown hair's going to make me a good catch? Is that what you're saying?'

'It was you who put the idea into my mind, Richard, and I

44

expect Lizzie Abercrombie's already hinted to Amy about my poverty-stricken state.' He pulled a wry face, then looked up to the sky at a sudden diversion. 'There's that dratted helicopter again. God knows what he finds so interesting around Wydale. This is the second week running he's been buzzing around like an oversized bumblebee.'

Richard Boden gazed up into the overcast sky. 'Lucky beggar! Wish I had the chance to be up there.'

Gif Weldon laughed. 'You could afford it, if you really wanted one.'

Richard gave all his attention to the old man again, and asked with a touch of humour, 'What on earth would *I* do with a helicopter?'

'Fly it, of course.'

'What a waste of money.'

'You're a prudent man, Richard. In *my* young day I spent money twice as fast as I earned it.' Weldon grimaced. 'That's how I landed myself in poverty street.'

'You still have Wydale.'

'Not much of an inheritance for Amy, though, is it? Not the state it's in.'

Richard leaned heavily on the bike's handlebars. 'Look – I can't just keep spending money on a place I'll never own. I'm a businessman, Gifford. I need to know just where I stand. I need some sort of security if I'm going to make a start on the Hall, and not just the pottering about in the chapel that I've been doing.'

The older man sighed, and his lean face was drawn and grey. He shook his head slowly. 'Marriage! It's the only way, Richard – as far as I can see. Amy would be your security, because Amy is going to inherit Wydale. And anyway, when I put the plan to you a month ago, you seemed to think it was an idea that could work.'

'A month ago she was on the other side of the Atlantic. Now she's here. Flesh and blood.'

'And perky and prickly as a porcupine,' Gif Weldon said. 'And with a mind of her own that I wasn't bargaining for.'

'But so far she knows nothing of your circumstances?'

Gif Weldon's head jerked up sharply. 'What do you mean by that?'

Boden closed his eyes and leaned his head back to stare up into the sky again, realizing his words had been taken the wrong way. 'Gifford – I'm sorry. I didn't mean what you thought I meant. Your life is your own affair – to lead in any way you choose. By "circumstances" I meant poverty street – as you said yourself a few minutes ago.'

The old man took in several deep, painful breaths of the damp air, and Richard couldn't help but feel sorry for him. 'You oughtn't to be out here on a day like this,' he said.

'I've got things to attend to. Duncan's expecting me. There are some accounts to go through and I'm worried about him. He's not at all well.'

'I'd better let you get on, then.' Richard's face darkened with a moment's irritation. He wished the old man would pay more attention to the state of his own health – *and* to the state of the house, which was in danger of rotting away beneath him – than he did to his old lawyer friend Duncan Ward, who lived in the custodian's cottage down by the road.

'Perhaps I'll drop in at the chapel later . . .'

'I'll be working on Gabriel.'

'Can't you call the damned thing by some other name?'

'Old habits die hard – Gabriel's the only angel I've ever heard of. I didn't go in for Sunday School when I was a lad. I was too busy with my dreams of being a champion boxer.'

The old man's laughter barked out on the still air. 'Too busy practising the art of fisticuffs on any Tom, Dick or Harry who crossed you, or so I've heard. It seems you were a right tearaway at one time. But not any more, eh?'

'Youth's energy had to be channelled into hard work after my father died, Gifford. I get my kicks now from blasting pieces of rock to kingdom come.'

'It pays, lad. It pays.'

'Aye, Gifford. That's what I've found too.'

Surprisingly, Amy found that she had slept well, and she woke ready to face her new life – whatever that might hold – at Wydale Hall.

Lizzie Abercrombie must have heard her knocking about in the bedroom above, because Amy found her breakfast was ready and waiting in a pan on the hotplate as soon as she entered Wydale's massive, stone-flagged kitchen. There was, however, only one place laid at the table.

'Aren't you having breakfast with me, Lizzie?' Amy's fashionable Reeboks made no sound as she stalked across to the stove and sniffed expectantly at the pan's contents.

'Had mine at seven,' Lizzie said.

'What about Uncle Gif?'

Lizzie ladled bacon, sausages and a fried egg onto a warmed plate and handed it to her. 'He never takes breakfast – just has a cup of tea.'

'That's right. Now I remember. I could never understand why Uncle Gif wasn't absolutely ravenous first thing in the morning – like I used to be.'

'Leopards don't change their spots, child.' Lizzie smiled grimly at Amy as she walked over to the table, carrying her

47

breakfast. She picked up the brown teapot and followed her, and as Amy sat down she poured out a cup of strong, hot tea.

'You've remembered that *I'm* a real pig at breakfast-time anyway.' Amy picked up her knife and fork and prepared to do battle with a pork sausage.

'You need some padding on them bones.' Lizzie looked her up and down. 'You were just the same as a kid, I remember – eat, eat, eat, yet you never put an ounce of weight on.'

'Thank goodness.' Amy grinned. 'I like being skinny.'

'Men like their women a bit more rounded, though.' Lizzie took the teapot back to the stove.

'I don't want a man.' Amy effortlessly disposed of a mouthful of sausage.

'You will.'

'Never!' Kip Weldon's handsome face still haunted her dreams. She mopped up runny egg with a slice of thick bread. Looking up, she asked, 'Where's Uncle Gif now, Lizzie. I think I was quite rude to him last night. I ought to apologize.'

Lizzie came back to the table and stood with arms folded. 'Miss Amy – maybe things were said that weren't meant by all of us yesterday.'

'You said some puzzling things,' Amy admitted.

'Things that were none of my business.' Lizzie looked downcast. 'I should have kept my mouth shut.'

Amy finished eating and took a long drink of her tea, grimacing as she put her cup down. At once Lizzie was up in arms.

'What was that sour face for, madam?'

'Sugar! Guess I've gotten used to not taking sugar. We always had coffee, you see . . .'

48

'In Yankee-land?' Lizzie pursed her lips. 'Call that civilized, do you? Coffee first thing in a morning – and on an empty stomach?'

Amy laughed softly and quoted, 'When in Rome, Lizzie, do as the Romans do!'

'Here we have tea.'

'So here *I'll* have tea. It won't poison me.' She rose to her feet and pushed her chair back.

'I suppose you've forgotten what a real egg looks like,' Lizzie groused. 'Did they have hens in New England?'

'We used to have pancakes for breakfast.'

'Pancakes! Huh! Pancakes are for Shrove Tuesday!'

'Pancakes and maple syrup. Great! I'm a real breakfast person. When I first went to live in the States, Kate and Marty took me on a visit to a sugarhouse near Maine, to see how the syrup was made.'

Lizzie started to clear the table. Amy began to help.

'Hey! This is my job,' Lizzie warned her. 'Why don't you get off and enjoy yourself around the place.'

'Alone? You still haven't told me where Uncle Gif is.'

'He told me he was taking a walk down to see Duncan Ward. Mentioned some hare-brained scheme about opening Wydale to the public, to try and rake in a bit of ready cash.'

'Does old Mr Ward still practise as a lawyer, Lizzie?'

Lizzie snorted. 'Do lawyers *ever* stop being lawyers? They're born lawyers and they die lawyers – with nothing but a great deal of talk and hot air in between.'

'You don't like him, do you?' Amy leaned back against the table, her legs stretched out in front of her.

'Your uncle's not going to like them trousers.' Lizzie glared across the kitchen at her.

'My jeans? Why not?'

'Because he's old-fashioned, that's why not.'

'You're just trying to change the subject so you don't have to answer my question about Duncan Ward.'

'No. I don't like him.' Lizzie banged the frying pan down on the draining board. 'Duncan Ward's done nothing to *make* me like him.'

'Does he still live on the estate? In that cute little cottage?'

'Yeah! Rent-free – as usual.'

'I should think Uncle Gif's pleased for somebody – anybody – to live in the old custodian's cottage, Lizzie. It would only have fallen into decay if it had been standing empty all these years.'

'I don't hold with it,' Lizzie snapped. 'Duncan Ward, for all his years, still has a smart brain in his head. Before we know it, he'll have your uncle building one of them theme parks, or else a holiday camp at Wydale.'

'But you said last night there was no money, Lizzie. Surely something's got to be done about that?'

'He'll persuade Gif to borrow from the bank again.'

'Uncle Gif wouldn't get into debt . . .'

'Wouldn't he?' Lizzie rounded on her sharply as she splashed hot water from the tap into a bowl in the deep porcelain sink. 'Wouldn't he just? I don't trust that man Ward as far as I could kick him.'

'Lizzie, why don't you just sit down and tell me what's going on around here, instead of throwing out vague hints?'

'It's not for me to say. I just wanted to warn you.' Lizzie clammed up and began swishing a dish mop around in the bowl.

'But . . .'

The housekeeper looked up. 'No buts, Miss Amy. I'm

not going to say another word except to tell you to keep your wits about you. You're older now. You might think you're grown up and can't be manipulated, but just be careful. You're a good lass but you're impulsive. I know you'd do anything you could to put Wydale on its feet again, but remember one thing: it's just a pile of bricks and mortar – well, stones and mortar really. And stones don't bleed – human hearts do!'

Wydale means more to me than that, Lizzie.' Amy pushed herself away from the table and walked over to the housekeeper, laying a hand on the older woman's arm. 'Look! I know you mean well, but if the place is in such a state as you say, I think we should consider *anything* that might help.'

Lizzie dropped the small mop into the hot water and sighed. 'Sometimes,' she said slowly, looking up into the girl's face, 'sometimes, it's best to let things be. It's *time* you see, Miss Amy, *time* that's eating away at the stones. The house is old. Wydale's been standing since the sixteenth century. You can't expect it to last for ever.'

'But I *do* expect that, Lizzie.' Amy's hand fell to her side again. 'You see, Wydale welcomed me when all my world was turning upside-down. Wydale took me to its great stone heart when I'd lost both my parents. And if time is doing its best to ruin Wydale and bring it down, then I'll do anything in my power to restore it.'

'Anything?' Lizzie's gaze had a curious kind of contempt in it.

For long seconds Amy held the housekeeper's stare, then she said calmly, 'Yes, Lizzie. I really do think I'd do *anything*.'

Lizzie turned back to the sink and tipped the bowl of greasy water carelessly down the drain. 'You do that,

51

then,' she muttered. 'You just go ahead and do that, missy.'

'I'll talk to Uncle Gif.'

Lizzie seemed relieved. 'Yes,' she said. 'That'd be best.'

Amy brightened visibly. 'I think I'll mosey on down to Duncan Ward's cottage myself. I could walk back with Uncle Gif, then . . .'

Lizzie rounded on her. 'You'll do no such thing girl!' She stood, her work-roughened hands planted firmly on her scraggy hips, and glared.

'Why not?' Amy jerked her head up in a gesture of defiance.

Lizzie's face flushed. 'Because!' she said, her whole attitude becoming aggressive.

'Because what?' Amy shrugged. 'Come on, now,' she teased, 'give me one good reason why I shouldn't go down there and ask Mr Duncan Ward what's happening to my inheritance.'

'Is that all you're concerned with, girl? Your damned inheritance?'

Amy was incredulous. 'Of course it isn't, Lizzie. Can't you tell when I'm joking?'

'Nobody jokes around here any more.' Lizzie turned back to her washing up bowl and began scrubbing at it with a scrunched up piece of scouring wire.

'Oh, Lizzie!'

Lizzie glanced up. ' "Oh, Lizzie!" ' she mocked, then went on, 'Why don't you take a look round the place before confronting your uncle? Don't you think that would be a better idea than baiting him at the cottage in front of Lawyer Ward?'

'Hey! That's a good idea. I'll start with the chapel.'

Lizzie's voice rose an octave. 'What's wrong with

starting with the house? Why do you have to go prancing out there to a mouldering heap of stones?'

'Because I want to see the damage. I need to know if there's anything that can be done for the place. If it's a danger to anybody, then it should be razed to the ground and the rubbish gotten rid of. Don't you agree?'

Lizzie Abercrombie began drying her hands on a tea towel, then said in an almost off-hand way, 'There's somebody else interested in the chapel, Miss Amy. A Mr Boden. He's been doing some restoration work there.'

Amy's interest was stirred. 'Why? What right has he to do that, Lizzie?'

'He's a friend of your uncle, is the man of stone, so that gives him the right,' Lizzie answered sharply. 'And as to your first question, girl – well, I reckon as how he's in love with that bloomin' Angel Gabriel.'

'Man of stone?' Amy gave a mock shiver. 'How creepy! Is that what this Mr Boden's like? A gaunt, grey statue? Man of stone! I like it, Lizzie. But who is Angel Gabriel?'

Lizzie threw a glance of resignation to the ceiling and stated, 'Mr Richard Boden is a widower who works a quarry over at Hatton-in-the-Dale, and Gabriel is the alabaster angel that used to be poised above the altar in the old chapel.'

'Heck! I remember that angel . . .' Amy's brow furrowed 'But I don't recall anybody by the name of Boden from the old days.'

'You're not going to let up till you get all the details, are you?' Lizzie sighed, walked over to the huge iron fire-gate and settled herself in an old wooden rocking chair beside the blazing hearth.

'Heck! I forgot all about that chair . . .'

53

'Do you *have* to keep yelling "*Heck!*" at me all the time, missy?'

'Sorry.' Amy strode over to the housekeeper and sank down on the hand-pegged rug at Lizzie's feet, begging, 'Come on, Lizzie. Tell me more about the man of stone.'

'Don't call him that.' Lizzie frowned at her. 'It was just an expression I used. He's okay, is Richard Boden. Nice. Quiet-spoken. Hard-working.'

Amy grimaced. 'Boring!'

'No, he's not.'

'I like Uncle Gif's chauffeur – "Plain" Graham.'

'Plain?'

'He gave me a telling-off for calling him Mister – said he was just plain Graham.'

'He was right, girl. Gif wouldn't like you getting familiar with the servants.'

'He's a chauffeur, for God's sake, not a slave in chains.' Amy rocked to and fro on her denim-clad bottom, her arms linked round her knees which were bent up in front of her.

'As well as not saying "Heck", don't say "for God's sake" either. Gif'll be on at you for blasphemy.'

Amy let out a huge sigh and felt decidedly repressed. 'Lizzie, I'm nearly twenty-four, and that's far too old to keep getting reprimanded all the time over what I should and shouldn't say.'

'He's still your guardian.'

'No! He's not. Oh, don't get me wrong, Lizzie. I respect Uncle Gif. I wouldn't do a thing to hurt him. But his guardianship ended when Kate and Marty adopted me. And that's a long time ago. After Christmas, if Uncle Gif wants me to stay here a while longer, I'll see if I can earn some money. I've trained to be a teacher, Lizzie, and I'm a

54

good one. I like kids – especially the tiny ones who are so cute.'

'You need kids of your own . . .'

Amy hooted with laughter. 'I need kids of my own like I need a wooden leg, Lizzie. There'll be plenty of time to think about a husband and kids when I get to thirty.'

Darkly, Lizzie warned, 'At twenty-three you should be looking seriously at your future.'

'Oh, Lizzie.' Suddenly Amy was impatient with the woman. 'Don't be so boring.'

'You're winding me up, aren't you?' Lizzie shook her head. 'I can see through you, my girl. You're just a-winding me up.'

'Maybe I'll fall in love with the enigmatic man of stone.'

'Huh! That'll be the day, girl – though it would please Gif.'

Swift as a shot, Amy asked, 'Why would it please Uncle Gif?'

Lizzie looked uncomfortable. She got abruptly to her feet and said, 'I don't have enough time to sit around gossiping.'

Amy scrambled up too, and laid a hand on the house-keeper's arm to detain her. 'Lizzie! What did you mean by that? Why would it please Uncle Gif if I fell in love with the man of stone?'

Lizzie crossly slapped the hand that held her, and Amy said, 'Ouch! What was that for?' as she jumped away.

'You ask too many questions, girl.' Lizzie went over to a cupboard and started reaching down saucepans.

Amy would not be put off. She followed, and said, 'Okay! I'll go and ask Uncle Gif.'

'No!' Lizzie spun round to her and dropped a saucepan in her haste to stop her leaving the kitchen. It clattered onto the hard paved slabs of the kitchen floor, and its lid rolled over to Amy and spun itself to a standstill against her feet.

Slowly, she bent down and picked it up, then straightened and looked at Lizzie Abercrombie, who appeared to be more dishevelled and awkward than ever before.

'Well?' Amy cocked her head on one side.

'Wells have water in them,' Lizzie grunted.

'You know what I asked you. Now, are you going to tell me?' Amy walked purposefully over to the table and placed the saucepan lid on it.

Lizzie, her face a dull red, muttered, 'He's got money. That's all I meant, girl.'

'Are you saying Uncle Gif would sell me to the highest bidder?' Amy's laughter pealed out. 'Oh, my God! Are we living in the Dark Ages or something?'

'Nobody mentioned anything about "selling" you.' A look of pain flitted across Lizzie's lined face.

'Hey! You're upset? What have I said?'

'Nothing.' Lizzie came and retrieved the saucepan lid, then walked over to the kitchen sink.

There was a prolonged silence. It lasted one minute, maybe two, while Amy thought back over what had been said. Suddenly things began to make sense. But it was preposterous, she reasoned. Marriages weren't arranged in England any more – at least, she hoped they weren't. Lizzie had her back to her. Amy watched her, wondering if she was going to say any more about Gif Weldon or Richard Boden. After a while, it became apparent that Lizzie had decided she'd said more than enough.

Quietly, Amy walked over to her. 'Seems I hit the nail right there on the head, doesn't it?' she said at Lizzie's side.

56

Lizzie turned her head away.

'You think you've let Uncle Gif down, don't you?'

After a pause for thought, Lizzie said, 'You don't know the half of it.'

'And you're not going to tell me? Right?'

'It's not my place to. I've said more than I ought already.'

'I'm going out, Lizzie.'

Lizzie nodded. 'Be careful near the river – it's almost in flood.'

'I'm not a little girl any more.' The words were kindly spoken.

Lizzie didn't answer.

Amy emerged from the courtyard archway and stood looking down on Wydale's parkland. Below her the River Eston skimmed like a black snake through the meadows, bending itself round clumps of willow, forging through reeds and laughing in triumph as it washed over the half-submerged stepping stones that sought to halt its headlong rush down into the valley.

Her gaze wandered to the quaint pack-horse bridge she'd been driven over less than twenty-four hours ago. It was constructed from large, flat stones and had no parapet. It was barely the width of a farm cart, and in the old days she remembered Uncle Gif had often said he'd do something about it when he had the time, but he never had. She wondered if the chapel would have been so badly damaged if a fire engine had been able to get near, and frowned as she realized how vulnerable the main house was, cut off so completely from the rest of civilization by that inadequate and out-dated little structure spanning the river.

It wouldn't take much effort by somebody who was experienced in such things, she reasoned, to widen the bridge and the tree-flanked avenue that led down to Duncan Ward's cottage and the main road.

A buzzing noise had her tilting her head and twisting round to watch a helicopter that seemed to be circling the house. She shaded her eyes and watched it for a few moments, then, her hands beginning to freeze, she pushed them inside her duffle coat pockets and began to walk towards the copse at the bottom of the hill that had always sheltered the chapel.

It was a bright, cold morning, with white fingers of cloud reaching out to her across the valley from Aspen Tor, the highest hill in that part of the county. Down beside the river, she turned her footsteps towards the chapel, determined that if Mr Richard Boden happened to be there she'd confront him and question him . . . But question him about what? she wondered suddenly. She couldn't just go up to him and say, I've heard a rumour that you're the highest bidder for my hand in marriage, Mr Boden, could she?

She scowled up at the winter-bare branches of beech and oak and caught a glimpse of the grey slate-clad steeple. Her heart leapt because if that part of the chapel was still standing, it couldn't be a complete ruin.

When she eventually saw it more fully, however, she came to an abrupt standstill and just stared in horror. It was a shell. A burnt-out wreck. And, although the main walls were still erect, there were gaping holes where exquisite stained glass windows had once been a feature of the place. The great mitred door was seared with scorch marks, and its splintering wood hung grimly onto a single hinge. Stone supports and arches had disintegrated into

heaps on the ground, with icy moss welding them together. The roof had lost its covering, but its rib-like
structure was still intact, though charred and scarred
throughout.

In the scorching heat of the fire, lead from the roof had
melted and wept itself into formless images among the
debris. Had it been springtime, it wouldn't have looked
quite so desolate, she knew. The grass would have been
ablaze with daffodils and aconites, and bluebells would
have swarmed round the boles of the ancient trees. The
carpet they made would have smoothed out the ridges
where the land dipped and dived its way down to the river.
As it was, though, the place looked utterly deserted, and
Amy had no desire to fight her way over those mounds of
rubble.

She was about to turn away and go back to the Hall to
wait for Uncle Gif when she heard a noise – a faint
scraping from the very depths of the chapel ruins. She
listened. It came again – distant but unmistakable. Silently
she flitted towards the door and eased through the gap
where the support had all but collapsed. The sound now
was rhythmic – like somebody using a saw. But not on
wood; it was too harsh for that. She picked her way round
the smashed timber which was all that was left of the pews,
then stood still again, holding her breath.

The grating and the scraping was coming from what had
once been the chaplain's room at the far end of the chapel,
where the one remaining piece of roof looked sound.
Slowly now, she moved towards the screen passage; at
the end of that was the door of the chaplain's room.

All was quiet as she inched into the passage, which was
claustrophobic in its narrowness and smelled horribly of
damp. No sound at all came now from the room she

approached. It was almost as if somebody else was standing on the other side, just as she was doing on this, listening. Inwardly she laughed at herself. It would be the man of stone. It had to be him, she told herself. She grasped the iron ring of a doorhandle and leaned her weight on it.

And, with a hideous drawn-out creak, it swung inwards.

CHAPTER 4

He didn't look up as she watched him from the doorway.

The alabaster angel was lying prostrate in front of him, on some sort of a bench, and the man was leaning over it, half facing the door, intent on measuring a minute part of one of the wings. Richard Boden – for it had to be him – had a pair of curved callipers in one hand and a pencil in the other.

'Come in and sit down, Gifford,' he murmured. 'I've put you a chair over by the stove.' He gave a slight inclination of his head towards a corner of the small room.

Man of stone, he was. Amy's sense of fun came to the fore. 'I've been called some things,' she drawled softly, 'but never have I been mistaken for a man in his sixties.'

His head jerked up at the sound of her voice. 'Hell and damnation!' His concentration lost, the pencil slipped out of his fingers and bounced on the floor.

'I hope Gabriel will forgive you those two choice words,' she said, her eyes alert as she walked into the room and closed the door. She held out her hand. 'I'm Amy Weldon. And you, I take it, are Mr Richard Boden.'

He looked like a man who'd just been hit squarely on the head with a mallet and was going to slide into unconsciousness at any moment.

'I sure am having some effect on you, aren't I?' She took a few steps towards him, her hand still out-stretched. 'I understand this is the way English people say hello – or should it be a prim and proper "How do you do?"'

He sprang into life and a big hand shot out and closed round hers. 'Heck! I'm sorry. I just wasn't expecting you.'

He let go her hand after giving it a vigorous shake. 'Should I have made an appointment to see you?' she asked in a teasing voice.

'Heck!' he said again. 'Heck, no!'

'Mrs Abercrombie tells me off for using slang like "Heck"! I thought I was the only person in England who said "heck" – and now I find a guy just down the road saying it too.' She grinned. 'Seems like you and I speak a universal language Mr Richard Boden.' With the words she walked over to the bench and gazed down on the angel. 'What are you doing to Gabriel?'

She lifted her glance to the man's face then, immediately liking what she saw – a strong jawline, steady brown eyes and well-defined features. Was this really the man who was planning for her to marry him? She decided to keep quiet for the moment on that score.

'Er . . .' He seemed put out by her presence, but quickly collected his thoughts. 'Didn't your uncle tell you? I'm trying to get the wings right. One was chipped when the angel fell during the fire. I've smoothed it down and carved it, but vital inches were lost, so now I have to match the other wing up to it. Look . . .'

He moved out of her way and gave his attention to the alabaster figure once more. He leaned down low to line up the angel with his eyes. His big hand reached out and one finger traced an imaginary line at the base of Gabriel's wing. 'See this part here?' He twisted his head round so he was looking intently up into her face.

She nodded. 'I guess so.'

'It has to come off. I was just measuring how much when you came in.'

'How will you take it off?'

'With a forged flat chisel, I think. I don't want to risk damaging this side – it's relatively unscathed.'

His voice was pleasantly soft. He sounded well educated. She said, 'May I touch it – the wing?'

'Of course.' He made as if to step away from her, to give her more space, but, impulsive as ever, she was already reaching past him and her hand brushed his.

A prickling sensation along her knuckles reminded her of the times she brushed her hair and it crackled and clung to the bristles. 'You're loaded with static, honey,' Kate Weldon had said. 'Just goes to show I must have been feeding you properly all these years. You're bouncing with health!'

She laughed up at Richard Boden. 'Sorry about that. Guess I've been overdosing on the vitamins.'

His eyes were amused. He had expressive eyes, she saw, and not many men did. And a lot of men wouldn't have been talking to her as this man was – as if she were a person who was able to understand the work he was doing and not just a good-looking dame he was out to impress. It was refreshingly different to talk to a man like Richard Boden. And she had to admit he wasn't turning out to be anything like the guy she'd imagined him to be – and *that* was a sobering thought!

'It's warm. I expected it to be cold.' She smoothed the flat of her hand over the angel's wing. I always thought marble was cold.'

63

'It's alabaster,' he said. 'Alabaster's a softer substance. Much easier to work with.'

'Yeah?' She tilted her head to look up at him. He was a big man, well over six feet in height. He made her feel feminine and small – not at all like her usual gawky five feet eight inches. A smile sprang naturally to her lips. 'You like alabaster, don't you?'

In a sarcastic way, he said, 'How did you guess that, ma'am?'

She answered, seriously. 'You talk about it like it's a woman.'

She saw a wariness come into his eyes.

'Don't mind me,' she said. 'I'm the dumbo who invented the tactless remark, Mr Boden.'

'Can we do away with the mister?' His eyebrows shot up. 'I'd like to think we could become friends.'

'What do your friends call you? Richard? Dicky?'

He had trouble trying not to laugh, though his eyes smiled. 'What would they call me in the States?' he asked.

She thought about that for several minutes, then said, 'Bodie, I guess. It's a nice strong name, isn't it?'

'Do you want to call me that?'

Slowly she shook her head. 'Uncle Gif would have a fit.' She grimaced. 'What does *he* call you?'

'Richard, most of the time. Sometimes "my boy" . . .'

'Oh, my God!' She burst out laughing.

'I know. I know. Hardly appropriate – I'm well out of boyhood.'

'You're not so old, Richard.' Suddenly she was serious. She prided herself on being a good judge of character and there was something about Richard Boden that had made him so he'd never completely grow up, even though he must be in his late thirties right now, she decided. It would still be there when he was eighty. He was that kind of man.

'I was going to come up to the Hall and introduce myself today,' he said.

She grinned at him again. 'Then I saved you the trouble – poor old man. Can you really still manage that steep hill up to the courtyard?'

His easy laughter rang out around the old stone walls. It was genuine. She liked a man who could laugh at himself.

He said, when he'd sobered a little, 'Somebody told you about me, though. You knew my name.' He moved away from her, bent down and picked up the pencil he'd dropped earlier.

'Lizzie Abercrombie!' Amy could see the whole of the angel Gabriel now, and she was impressed by the sight. 'I guess old Gabriel here must have been in quite a mess?' She met his eyes over the alabaster figure.

'A bump on the nose, a few scratches and that damaged wing, but he was lucky. By some chance he toppled backwards out of his window niche, escaping a lot of the heat by doing so.'

'What are you going to do with him? He can hardly stand aloft in all this chaos, can he?'

He began measuring the tiny detail on the wing again. She moved round the head of the angel and to his side, tilting her head to watch more clearly what he was doing. He made a few scratches with the pencil then turned to a battered table underneath the one mitred window in the room and placed the callipers down among other tools.

He stood weighing up different sized chisels in his hands, and, not looking directly at her, answered, 'I aim to rebuild the chapel in my spare time.'

She laughed outright. 'You say that as though it's a five-minute job.'

65

His head twisted towards her again and he was smiling, the skin at the side of his dark eyes crinkling into a score of tiny merriment lines. 'I'll need help, of course, but there are plenty of lads at the quarry who wouldn't mind a bit of overtime.'

'You'd pay them to come here?' she asked incredulously.

'It's a promise I've made to myself,' he replied with a shrug. 'Anyway, a man needs a hobby – and, since I didn't have one before, I've made the chapel into mine.'

'How did you meet Uncle Gif?' Suddenly she was curious.

'I'm a quarryman, Amy. I sell gypsum for building purposes, and I also deal in the local stone that Wydale's built from. Your uncle asked for an estimate on one or two jobs up at the Hall. I don't know if you've noticed but . . .'

'The place is disintegrating around our ears!' She pulled a wry face. 'Yeah. Lizzie Abercrombie told me.'

'Gifford wanted the west wing renovated, but it needs underpinning; it's not safe.'

She nodded.

He faced her, chisel in one hand, a small mallet in the other. 'It was only the tip of the iceberg,' he said. 'When I saw the state of the Hall in its entirety, I told your uncle it would be wiser for him to concentrate on more essential repairs than the west wing. After all, the west wing *could* be demolished without it having a detrimental effect on the rest of the place. I didn't see the point in Gifford wasting money on something that's so obviously beyond repair.'

Pensively she asked, 'How much would it take to put Wydale back into shape?'

66

He walked slowly back to the bench and looked down on the angel. Pursing his lips, he said, 'Shall I tell you to the nearest hundred thousand, or do you want it more precise than that?'

'Phew!' She pushed her hands into the pockets of her coat and considered his words. She was glad he'd been straight with her, though. 'It really is serious, then?' She glanced up at him.

He met her eyes with a straightforward and honest look and said, 'We'll go over the place together – with Gifford, of course – if you like. I can give you an inventory of what needs doing. And you can always get another independent estimate.'

Slowly she nodded. 'I don't think we'd need another one. I guess we can trust you, Mr Boden.'

He was about to start work on the angel's wing when suddenly he downed his tools and said, 'Damn! I nearly forgot. I've got something for you. I was going to bring it up to the house this afternoon and leave it with Lizzie Abercrombie.'

'For me?' She looked at him in surprise.

'A little homecoming gift. If you'll accept it, of course.'

'Mr Boden – how kind.' Was this a sweetener? she wondered. And then she felt guilty for thinking such a thing. He didn't seem at all the kind of man who would stoop to subterfuge. He'd been incredibly nice to her so far – *and* down-to-earth honest as well.

He said in a serious tone, 'I really do think I'd rather be called Bodie than *Mr* Boden, Amy.'

A little self-consciously she said, 'Richard would be more polite, don't you think?'

'It doesn't come naturally to you, though, does it?' He was remarkably intuitive, she realized. She laughed softly and replied, 'No! To be perfectly honest, it doesn't. It puts me in mind of a big brother.'

'I'd hate to be your big brother.' His deep voice was amused. Bodie would take years off me. I trained to be a boxer you know, when I was young. If I'd known you then, I might have gone into the ring as "Big Bad Bodie"! What do you think?'

'It would have suited you.' She laughed.

He stood and looked at her for a few seconds more, seeming deep in thought about something, then abruptly he turned and strode to a corner next to the alcove, where a small, round black stove was throwing out more fumes than heat. He picked up a plastic carrier bag and carried it over to the bench. Handing it to her carefully over Gabriel, he said, 'Take a look. Tell me if you like it. If not, I can do something different.'

She peeped inside. 'Marble! No – don't tell me – it's alabaster, isn't it?' She'd thrust one hand inside to feel at the awkwardly shaped articles inside the bag. 'It feels warm – just like Gabriel's wing.' She grinned across at him. 'What is it? Or ought I to say, what *are they*? There are two pieces of alabaster in here.'

'Bookends. I figured if you were going to be a teacher in the United States, then you'd enjoy reading books.' He leaned over Gabriel again and said, 'Here! I'll get them out for you, shall I?'

He helped her extricate the two pieces of alabaster and, when both were in his capable hands, allowed her to place the carrier bag to one side and take one bookend from him.

She drew in her breath as she examined it. On the opposite side to the square-cut end were carved minute faces of children of all nationalities. Gazing across the prostrate angel, she saw that the matching other half which he held was just the same. Happy little faces were intermingled, with the marking in the alabaster being used to full effect in order to create light and dark skin-tones. Amy had never seen anything so beautiful before. Shyly, and not at all in her usual brash manner, she said, 'I've never been given anything so lovely in my whole life.'

He shrugged off her thanks and picked up the bag. 'I hoped you'd like them.' He replaced the one he was holding inside the bag, then held out his hand for hers. She gave it to him. 'In fact,' he said, 'I carved those faces thinking they'd perhaps remind you of the kiddies you were going to teach in school. Gifford told me you'd given up the job to come over here, you see . . .'

'*You* carved these?' Her eyes widened.

He went and placed the carrier bag beside the door, then stood up and dusted his hands down his cord trousers. 'Well,' he said matter-of-factly, 'I'd hardly go out and buy alabaster in a shop, would I? Not when I make my living out of stone.'

She whirled to face him as he was returning to Gabriel. Her eyes were alight as she spontaneously stopped him with a hand on the rough wool of his much too large navy knitted sweater. 'In the States you could make a fortune with a talent like that.'

'It's just a hobby!' He dropped his gaze to the hand that was detaining him.

She felt a bit stupid for being so familiar as to touch him like that. But it had seemed the natural thing to do – and not at all premeditated, she told herself. She was surprised at herself. Naturally garrulous she might be, but she wasn't usually so effusive in showing her feelings. She let her hand fall away from him, and straight away it forced

69

itself into her duffle coat pocket again, where it clenched into a tight fist.

She was a fool, she thought. He *could* be trying to get into her good books by giving her such a gift. He *could* be softening her up so she'd be more amenable to him . . . Maybe he'd spun Uncle Gif some schmaltzy story about needing a wife to look after him in his declining years. Yeah! This Bodie fella would be reluctant to part with his cash – and Uncle Gif would be distraught at not being able to afford the repairs Wydale needed. So – wouldn't it be only natural for Bodie to suggest a merger?

She could just hear the pair of them, planning it all. 'Marriage with Amy, Gifford, old chap? And in return my money for Wydale?' And Uncle Gif must have agreed! 'What a good idea, my boy. Amy's almost twenty-four. Time she got herself settled down . . .'

'You look deep in thought, Amy.'

Startled, she jerked her head up. They were standing very close still. She felt her cheeks flaming. Had she given anything away? She hoped he hadn't been able to read what she was thinking. Uneasily she backed away, towards the door. 'I – I guess I should be getting back.'

'It's been nice meeting you.' He didn't attempt to stop her.

She came up against the door.

'Don't forget the bookends. I hope they come in useful.'

Useful! He had to be joking. They were exquisite. She doubted she'd ever dare use them for fear of damaging them. She smiled at him, bent down and picked up the bag – gingerly, cradling it in her arms lest the flimsy handles should give way. 'I sure appreciate the gesture.' She smiled in what she hoped was a purely convincing way.

'Can you find your way back?'

70

'Sure! I won prizes for tracking in high school.'

'Come and see me again.'

She nodded. She'd have liked to stay longer, but realized she had to go now she'd made the move to leave. 'Are you here every day?'

'Heck, no. I've got a business to run – the quarry up at Hatton-in-the-Dale. Usually I only manage weekends down here.'

'I won't see you for another few days, then?'

'Looks like it, doesn't it?'

She felt suddenly disappointed. She'd enjoyed talking to Richard Boden; she had the feeling he could be a good friend – if it were indeed friendship she wanted from him.

'You look laden down with that carrier bag.' He moved away from the angel and came over to the door. 'Here! Let me help.'

He had opened the door with the words and she passed out into the narrow passage. Once there, she paused for a second and said, 'By the way, maybe I should put you right about one thing.'

'Yes?' He was wary, she could see.

'You seem to have gotten the idea from Uncle Gif that I've given up the job at Paisley Junior in Boston.'

'Well, yes. Gifford said – '

She broke in abruptly. 'They're holding it for me for six months.' She flashed him a brilliant smile. 'I've no intention of staying in England for good, you see. I'm just over here for a visit – nothing more.'

Very calmly he said, 'Maybe, then, Amy, you should put your Uncle Gif straight on the matter.'

'Yeah.' She smiled, then said thoughtfully, 'I guess I'll just go and do that.'

CHAPTER 5

'My dear girl – you are talking out of the top of your pretty little head.' Gif Weldon's smile was as foolishly benign as if he were talking to a five-year-old, Amy thought as he faced her across the dinner table that night.

'Uncle Gif, I'm serious.' Actually, Amy was furious at being talked down to in such a manner. But it was what she should expect, she supposed, from this man who had once been her guardian, and who, it seemed, still thought he could control her life.

He carried on eating his dinner, poking around the potatoes on his plate and cutting them into minute pieces before popping them into his mouth. 'But you can't go back to America. You've only just arrived over here.'

'I didn't say I was going back immediately. I said that Paisley Junior's principal is keeping the job open for me until the summer vacation. And I intend to return then, Uncle Gif. I mean it.'

'Eat up your dinner, there's a good girl.'

His smile was beginning to irritate her. She slammed her knife and fork down on her plate and took a deep breath, ready to lambaste him again. Somehow she had to make him see she wasn't a little girl any longer . . .

'Eat up your greens, child. And the chicken is excellent.

72

I shall have to congratulate Mrs Abercrombie on her culinary expertise.'

He really was insufferable. Culinary expertise, indeed. 'If I were Lizzie I'd tip the gravy boat over your head if you said that to me,' she said in a tense voice.

He looked only mildly surprised at her comment. 'But it's a compliment, Amy. Don't you like compliments? I'm sure Lizzie will take it as such.'

Amy was sure Lizzie Abercrombie wouldn't. She realized, however, that Uncle Gif had adroitly changed the subject.

Well, she decided, she'd told him now, hadn't she? And if he chose to ignore the fact that she would be going back to America, then that was his fault. He couldn't put her in chains and keep her here, could he?

His eyes twinkled. 'It's a pity we don't have a dungeon here at Wydale. I could have you thrown into it, my dear, until you'd cooled down a little.'

She took the remark as a joke and laughed in a bitter little way just as Lizzie Abercrombie came in through the door to clear the things away.

'Pudding?' Lizzie looked from one to the other of them.

To Amy, who was aware that the atmosphere in the dining room could have been cut cleanly through with only the minimal effort, the one word uttered by Lizzie was so incongruous it set her off in a fit of the giggles.

'Oh, Lizzie!'

'What have I said now?' Lizzie stuck the bunched up knuckles of both hands on her hips and glared.

'Pudding!'

Gif Weldon said, 'Take no notice of Amy, Lizzie. She's in a funny kind of mood.'

'He wants to lock me up in a dungeon. And then you come in and ask if I want pudding.'

'You're talking way above me,' Lizzie muttered. 'Now, do you want steamed ginger or not?'

'That will be delightful, Lizzie.' Gif Weldon's voice was sickly sweet. 'And I must compliment you on the dinner . . .'

'It was chicken. Just plain chicken,' Lizzie snapped. 'So don't you think you can get me on your side with your so-called flattery. Women have rights now, Gif Weldon. Women don't have to put up with patronizing behaviour from their employers.'

'You're more than just an employee, Lizzie, surely you know that?'

Lizzie's voice boomed out. 'You pay me a wage. I skivvy for you. Okay?'

Amy rose from her seat and started helping to clear the plates.

Lizzie Abercrombie waved her help aside. 'Sit down, girl.'

'But I don't want any ginger pudding, Lizzie. I'll come to the kitchen and start washing up with you.'

'It isn't your job.'

'Have you never heard of job-sharing?' Amy beamed at the housekeeper and scooped up two vegetable dishes from under her nose.

In the kitchen, Lizzie said. 'What were you upsetting him about?'

'I told him I'd be going back to the States in a few months' time. He seemed to have gotten the idea I was staying here for good.'

'Bad move, that.' Lizzie walked over to the old fash ioned fireplace and scraped the unwanted scraps off the

74

plates into the fire. The chicken bones and skin sizzled and spat. Lizzie straightened up then, and asked, 'Why did you have to do that? Don't you know he wants you to stay here indefinitely?'

'Well, I can't. I have a job waiting for me in Boston.' Amy turned the hot water tap full on.

'He's an old man. Can't you mollycoddle him a bit.'

Amy laughed as steam drifted up from the dirty crockery in the bowl. 'What on earth does mollycoddle mean, Lizzie?'

'Spoil him! Let him have his own way?'

'At the expense of my own life?' Amy's head jerked up.

'*His* life's nearly over, girl.'

Amy spun round from the sink, where she'd been swirling the bubbly water round and round with a plastic brush. 'Lizzie! You shouldn't say things like that.'

'I meant it. Why do you think I sent you that letter?'

'I thought Uncle Gif was at death's door when I read it.' Amy frowned. 'But he isn't, is he, Lizzie? Did he put you up to sending it? Just to get me back over here?'

'He didn't know I'd written. I let him think you wanted to come over for a holiday.'

'That was a bit devious.' Amy leaned against the spartan fitted kitchen units that were the only bit of modernization Wydale possessed, and watched as Lizzie came back across the room and clattered the plates into the bowl. She turned away then, and started dishing up steamed ginger pudding for Gif Weldon's dessert.

'Just don't go mentioning it again, missy – going back to the States.'

'If you must know, it was Richard Boden's idea to tell Uncle Gif.'

75

Lizzie stared hard at her. Then her eyes narrowed. 'Didn't take you long, did it? To hunt *him* out.'

'He was at the chapel. I didn't deliberately go on a man-hunt, for God's sake.'

Lizzie wagged a finger at her. 'I've told you not to say "God's sake" around here.'

Amy struck a pose and said, 'Richard Boden doesn't nag me about my accent. And Richard Boden says 'heck' just as much as I do.'

Lizzie mimicked her American accent and said, 'Richard Boden's got into your good books, then, has he, Miss Schoolmarm?'

'He's okay!' Amy turned back to the washing up and started splashing water about. She heard Lizzie leave the kitchen and go down the long stone-flagged passage towards the dining room with the ginger pudding.

When she came back, Amy asked, 'Why can't we all eat in here? The three of us? It's more cosy than that dreary boarded-up dining room.'

'Boarded-up?' Lizzie almost choked with laughter. 'That's wainscoting, my girl. Don't let our lord and master hear you calling it boarded-up.'

'It's dark and dismal, and it's got a horrible blue haze on it.' Amy shivered.

'The blue haze is caused by damp. Richard Boden says we need a proper damp course. Apparently they didn't know about such things when Wydale was built round about three hundred years ago.'

'You shouldn't have to eat on your own, Lizzie.'

'I'm a servant, Miss Amy.'

'Don't call me Miss Amy, for God's sake,' Amy stormed. 'I hate it, Lizzie. I really do.'

'You've said it again, girl. "God's sake".'

76

'I feel as if I've been time-zapped back into the Middle Ages,' Amy grumbled. 'Can you blame me for cussing once in a while?'

Lizzie shrugged her broad shoulders. 'I suppose not.' She picked up a crisp, clean teatowel and started drying off the plates and cutlery as Amy washed them. Slyly, then, she asked, 'So! What did you think of him, then? Richard Boden?'

'Ah, the man of stone,' Amy said mysteriously.

'You do have some imagination.' Lizzie reached effortlessly into the top cupboards and stacked the plates away. 'Man of stone.' She snorted. 'I should've known better than to ask, I suppose.'

'He's okay. Actually, I liked him. He gave me some bookends he'd carved.'

'Bookends?' Lizzie's hands flew to her hips again. She stood rigid in the middle of the kitchen and gaped – there was no other word for it.

Amy started to laugh. 'Don't you approve of me getting gifts from Richard Boden?'

'Well! I never expected it. Usually he seems so kind of shy.'

'That wasn't the impression I got.' Amy turned back to her pot-washing. 'But tell me, Lizzie, what happened to his wife?'

'He told me she died – oh, it must have been way back in the mid-eighties. Some sort of complication in pregnancy.'

'Pregnancy!' Amy spun round to confront Lizzie Abercrombie again. 'Heck! I never thought of kids. He doesn't have any, does he?'

'No. It would've been their first – if Grace and the child had lived. He once brought a photo of her up to the Hall to show me.'

77

Amy's eyes narrowed. 'So – you and Richard are on quite good terms, eh, Lizzie?'

'You could say that.' Lizzie concentrated on drying the cutlery and placing it neatly away in a baize-lined box in one of the kitchen drawers.

'Aw, come on, Lizzie. Tell me about him. I'm having to drag every bit of information out of you.'

'I don't know no more.' Lizzie lifted her big shoulders in a shrug. 'He comes up for a cup of tea sometimes, when he's working in the chapel.'

'Can I invite him for dinner one night?'

'Why not? You seem to be taking over as boss around here, Miss America.'

'Are you trying to tell me something, Lizzie?'

'You ask too many questions. That's what I'm trying to say.' Lizzie slammed the drawer shut and hung up the teatowel, 'Now – if you don't mind – I'm going to my room to watch *Coronation Street*. Any objections to that?'

'*Coronation Street*? Is that one of those fly-on-the-wall programmes about the Queen?'

Lizzie said drily, 'Come and see for yourself, Miss Know-it-all. I think you'll enjoy it.'

'I will?'

'Yeah! Some of the characters are just like you – poking their noses into other folks' business whatever the cost. So you never know, you might just learn something new.'

Gif Weldon had agreed to Richard Boden coming over for dinner, but said he'd issue the invitation himself. Amy was disappointed. She'd hoped to be able to phone Richard herself, but Uncle Gif wouldn't hear of it.

'Not your place, my girl. As host, it's only right that I do the asking.'

'But I'll be your hostess.'

'You, Amy, are my visitor.'

Gif Weldon had been emphatic. There could be no argument. Amy realized she was, indeed, nothing but a visitor – even if she did stand to inherit Wydale at some distant date in the future.

Snow started to fall two weeks before Christmas. Looking out of her bedroom window on the bitterly cold and cheerless first day of it, Amy shivered, thinking longingly of the central heating they'd had in Boston. She dressed quickly, pulling on the first things that came to hand from the double-doored antique wardrobe: a polo collar black shirt, black jeans and a thick, lined red sweatshirt. Boots, she decided, were a must – especially if she intended going out walking, as she had done every day for the past week since she'd arrived at Wydale. She'd covered miles on foot – to the despair of Lizzie Abercrombie *and* Uncle Gif.

After breakfast, which she'd eaten alone in the lofty kitchen because Lizzie was occupied with the two women who came up from the village to clean twice a week, Amy sauntered out into the great hall. She caught a glimpse of her uncle disappearing into his study, which was situated off a draughty stone passageway leading out of the hall, but decided not to disturb him.

She looked up at the portrait of Barbara Weldon above the empty, cleaned-out firegrate and shrugged. 'Well, Babs, old girl,' she said, 'looks like my company's not top priority in anybody's diary this morning. Guess I'll go climb that diddy little mountain out there, huh?'

'Who d'you reckon you're talking to?'

Amy spun round. Lizzie Abercrombie usually made a clatter when she was near. Today she'd appeared silently, and apparently out of nowhere.

79

'Hell's bells, Lizzie. You scared me.' Amy's attention, though, had been caught by the incongruous pair of fluffy pink slippers Lizzie was wearing. Anything more feminine on the Amazonian Lizzie she couldn't imagine. She laughed. 'What on earth have you gotten on your feet, Liz?'

'Slippers! Ain't you got eyes in your head, girl?'

'I usually hear you coming.'

'Today I've got a bad case of chilblains.'

'Oh! I see.'

'And I've been supervising them two from Hawkwood. Setting 'em to work in different parts of the Hall. They get gossiping if not, and then no work gets done. If I wear slippers, I can creep up on them and surprise them if they start to slow down on the cleaning.'

'Do you want me to help any, Lizzie?'

'Nope! You're not here to work.'

'Is it okay if I go out, then?'

'Is that what you were asking madam up there?' Lizzie jerked her head meaningfully at Barbara Weldon's portrait.

'What happened to her, Lizzie?' Amy stared again at the portrait that had always fascinated her.

'She left. Or so I heard. It was before my time.'

'But why? Why did she go?'

Lizzie shrugged. 'How should I know?'

'Was there an argument?' Amy had the distinct feeling that Lizzie was holding something back.

'Look! He divorced her. What more is there to know?' Lizzie waved a hand aimlessly in the air.

'But he must have loved her. He still keeps her portrait hanging up there.'

'Love! Love doesn't mean a thing.'

80

'Well, I always knew you weren't the world's most incurable romantic, but . . .'

'But nothing, Miss Amy. Love's merely nature's way of telling a body that its hormones are working properly. That's all love is. It's all very well for you young 'uns, getting all starry-eyed, but there comes a time when you have to wake up to reality and admit that love isn't half the fun it's made out to be.'

'She looks kinda lonely up there, Lizzie.'

'So? She's lonely? Is that reason enough for you having a brainstorm and starting to talk to a picture?'

'I was telling her I intended climbing a mountain.'

'What mountain?'

'Aspen Tor. The big hill to the north of Wydale . . .'

'I know which hill Aspen Tor is, girl. You don't have to spell it out to me.'

'It used to fascinate me during the few months I lived here when I was a kid, Lizzie. I loved to see it covered in snow. When I went to America, I made a promise to myself that if I ever returned I'd climb right to the top.'

'You're stark, staring mad. What d'you want to do that for?' Lizzie's bunched fists flew to her hips.

Amy was beginning to have a theory about Lizzie and her hands-on-hips pose. She reckoned it was so Lizzie could take up a larger amount of space than usual, and therefore have more notice taken of her.

'I want to climb it because it's there. Isn't that why most people climb mountains?'

'Well, it's not going to run away. It'll still be there when the weather's better. And it's hardly a mountain. I've walked to the top many a time.'

'I want to take some film.'

'Snapshots?'

81

Amy spluttered with laughter. 'Oh, my God! Whatever are snapshots?

'Photographs. That's what we used to call them when I was a girl.'

'I'm talking about video film, Lizzie.'

'Video?'

'Yeah! Video! The little black box thing that we *don't* have at Wydale.'

'Well, what's the point of taking video film if we can't see the result?'

'I'm going to buy one. A video cassette recorder. We could connect it to your little television set, couldn't we?'

'Oh, no!'

Amy turned her back on the fireplace and confronted the housekeeper head-on. 'Why not?'

Lizzie's hand deserted a scraggy hip to wag a finger at her. 'You ain't connecting nothing electric to *my* telly, Miss Amy. I don't want nothing new-fangled blowing up my little TV set.'

Amy started walking towards the older woman. 'Oh, Lizzie. You are old-fashioned. Nothing's going to blow up, for God's sake.'

'Things have been blowing up ever since you arrived, child. Look at the way you took off – first at your uncle, then at me. You sure aren't noted for tact, you Americans, are you?'

Amy stopped dead, feet away from Lizzie Abercrombie, and said quite calmly, 'You got me here under false pretences, Lizzie. I expected Uncle Gif to be at least bed-ridden – and what do I find? An argumentative old man who seems to care for nobody and nothing except his precious house – that's what I find. So – while we're on this subject – will you tell me honestly just why did you ask me to come?'

82

'You wouldn't understand.' Lizzie stuck her nose in the air and pretended to be affronted.

'Lizzie! I want some answers. I'm not a child. You can't say, Do this, Do that, and expect me to obey every command without question.' She walked round the woman towards the staircase that led out of the great hall, and with her foot on the first stair turned back to the housekeeper and said, 'Lizzie! I *need* some answers.'

Lizzie Abercrombie moved round slowly to look at the girl. 'You think I'm crazy, don't you?'

'I'm beginning to think I'm the crazy one – coming hurtling across the Atlantic at a minute's notice on nothing but a wild-goose chase.'

Lizzie's usually sallow features were uncomfortably flushed. 'There was once a *Mr* Abercrombie,' she said at last.

Amy looked at her blankly. 'What's that got to do with it?'

'I dreamed a dream . . .'

Amy looked up at the ceiling. 'Don't we all, Lizzie? Don't we all?'

'Not that sort of dream. This was a bad one. A real one. And it wasn't the first I'd ever had, see?'

Amy was becoming impatient. Had Lizzie brought her all the way from America for this? She spread her hands. 'Lizzie – what the hell is going on here?'

'We were going through a bad time – me and Mr Abercrombie. His name was Tom, by the way.'

'Just when was this?'

Lizzie grimaced. 'Years ago. Twenty – twenty-two – who's counting after all this time?'

'And . . .?' Amy was getting impatient.

'I had this dream where a whirlwind picked me up and

83

sucked me into some sort of tunnel. There were trains whizzing past me at a hundred miles an hour, and then, just as I saw the light at the end of the tunnel, this brick wall came down right in front of me and shut it off. And I slammed right into it.'

Amy saw the glazed horror in the housekeeper's eyes. She said gently, 'We all have those sorts of dreams too, Lizzie.'

'Next day, Tom jumped off a railway bridge – into the path of an express.'

'God! No!' Amy slumped down onto the second stair and sat there just gazing in disbelief at Lizzie.

'I had another dream a couple of months ago.'

Amy felt her blood running cold. She couldn't speak.

'This time it was that little pack-horse bridge over the Eston I dreamed about.'

Amy still said nothing. A terrible kind of fear was surging through her.

'You were in the dream. You were a little girl and you came running up the avenue from Duncan Ward's cottage. There was a terrible storm raging – branches flying everywhere – and you were scared, I could tell. You know what it's like in a dream, Miss Amy, you want to go and help, yet you feel rooted to the spot, unable to move – except in slow motion.'

Amy nodded and said hoarsely, 'Go on, Lizzie. Tell me how it ended.'

'Well, just as you reached the river, and were about to set foot on the bridge, it was swept away. You were stuck there. You on one side of the river and Gif Weldon laughing like a maniac on the Wydale side.'

Amy shivered, but had to ask, 'What happened?'

Lizzie uttered what sounded like a sob. 'That damned

84

angel Gabriel – the one that Richard Boden's so obsessed with – it suddenly appeared, rearing itself up out of the swollen river, all life-like and kind of weird, swaying this way and that – not a bit like it really is – just a lump of solid alabaster. It looked first at you, and held its arms out, and I felt like screaming my blooming head off at you, telling you not to go to it. But I couldn't utter a word. And you put a hand out towards it, but . . .' Lizzie shuddered. 'But it seemed to change its mind then, and turned instead to your uncle. It reached out to him, and Gif just stood there as its wings opened up, and it went for him . . . And then I woke up.'

Amy felt as if melted ice were running down her spine. She lurched to her feet and rushed across to Lizzie. Lizzie's arms went round her, and they clung together. Neither spoke for several minutes. They stood locked together, rocking soundlessly.

Eventually Amy looked up and whispered, 'What does it mean, Lizzie?'

'Lord knows. I don't. All I know is, I had the same feeling when I woke as I did the time my Tom died.'

'And you say it had happened before . . . before your husband died?'

'Many a time, ducks. And always with the same result.'

'A death? Oh, God, Lizzie – you're giving me the creeps.'

'Did I do right? Sending you that letter, child?' Lizzie at last held her away and looked into her eyes.

Numbly, Amy nodded, then said, 'Lizzie – I have to get out of here for a while. Do you understand? I'm going out – up to Aspen Tor. I need time to sort things out . . .'

Lizzie's hands fell away from her. She nodded, but warned, 'Be extra careful near that river . . .'

CHAPTER 6

As Amy set out, huddled up in her warm duffle coat and bright yellow scarf, she heard again the sound of a helicopter in the skies above Wydale. On the riverbank, just past the pack-horse bridge, she halted and shaded her eyes to look up above the trees that bordered the burnt-out shell of the old chapel. Like Gifford Weldon, she too wondered why the helicopter always seemed to be hanging around the big house.

She heard a yell from behind her and turned to see Lizzie waving madly from the courtyard archway. 'Phone! America! You're wanted!'

'Hell!' Amy forgot all about the helicopter as she raced back up the hill to Wydale. In the big hall, with Barbara Weldon's black eyes staring down at her from the portrait over the fireplace, she took the call.

'Kate! It's lovely to hear your voice. Did you get my letter?'

'Not yet, kiddo. Didn't really expect one, though. After all, you've only been there a week – and you did call me that first night to let me know you'd arrived okay.'

'I made sure the letter was air-mailed.' Amy frowned.

'Don't worry. It'll come. What've you been up to, Amy?'

Amy smiled into the telephone. She missed Kate – missed Marty too. 'Not much! How's Marty?'

'Fine! He says I oughtn't to be a drag on you, but I couldn't help wondering if you'd gotten any clues to Kitty's identity yet, honey.'

Amy was guiltily aware that with a week in England behind her she'd made no effort yet to try and trace Kip's girlfriend. 'No news on that front yet, I'm afraid,' she apologized. 'Wydale's a bit remote. I haven't been able to get into any of the big towns where I might be able to make enquiries.'

'Shouldn't think you'd find anything out in Derbyshire anyway,' Kate said. 'Seeing as how this Kitty girl must be from Lincoln, where my Kip was stationed.'

'Yes, I suppose so,' Amy agreed. 'But Lincolnshire is also near Norfolk too, so Kitty could be from either of those two places. And, yet again, Nottingham could also be a possibility.'

'Honey – I've given you a mammoth task, I *do* realize that, but you will try to find her, won't you . . .?'

Amy heard the raw note of appeal in Kate's voice, and knew she ought at least to *try* locating the elusive Kitty. She thought quickly, then said, 'Kate, I'll go into Hatton right now – it's quite a big village near here. They must have a library and I'll be able to find out about local newspapers in the area where Kip was staying. I'll place an ad then, and see if I get any response. How's that?'

'Sounds fine by me, kiddo.' Relief poured out over the miles and Amy found herself wanting to put her arms round Kate and hug her.

'Take care of yourself,' she urged. 'I'll do all I can, Kate.'

'I'm a pest, aren't I?'

'Of course you're not.'

'I'll call you again. Next week, huh?'

'Great. I'll look forward to that.'

As Amy replaced the receiver she chewed pensively on her bottom lip, knowing she couldn't let Kate down. But it would be bordering on the miraculous, she knew, if the unknown Kitty actually saw a small advertisement in a newspaper. But how else was she to start the search? she wondered. And, looking further ahead than that, what would she do if the advertisement did, in fact, draw a blank?

The lumbering little bus must have been at least fifty years old, Amy reckoned. Its engine juddered and its brakes jammed on each time it halted to pick up passengers every half-mile or so. The village of Hatton was situated high above the hamlet of Hatton-in-the-Dale, where Richard Boden reputedly worked his quarry, she remembered. And the journey, which couldn't have been much more than eight miles from Wydale, took more than an hour to complete.

Amy had to admit to herself that she did miss having a car at her disposal; in Boston, after Kip had gone into the Army, she'd used his convertible to get about. She could imagine it was going to be somewhat frustrating here in England without her own transport.

Hatton was a busy and quite modern village, with pedestrianized areas and shops. The library, though small, was up to date, and Amy found telephone directories for every part of England on its shelves. She quickly made notes of the addresses and telephone numbers of all the newspapers in the Lincolnshire and Norfolk areas nearest to that part of the coast where Kip had been stationed. That done, she spent a lazy hour looking at the shops after finding out she had quite some time to wait for her bus back to Hawkwood. In a chrome and glass burger bar, sipping coffee, she watched the people passing by outside the window. Suddenly, though, she became aware of somebody out there watching *her*.

'Richard!'

The big man, huddled on the paving stones in his substantial tweed coat, saw her up-tilted lips form his name. Her eyes lit up in recognition, and a rush of pleasure assailed him. He was immediately glad that he hadn't just walked on when he'd spotted her. She beckoned to him, her smile wide and welcoming.

He'd never been in a burger bar before; it made him feel suddenly young again, and reminded him of his teenage years. He asked for a coffee at the counter, then carried it carefully over to her table.

'Hi!' Her elbows were resting on the table top, her hands supporting her chin. She looked like a kid, he thought, in that duffle coat – unbuttoned and showing a glimpse of red sweater – and a long yellow scarf that was pushed back on her shoulders, its ends almost touching the floor.

He sat down opposite her. 'I thought I must be dreaming when I saw you. What on earth are you doing here?' Carefully he eased the lid off his plastic coffee-cup. 'This looks hot.' He raised his eyes to meet hers and grinned at her.

'It is. Hot, I mean. The coffee.' She seemed to be glad he'd joined her, Richard thought. She took a long sip out of her own cup, appeared to be savouring it, and closed her eyes. 'Mmm. I don't get coffee at Wydale, you know. I'd almost forgotten what it tasted like.'

He laughed and she opened her eyes again and looked straight at him. Under the glaring lights of the burger bar her hair gleamed golden and her skin echoed the sun-drenched sheen of it in the healthy honey tan she'd brought with her from America. She was the most beautiful girl he'd ever known, he realized – well, not exactly beautiful in the classical sense of the word, but she had good bone structure, her skin was fine and clear, and her mouth was wide and generous. 'Have you been shopping?' he asked.

Her shoulders lifted in a shrug. 'Just browsing around.' Her grey eyes searched his face. 'And you?'

'My freezer was nearly empty.'

She grimaced. 'Lizzie Abercrombie's going to have kittens. I'll be late back at Wydale. She'll think I've gotten myself lost. I didn't know I'd have to wait going on two hours for a bus back.'

He pulled his mobile phone out of his back pocket. 'Here. Ring her. She won't worry then.' He laid it on the table.

'I expect she knows how slow the buses are around here.'

'Blame me for making you miss the earlier one, if you like. My shoulders are broad. I can take a telling-off from Lizzie Abercrombie any day.'

She picked up the phone and looked at it. 'Do I just dial the number?'

'You need a code from here – zero, one, two, nine, eight.'

He watched as she spoke to Lizzie and put the house-keeper's mind at rest. Then, as she was about to ring off, he held out his hand for the phone. Raising her eyebrows, she said, 'Hang on a minute, Lizzie. Mr Boden wants to talk to you.'

Richard said, 'I'll run Amy back in the Land Rover. Don't keep dinner waiting for her. We'll have something at this end.'

'Well! That was a cheek.'

He was startled to see something resembling anger flash into her eyes as he put the phone back in his pocket. She slumped back in her chair and cocked her head on one side. 'What happens if I say I don't want you to run me back?' she asked. 'I might just prefer going back on the bus? Did that thought ever cross your mind, Mr Richard Boden?'

'It'll be pitch-dark by the time the bus drops you off at Wydale,' he said patiently. 'And anyway, I don't like the idea of you walking up that long drive all alone. More snow's been forecast. If there's a heavy fall the bus might not even get that far.'

'You still have no right to organize my life.' There was a high spot of colour on each of her cheeks, he saw. And there was an undertone of impatience in her voice.

Richard Boden hadn't intended being high-handed with her. He said simply, 'I'm sorry, Amy.'

'You're not my damn keeper, for God's sake.' She stood up, fastened the toggles on her duffle coat and knotted the yellow scarf at her neck.

He glanced up at her. 'You should get yourself a set of wheels.'

'Try telling my uncle that.' Her mouth twisted wryly. 'He just tells me I can give orders to John Graham to chauffeur me any time I want to go somewhere.'

'So why catch the village bus?' Richard said. 'Why *didn't* you use your uncle's chauffeur?'

'I don't like giving orders, Mr Boden.' Her voice was ice-cool.

'You don't like taking them either.' Richard cursed himself the moment the words were out. He hadn't intended to annoy her, or to be so overbearing and patronizing towards her. It was just that he wanted to see her safely home. But he should have known better – he should have known she wouldn't take kindly to being bossed about. He didn't want a full-scale argument, so he decided to bow out while tempers were still comparatively cool.

He rose to his feet and said, 'Okay, Amy. Have a good journey home.' With the words, he swung away from her and went striding out of the café.

Outside he hesitated, half turning to see if she was following him. She wasn't. Through the window he glimpsed that she had seated herself at the table again and was finishing off her coffee.

A bleak feeling of irritation hit him. This was no way to carry on – not if he wanted to get the girl to marry him. But did he *really* want a wife who was so bloody-minded? She was nothing at all like Grace had been . . .

'Hell!' He hunched his shoulders and pulled up the collar of his thick overcoat. She was a bitch! And *he* was far too old for playing games. So let her catch the damn bus home – and let her walk half a mile up that long, dark alleyway of trees that led to Wydale. She was one girl who could take care of herself, of that he was in no doubt at all. She probably had a degree in karate, or something of the sort, in case she was set upon by muggers.

He made his way through the dwindling shoppers until

92

he reached the old market square that served as a car park on weekdays. The four-wheel drive was parked next to a puddle. In the dark he didn't see it until his boots skidded on the ice that had formed. 'Hell!' He swore again, and brought the flat of his hand down in a hefty swipe on the bonnet of the Land Rover. The alarm went off. 'Hell and damnation . . .!'

It was long minutes before he managed to get the door open, lean inside and stop the piercing wail that was filling the car park. But then he became aware of another noise nearby – somebody was laughing. And she was there, not three feet away from him, mocking him, throwing back her head and honking away like a seal. He'd never heard a woman laugh like that before, and his ill temper just melted away at the sight of her – and the sound of her.

He straightened and looked right at her. 'Who needs a car alarm with a laugh like that?' he asked, straight-faced.

She bent over double, trying to stop the raucous noise but almost choking in her efforts to appear more ladylike.

'Don't mind me,' he said, folding his arms and leaning against the vehicle. 'I can just stand here and freeze to death while you do your impersonation of Sammy the Seal.'

Eventually the fit of laughter passed, but she still had trouble keeping that mobile and expressive face of hers under control. She shoved her hand in her pocket and found a wool glove that she used to wipe her eyes. 'You looked so funny . . . slipping on that puddle . . .'

He wanted to laugh too, but managed to keep his own face straight. 'You like that sort of comedy? Slapstick? Remind me to throw a custard pie one of these days.'

'Oh, Richard!' She shook her head. 'That's the best laugh I've had since I left Boston.'

'Call me next time you're in a deep depression. I'll do my slipping on a banana skin routine.'

All animosity dispelled, she said, 'Richard Boden – with my zany humour and your dead-pan expression, I guess we'd make a great double act.'

'Double act?' His eyebrows shot up. 'I could misconstrue that as a proposal of marriage, you know.'

She sobered instantly. 'Look! I'm not sorry I laughed at you – but I am genuinely pleased you didn't break a leg or anything when you slipped.'

'I'm pleased too,' he said. 'The way you were laughing, you wouldn't have been much help in an emergency, would you?'

'Oh, I'm real good on the first-aid front, Mr Boden,' she mocked.

He drawled softly, 'I'm glad to hear that, Miss Weldon.'

'I really would appreciate a ride home. If the offer still stands.'

'It'll have to be a "ride" to *my* home first,' he told her, amused. 'I have shopping in the back seat – freezer stuff.'

She shrugged carelessly. 'Okay!' She said, and made her way round to the passenger door. Cocking her head on one side, she went on, 'I'd like to make a bet that you have central locking.'

He nodded.

'I knew it! You're all geared up on the modern stuff, aren't you? Mobile phone, truck alarm. I think it must just be Wydale Hall that's in a time-warp. Everybody else seems to have moved into the twentieth century round here.'

'Truck?' he growled, then raised his eyes to the snow that was falling quite heavily now from the dark evening sky. '*Truck*?' He shook his head at her. 'We really shall

94

have to teach you some manners, Amy. My trusty old Land Rover will object to being called a common or garden *truck*!'

She sat humming beside him as he drove out of Hatton village and they started the short five-mile journey to Hatton-in-the-Dale. Snow was battering the windscreen and sticking to it before they were even half-way there.

'What's the tune?' he asked.

She stopped humming and twisted her head round to look at him. 'Is my humming so bad?' she asked. 'Don't you recognize the theme from *The Bodyguard*?'

'*The Bodyguard*? Is that something on TV?'

Her easy laughter rang out. 'It's a film! Surely you've heard of it? Heavens, man, it's even out on home video now, it's so old.'

'Can't say I have.'

'Richard, you've just got to be kidding.'

He glanced at her. 'I don't see many films.'

'Oh, my God. Don't you have multi-screen cinemas around here?'

'Not in Hatton – and certainly not in Hawkwood. Do you know, there's only one *pub* in Hawkwood.'

'Heck! No cinema? And with winter closing in.' She screwed up her forehead. 'What on earth am I going to find to do with myself?'

'Not much, if this snow settles.' He nodded at the windscreen, where the wipers were clearing two half-moons of glass and leaving all the rest snowy.

'Do you have a spare bedroom if I have to stay the night?' she asked in the darkness.

'I have three spare bedrooms, but you most definitely are *not* going to stay the night,' he replied.

'Why not? Surely you wouldn't turn me out into the snow?'

He glanced across at her. 'If you stayed, your uncle would be banging on my door in the morning with a shotgun and the vicar,' he said.

'But wouldn't it be worth it?' she couldn't resist taunting. 'You'd be awarded Wydale as consolation prize if you took me on.'

He was quiet for a minute or two, then he said, 'Somebody's been talking, I take it.'

'First day I was back,' she replied glibly.

'So now we know where we stand.'

'Oh, I knew that before I even met you,' Amy said. 'I just needed the opportunity to bring it up with you.'

He didn't answer, and soon the Land Rover drew up outside a large squat detached house that was located halfway up the main street of Hatton-in-the-Dale. The house was built of grey brick, with a slate roof and high chimneys. It looked solid and square, with oversized bay windows on either side of a wide oak door and conventional sash windows upstairs. There were other houses built of the same grey brick along the same stretch of road, but they were built in pairs and were not so large as this one. Across the road was a long row of stone cottages stepped into the hillside. One of them had a Christmas tree in its window, with fairylights twinkling, and a 'For Sale' board hanging by the side of its door.

Amy, looking at her watch, noted that it had taken less than ten minutes to drive there from the larger village of Hatton, and in that time, although she had peered out into the darkness, she'd seen no sign of a limestone quarry.

With the vehicle parked neatly at the side of the road, Richard Boden got out himself and then swung two plastic carrier bags out of the back seat. Amy jumped down onto the pavement amid a flurry of snow and said, 'Can I help?'

'No. This is all I've got.' He hurried round to her side then, to where a small walled garden fronted the house and a concrete path, fast being covered with snow, led to three steps and the solid front door.

'You're laden down with those bags. Give me your key. I'll open up,' she offered.

He slipped one plastic bag handle round his wrist and dived a hand into his pocket. 'I can manage.'

She didn't argue. She followed him up the little path and then waited at the bottom of the three steps while he unlocked.

The house was dark inside. 'Wait there,' he said as he stamped snow off his boots on the rough matting just inside the door. 'I'll switch a light on so you can see where you're going.'

The light dazzled her as she followed him inside. Once there, she was impressed. Long and wide, the hall had a lovely old central mahogany staircase, with matching panelled doors leading off all over the place. The light was so bright because it was encased in a mass of glittering Victorian crystal. She went and stood underneath it, and looked up admiringly.

Richard dumped the supermarket bags on a chair beside a bureau and watched her.

'It's genuine, isn't it?' She shaded her eyes with one hand.

'You know something about antiques?' he asked.

'A bit. Not as much as Kate, though. Kate would give her right arm for this crystal. It's her idea of heaven to spend a day at Beacon Hill hunting for a bargain.'

'Kate?'

'Kate Weldon – she and Marty adopted me when Uncle Gif couldn't cope with a kid under his feet.'

'And Beacon Hill?'

'Charles Street, actually – the flat part of Beacon Hill in Boston. It's a paradise for antiques-hunters like Kate. Me, I like the bookshops, but with Kate it's anything Victorian – and that's what your glass is, isn't it? Victoriana?'

'So my mother used to tell me.'

'This was your mother's house?'

He smiled gently. 'A long time ago. Mam's been dead nearly twenty years. Dad went a couple of years before that.'

'Mam!' She warmed to him. 'That sounds nice. Nice and homely.'

'Mam was like that.'

A sudden draught had her turning round to close the heavy front door. Snow had blown inside and onto the mat. It started to melt into glistening drops of water in the heat from a large, modern radiator fastened to the wall next to the door.

'Gee! Central heating.' She rubbed her hands together. 'I'd forgotten what it was like.'

He laughed and picked up the plastic bags again. 'Follow me through to the kitchen. I'd better get this lot dumped in the freezer.'

She stood in the doorway and watched as he deposited bags of frozen vegetables and packets containing ready meals into the substantial chest freezer on the other side of the great, comfortable room he called a kitchen.

It was a cheerful place, painted mainly yellow, and it had obviously been sympathetically planned to keep the character of the place. Copper was a gleaming feature –

copper and cast-iron. The stove was a warm cream colour and was fuelled by coal. When Richard Boden had put his shopping away, he opened up one of the heavy stove doors and swung a big copper bucketful of coal into it. The fire hissed and glowed red as it swallowed up the fuel and started to burn right through it.

Amy could feel the heat reaching right across the kitchen to her. She went into the body of the room.

'Do you like it? Not quite America, I'd imagine, but it's me.'

Big, solid and dependable were the three words that came to her mind when he said that. Yes. The house most definitely had the stamp of Richard Boden on it.

'It's great. Can I see the rest of it?'

'When we've eaten you can, if you like. It's a very ordinary house, though.'

'It isn't what I imagined – for you.'

'What had you imagined?'

'Something really new. Something big and rambling, and standing in its own land. Probably with a swimming pool too.'

He gave a mock shudder. 'How awful.'

'You seem like a guy who moves with the times, though,' she said. 'I thought you would have designed your own house – instead, I find you living in the old Victorian family home.'

'My grandad built it. He built all the street.'

Interested, she said, 'Wow! Tell me more.'

'No more to tell,' he said. 'Take your coat off; you're starting to steam.'

She took off her duffle and scarf and handed them to him. He said, 'Your hair's all wet – the snow looks like diamonds in it.'

'Yours is the same.' She laughed and reached up a hand to ruffle his dark hair and scatter melted snow all over his wide shoulders.

He caught at her hand to stop her, laughing at her, gazing down into her eyes. Her hand twisted and locked round his wrist. His skin was warm to her touch, yet underneath she could feel the power in the rigid sinews as he fended her off.

His other arm was clutching her coat and scarf, but he was holding her away from him effortlessly. With one hand he prevented her getting near to him. And all the time he laughed down into her face.

'You're strong.'

'I have a physical kind of job.'

'Man of stone,' she taunted softly.

His laughter died away. 'Could you marry me?' he asked.

Shocked at his forthright question, her fingers tightened round his wrist for a moment, and then her hand fell away from him.

She couldn't take her eyes off his face, however, and he asked again softly, 'Well, Amy? Could you marry a man like me?'

'I don't intend marrying anybody,' she said, mesmerized by his stare, but not willing, for the moment, to give him the satisfaction of knowing she found him attractive.

'Not even to save Wydale Hall?'

'Wydale's my uncle's responsibility,' she flung back at him, more composed now, and making an effort to steady her voice.

'But it's *your* inheritance. Doesn't that mean anything to you?'

A shiver ran down her spine. With her hand disengaged

from Richard's arm she felt suddenly alone – and quite cold. 'Did you put Lizzie up to sending for me?' she wanted to know.

Slowly he shook his head. 'Not me, Amy. Not me.' He smiled, but the smile didn't quite reach his eyes.

She looked away at last, away to the table. 'We shouldn't have gotten into this kind of conversation,' she said.

He turned and walked away to arrange her coat over the back of a chair. He pulled it over towards the stove then, to where the heat would dry off the melted snow. It was a caring kind of gesture, the sort that a mother might carry out for her child.

'Do you like hot-pot?' he asked. 'It's been simmering in the oven all afternoon.'

He took his own coat off. Underneath he was wearing a plain beige wool sweater. He looked good in it. He was a no-frills sort of man. There wasn't even a cable stitch to relieve the absolute simplicity of the sweater. He was unlike anybody she'd ever met before. He fascinated her.

'Sounds fine.'

She walked over to the stove, needing to put some distance between herself and the man. Close up, his size dominated her; his presence invaded her thoughts. There was much about him which made her think of the majestic Balsam firs and the white mountains of home. Richard Boden was a man of the outdoors; Kate and Marty would take him to their hearts.

'Do you eat in here?' she asked, turning to him again with almost half the width of the kitchen – a safe distance – between them. 'I love meals in the kitchen with Lizzie at Wydale.'

'And in America?' He started getting plates, mugs and cutlery out and laying places at the polished solid oak table.

101

'We had a breakfast bar. And TV dinners at night.'

'TV's okay in its place.' He filled an electric kettle with water and switched it on.

'You have a TV set?'

He threw back his head and laughed. 'My name isn't Gif Weldon. Yes. I have a TV set. It's in the sitting room. I've just never been able to get into the habit of eating and watching TV at the same time.'

'I never saw your limestone quarry as we drove here.' Amy went over to the table and seated herself on a cushioned carver chair.

'That's because we didn't go anywhere near it. It's on the other side of the village. The planning moguls don't take kindly to limestone quarries encroaching on private housing.'

'I guess not.' She laughed.

The kettle boiled and he made a pot of tea. Would she ever get used to these everlasting cups of tea? Amy wondered. But, truth to tell, she was getting quite a taste for it.

Richard Boden then transferred a heavy-looking brown casserole dish from the oven to the table. He lifted the lid slightly and the aroma that escaped made Amy feel hungry.

'Mmm. That sure smells good.'

He replaced the lid and then leaned forward to place both his hands flat on the table, where he stood looking at her. 'Amy . . .' he began, then stopped and looked down at his hands.

'Do you want me to pour the tea?'

His head came up slowly, and his eyes looked incomprehensibly at her. 'What?'

'You said my name. You said "Amy", and then you

102

stopped – just as if you'd forgotten what you were going to say next,' she explained. 'I just wondered if you wanted me to pour the tea while you dished up the stew.'

'Heck, no,' he said. 'I hadn't forgotten what I was going to say. I was just wondering how to say it.'

'Just use simple words,' she said, grinning. 'They're the sort I understand.'

'I don't want any misunderstanding between us, Amy. I don't want any secrets. Secrets always seem to have a way of leaking out at the most inopportune times, don't you think?'

'I'm not a secretive person.' She grinned at him again. 'With me, Mr Richard Boden, what you see is what you get. So if you don't like it . . .'

'Don't joke about it, Amy.' His voice was ragged.

'Hey! What have I said?'

'It's *me* I'm talking about.'

'Oh! You have a secret, Richard?'

'Only from you. Everybody else knows about it.'

'So why hasn't it reached me?'

'Because *I* haven't told you – and I doubt whether Gif or Lizzie Abercrombie will have told you either.'

'Should they have told me?' She looked puzzled.

'Gif wouldn't. Gif wants you to believe I'm marriage material. Gif wants my cash for Wydale.'

'I know that. It's ridiculous really . . .'

'And I won't put money into something on which there's no return.'

She nodded. 'Yes. I figured that out too. I can't blame you . . .'

'Will you let me finish?' He pushed himself up straight and banged one clenched fist on the table. 'For heaven's sake, Amy, will you let me tell you?'

'Tell me what? Just what *is* this big secret? That you want to marry me for my inheritance – such as it is?'

'Heck, no.' He pushed an impatient hand through his thick dark hair. 'No, no, no!' he stated fiercely. 'It's just something I think you should know before you and I become more involved with one another.'

'You're Count Dracula in disguise?' she teased. 'Is that your big secret? If so, I'll let you into one too – I've always loved Dracula.'

'Are you *ever* serious?' He sighed.

He looked worried. She was instantly sorry for playing him up. 'Drat my sense of humour,' she said. 'Go ahead and tell me, then. I don't suppose it'll shock me, whatever it is.'

'I killed a man,' he said. 'You're sitting down to supper with a murderer.'

CHAPTER 7

Thoughts ran swiftly through her mind – the first being that she was in the house alone with him, snow was falling outside and, if she was to believe all she'd heard about English winters, she *could* in fact, be stranded here for days.

Then thought number two struck her. She was hungry. And that hotch-pot – or whatever it was he had called it – was not going to go to waste if she could help it.

Ever practical, she said. 'So sit down and tell me about it. But first will you serve up some of that hotch-pot stuff?'

'Hot-pot,' he corrected gently, his eyes softening into that look she found so attractive, where those tiny creases fanned out from their corners. He sat down and filled wide-bordered soup plates with cooked lamb and vegetables and handed her one of them.

'Thanks.' Her own hands were steady as a rock as she took the plate from him.

'You aren't shaking in your shoes, I note,' he said.

She glanced across the table at him. 'I guess you'd be inside doing time if you'd been found guilty,' she reasoned.

'Thank God, it didn't come to that.'

'So who did you kill?' She tasted the food he'd spooned out for her. It was steaming hot and delicious.

'A man I was fighting.'

'Over a woman?' she flashed.

'Heck, no. I told you, I did a bit of boxing in my youth.'

'So it was legal?'

'Killing's never legal, Amy.' He wasn't smiling any more, she noted.

She nodded slowly. 'Guess I didn't mean it that way. What I did mean was – it wasn't premeditated murder, was it?'

'I went a bit mad. He'd made a crude remark about the girl I was going to marry just before the fight. I shouldn't have gone through with it. You're not supposed to hate the fellow you're fighting. Boxing's a sport, not something you can pour your hatred into.'

'Tell me about the girl.'

He fell silent and, looking across at him, she saw he was frowning.

'Lizzie told me you were a widower,' she said gently. 'But if it hurts to talk about her . . .'

'I was the one who said I wanted no secrets.' A glimmer of a smile touched his stern features. 'And Grace is no secret. She died ten years ago.'

Amy, halfway through her plate of hot-pot, stopped eating to say, 'You loved her.' It wasn't a question, it was a statement. She knew from the expression on his face that he had indeed loved Grace.

'Yes,' he said. 'I worshipped her.'

'It made no difference to *her* that you'd killed some-body, then?'

'She made me stop fighting. I would've done anyway, but she threatened she wouldn't marry me if I didn't give it up.'

'Were you a good fighter?' Amy carried on eating.

106

'A bloody good one.'

'Do you regret giving it up?'

He grimaced. 'No. Not now. I'd have met my match one day, and when you hear of the awful things that can happen to boxers – well, I suppose I had a lucky escape. It made me realize how precious life is, though. I vowed then, all those years ago, that I'd never, ever lift a finger to hurt anybody again – no matter what they did to me.'

'I can't imagine *anyone* enjoying a fight.'

'But you're a fighter,' he teased. 'Look how you're fighting your Uncle Gif – and me!'

'That's different – I'm using brains, not brawn.'

'Is your brain telling you right now to get the hell out of Richard Boden's life?'

She thought over his words for some seconds, then said, 'I wish it were as simple as that. I like you, Richard, but I'm not going to be forced into something as important as marriage – not for you, not for my Uncle Gif and certainly not for Wydale.'

'Have you left somebody you care about in America?' he wanted to know.

Thoughts of Kip Weldon flew in and out of her mind like butterflies: Kip teaching her to ride a bicycle when she was a gangling teenager; Kip lounging alongside her at the Hayden Planetarium; Kip taking her to hear the Boston Symphony Orchestra at Symphony Hall; Kip buying home-made ice cream on Massachusetts Avenue; Kip wearing the uniform of the United States Army; Kip leaving for England . . .

'No,' she was able to say in all honesty. 'There's nobody in my life I care for in that way.'

'Was there ever?'

She looked down at the food in front of her and suddenly wasn't hungry any more. She forced herself to go on eating, however, until every bit had gone.

'Amy?' He was waiting for an answer.

'You don't really have any right to ask me that, do you?' She lifted her head and stared angrily at him.

'I don't want to step on anybody's toes. I just want to know if the way is clear.'

'Clear for what?'

'Clear for me to try and get to know you.' His voice was steady and calm.

'You're like a dratted dog with a bone, Richard Boden. You know that, don't you?' She pushed her plate away, sat back in her chair and thrust both hands into the pockets of her black denims.

Slowly and very clearly, he said, 'Amy, I want to marry you.'

She leaned her head back till she was looking up at the ceiling. Then she muttered, 'I don't love you. I'll never love you. I can't love you.'

'How do you know that?' he asked.

She brought her attention slowly back to him, knowing that the next few moments were going to be harrowing. 'Kip Weldon was to all intents and purposes my brother,' she said. 'I told you, I was adopted by Kate and Marty Weldon. Marty is Uncle Gif's younger brother.'

He nodded, sat forward and linked his hands in front of him on the table-top. 'I know all that. But Kip Weldon wasn't really your brother. He was just Kate and Marty's son.'

'I know,' she said. 'But the fact that we'd almost been brought up together stopped me from telling him how I really felt.'

'You fell in love with him, huh?'

It sounded so simple, so trite. *You fell in love with him.* 'You make it sound like I just had a simple accident,' she flared. 'You put it in the same category as falling off a bike or falling in the water.'

'Falling in love has the same set of consequences,' Richard said evenly. 'When you fall off a bike you get hurt, when you fall in the water you think you're drowning. In my experience love hurts, and love makes you go under at times.'

'Yeah!' she said. 'That's just about it, isn't it? Hurting and going under. But when does it stop hurting? And when do you come up for air again?'

'You come to terms with it – eventually,' he said.

She dragged her hands out of her pockets and with one clenched fist thumped at her chest. 'It still hurts, though,' she cried. 'After more than two damn years, it still hurts that I never told him. And now he's dead. And what makes it worse is that fact that . . . that . . .' She stopped, already knowing she'd said more than she'd intended saying, and realizing that *he* had gone through it all as well. He must be knowing how she was feeling, even though he'd had ten years to 'come to terms with it'.

He leaned forward and thrust out a hand across the table. She ignored it.

'Come on,' he said. 'Put your hand in mine.'

'Why?' She scowled at him and slumped in her seat.

'Just do it.'

Reluctantly she sat forward and slapped her hand down in his. 'Okay,' she said, 'now what?'

His hand curled round hers, holding it tight. 'What do you feel?' he asked.

'What do you mean?'

109

'Just tell me. I'm holding your hand. What do you feel?'

'Physically or mentally?'

'Physically.'

She entered into the spirit of the game – for a game was what it was for her. It meant nothing, holding his hand like this. She was beyond the boy-and-girl-holding-hands stage. 'It's warm,' she said. 'It's warm and hard and callused. You work with your hands. That's what I feel – a working hand. Strong. Big. So how many marks do I score for that?'

'You forgot to say "alive",' he said. 'And that's what I am, Amy. Alive. And Kip Weldon's dead.'

She pulled her hand free of him. 'Yes,' she said flatly. 'But even if he were alive, he wouldn't want me. He'd gotten a girl pregnant over here in England while I was languishing in America and dreaming golden dreams about him.'

'As I said – love hurts,' he reminded her.

'I know. I also know that I'll never get into a situation where I care for somebody like that again. That's why I said I'd never love you. I won't let it happen again, see? I've got more sense now.'

'I know how you feel.'

'Yeah!'

'Okay. Don't believe me. But I too have my hang-ups.'

She grinned across at him, her good humour surfacing briefly. 'You're too sensible for hang-ups.'

'If I were sensible, I wouldn't have killed that man, Amy.'

'That's different. I still say that was pure chance. An accident.'

'If I were sensible, I wouldn't have made Grace pregnant. If she hadn't been having a baby, her blood pressure

110

wouldn't have rocketed as it did. Today they might have saved her. Ten years ago they didn't have the same technology in hospitals as they do now, and by the time they discovered what was wrong she'd suffered a severe stroke.'

'Richard – I'm sorry.' She sat forward again, knowing no words of hers could be of use, but wanting him to know she understood.

'It's okay,' he said. 'Ten years is a long time, and I've struggled to the surface after going under. But one thing you have to know, Amy – although I want to marry you, I don't want to have kids. I couldn't go through all that again.'

'Then we're through before we even start,' she said, giving a shaky little laugh. 'Because I adore kids, Richard. In Boston, I was just about to start what I hoped would be a lifetime of caring for kids. I'd trained to be a teacher. I've got a good job all ready and waiting for me – teaching the really young ones. And, if I ever get married, I'll want kids of my own – four at least.'

'Then I'm not the man for you,' he said, lolling back in his chair and fixing her with a grim smile.

'I never thought you were.' She pushed her chair back from the table and started stacking up the plates they'd used.

He sprang to his feet. 'Leave them,' he said. 'You don't have to do that.'

'I always help Lizzie wash up at Wydale.' She walked over to the kitchen units with the plates.

'No.' He stopped her with his hand on her arm.

'Don't order me about – not again,' she snapped.

'I have a dishwasher,' he said. 'I wasn't going to order you about, Amy.'

111

She put the plates down, feeling foolish. 'I might have guessed,' she said. 'Mr Up-to-date, that's what you are.' She started to laugh. 'Richard, I've never met anybody like you in the whole of my damn life.'

She turned to him, still laughing, and then it all happened in an instant. He gripped her shoulders and his dark head swooped down. She was taken by surprise as his hard lips descended on hers in a fiercely calculated kiss. She clung to him, afraid of being knocked off her feet by his ferocity, then she kept on clinging to him because she liked the feel of his body moulding itself against hers.

Basically, she realized, this had been brewing up all evening. And she had a good feeling flowing through her right now. It had been a long time since she'd allowed anyone to take liberties with her – and never like this. Sure, she'd been on dates, and there'd been the occasional kiss and fumble in the dark, but it had never gone further than that.

Her lips clung to his. She closed her eyes and felt his arms sliding down and around her back. He was aroused. She could feel that too. He kissed her face all over, and her neck, and round the back of her ears, before coming back to her lips again. She entered into the spirit of the thing that was happening. She wasn't a prude, but she was a virgin. And it was going to stay that way, she told herself. There was no way she'd lose control. She knew exactly what she was doing.

And he did too. After long minutes, he dragged her head down against the hollow of his shoulder and held her tenderly, stroking her hair, laying his lips against it. His body was still tense. She kept still against him. She wasn't a tease. After a while he began to relax, and then whispered gently against her hair. 'It's time I took you home.'

She said, 'Yes,' and was glad he hadn't apologized for what had happened.

They came apart slowly. Her hands reached up to thread themselves through her hair and straighten it. She looked at him. He was composed and cool. 'You're starting to surface out of that drowning pool,' he said.

'Yeah. I guess so,' she replied.

But love had not played a part in it, she realized.

CHAPTER 8

By the day before Christmas Eve the snow had vanished and the weather turned mild.

Gif Weldon had invited Richard over for dinner on Christmas Eve. It was nearly two weeks since Amy had last seen him. That had been when he'd dropped her off in Wydale's courtyard on that snowy night after driving her back home from Hatton-in-the-Dale.

There had been much to do in the past fortnight – presents to buy for Lizzie and Uncle Gif, and parcels to send off to America for Kate and Marty too.

That day she asked Lizzie about decorating the Hall, and Lizzie laughed and called her crazy. Nobody celebrated at Christmas, she told Amy. Not at Wydale, anyway.

'But tomorrow is my twenty-fourth birthday,' Amy said. 'And in Boston we always have a lighted tree and lots of silver decorations around the place.

'Christmas is for children,' Lizzie argued. 'And it's downright awkward of you to have a birthday on Christmas Eve.'

'But I'm the biggest kid in the world,' Amy said.

And, not heeding Lizzie, she caught the little bus down into Hawkwood village and bought a Christmas tree at the market.

'It must be all of six feet tall. How did you get that thing home?' Lizzie demanded when she saw it.

'On the bus.' Amy grinned and sank down onto the hard-backed settle in the hall to get her breath back, while the tree lay stretched out at her feet. 'I smiled in a sickeningly sweet way at the driver and he got out and helped me prop it up in the baggage compartment under the stairs.'

'You've got the cheek of the devil. Nobody ever helps me with my bags when I've been shopping down there, yet that thing's bigger than a dog. Did you have to pay full fare for it?'

'You have to look kinda helpless,' Amy explained, starting to laugh as she tried to envisage the capable and Amazonian Lizzie looking anything of the sort.

Lizzie shook her head and said, 'Well, now you've got it here, what're you going to do with it?'

I'm going to plant it in a bucket or something, and we'll have it in the sitting room. Then we'll put some lights on it. I bought a box of forty when I went over to Hatton to do some shopping yesterday.'

'It's as well you took John Graham and the car with you,' Lizzie said. 'You came back laden down with stuff.'

'Yes,' said Amy, knowing full well that she'd taken John Graham for quite another reason. She hadn't intended bumping into Richard Boden again – and having to accept a lift from him like last time. She'd had two whole weeks to think about that last visit to Hatton and now Richard was coming over tomorrow night, but it didn't worry her – not with Lizzie and Uncle Gif around. But what she didn't want was to be entirely on her own with him again. Not yet anyway.

The outside door suddenly banged open, making both her and Lizzie jump. Gif Weldon came in, rubbing his

115

hands together and complaining of the cold weather. Her uncle was always cold, Amy thought, hoping he wasn't going down with flu or something. She levered herself up from the settle and said, 'I'll make you a cup of something hot, Uncle Gif. Come and sit over by the fire.'

Weldon turned back to the door and looked outside before closing it. 'That damned helicopter,' he said. 'It's still buzzing around up there. It's making me feel as if somebody's spying on Wydale. Now, why would they do that, I wonder?'

Lizzie said, 'Look! *I'll* go and make some cocoa. There's nothing warms you up quicker than cocoa made with boiling milk.'

Gif Weldon came into the room, his eyes fixed balefully on the tree lying across the floor. 'What in the name of heaven is *that*?'

'It's a Christmas tree, Uncle Gif.' Amy took hold of his arm and steered him round it and over to the fire. Logs were blazing in the grate.

Apparently John Graham was still sawing up the trees that had been taken down after the storm that had destroyed the chapel two years ago. Lizzie had said there was enough wood down there to last them for the next decade, but Amy doubted that was true. Graham had brought up stacks of it, though, and had piled it round the back of the house near the coal cellar. Amy had been delighted. She wanted to experience a real English Christmas, and logs on the fires would make it just perfect.

She helped her uncle off with his coat. He seemed dazed as he stared again at the tree. 'Why?' he asked, when Lizzie had gone back to the kitchen. 'Why do we need a tree? There hasn't been a Christmas tree in this house for the last twenty years.'

116

'It's high time we restored the tradition, then,' Amy said. 'I bought some lights for it, Uncle Gif, and I'm going to persuade Lizzie to help me decorate the sitting room this afternoon. You don't really mind, do you?'

'It's your birthday tomorrow, child, so I don't suppose I can refuse you anything, can I?'

He seemed more human at that moment than he'd been since she'd arrived in England. She smiled fondly at the old man as she draped his tweed coat over her arm. 'I thought you'd forgotten my birthday.'

'No. I wouldn't do that.'

She said, 'I'll just go and hang your coat in the passage, shall I?'

He nodded absently, gazing down at the blazing fire, and said, 'Yes. Yes, child. You do that. Then come back here. I've got something for you.'

When she came back he was standing in the middle of the room looking down at the Christmas tree again. 'There'll be pine needles dropping everywhere,' he said in a petulant tone.

'Well, *I'll* clean them up if they do drop,' Amy offered.

He tut-tutted for a few seconds more, then turned and looked up at the portrait of Barbara Weldon over the fireplace.

Amy walked over to him, wondering if he was thinking of old times, when he'd had a wife, wondering too if he was sad because he was alone now.

He had his hand in his pocket. He drew it out and gave her a small tortoiseshell box. 'It's not new, I'm afraid. But we couldn't let your birthday pass without a memento, could we?'

She opened the snap fastener on the box and the lid carefully. Inside was a brooch in the shape of a thistle. It

117

was made of heavy gold and amethyst, and very beautiful. 'Uncle Gif! It's lovely.' She smiled at him. 'Thank you.'

He waved her thanks aside. 'I hope it brings you luck.' Grimly he turned to look up at the portrait again. 'More luck than it brought her, anyway,' he said.

'It . . . it belonged to . . .?'

'Barbara. Yes.'

It was the first time ever he'd mentioned the woman in the picture to her. 'Are you absolutely sure you want me to have this?' Tentatively Amy held out the brooch. 'I mean – it must have memories for you.'

'Memories!' He gave a bitter laugh. 'Yes. It has memories. But I don't want it, Amy. I bought it for her – and she didn't want it either. She left it behind when she went back to Scotland.'

She touched his arm but he flinched away from her and reeled towards the fire. His gait was unsteady. She cried out, 'Uncle Gif . . . be careful . . .'

His head ached and the whole room was spinning round and round. He looked up at the portrait and she was smiling down at him in triumph. 'You tricked me . . .' he could still hear her screaming. 'I hate you . . .'

But it hadn't always been like that . . .

Duncan had been in a foul mood when he told him he was going away for a month.

'You're a fool, Gifford, a bloody fool to listen to gossip.'

'If I'm hearing it, others are too,' Gif said as they walked through Hyde Park on a September Sunday evening.

'Then be like me and take no damn notice of it.

'I can't. I've got my career to think about. Who's going to want a surgeon like me touching them . . .?' His voice

118

tailed off. He made an effort to explain however. 'Look here, Duncan, I'm forty-two. I can't afford to have scandal spread about. I've got Wydale to look after; it costs the earth for the upkeep of the place.'

'Then sell it, and get a flat here in London.'

Gifford shuddered. 'I couldn't bear to live in London permanently. I need a bolt-hole – a retreat. Sometimes I feel like chucking it all in, and Wydale puts things back in perspective for me.'

'Do you want to finish things between us?' Duncan Ward had a shock of red hair that matched his temper. He was forever flying off the handle at some little thing or other. Sometimes Gif wondered why he put up with the damn man. But he knew the answer to that. Of course he did. He loved him . . .

A walking holiday in Scotland was the answer. He had to get away from London, away from Wydale too – Wydale that was eating up every penny he earned. He needed a complete break while he decided what he could do to stop the whisperings about his suspected homo-sexuality. He couldn't go on as he had been doing for all these years. Being a medical man, he knew the signs. He was heading for a complete nervous breakdown and he couldn't afford that on top of his other problems.

He'd been to the farm in Perthshire before – but that had been five years ago. He wouldn't write or even telephone now to see if they could put him up again. Instinctively he knew he'd be welcome, and he looked forward to seeing Ross and Alison Mackenzie and their daughter Barbara again. During the month he'd stayed with them five years before a warm friendship had blossomed between him and the feisty Barbara. Gif knew she'd been attracted to him – and who knew what might

119

have happened if he'd been capable of having as meaningful a relationship with a woman as the one he enjoyed with Duncan Ward?

The train pulled into the little railway station nestling in the shadow of pine-scented hills. In a whitewashed shack beside the main line to Inverness he knew he could order a taxi to transport him to Mackenzie's farm at Glenochry, some ten miles east in the wilder hill country.

His first glimpse of the granite-built farmhouse squatting squarely in the heart of the valley had him sitting forward in his seat as the taxi cruised carefully down the track to it. But as the taxi drew nearer he could see no sign of human life – nor animals for that matter – and a sense of foreboding gripped him.

'The auld croft yonder looks deserted.' The driver half turned his head towards the back seat for a second. 'Is anybody expecting you, maister?'

'Not exactly.' Gif Weldon frowned as the man brought the car to a halt against the gate across the yard. 'Look, can you wait here – just while I go and see if anyone's around?'

'Aye! Ah've nothin' else on till th'next train comes along, and that's not for hours yet.'

Gif went up to the door and knocked loudly. All was silence within the house. He walked round to the windows and tried to peer inside, but curtains were drawn across every one. He tried the back door, but found it locked, then turned away to the cow byres – and surprisingly heard a noise.

'Is anybody there?' He stood outside and listened. There was a scuffing sound and then an old wooden door creaked slowly open.

'Barbara!' He heard the relief in his own voice, but then, on looking closer, saw she'd obviously been crying. 'Barbara? Don't you remember me?'

She wore down-at-heel shoes and a black woollen dress that barely covered her knees. She'd aged far more than five years. When he'd last seen her she'd been eighteen; now she looked far older than he was himself.

'Gifford?' Her black eyes suddenly came to life.

'Is your father at home? Or your mother?' He made a useless little gesture with his hands. 'Maybe I should have written to see if it was convenient . . .'

'To stay with us again?'

'Yes. The place looks deserted, though.' He glanced away to the house. 'I couldn't get any reply when I knocked on the door.'

'You wouldna,' she said. 'There's nobody around.'

'Nobody . . .?' He was bewildered.

She walked towards him. 'I was just leaving myself – just having a last look round.'

'But why? Has your father sold the farm? And where are you going?'

She gave a hollow little laugh. 'Bide yourself awhile, Gifford. One question at a time. First of all, Dadda died last spring.'

'Barbara – I'm so sorry, my dear.'

She held up a hand to quiet him. 'It's been a bad year. Mamma wore herself out with all the running around. Her heart gave up – just a month ago. We'd struggled to keep the place tidy-like, but it beat us in the end.'

'You've sold the farm?' he asked incredulously. 'Just like that? You've turned your back on it?'

'I canna' manage it myself, Gifford – and anyroad, it wasna mine to sell. Dadda was a tenant. The croft was only leased to us, and now the factor wants it back.'

'But where are you going to live?'

She shrugged her thin shoulders. 'At a hostel.'

'A hostel?'

'I'm homeless, Gifford. I have to go somewhere.'

He took her to a guesthouse in Edinburgh. They had separate rooms. She seemed to have lost all interest in life. She had no family, no home, and, after living in so remote a spot for all her life, there were no close friends for her to turn to.

An idea formed in his mind as they whiled away the days in Edinburgh. It would stifle the gossip that was becoming rife about Duncan and himself if he had a wife. His career would be safe. He'd be respectable and above reproach. And he'd still have Duncan . . .

He broached the subject, only telling her what was necessary – that he needed a housekeeper at Wydale Hall in Derbyshire's Peak District. That was all she need know. He offered marriage. He had nothing to lose and everything to gain by taking a wife home, he knew.

At first she didn't want to leave Scotland, but after a few days she'd obviously thought the matter over.

'I don't expect you to . . . to love me, Gifford. Not yet at any rate. But maybe one day . . .'

He tucked her arm in his as they hurried back to the guesthouse in a shower of rain. 'It's settled, then? You'll become Mrs Weldon – and make me a very happy man?'

'Aye!' She smiled up at him, her eyes dark and glistening in the autumn dusk. 'Aye, Gifford. And I'll make you a good wife, I promise.'

Amy yelled for Lizzie Abercrombie. 'Lizzie! Lizzie! Help me. Quickly!'

Lizzie's footsteps clattered down the stone passage from Wydale's vast kitchen. 'Lord, child. What's the commotion for . . .?'

'He's fainted or something.' Amy's taut face looked up at the housekeeper from the fireside, where Gif Weldon lay inert.

'Heavens, child.' Lizzie rushed across the great hall and dropped to her knees on the other side of the old man.

Amy's voice trembled. 'I put him in the recovery position. He's still breathing. Did I do right, Lizzie?'

Lizzie felt for a pulse in Weldon's neck, and nodded. 'What happened?'

'He was looking up at the portrait and then he just seemed to black out. I managed to steady him as he fell, but though he's so thin, Lizzie, he was too heavy for me to hold onto.'

'He'll be okay.' Lizzie sat back on her heels and started chafing one of Gif Weldon's wrists between her hands.

'How do you know? Oughtn't we to send for the doctor?'

'It's happened before. Some sort of seizure. We'll give him a few minutes. His pulse is weak, but it's steady.'

'Oh, Lizzie . . .'

'Don't fret, child,' Lizzie soothed. 'He's an old man.'

'He's *not* old, Lizzie – he's only in his sixties. That's not old by today's standards.'

'He's sixty-eight, Miss Amy. And some men are old way before that age. Gif Weldon's one of them. He was old when I first came here, and he couldn't have been much more than fifty then.'

The old man stirred and groaned. His eyes fluttered, and Lizzie stopped rubbing at his wrist and smiled over the top of him at Amy. 'There! He's coming round. What did I tell you? He'll be okay.'

'I still think he should see a doctor . . .'

Lizzie shook her head. 'He won't see no doctor, so don't go worrying him – else he might black out again. Just let him come to. Then we'll have a nice hot drink and all this can be forgotten.'

Amy couldn't believe how quickly Gif Weldon rallied once he'd regained consciousness. He sat up on the cold flagstones of the great hall and pushed their helping hands away.

'What a fuss. What a fuss,' he grumbled. 'I only tripped over the hearth, for goodness' sake.'

'Uncle Gif – you were – '

'Knocked out for a couple of seconds,' Lizzie broke in. 'But you're all right now, so let's get you over to a chair or something, shall we?'

Gif Weldon rubbed at his forehead, then slapped Lizzie's hand away from him. 'Woman! You're a menace!' he shouted at her. 'Leave me alone. I'm perfectly capable of using my legs.'

Lizzie rose to her feet in none too gracious a manner. 'Right!' she snapped. 'See to yourself, old man. I'm going back to my kitchen.' She glared at Amy. 'And you, madam – you'd better come with me.'

'But . . .'

'I said, you're coming with me. Understand? We'll leave this old bugger to his own devices.'

'Lizzie – we can't do that.'

'Yes, we can.' Lizzie marched over to her and grabbed her arm, bending to whisper in her ear, 'Be a bit tactful, love. He's embarrassed because you've seen him weak and vulnerable.'

Amy's eyes met those of the housekeeper in understanding. 'I – I'll come and help you,' she stammered.

And Lizzie led her out of the room while, grumbling quietly, Gif Weldon staggered to his feet and watched them go.

CHAPTER 9

On Christmas Eve, Richard Boden joined Amy and her uncle Gif for dinner at Wydale, and, for once, Lizzie sat down at table with them. Amy had helped her prepare the meal, which was eaten by candlelight in the austere oak dining room which Amy disliked so much.

She'd been a little apprehensive about meeting Richard again, but soon found she needn't have been. He made no reference to what had happened in his house at Hatton-in-the-Dale, and by the end of the evening she was beginning to believe that she'd imagined him holding her in his arms and kissing her on that snowy winter's night just over a week ago.

Uncle Gif was in a good mood. Richard had driven to Wydale in his Land Rover, so didn't drink. Lizzie suggested a game of cards when the meal was over, and Amy was on a winning streak. The evening passed quickly, with good food and pleasant conversation. She went to the door with Richard at around eleven o'clock, when he was leaving. As he pulled his coat over his dark suit he fished a brown paper package out of one deep pocket.

'Open it in the morning,' he said, handing it to her. 'I didn't realise it was your birthday today, or I'd have brought flowers too.'

125

'There's no need. Birthdays stop getting exciting after you've had more than twenty.'

His eyes twinkled. 'You make me feel very old, saying that.' He leaned forward and kissed her lightly on the forehead. 'Goodnight, Amy.'

'Is that all I get? A peck on the forehead?' she asked in a teasing sort of way.

'Uh-huh! For the time being.'

They were alone. Uncle Gif had gone up to bed and Lizzie was away down the long stone passageway tidying up the kitchen. 'Fine!' She wouldn't let him see she was disappointed. 'Maybe we'll see you again some time over Christmas.'

'It's doubtful – unless I come over to do a bit more work on Gabriel.'

A tiny frown settled between her eyes. 'That dratted angel!'

'Jealous?' he asked, amused.

'Oh, yeah!' She clasped the package against her and said, 'What's in this parcel?'

'You must surely know what it is from the shape.' He buttoned up his jacket and turned towards the door.

'A book, I guess.'

'Right first time. *Stone Grinding and Quarrying in the Peak District*,' he said.

'It is?' She was slightly disappointed.

'No, it's not, so you can take that look off your face. I was just kidding you.'

'Richard!' She swiped at him with the book.

'You'll lie awake all night now, wondering what it is, won't you?'

'Nope! As soon as you've gone I'll open it and find out.'

He grimaced. 'Thank goodness I didn't waste good Christmas wrapping paper on it, then.'

'I don't have anything to give *you*.' Suddenly she felt at a loss. She hadn't expected him to bring her a present for Christmas.

'Don't worry,' he said cheerfully. 'It puts you under an obligation to me, doesn't it? And I rather like the thought of that.'

He opened the door and a chill wind blew in, making her shiver. 'Don't come out,' he said. 'You'll get cold in that cute little slinky frock.'

She didn't want him to go. She stalled him. 'Do you like me in a frock, Richard?'

'You look great to me in anything.'

'You sure know how to *not* pay a girl compliments, don't you?'

In another minute he'd be gone.

'Kiss me,' she said. 'I don't know how to take you when you're in this mood. Be like you were the other night. I know how to handle you then.'

He faced her. 'You want me predictable, lady?'

'I want you to hold me – to kiss me hard, and well and truly,' she answered.

It only took two steps for him to reach her. She looked up at him expectantly, her eyes bold and bright. She felt in control of the situation, just as she'd been that night at Hatton-in-the-Dale.

His arm slid round her waist and he pulled her close to him. 'Hard, and well and truly?' he said.

She nodded and leaned towards him, closing her eyes, then braced herself for the bruising strength of his lips on hers. It was a game to her, and they'd established the rules already. Hard, and well and truly – that was how he'd kissed her on a snowy night in mid-December. And she'd kept her heart hidden from him because it had already been given once, and freely, to Kip. But Kip had never known that she loved him.

Richard Boden's hand was pressed firmly in the small of her back, and his other took hold of her jaw and positioned her face at just the right angle. Her body was tense, full of anticipation for the light-hearted bit of fun his kiss had been before.

His lips touched hers, but this time they were gentle. There was none of the rough hunger she'd felt before. His mouth moved like that of a lover against hers, barely touching her at all, even, but this kiss made her gasp at the sweetness of it. Her body reacted violently, wanting more than this, making her hands tighten on his shoulders and pull him closer to her. He was big and protective. He could make the rest of the world go away if he wanted. His mouth was covering hers now, and she drew in a deep breath, parting her lips to allow him even greater intimacy.

Strange longings were sweeping through her, and they weren't the simple kind she'd once felt for Kip. This was no 'boy meets girl' stuff, she realized, this was physical – carnal, even – and it wasn't what she'd expected or wanted, this searing, flame of lust burning right through her . . .

Suddenly she felt disgust with herself for what she interpreted as her betrayal of Kip. Her love for Kip had been of the innocent kind, whereas Richard Boden's masculinity, as potent as earth and fire and sun and moon, was stripping away her innocence. Man of stone! It was appropriate. She made herself react violently to his embrace, and to his kisses that were now too intimate and lingering. She dragged herself out of his arms and staggered away from him, flinging the back of her hand across her mouth, as if by doing that she'd be able to rub his kisses away.

He laughed very softly. 'You see now why I kissed you on the forehead,' he said. 'I guessed it was safer that way.'

She turned and ran from him, and didn't stop until she'd slammed her bedroom door and was leaning against it, her head tilted back against the hard wood, and her eyes blinded by the glaring electric lightbulb hanging over her bed.

Her lips still tingled long after she was in bed, curled up like a shivering embryo, and trying to sleep. But her mind was too active for sleep, and every time she closed her eyes she saw Richard Boden's face.

Amy was glad when the New Year came and Christmas was behind them. Daily she waited for a reply to the advertisements she'd placed in half a dozen newspapers on the east coast of England, but it seemed that Kitty was as elusive as ever.

Kate called from Boston again, and Amy felt guilty because she had not so far been successful in tracing the girl.

Uncle Gif seemed more frail than ever as the weather turned icy and fog topped the summit of Aspen Tor for the most part of every day. Mist and damp seeped up from the river, and cobwebs hung like silver lace on the evergreens in the garden.

Even the little helicopter stopped its daily fly-over, and Amy found she was missing the buzzing oversized insect that had droned incessantly overhead almost every day since she'd been at Wydale.

She walked a lot and took endless video film of the

English winter, so she'd be able to show it to Kate and Marty when she returned to America. If she went into Hatton shopping, she always asked John Graham to accompany her. At Wydale, she avoided the old chapel, and, if the phone rang, she ignored it until either Lizzie or Uncle Gif answered it. But it was never Richard Boden who rang, and her days started to be appallingly long.

But at the beginning of the second week in January a letter arrived, and she could see that Uncle Gif was mystified when he called her downstairs and handed it to her. 'Read this and tell me what you make of it, Amy,' he said.

She read, then re-read the letter. 'How odd,' she said.

'Have you ever heard of this magazine called *Diary* – because I haven't?'

She gave a soft little laugh. 'You wouldn't have heard of it, Uncle Gif. It's one of those glossies that's aimed at the career-conscious woman. I *have* noticed it in the newsagents in Hatton. It's a fairly new monthly, and it seems quite popular.'

'But why on earth would they want to write about Wydale Hall, child?'

'The editor says in the letter that each month they plan to do a feature on an outstanding property – not the usual stately homes, that Dukes and landed gentry inhabit, but a house where *real* people live.'

'But how did this editor – this *Ms* Catherine Blake – come to know about us?'

She shrugged, and handed the letter back to him. 'I don't know, Uncle Gif – but I think it's a great idea.'

'You do?' He frowned deeply at the single sheet of paper with its elaborate heading. 'I wonder what Lizzie Abercrombie would think. Perhaps I ought to ask her.'

'If they decide to do the feature, Uncle, they say they'll pay for the privilege of taking a few photos and talking to you. A thousand pounds seems too good a chance to miss,' Amy said thoughtfully, knowing the state Wydale was in. Her mind was busy, wondering how much damp-proofing a thousand pounds would buy, even as she realized that a thousand pounds, where Wydale was concerned, was merely a drop in the ocean.

Gid Weldon sighed. 'I don't think a thousand is going to go very far, Amy.'

'But it could be fun,' she said.

'Fun? Having our lives disrupted by people flashing camera bulbs at us and asking prying questions?'

'It's only for three days, though. And some of these magazines are very discreet,' Amy soothed. 'Honestly, Uncle Gif, I don't think you need worry. And it would be nice to see Wydale splashed all over the cover and the centrefold of a really classy magazine, wouldn't it?'

'I don't know . . .' He walked off towards the kitchen, shaking his head. 'We'll see what Lizzie says. Lizzie's pretty sensible about things like this . . .'

The lounge bar of the Hawkwood Arms was fairly quiet, Catherine Blake saw, as she peeped through the open doorway at the bottom of the stairs. She felt refreshed and ready for anything after the best night's sleep she'd had in ages, and was glowing from the deep, steaming bath she'd taken on rising. She smiled as she recalled asking for a room with a shower on the phone a couple of days ago, and being told that the Hawkwood Arms wasn't the sort of place that went in for *ensuite* facilities.

She'd had misgivings, and had wondered whether to book into the nearest large town, but that was ten miles away, and she wanted to be nearer Wydale than that. She knew there wouldn't be any time to waste, and Hawkwood – on the map – looked as if it might be only a few minutes' drive from the old Hall she was so interested in. So she'd decided to give the pub a try, and now she was glad she had.

She wondered if he would be around this morning. 'He' being the black-haired, black-eyed mystery man – the only other resident at the inn in this quiet Derbyshire valley. He'd been sitting alone in a corner against the door when she'd checked in last night, and he'd looked deep in thought. Morose, almost. And he'd been the only man in the place who hadn't ogled her. That, she assumed, must have been what had made her take special note of him. Catherine was accustomed to being looked at, and she knew that in this tucked-away village in the heart of the Peak District, a tall, striking brunette – and a fashion conscious one too – must be something of a rarity.

Outside in the car park when she'd arrived, a notice-board had proclaimed: 'HIKERS AND COACH PARTIES CA-TERED FOR'. It was that kind of place, she supposed – off the beaten track. Hikers and coach parties must be good for custom, because all in all the village itself couldn't consist of much more than fifty or sixty dwellings from what she'd seen of it.

He was sitting at a small table by the window when she walked into the lounge. He was eating breakfast and didn't seem to notice her as she slipped quietly into a seat at the only other table laid for a meal – also beside the window, but opposite him.

As he looked up briefly she smiled, but he frowned and acknowledged her with a nod of his jet-black head. In daylight she could assess him better than last night in the subdued lighting of the bar. His hair was cut short, his face the pale and interesting kind. He was thin – skinny, almost – with long legs curled under his chair and white, well cared for hands with short fingernails, which were manipulating his knife and fork as if he were dissecting a body and not merely a piece of bacon.

'It's a lovely morning.' She felt she had to say something. If they were to be thrown together like this for the next couple of days, the atmosphere could become quite strained if they consistently ignored each other.

He'd finished his meal. He sat back and looked through the window at the surrounding hills and said, 'Yes.'

Catherine was distracted then by the landlady bringing her breakfast to the table – a huge pot of tea and a plate laden with everything her figure was going to go into blind panic about when it realized what she intended doing with it. When she was alone with the mountain of food she just sat and looked at it and wondered where to start. Never, since leaving her fenland home eighteen months ago, had she seen a breakfast resembling this one.

She heard a soft laugh and glanced up and across at him. 'Do I look as if I need my strength building up or something?' she asked.

'Not to me,' he replied, his voice reminding her of heather-clad hillsides, the scent of pines, and the lochs and glens of Scotland, where she'd spent holidays as a child. 'But,' he warned, 'you'll be questioned unmercifully by Mrs Hillaby if you don't eat it.'

She groaned. 'Oh, no.'

'They do say around here that a layer of grease on your chest helps keep out the cold.'

'Don't,' she pleaded, picking up her knife and fork. 'For heaven's sake don't put me off. I can't bear being inter-

133

rogated if I leave a smidgen of food on my plate – and really it's just the sort of breakfast I used to have at home in the old days . . .'

'But now you're the smart city girl.' He even managed a sort of smile.

'Yes. Does it show?'

'Girls in boots and rucksacks are all I've seen in the few weeks I've been staying here.'

'The few *weeks*?' She started work on the sausage, then paused to reflect, 'Well, the grease on *your* chest hasn't given you a premature middle-age spread.'

'Nor have I caught a cold.' He drank up his tea, pushed back his chair and stood up.

Catherine carried on eating.

'I'll see you around, then?' He hesitated as he was about to walk out of the room.

She smiled. 'I suppose so.'

Mrs Hillaby – the landlady of the Hawkwood Arms – was in a talkative mood when she came to fetch the breakfast things.

'Did you speak to Mr Powell? He's a nice young man when you get to know him.'

Catherine nodded. 'We exchanged a few words.'

'From Scotland, he is.' Mrs Hillaby made a clatter as she banged cutlery down on the tray. 'A photographer! Apparently he's quite well known for his pictures – taken from the air they are. He's taken one of this place. I can't wait to see what the old pub looks like from way up there.'

Catherine was interested. 'You say his name's Powell?' She wrinkled her forehead. 'He's not *Mark* Powell, is he? The Mark Powell we deal with has a photo-library in London, and we often use his pictures in our magazine.

134

I've never met him, but I always imagined him to be much older than the man I've met today.'

'I don't know nothing about that, Miss Blake. You'd have to ask him if he's one and the same, I suppose.' Mrs Hillaby chuckled. 'He might take you for a ride in his helicopter if you ask him nicely. He says he's been flying around Derbyshire taking photos for another book he's writing. Seems quite taken with Wydale Hall. He's forever asking questions about it.'

'What a coincidence. That's where I have an appointment this morning – at Wydale Hall.'

'Well, I never!' Mrs Hillaby gave her a wink and a nod. 'You two should get together.'

Catherine laughed, but said nothing. There were more important things in her life at the moment than catching herself a man.

He caught her off-guard an hour later, just as she was unlocking her car. He sauntered over from where a huge black and silver motorbike was parked and leaned against the dry stone wall which bordered a meadow that stretched down to the river and marked the boundary of the Hawkwood Arms car park.

'You're off to Wydale Hall, I hear.'

Obviously he'd been talking to Mrs Hillaby. Momentarily Catherine was annoyed with the woman for gossiping about her reason for being here.

Drily, she said, 'You've been talking to the landlady, I take it.'

'Mrs Hillaby is the eyes and ears of the world.' He pushed himself away from the wall and came and stood at the front of her car. 'Nice car.'

'Yes.'

'D'you mind if I come along? I've flown over the old

135

Hall many times, but it would be nice to see it at ground level.'

'Sorry! I have an appointment with Mr Weldon. It wouldn't look too good if I turned up with a car-load of sightseers, would it?'

'You could pass me off as your photographer. In fact, I wouldn't mind getting a few shots of the Hall. I'd let you have your pick of them for your magazine.'

She was tempted. Photography wasn't her strong point. She was much better at interviews. And the camera she'd brought along wasn't really a professional type. She'd been told only to get an interview with old man Weldon and take a few pictures. At the moment there was nothing definite in the pipeline for Wydale Hall. It had taken some persuasion on her part for anyone connected with the magazine ever to be interested. *If*, however, she could make a good story of it, then they'd consider doing the feature.

Catherine knew she should be thankful for even getting this far. But she had desperately needed a reason for visiting Wydale, and this had seemed the only solution. The advertisement in the east coast newspapers had been puzzling. She remembered being distinctly uneasy when Aunt Mary had telephoned to tell her about it.

'Kitty, love – can it be somebody belonging to Kip Weldon's family in America who's trying to get in touch?' her aunt had asked.

Catherine's heart had given a sudden lurch. Kitty wasn't the name she was known by in London. That part of her life was done with, she'd long since decided. 'Oh, Auntie, I hope not. Not after all this time. I thought Kip's parents had given up on me.'

'Well, you'd think so, wouldn't you? Especially when

136

you never replied to their pleas in the Press to contact them right after the accident.'

Catherine had hesitated for a moment, then said, 'I couldn't risk it, Auntie. They might have tried to take the baby away from me.'

'How is the little one, love?' Aunt Mary had enquired fondly.

'Fine, Auntie. Just fine.'

'I'll send you the advertisement, shall I, Kitty?'

'If you would. That might be best.'

'You can at least read it for yourself – and then make up your mind about it.'

'Yes, Auntie. I'll do that.'

The address in the newspaper had been Wydale Hall in Derbyshire. Catherine had never even heard of it. The person to be contacted was a Miss Weldon. Kip, she knew, had had an uncle who lived somewhere in Derbyshire, but she hadn't been aware of the uncle having a daughter or a sister. So just who was this Miss Weldon of Wydale who was so intent on contacting her, she wondered? She'd decided to play safe, and, when she had discovered that Wydale was a centuries-old country house, had persuaded her editor to let her investigate it as a possible feature for the magazine.

From then on it had been easy. Now, though, as she weighed up the possibility of taking Mark Powell along with her, she couldn't help feeling a little unsure of herself. She hated having to be so devious. It would have been much better if she could have replied to the advertisement in an honest and straightforward manner. But always at the back of her mind was the fear that Kip's parents might start up trouble about the child. They'd lost their only son and it was natural, she supposed, that they'd want to know

137

a part of him still lived on. But at least they had the girl –
the daughter they'd adopted years ago. Kip had spoken
warmly of Amy. He'd adored his kid sister . . .

'Well? Do I get in on this story or not?'

She came back to earth with a jolt. Mark Powell was
waiting for an answer. It might be a help – having somebody with her, she realized. 'Okay,' she said. 'Only don't
go getting in the way. And if they object to two of us
turning up – well, you know what you can do.'

He grinned and swung round to the passenger side of
the car. 'I'll make myself scarce,' he said softly. 'You can
rely on me to do the right thing.'

CHAPTER 10

It was a clear, cold day at the end of January, and Amy stood at her bedroom window looking out over the valley to where the River Eston gleamed like a silver rippling chain in the winter sunshine. She was watching the winding tree-lined road that led up from Duncan Ward's cottage to Wydale Hall for the first sign of Catherine Blake.

There had been more letters since that first one – letters setting out schedules and details of what the magazine wanted – and telephone calls from London confirming dates and possible fees. Lizzie had all but stood over the two cleaning women from Hawkwood with a whip as they'd spent most of this past week scrubbing, disinfecting, polishing floors and furniture and banishing every cobweb from the place in readiness for Wydale's meeting with the media.

Amy saw a glint of sun on glass as a car suddenly appeared, wending its way between the two lines of bare trees. In an instant she was running across the bedroom then down the stairs, calling out, 'Lizzie! She's here. I saw a car . . .'

Lizzie, practical as ever, said, 'Well, she'll ring the bell, I s'pose, when she arrives. There's no point in opening the

139

outside door now and letting in a whole lot of cold air, is there?'

'Aren't you excited, Lizzie?' Amy caught at the housekeeper and whirled her round the kitchen table, hardly able to contain her enthusiasm.

Lizzie extricated herself, dusted down her apron and said, 'For heaven's sake, girl, she's only a reporter!'

'But it's something different,' Amy said, struggling to contain her enthusiasm. 'Wydale is going to be put on show. And it deserves it. It's a lovely old house.'

'And you, madam, if truth be known, are bored to tears with having nothing to do for the past month. Correct me if I'm wrong,' Lizzie said.

'Oh, Lizzie. Of course I'm not bored. Not with Wydale. But you must admit at this time of year, with dark nights and short days, it can be a bit . . .'

'Boring! Yes, that's what I just said. You're bored. Admit it.'

'I wasn't going to say "boring"! I was going to say it can be a bit lonely.'

Catherine Blake was not alone. A man got out of the little blue sports car's passenger seat as she slid out from behind the wheel. Amy walked out onto the courtyard to meet them.

The man was tall and too thin. His hair was almost black. He half turned away from the car, and for a moment she saw his face and was struck by a pair of gorgeous eyes which were so dark they were almost the same colour as his hair. If a woman had been the owner of those eyes she would have been a devastating beauty, but *he* wasn't even good-looking. His skin was too sallow and his hair too short. He didn't look as if he'd bothered to shave that morning, and his jeans, polo shirt and checked jacket had a slept-in look about them.

He did move with an easy grace, however, and, with an expensive-looking camera slung over his shoulder, was eyeing up the old house with a professional scrutiny. Amy knew he'd seen her, but he was deliberately avoiding the level gaze she directed at him.

Catherine Blake was almost as tall as Lizzie Abercrombie. But where Lizzie was gaunt and angular Catherine's features were softly rounded – as was her figure. Her clothes were simple: a beige flowing skirt and long jacket to match, with shoes that were designed more for comfort than fashion. She wore little make-up, and her brown hair curled upwards where it touched her shoulders. She came forward eagerly, and Amy shook hands with her.

'You must be Miss Blake.'

'Call me Catherine.' The woman, who couldn't have been much older than Amy was herself, looked beyond Amy, towards the great oak door of Wydale, almost as if she expected somebody else to greet her.

'My uncle Gif's inside the house. This cold weather plays havoc with his lungs.' Amy grinned. 'My name's Amy, by the way – Amy Weldon.'

Catherine Blake looked stunned.

Amy said, 'Is anything the matter?'

'No . . . no!' The girl seemed to recover herself quickly and said, 'You're American. I wasn't expecting . . .'

Amy's easy laugh rang out. 'Oh, don't mind me. I'm only here for a vacation. I think it's just great that Wydale is going to be put on the map, so to speak.'

Catherine said weakly, 'Yes. I hope things work out. I'm sure my editor will be interested, though, when she sees how impressive the old house is.'

'You've brought a photographer, I see.' Amy's gaze flew

141

once more to the dark, brooding figure, who was distancing himself from them deliberately, it seemed.

Still a little flustered, Catherine said, 'I hope you don't mind, but I met Mark Powell down at the village pub in Hawkwood, where I stayed last night. Apparently he's been lodging there for some time. He's a very good photographer, and very well-known in London. He's a real professional – not a rank amateur like me.' More composed now, she grimaced and called out, 'Mark, come and meet Miss Weldon.'

'Amy, please.' Amy said to the girl.

The man didn't move from his stance, which was fully ten feet away from her. 'Don't mind me,' he said in a soft north-of-the-border brogue, 'I'm only here for the ride, Miss Weldon. If you or your uncle don't want anyone else hanging around, I'll be okay wandering downstream for the next couple of hours.'

Amy thought he was being deliberately anti-social by not even coming over to be properly introduced. She said sharply, 'It's not a stream, Mr Powell, it's a river. The River Eston, to be exact.'

He looked at her then, interested. 'You're not from around these parts, are you?'

'No. I'm from Boston, USA.'

'A bonus for the magazine,' he said, his attractive voice taking on a caustic note. 'What could be better for an eye-catching title for the piece, eh, Catherine? "A Yankee at the Court of King Weldon"!'

Catherine Blake's gentle expression turned hard. 'Mark! That's enough,' she said. 'I think I'm in a better position than you to know what the public wants – and they don't want that kind of clichéd rubbish, thank you very much.'

'I think you'd both better come inside,' Amy said,

142

though not really wanting anything more to do with the man. She didn't like him. He was both surly and supercilious. She led the way into the great hall, where Lizzie and Uncle Gif were waiting to meet Catherine Blake – *she*, after all, was the one who mattered. Amy turned, after introducing Catherine to Gif and Lizzie, and found to her surprise that Mark Powell had not followed them inside.

'Your companion must have gone downstream as he threatened,' she said to Catherine with a smile.

'Good!' Catherine's smile was a little too bright, her relief too obvious, Amy thought. And she couldn't help wondering if Mark Powell had perhaps been a bit too pushy in assuming his presence would be welcomed at Wydale.

'He's a good photographer,' Catherine said, as if she knew what Amy was thinking. 'He's one of the finest aerial cameramen around today.'

'Aerial?' Gif Weldon and Amy chanted the word in unison.

Catherine smiled. 'He has his own helicopter, I understand.'

Amy looked over towards her uncle. Gif Weldon was tight-lipped and unsmiling. 'So that's the man who's been such a menace around here for the last few weeks,' he said.

Amy had a strange sensation in the pit of her stomach. Something was telling her that Mark Powell's arrival today hadn't been entirely accidental. It had been planned – just as all that circling round and round Wydale in the helicopter had been for a reason.

'How well do you know him?' she burst out.

Catherine looked taken aback. 'I don't know him at all,' she said. 'In fact, until yesterday, I'd never even set eyes on him – though I must admit I recognized the name when

143

I heard it. His photographic work is second to none. And when he offered to come here and help me out – well!' She spread her hands helplessly. 'What could I say? Especially when he asked me straight out if he could take a ride out to Wydale with me this morning.'

Amy said, 'Look, I'll leave you with Uncle Gif for a while. You'll have things to talk about.'

'I'll make a nice cup of tea,' Lizzie said.

'Not for me, Lizzie.' Amy strode over to the stairs. 'I think I'll have a walk down to the chapel and see if Richard's around.'

Gif Weldon and Catherine Blake walked down the corridor leading to his study, chatting about the weather. Gif seemed to have taken to the girl.

Lizzie hurried over to Amy and whispered, 'I don't like that fellow who came with her.'

'Neither do I, Lizzie. But it looks as if he's taken himself off for the day.'

'I hope so. I can't say I like the thought of *him* creeping about the house.'

'I guess Uncle Gif and Miss Blake have things to talk about. They won't miss me for half an hour or so.'

'So you're going to look for the man of stone, are you?'

'Not really, Lizzie. I just thought Uncle Gif and Catherine ought to be left alone to sort out how the feature is going to be presented,' she said.

Lizzie's eyes narrowed. 'Are you getting on all right with Mr Boden?'

Amy's toes curled into the soles of her Reebok boots, but she made her voice sound nonchalant as she replied, 'I guess so.'

'Have you seen him since Christmas Eve?'

'No. Have you?' Amy's chin jutted defiantly. She didn't

144

want Lizzie starting all that nonsense about marriage again.

'No, I haven't! Maybe you should phone him. He doesn't usually stay away from Wydale this long.'

Amy gave a wild laugh. 'Why on earth would I want to phone him, Lizzie?'

Lizzie's big shoulders lifted in a shrug. 'He *could* be ill, I suppose – all alone in that big house at Hatton-in-the-Dale.'

'He's got a telephone. He also lives in the main street of the village. He could attract the attention of any passer-by if he were ill.'

'Not if he'd fallen downstairs and broken his leg.'

'Well, if he did that on Christmas Eve, he'll have starved to death by now. It's nearly a month ago,' Amy retorted, deliberately hardening her heart.

'You're hard as nails. That's what you are, madam!'

'Yeah!' Amy took the stairs two at a time.

'Where're you going?'

'To get my duffle and a scarf. I'm going out for a walk.'

Richard wasn't at the chapel. Amy had thought about him a lot during the past weeks. With time, though, those invasive Christmas Eve kisses were fading from her memory. She smiled as she walked away from the chapel.

The book of romantic poetry hadn't been what she'd expected when she'd opened the brown paper parcel in the privacy of her own room on Christmas morning. It was the last thing in the world she'd have expected from such a practical man. She'd placed it between the alabaster bookends on her desk under the window, but it had looked lonely there, so she'd shoved a dictionary on one side of it and her diary on the other. It still looked lonely!

She'd lain in bed at night and read some of the poems. It was an old book, beautifully bound in brown leather with gold tooling on the spine. There had been a bookmark inside inscribed, 'Too long a sacrifice can make a stone of the heart'. And Richard had signed his own name underneath the words written by William Butler Yeats so many years ago.

She knew the message was meant for herself alone. Knew too that he was referring to her steadfastly clinging to the memory of Kip Weldon. She'd also swear it was why he'd stayed away from her all this time. He was playing a waiting game. But two could do that just as well as one, and she certainly wasn't going to be the first to make a move to further the friendship. She liked things just as they were, and, though she had to admit to herself that she was attracted to the man, she certainly wasn't going to let him know that.

Once clear of the wooded area around the chapel, she shaded her eyes with one hand and sought the gathering mist for the summit of Aspen Tor.

'It's not a guid day for photographs.' The voice was soft and faintly mocking.

She spun round. Mark Powell was lazing against a mossy tree trunk watching her.

'Where did *you* spring from?' she snapped, making the question sound as though he was something that had just crawled out from under a stone.

Mark Powell sauntered towards her. 'I'd just got beyond the chapel – deeper into the wood – when I saw the flash of your yellow scarf through the trees.'

'I really ought to be getting back to the Hall.'

'Don't go.' His camera was half-in, half-out of its leather case and hanging lop-sidedly against his chest.

He grabbed hold of it, lifted it up to his face. She turned her back on him, seething because he was taking it for granted that she wouldn't object to him photographing her.

'Turn round!' His voice was imperious. Commanding.

She began to walk away from him, not once turning to look at him.

She heard his boots scraping on the gritstone beside the river as he followed her. She knew he was trying to provoke her into looking at him. 'Camera-shy, are we?' he taunted as he came close up to her.

'Get lost!'

'Don't you want to see yourself portrayed as lady of the manor in a smart centrefold?'

'No! I'm not lady of the manor.'

'I hear you will be – one day.'

She quickened her steps beside the swollen river.

'Aw! Come on,' he pleaded. 'Talk to me, will you?'

'Put that camera away, then.' She gave him a swift glance, knowing he wouldn't have time to click the shutter. It was the kind of camera that needed adjusting to the ultimate degree for perfect light and shade. The speed would need to be just right too, in a misty landscape such as this.

She heard him fumbling with the leather case and the mass of instruments he had dangling from it. 'Okay,' he said. 'You're safe now.'

She came to a halt against the stump of a tree that must have been felled years ago. She stepped up onto it and looked down at him.

'Queen of all you survey,' he said mockingly.

'Why do you resent me?' she asked.

His sallow cheeks darkened with a flush of annoyance.

'Who said I resented you?' He shoved both hands into the pockets of his checked jacket and stared up at her.

Standing on the tree stump as she was, she felt she had an advantage over him. Her head was marginally higher than his, and, added to that, she knew by the flush on his face that she'd embarrassed him – if such a thing were possible with such an arrogant man.

'You have an attitude,' she said. 'And I don't like men who have an attitude towards women.'

'You prefer mealy-mouthed men who pay compliments all the time, do you?'

'I prefer men who are genuine,' she said, keeping her temper under control with difficulty.

'And I'm not in that category?'

'I don't know you,' she said. 'But I'd hope that this isn't your *real* self I'm seeing. If it is, I think you have quite a problem.'

'Quite the little psychoanalyst, aren't you, Miss Weldon?'

'I like to think I'm a good judge of human nature, that's all.'

'We're getting away from the point, though.' He walked down to the edge of the riverbank and stood looking at the water rushing down into the valley. Over his shoulder, he asked conversationally, 'Are you over here for long? In England?'

She jumped down from the tree stump and joined him beside the water. 'A couple of months, I guess.'

'It's a holiday, then?'

'Something like that. I hadn't been back in over twelve years.'

'It must seem very different to Boston.'

'Yes. Do you know Boston?'

'Only through the eye of the camera.' He turned to her

and smiled, but the black eyes were hard and calculating. The smile didn't reach them. Something about those eyes unnerved her. It was as though she'd known him before, but in a different lifetime. 'I was commissioned to produce a book of pictures of the New World eighteen months ago,' he said.

'America?' she asked, surprised.

'Mmm. Not my usual thing. Tacky. Old and new. You know the sort of thing – two pictures to a page, one a sepia taken a hundred years ago, the other a modern colour one of the same place.'

'Sounds interesting to me, Mr Powell, and not at all tacky.'

'It doesn't need brains to do that kind of work, though.'

'I see. You thrive on challenge, do you?'

'A good photographer is an artist.'

Uncaring of his feelings, she said, 'I prefer video.'

He snorted. 'Aye. Y'would.'

Annoyed at his sneering remark, she said, 'I'll ask you again – why the resentment towards me?'

'Poor little rich girl,' he taunted. 'I can't stand women who sit back and reap the rewards of others, yet never lift a finger to help themselves.'

'You've lost me,' she said, starting to walk back to Wydale. 'You don't know a thing about me, yet you're making wild allegations all over the place.'

'Well, you're going to step in and inherit all this when the auld man dies, aren't you?'

'I guess so. Dry rot included,' she said meaningfully.

'It's one hell of a place, all the same. Woodland, God knows how much acreage in pasture, and a dream of a house. But,' he said with contempt, 'the best-laid plans, etcetera, etcetera.'

She stopped walking and faced him full-on. 'Just what are you getting at?' she wanted to know.

He kicked at a tuft of icy grass, looked at it hard and long, then lifted his head to say, 'We can never be a hundred percent certain of anything in this life, can we, Miss Weldon?'

Richard Boden drove the Land Rover carefully over the pack-horse bridge, then headed for the old chapel. The track petered out before he reached the wrecked building, so he drew his vehicle onto a rocky patch of ground on which nothing much grew except coarse grass and clover, and parked it there, under the trees.

Outside, in the fresh cold air, he looked towards Aspen Tor in the distance. Low cloud obscured its summit. Further down the valley, however, beside the fast-flowing river, he caught a glimpse of something brightly coloured.

He walked out into the open, a smile touching his lips. It had been a long time since he'd seen her, but that cheerful yellow scarf just had to be hers.

He cupped his hands to his mouth and called, 'A-m-y! A-m-y!'

She was too far away for him to see her expression, but her head jerked round, and then he saw her lift a hand and wave. She'd seen him. She'd started coming towards him.

But there was someone else there too – someone who must have been with her, and who was following her now. A man? Richard frowned and focused his eyes, trying to get a better look at the figure loping along in her wake. It wasn't Gif Weldon! It was too light-footed for the old man. Gif Weldon would never wear such a loud red and white checked jacket either.

She ran the last fifty yards towards him. Her cheeks were flushed and the yellow scarf streamed out behind her. The man accompanying her slowed down, coming up the last and steepest part of the river path at almost a saunter.

'Richard.' She was panting as she reached him. 'Richard. You're quite a stranger around here nowadays.' Her breath was misting on the icy air in front of her. She stood still, pushed her gloved hands deep into the pockets of her grey duffle coat, and smiled broadly.

She seemed pleased to see him, he thought, and it warmed his heart, seeing that wide, infectious smile again. It had been hard keeping away from her these past weeks, but it had been necessary. The message he'd left on the bookmark had been obvious. The ghost of Kip Weldon had to be well and truly laid, he knew, before he could embark on anything more serious than a flirtation with her.

He wondered who the stranger was – the dark-haired young man who was now leaning against a nearby tree-trunk fiddling with his camera. His brooding eyes were on Amy, though, and Richard didn't like the way they were watching her – almost caressingly.

His big hands clenched into fists at his sides. Once before he remembered feeling like this – and look where that had got him. He fought down the urge to smash that cynical smirk off the stranger's face with his bare hands. No one had the right to stare at Amy in that way – almost as if he owned her. Who the devil was he, anyway?

Richard said in as casual a manner as he could muster, 'I didn't know you were with somebody, Amy. I wouldn't have called out to you if I'd realized.'

She glanced across at the man beside the tree and tossed her head. 'Things have been happening up at the Hall since Christmas Eve, Richard. It's a long story, but this is Mark Powell. He's a photographer.'

The man acknowledged her explanation with one word in Richard's direction. 'Hi!'

Amy swung round to him. 'Mr Powell – Richard Boden.'

Richard was glad she wasn't on first-name terms with the stranger. His initial irrational feelings towards Mark Powell began to subside a little. 'A photographer?' he said. 'That must be interesting work. Perhaps you'd like to see inside the old chapel.'

'I was there earlier – took almost a reel of film of the place.'

The Scottish accent was unmistakable, and, Richard noted, the man was obviously well educated. He saw Amy suck in her breath before retorting, 'You never told me you'd done that.'

'What you mean is, I never asked permission,' Powell replied, almost insolently.

Amy seemed intent on not stirring up trouble. She deliberately turned her back on him, pulled one hand out of her pocket and rested it on Richard's arm. 'Are you going inside?' she asked him. 'If so, I'll come with you, and Mr Powell can make his way back to the Hall alone.'

With a polite nod at the stranger, Richard led her through the mass of brambles and strewn debris littering the ground towards the chaplain's room.

Once there, he put a match to the little oil stove and pulled a chair close up to it for her. 'Here. Sit down. It's cold today.'

She wandered over to the window. 'I hope he's taken the hint and gone,' she said, sounding uneasy.

'Do you want to tell me why he's here?' Richard was wearing a green waterproof jacket. He shrugged his shoulders out of it and tossed it aside. It landed on an upturned cardboard box in a corner of the room. Heat was slowly stealing out from the stove. He pushed up the sleeves of his thick khaki sweater and then removed the dustsheet from the angel, which was still lying on the trestle table in the middle of the room.

She turned towards him and told him of the happenings up at Wydale since she'd last seen him.

He listened in silence, and when she'd finished asked, 'And all this came completely out of the blue? No one had ever approached Gif for a story on Wydale before?'

She shook her head. 'He was completely taken aback by the letter.'

'Strange!' He frowned. 'Stranger still that fellow Powell circling the place for weeks beforehand in his helicopter, don't you think?'

'But the girl seems genuine. And *Diary* magazine certainly is. It's in all the shops, and seems to be quite popular.'

'Where is this Catherine Blake right now, though, Amy?'

Amy walked across to the angel and looked down at it. 'She's up at the Hall – talking to Uncle Gif.'

'Has Gif seen the colour of their money yet?'

'Five hundred pounds will be paid to Uncle Gif when a contract is signed, and the remaining five hundred on publication.'

'Maybe we shouldn't worry, then.'

'That's what I keep thinking.' She laughed up into his face. 'Usually I'm so trusting, but with this . . . I don't know.' Her laughter faded, and she frowned. 'Richard, something seems not quite right. I guess it could be because of the guy. I can't get to grips with him. He makes everything he says sound like a question; he gives me the creeps. Lizzie doesn't like him either.'

'He didn't seem the friendliest thing on two legs, I must admit.' Richard leaned back against the trestle and folded his arms.

'It's those eyes. Black as night.' She gave a little shudder. 'They make him look mean as a skunk at times – and yet they're beautiful, really.'

'Are you trying to make me jealous? "Beautiful", indeed!'

'Heck, Richard, you don't think I'm falling for him, do you?'

'Heck, I hope not,' he said, mocking her and laughing.

'He never laughs. Not like you do.' Her face softened as she looked up at him, then she cocked her head on one side and said, 'I seem to know him from somewhere, though.'

'Lots of people bear a resemblance to somebody else,' Richard said.

'But I swear I've seen him before – or somebody very like him.'

'Probably around town. You've been to Hatton quite a few times.'

'I guess so. And he *has* been to Boston. He told me he was in America eighteen months ago.'

'There you are, then. There's nothing sinister about him after all.'

It was still quite cool in the little chapel room. He saw her shiver. 'But he knew all about me, Richard. He even knew I was going to inherit Wydale one day.'

'That's no great secret, Amy.' He pushed himself away from the trestle and came over to her, taking both her

154

hands in his and looking down into her eyes. 'Your uncle talks to people. He told me a year ago that he'd made a will leaving everything to you. Duncan Ward must know about it too. I'd assume that, being a lawyer, he would have drawn it up. And Lizzie knows – and probably John Graham the chauffeur does too. Don't you see? Anybody could have passed on *that* information to this Mark Powell.'

She shook her head and pulled her hands away from him. 'I don't get it,' she said. 'He's a stranger around here – a stranger to all of us at Wydale – yet he said something quite chilling, Richard. He said we can never be a hundred percent certain of anything – just as if he was issuing some kind of threat. Just as if he *knew*, somehow, that I would never inherit Wydale.'

'Amy! My advice is that you shouldn't take any notice of him.'

'It's easy for you to say that . . .'

'Amy. You have to forget what he said. It sounds to me as if he's a bit of a lad who likes to stir up the dust just for the sake of it.'

'To me it sounded like a threat,' she said. 'But why should a stranger want to see me disinherited, I wonder?'

She thought about Mark Powell as she walked back up the hill to the Hall around lunch-time. The little blue car had gone, she noticed as she went into the courtyard. She hoped with all her heart that Powell had gone too – *and* that he wouldn't return.

'It's given your uncle a new lease of life,' Lizzie said. 'Having that attractive young woman showering him with so much attention.'

'Catherine Blake's nice, isn't she?' Amy took her coat off

and draped it over a kitchen chair. Lizzie was bending down at the oven, taking over-sized potatoes baked in their jackets out of it.

Looking over towards the table, Amy saw that two places had been set, and she was just about to ask where her uncle was when Lizzie informed her, 'Gif's gone out for lunch. Miss Blake bundled him into that little car and said she was taking him for a pub lunch down at the Hawkwood Arms.'

'She did?' Amy's eyes widened with surprise. 'Heck, Lizzie, how did he take it?'

'Lapped it up.' Lizzie straightened up from the oven and carried the hot potatoes in an ovencloth over to the table, where she placed one on each of the two plates.

'Lizzie Abercrombie – you're kidding me.' Amy began to laugh.

Lizzie, keeping her face straight, said, 'Can you see Gif Weldon taking kindly to a ploughman's platter?'

'What in the world is that?'

'Crusty bread. Lump of cheese. Salad and pickle.'

'We – ell, he just might – for a pretty face.'

Lizzie gave her a strange look and raised her eyebrows. 'I think not, Miss Amy. Indeedy, I think not.'

Wydale Hall had been built on several descending levels and followed the line of the hillside on which it sat, with small flights of stairs leading to different rooms and wide landings with leaded windows giving panoramic views of the spectacular Derbyshire countryside. The gardens were similarly laid out, in a series of wide terraces, each one supported by low dry stone walls and balustrading. The gardens had no particular pattern to them, each one being connected to the next with wide, shallow steps hewn from local limestone. The hillside above Wydale was densely wooded, mainly with evergreens and the trees fanned out into a giant half-circle that seemed to enfold Wydale and all its surrounding land in a mantle of green, summer and winter alike.

Amy liked the winter garden best of all. It was well secluded and could be reached only by a path that was lined with yew. Flowerbeds here were boxed in by stone kerbs, with little pebbled walkways between dahlias and crysanthemums. From the old days, she could remember a blaze of daffodils under the ornamental trees, and purple aubrietia tumbling down over a rockery splashed with enormous clumps of white heather. Today it was bare of colour, except for a few green tips showing through the soil – the daffodils and hyacinths of tomorrow.

The afternoon sun had no warmth in it but she'd dispensed with her thick yellow scarf and duffle coat, preferring, instead, a heavyweight sweater, jeans and calf-high boots to work in. She had studied her reflection in the long wardrobe mirror in her bedroom before setting out for the garden. Her friends in Boston wouldn't recognize her, she'd thought with a wide grin. She'd never looked so rural – so incredibly *English* before. The deep turn-over collar of her sweater might be a hindrance to gardening, though, she'd realized.

She had leaned forward slightly and noticed how the cowl neck unrolled itself and flopped forward against her chin and cheeks. 'Not a good choice for an afternoon's gardening,' she had muttered to herself, but time had been getting on, and soon there would be nothing left of the daylight. She had gone over to her dressing table and seen the little tortoiseshell box still sitting there. Every day she dusted it, looked inside at the brooch Uncle Gif had given her, then closed it up again. Today she had taken it off its tiny satin cushion and held it up to the collar of her sweater. The purple amethyst in the shape of a Scottish thistle had nestled into the creamy whiteness of the wool. On impulse she had fastened it right through the thickness of the cowl neck and anchored it securely to the body of the sweater underneath.

She'd leaned forward again and the collar had stayed put. Uncle Gif might not look kindly on her using the brooch for such a purpose, but it had saved her asking Lizzie for a safety pin and then having to rummage through the housekeeper's sewing basket to find one. Now, as she cleared out the dead-headed crysanthemums and piled them in a corner of the garden where she remembered the bonfire always used to be, the sweater was no problem at all.

She was glad to be actively employed in doing something worthwhile, for there were no gardeners at Wydale now. Uncle Gif had told her that the chauffeur John Graham had little to occupy him, so he had taken on the weeding and the hedge-cutting. Lizzie too, helped out when she had the time. Lizzie admitted to loving a bonfire, and, when Amy had said she was going out to do a bit of clearing up in the gardens, Lizzie had promised to come out later and bring some old newspapers and a box of matches.

Amy worked methodically, starting on the lower level and working her way across it. She snipped off dead flowers and carried them, overflowing in a garden trug, to the bonfire area, then returned and filled and refilled the trug several times more. She turned her attention then to the rambler roses, but almost lost her footing when one of the small terrace walls suddenly gave way under her

158

weight. She stopped working to examine the damage and found that the soil had worked loose around the foundations of the stones embedded in the earth. She sat back on her heels and looked at the rest of the wall. Stones were loose all the way along it, she saw. She decided she'd have to ask John Graham's opinion as to what could be done to safeguard the roses.

She made her way carefully out from between the prickly branches of the sprawling ramblers. Thorns tore into her thick gardening gloves and refused to budge even when she tried to shake them off as she reached the path once more. Looking round the silent garden, she was struck by the decay of it all. Lizzie had been right when she'd said that it was time that was eating away at the stones of Wydale. The old house and its gardens had been neglected for far too long.

Mark Powell had been standing in the shadow of the yews for more than five minutes before she saw him. Even then, he doubted she would even have looked up if it hadn't been for the camera's almost inaudible click as he captured her on film.

The look she shot at him spoke volumes.

'Guilty!' he called out softly. 'Forgive me. I couldn't resist just one picture.'

She tore off the prickly gloves and tossed them onto an ornamental stone bench, then, with mud caking her leather calf-length boots, she came striding towards him. 'Get off my back, will you, Mr Powell?' she stormed as she stopped right there in front of him, her eyes sparkling with indignation. 'You have absolutely no right to come poking and prying around here.'

He felt a bit of a louse for creeping up on her as he had

159

done, and he heard his own laugh sounding brittle and artificial as he replied, 'I only wanted a couple of pictures, for heaven's sake.'

'I don't give a hoot what *you* wanted. You're trespassing here, so get out and give me some space, will you?' She flung out an arm and pointed back up the path. 'Go on. Get out. You're nothing but a damn creep – first of all spying on us from the air, then barging your way in on the pretence of helping Catherine Blake with her feature – '

'You have no idea . . .' he broke in, and then his voice tailed off as he saw the amethyst brooch. Anger threatened to overwhelm him, and it was only with difficulty that he stopped himself from shooting out a hand and ripping the tiny thistle off the collar of her sweater. It wasn't hers to wear, he reasoned. She had no right at all to be in possession of it. But he couldn't tell her that, could he? Couldn't tell her that for as long as he could remember a faded photograph of a young woman wearing that brooch had been standing on his mother's dresser. That the young woman *was* his mother . . .

'No idea, huh? No idea of what, Mr Powell?' Hands on hips, she faced up to him, her jaw obstinate.

He dragged his eyes away from the brooch and said quietly, 'I'm the bad guy in your eyes, aren't I?'

'You're a snoop. I don't like snoops.'

'I'm doing no harm.'

She'd fastened her shoulder-length hair back with a thin black ribbon. Now a golden strand broke loose and fell forward over her eye. She dashed it back impatiently. 'You have no right being here,' she said. 'You wormed your way in and you can just crawl right back out again.'

'Hold on a minute.' His voice was quite calm. He prided

160

himself on never yelling or shouting. Usually he could get a point across without all that sort of fuss. Today, though, he felt like bellowing at her, telling her he had every right to be here – more right than she had, in fact. He wanted the world to know – not just this girl – that he was Gifford Weldon's son. He wanted the old man to know most of all, though. That would hurt him – knowing he'd had a son all these years and had never even realized. It would pay him back in some small way for the hurt he'd inflicted on Barbara Weldon.

'Why should I hold on a minute? Tell me, why should I do that?' Her hands fell to her sides. Suddenly, to him, she looked weary and vulnerable. Her face was daubed with mud, her clothes were dusty. Dead leaves and bits of wood had stuck to her creamy white sweater. Wydale obviously meant something to her, he realized. She wouldn't be out here now, looking like something the cat wouldn't drag in, if she didn't care about the old place.

He'd been about to tell her the truth, but now he knew he couldn't do it. But he had to say something.

'What interest does that guy down at the chapel have in Wydale?'

Looking surprised, she said, 'Richard's been doing some restoration work at the chapel. There's a possibility he might do a whole lot more on the Hall itself in the future.'

'Why would he want to do that? He has no claim on it, does he?'

Obviously without thinking, she blurted out, 'If I marry him . . .'

'If you what?' Mark Powell was thunderstruck. 'God! He's too old for you.'

She lifted her shoulders in a couldn't-care-less shrug.

161

'It's none of your business,' she said. 'And anyway, what's age got to do with it?'

'You're crazy,' he said, thinking what a waste it would be if she were indeed seriously considering throwing herself away on somebody ten years or more her senior. Then he narrowed his eyes thoughtfully. 'But he could be onto a good thing, couldn't he – this Richard Boden? He gets the girl and the house all in one easy swipe. Is that the idea?'

'Mr Powell, I think you should just go,' she said.

'You haven't answered my question.' Hostility burned in the black eyes.

'There's nothing to answer. I don't have to ask your permission for anything I do.'

'No,' he said, 'but maybe you should ask *yourself* a few questions before you dive headlong into a marriage of convenience.'

'I don't know what you mean.' She stuck her hands on her hips and glared at him.

'I think you do know what I mean,' he said. 'I think you must have asked yourself a dozen times – if you're seriously thinking of marrying him – if it's you he wants or the old Hall back there.'

She stared stubbornly at him, but he knew his words had hit home. It was obvious, however, that she wasn't going to enter into any kind of an argument with him. 'Please go,' she said.

'I'll be happy to.' He didn't trust himself to say any more, yet there was so much that needed saying, he knew. Would it make any difference to her, he wondered, if she knew that *he* himself was old man Weldon's son? Would the marriage still go ahead if she had no inheritance?

Hell! She was a good-looking girl with a future ahead of

162

her. And she was thinking of tying herself down to a man nearly twice her age. He felt like getting hold of her and shaking some sense into her. He wanted to set things to rights, to tell her – and the world – that Wydale belonged rightly to *him*! But how could he? What right had he to snatch everything away from under her nose – everything she had been promised?

He found he couldn't face her any longer. With set jaw and one last hard glance at her he swung away, then started running as he reached the avenue of yew, knowing he had to put a safe distance between the two of them while he thought about what to do next.

CHAPTER 11

Mark Powell fed several fifty-pence pieces into the telephone in the long passage between the bar and the lounge of the Hawkwood Arms.

'Mother?'

'Son, this is nice. How's the weather down there?'

'Mild. Mild for February anyway.' His usually harsh features relaxed into a smile. Trust her to worry about the weather.

'We've had some snow in Blairgowrie. The skiers are making the most of it at Glenshee . . .'

'Mum, I'm coming home for a while – if that's okay by you?'

The woman's voice held delight. 'That'll be fine, son. You know you don't have to ask. Are you sure you're all right, though? I thought the photographs you're taking of Yorkshire would take a lot longer than this?'

His low laugh was forced, though only he knew it. 'I've had a dose of the English flu. I need pampering,' he told her, deliberately ignoring her query about his work. Guilt welled up inside him. He hadn't told her he was coming to Derbyshire. Nobody knew about that. And he suddenly found he wasn't proud of his snooping activities during the past few weeks.

'I'll air the bed, then,' she said. 'When will I expect you, lad?'

'Tomorrow. I'm getting the bike ready for the long haul north.'

'Be careful, then. I worry about you . . .'

'Don't worry. I'm a big boy now.'

Barbara Powell placed the telephone back on the receiver and then leaned heavily on her walking stick. The arthritis was bad today; it was making an old woman out of her before her time. Moving slowly over to the window of her bungalow, she caught sight of her reflection, and the expression of pain on her face made her draw in her breath and straighten her back. It wouldn't do to let him see her like this – all peely-wally, as her dadda used to say – and she not yet fifty. She'd take one of those pills the doctor had prescribed before tomorrow. And a bit of make-up wouldn't go amiss.

She turned back to the interior of the room and was pleased at its simplicity and lack of clutter. She couldn't abide confusion; Lord only knew she'd had enough of *that* in her life before Derek Powell had died. Men only brought upheaval and unhappiness to a woman. Well, perhaps not *all* men. Mark was different – but Mark was a part of her, and a son to be proud of. Derek had driven him away. Away from her and away from Scotland.

But Derek hadn't been able to drive the love out of him, and now Derek was dead Mark had a home again. It warmed her to remember how he'd said on the telephone, 'Mum, I'm coming *home* for a while . . .'

What would she do without Mark? She supposed she must be thankful to Gifford Weldon for that one thing at least. As she made a pot of tea in the kitchen, and heated

165

up a can of soup for lunch, her mind went back over almost a quarter of a century, and the hurt she'd secretly nursed gradually began to seep away so that within minutes she was able to pull open the top drawer of the sideboard and take out a large brown envelope.

Carefully she drew the card-mounted photograph from its covering. Her lips curved upwards into a smile. My, but she'd made a bonny bride there at the wedding in Wydale's little chapel. It had been a quiet affair – just a handful of guests, all acquaintances of Gif's because *she'd* had no family – but it had been a nice little do. It had only been after the guests had gone home that the dream had started to fade.

Duncan Ward had been best man. He was a red-headed, cold fish of a lawyer who'd had a lofty disdain for women and never failed to let his views be known. Barbara had detested him – not for his opinions but merely because he was Gifford's best friend who, in the three weeks before the wedding, had monopolized the bridegroom and spent long evenings with him either playing chess or just lounging about drinking copious amounts of whisky.

Barbara remembered how she'd been forced to turn to Mrs Tilly, the mouse of a housekeeper, for company in the long dark nights of autumn. There'd been two other girls who had lived in at the Hall, but they had only been teenagers, and Mrs Tilly had been hard-pressed to get any work out of them at all.

Mrs Tilly had been due to retire at the end of that year, and Gifford had made it plain that Barbara must learn all there was to know about keeping staff in order.

The marriage, she could see now, had been over before it began. Duncan Ward had made sure of that. She could look back now, though, without bitterness. That brief interlude at Wydale Hall had opened her eyes to a lot of things that at twenty-three years of age she'd never even dreamed about. She didn't blame herself any more now. She knew the marriage had never stood a chance of surviving whatever she might have done – or not done – to make it work. And at least she'd come out of it with her son. But at what cost to her own self-esteem?

Her second wedding anniversary. Barbara gazed at the portrait hanging over the fireplace in the great hall at Wydale. It was all a sham – her marriage. She recognized that now. And that portrait was the biggest sham of all. It branded Gifford Weldon as a solid pillar of society, a married man – a respectable man. A portrait of the lady of the house couldn't be anything else but respectable, could it? All the best county families had such portraits!

He was coming in now. She heard him giving imperious stabling instructions to the groom in the courtyard, then the hollow ring of hooves sounded on the slabs out there. He came in silently and she knew he was standing just inside the door and watching her.

'It's an excellent likeness, my dear. Do you like your anniversary present now it's finished?'

She said, without moving, 'Yes. The grouse moors in the background remind me of home.'

'But this is your home.'

She caught the note of censure in his voice. He'd taken lately to talking down to her – almost as if she were a servant. And in truth, she knew now that she was more servant than wife. Hot shame raced through her as she remembered the night only two weeks ago when she'd finally realized that she couldn't stay with him and be humiliated any more.

They'd been godparents to a colleague's baby. Little Amy Rawle had snuggled deeply into Barbara's arms – and also into her heart. She'd gazed down fondly at the child, at the tiny, wrinkled face and big solemn eyes. She longed for a child of her own, but how was that to be when her husband didn't even sleep in the same part of the house as she did?

It had worried her constantly that she didn't have a proper marriage. After the baby's christening Dr Rawle and his wife had invited them to stay the night. Gifford had tried to make excuses, but in the end the Rawles had insisted, and from that moment on Gif had hit the bottle as if there were no tomorrow.

Sharing the big double bed with her husband at the Rawles' house that night, she'd snuggled up close to him and whispered, 'Gifford, I want to be a proper wife to you. We could have a bairn of our own.'

'No!' He'd pulled away from her and turned his back. She'd touched him gently on the shoulder and he'd shrunk even further into himself.

Gifford . . .' she'd pleaded, 'we're man and wife – and have been for nearly two whole years.'

He'd groaned and told her to go to sleep. His speech had had a whisky-induced slur.

'Please, Gifford . . .' Her hand had moved gently against his spine. It was the first time ever she'd touched him like this. There was a burning, gnawing ache coursing through her whole body. She wanted to be loved. She needed him to take this pain away and give her a child of her own. She'd felt his body go tense, then without warning he'd flung himself over to face her and snarled, 'Leave me alone. I don't want you. Can't you understand?'

She'd recoiled from him, seeing his face livid in the pale

168

light of the moon which was shining in through the uncovered window. 'Gifford . . .?'

'Haven't you guessed, woman? After two years don't you know what's going on right under your nose?'

'I – I don't understand . . .' She'd pushed herself up in bed and rested an elbow on the pillow as she'd looked down on him. 'Gifford – we ought to talk – we can't go on like this.' A sudden thought had flashed into her mind. 'Is there . . .?' she'd hesitated, then asked, 'Is there another woman? Is that what you're trying to tell me?'

His laugh had been ugly. 'A woman? What would I want with another woman? It's Duncan, you stupid bitch, Duncan! Duncan! Duncan! He's all I want – all I need. If you can't accept that, then you can always get out of my life – go back to Scotland. Maybe that would be the best thing of all.'

By the following morning a plan had formed in her mind. And now, tonight, she went about her task methodically, first of all cooking a celebratory meal for their anniversary and then plying him with champagne and whisky. He was unable to climb the stairs unaided when it was time for bed, and he didn't resist when she went into the bedroom with him. He slumped onto the bed – an elegant mahogany four-poster with red drapes. A large oil lamp burned brightly on a lacquered cabinet. Wydale had no electricity, but that fact didn't worry Barbara. There'd been no modern amenities at the croft in Glenochry where she'd been brought up. 'What a body niver has, a body niver craves,' her mother had often said to her.

Her mother had been wrong.

Barbara, after two years of marriage, felt cheated. She'd been duped. And now she wanted a man to hold her, a man to love her, a man who would make her into a whole woman. She yearned for motherhood. Her whole body was craving fulfilment. She needed to become as other women were. To be rid for ever of the burden of virginity that had been forced upon her by her marriage to Gifford Weldon.

Barbara looked down on her husband with disdain. His eyes were closed. He was snoring quietly. She began dragging off his clothes and tossing each item onto the floor. When that was done, and he didn't wake up, she took off her own things and lay down on the red silk coverlet beside him.

His body was strong, athletic and warm. She could persuade herself it wasn't Gifford Weldon if she closed her eyes. She pressed herself close up against him and allowed her hands to caress him. He moaned softly once or twice, but never once opened his eyes. It didn't take long to bring him to erection. His back arched and he murmured, 'Duncan . . .' on a long, drawn-out sigh.

Barbara despised herself for what she was doing as she climbed on top of him, then lowered herself down onto his writhing body. This way she could control the pain she knew was bound to come. He started to move rhythmically, and gently she eased over until it was she who was lying on her back and he on top. It was too late to go back now. She thrust herself upwards and he threw his head back with a terrible cry. A surge of victory flooded through her. It was over in a matter of seconds, and he was fully awake now and panting. His head fell forward, his open with stark horror as he gazed down at her.

When he realized what had happened, he tore himself out of her body and rolled off the bed. She heard the crash of the bedside table as he hit it and knocked it halfway across the room. He stumbled to his feet and she

170

saw the muscles of his stomach starting to heave. He began retching and crying. The tears flowed fast down his haggard cheeks as he looked at her in revulsion. He reeled away from her and was violently sick on the Indian carpet.

She lay still and watched him, triumphant in her one moment of glory. There would be a child; instinctively she knew that it would be so. She'd read all about it in a book. All she had to do was choose the right time of the month and then lie still afterwards for half an hour . . .

She left Wydale the next morning, summoning a taxi and making the driver fetch the luggage from her room. She wouldn't take any risks like carrying heavy bags herself. This baby was precious. It was the only thing that mattered in her life at that moment.

Amy showed Richard the broken wall in the winter garden. He got down and examined it, then stood up, looking uncertain, with a frown etched across his forehead.

'I meant to ask John Graham to take a look, but Uncle Gif's keeping him real busy at the moment.'

'It seems there's been a small landslip.' He climbed back to the path, dusting his hands together, then looked back at the wall and said, 'Maybe you should get somebody to do a survey.'

'But you know all about such things, surely, Richard.'

'Rock quarrying's quite a different kettle of fish from this.' He smiled gently at her. 'Amy, it might be something and nothing, but, considering how badly the western tower's subsided, I really think a survey of the land Wydale's built on is necessary.'

'That would cost money,' she reminded him. 'And Uncle Gif doesn't have any.'

171

'There's the money from the magazine feature,' he said.

She sighed. 'I can't prise that out of him. Heck, Richard, it's hard enough getting him to pay the essential bills around here.'

'Do you want me to talk to him?'

She looked up at him gratefully. 'Would you? He'll take notice of you. He thinks women are just empty-headed little creatures.'

He held out a hand to her. It came naturally now for her to place hers in it. In the past two months she'd come to rely on him. Their friendship was the most natural thing in the world. He'd never attempted to kiss her again like he had on Christmas Eve. He seemed to be letting her set the pace of their relationship, and if friendship was all she wanted, that was precisely what she got.

She felt easy and happy with him. It wasn't love, as she reminded herself constantly, but it was a nice feeling being with him. She visited his home and he cooked meals, and he took her to the theatre in Hatton, and once to Derby. He still spent a good amount of time at the ruined chapel. The angel Gabriel was restored too – if not to its former glory, then to a good imitation of it.

They walked back towards the house. 'I'm going away for a few days,' she told him. 'You remember I told you that Kate Weldon asked me to try and find Kip's former girlfriend?'

'Yes.' He looked down at her as their locked hands swung companionably now the path had widened. '*Have* you found her, then?'

She shook her head. 'Not a chance! I placed ads in the east coast newspapers, as you know, but nothing came of them, so I've decided to mosey on down there and have a look round myself.'

'It might work. If she still lives there. But it's one heck of a big area to cover, you know.'

'I thought I'd try local libraries and records offices. They have microfilm of old newspapers, don't they? Kip's accident *must* have made headlines, so there's bound to be a report of it somewhere hidden away.'

'And you think there might be mention of this girl? Kitty?'

'I don't really hold out much hope.' They were almost up at the Hall now. Amy tugged on his hand and brought him to a halt. 'Look – I don't want Uncle Gif to know about this. He wouldn't understand about Kip, but you do – '

'I understand that you loved him. Still love him,' Richard broke in, shaking his dark head at her. 'Oh, yes, Amy. I understand perfectly. You want to trace the baby for yourself, don't you? Kitty is just the bait in the trap. Once you've traced her, you'll have got what you want.'

'I'm doing this for Kate and Marty Weldon!' she cried. 'Can't you understand that?'

Softly he quoted, '"Too long a sacrifice", Amy. Have you forgotten so soon the message in that book?'

'My heart is not made of stone.' She dragged her hand out of his. 'And, yes – I had forgotten the message. And you should forget it too. It was unkind to say that about me.'

'There'll be no future for you with anyone until you get rid of that obsession,' he said in a hard voice.

'All I want you to do is keep it from Uncle Gif,' she insisted. 'Richard – ' she held out a hand pleadingly ' – Richard, please don't make things difficult. As it is, I've got to think up some logical excuse to tell him why I

173

want to go visit the east coast at this time of year.'

A smile creased his face. 'Early March isn't exactly the peak holiday season, is it? But why not tell him half a truth, instead of a downright lie?'

'Half a truth?' She tilted her head and looked warily at him.

'With your second obsession – making video films – why not say that you want to see the place where Kip was stationed, and take some film to send to Kate and Marty in America?'

Her face brightened. 'Richard! You're a darling.'

'I sure try to be.' He grinned at her. 'It's hard work where you're concerned, though.'

They fell into step again and walked round the kitchen garden and into the courtyard. 'I guess I could get a train from Hatton,' she said.

'A train!' He stopped dead in his tracks. 'Good grief, girl – why do you want to go by train?'

'Because,' she said patiently, 'I don't have a car, and a couple of hundred miles is too far to walk.'

'I have an idea,' he said.

Her ready laughter pealed out. 'You're full of good ideas today.'

'This is serious. But it's the best idea I've had all week.'

'So, tell me, Mr Boden.'

'I could take you. I have wheels.'

'You also have a quarry to run.'

'I have a very efficient foreman.'

Her eyes lit up. 'You mean it? You really mean it, Richard?'

He crossed his heart solemnly. 'I mean it, my little Bostonian. I really and truly mean it.'

Practicality took over. 'Where would we stay?'

'A room in a hotel might be a good idea.'

She raised her eyebrows. 'Two rooms,' she corrected him.

'Okay. Two rooms.'

'On different floors.'

'Heck! You're a pest of a woman. You really try my patience sometimes.'

'I trust you really.' She walked into the courtyard, then turned and faced him again.

He followed her, and asked on a surprised note, 'Do you?'

'Uh-huh.'

'You make it very hard for me to be a cad, Amy Weldon.'

' "Cad" 's old-fashioned. Make it "heel" or "jerk" – and if you still mean it about two rooms, you're on.'

'Heck,' he said, 'aren't I the lucky one?'

'Heck,' she replied, in a voice heavy with sarcasm, 'this is one crazy guy I've gotten myself lumbered with.'

CHAPTER 12

It was a fine spring-like morning when Richard called to collect Amy from Wydale for the longish drive down to Norfolk. At just after seven o'clock the roads were relatively clear of traffic. Later in the day the limestone lorries would begin their heavy lumber to and from the deep, white quarries of Derbyshire – and Richard Boden's would be among them.

'Sure they can manage without you for a couple of days?' she asked as she sat beside him in the Land Rover, bright-eyed and confident that this trip would bring something to light and put her on the track of the elusive Kitty.

He shot her a twinkling glance. 'The place won't grind to a standstill just because I'm not there. Anyway, I'm long overdue for a holiday.'

She studied his profile as the Land Rover started to climb towards one of the highest points around Wydale. The notorious Blackthorn Pass never failed to impress her, but, unlike John Graham, she wasn't afraid of its loftiness and majesty. Today there was no mist to speak of, but swirls of fine cloud hovered round the higher peaks. Across the valley, bleak moorland could be seen, its close-packed heather – darkened and dank now – stretching endlessly to the northern peaks from a long, shallow outcrop of gritstone. Blackthorn Edge, across the valley, could have been chiselled out of those ancient hills by nothing short of a giant's hand.

Amy noted that Richard kept his attention firmly on the road at all times. It was as well to be wary, though, with a highway that was barely the width of two vehicles in some places and which on Amy's side was a sheer drop measuring hundreds of feet. She looked out of the window with interest, and said, 'Wow! I wouldn't like to get a dizzy attack up here, would you?'

He laughed. 'The road widens out a bit further on. Do you want me to pull into the observation bay so you can take a look around?'

'I'd sure like to take some film – if we have the time.'

He drove on for half a mile or so, then pulled over onto a jutting promontory that was just big enough to take perhaps five or six cars.

Outside in the fresh air, she laughingly steadied the camera as a sharp, unmerciful wind buffeted her about. Richard leaned his hands on top of the dry stone wall which was all that separated them from that terrifying drop into eternity. She caught him watching her several times as she panned the camera round from the high gritstone edge across the valley, to follow several little craggy pathways on the opposite hillside that led down to the valley floor.

'That little river down there looks cute.' She put the camera on hold for a second or two as she glanced at him. 'I'm going to close in on it and take a better look. There's a flat stone bridge across the water that looks like the one at Wydale.'

'I've got a pair of binoculars in the back of the vehicle,' he said, but she shook her head.

177

'No thanks.' She grinned. 'The camera does the trick just as well, and I can see what I'm actually getting on the picture.'

He shrugged. 'Okay. Suit yourself. You're the expert.'

She filmed the river – which was actually no more than a wide, shallow stream running through the valley – smiling in delight at the tiny packhorse bridge that spanned it, and wondering who on earth had gone to the trouble to build it when it seemed the whole area was deserted down there. She swung the viewfinder upwards again then took more film of the whole of the winding road they'd travelled along that morning, right up to the point they'd reached now.

And then the camera focused on Richard, and he shook his head and laughed and said, 'I hope this bit is going to be edited out.'

'I want to record every second of my time in England. I'm even keeping a diary for the first time in years.'

'Is that because England is the place where you were born?' he asked gently.

She faded Richard out of the picture, switched off the camera and lowered it. 'Usually I'm not the sentimental sort, but something's taken a hold of me while I've been here.' She lifted her shoulders helplessly. 'It's like I've come home. Know what I mean?'

'It's natural, I suppose. You must have memories of when you were a child in England all those years ago.'

'I guess so. But I can't stay here, Richard. I promised Kate I'd go back. I can't let her down.'

'It's your decision.'

His reply brought her no comfort. She shivered, suddenly feeling the full impact of the biting wind that was numbing her fingers and raking through her hair.

'You're cold,' he said, coming up to her. 'Come on. Get back in the car.'

She looked at him. He was standing about four feet away from her. He could warm her, she knew – if he wanted to. She recalled the feel of his arms around her, and the solid strength of his body close up against her on Christmas Eve. Suddenly, going back to America, and Kate, and Marty, wasn't what she wanted. She wanted to stay here. She wanted Richard to *make* her stay here. She felt very vulnerable. Her eyes swept up to his, pleading with him. Silently she begged, Give me a reason – a reason to be with you. But he didn't know, couldn't even guess at her feelings – could he?

He swung away and strode over to the Land Rover. He held open the door and yelled, 'Come on. We've got a long way to go.'

She went over to him, cocked her head on one side and said, 'Are we in a hurry all of a sudden, Mr Boden?'

He looked at his wristwatch. 'It's taken us twenty-five minutes to drive twelve miles. At this rate we might just reach Norfolk next Friday.'

She stuck out her tongue at him and hoisted herself back inside the Land Rover. He laughed out loud and slammed the door shut, then walked round to the driver's side and got in beside her.

'Did you have any breakfast before starting out?' he wanted to know.

'A piece of toast. Lizzie went mad at me. She said I needed a good breakfast but I was too hung up on getting started, I guess.'

'We'll stop somewhere around Grantham, shall we?'

She grimaced. 'If I don't sink through the floor before that. I'm starving now.'

179

He started up the engine again and pulled carefully back onto the road.

'You call the tune. You tell me where you'd like us to make camp,' he said as they drove through flat Lincolnshire, which seemed to Amy to consist mainly of sky and vast open space.

She studied the map on her knee, and crunched an apple as she tried to pinpoint exactly where they were.

He stabbed a finger at the map. 'Try that area,' he suggested.

'I *do* know how to read a map.' She shot him an impatient glance. 'We're not near enough the sea yet. I want to get really close to the place Kip stayed at. I need to know if there are dance-halls, cinemas, somewhere – anywhere – where he might have met up with Kitty. I mean, this is all very well – all this wide open space we're driving through – but it doesn't make a good hunting ground for young, virile American service boys, does it?'

'Not unless they're into bird-watching of the feathered kind – no!' he agreed. 'I get your point.'

'Can we drive round this bit of land that's got a square of sea in it?' She held up the map so he could slow down a bit and glance in her direction.

'That's the Wash,' he said. 'There aren't many roads around it.'

'Great!' she said with derision.

It was almost midday. 'We need to get a base,' he said. 'I think we should book into a hotel, then we can start looking around Kip's old hunting grounds.'

'Okay,' she said. 'Let's do that.'

But finding accommodation wasn't as easy as they'd imagined it would be. All the hotels were full.

'A trade fair,' Richard explained to her. 'It's a dead time of year for visitors to these parts, so they hold a trade fair the first week of March each year.'

'A trade fair?'

'A kind of convention for all kinds of trade. Buying. Selling. Conferences. Receptions.'

She sat in the Land Rover and looked at him. 'So what do we do now? Move on?'

He snapped himself into his seat belt. 'They said at this last place I tried that we might get a caravan or beach cottage in West Norfolk.'

'A beach cottage? That sounds cosy. We had those in New England – built on legs on the sand – wooden buildings. I didn't know you had them over here.'

Richard smiled. 'I don't really think we're talking about the same thing. After the flooding they suffered here in the fifties, I doubt anyone in their right senses would build wooden houses on English beaches.'

They sat in the crowded car park of the latest hotel and consulted the map again. 'Here,' he said, indicating a tiny road leading off from the main one. 'This is the place they said I should try. It's just a village. Way off the beaten track.

'Corrie Creek!' Her eyes lit up as she looked at him. 'Sounds quaint. I like it.'

'You don't mind a cottage?' He was serious all of a sudden.

'I trust you,' she said, 'if that's what you're hinting at. I shan't get all girly and shy because we have to share a bathroom.'

'You're a funny one,' he said, grinning at her.

'I guess so.' She folded the map and asked innocently, 'So what are we waiting for, Mr Boden?'

* * *

181

Cottages, Amy decided, were a whole lot easier to rent than hotel rooms – and they were more fun.

She poked around the cupboards in the tiny kitchen of number three, The Lane, and yelled over her shoulder, 'Richard – we need some food. There's absolutely nothing in here.'

She heard him coming downstairs, then he stood in the doorway and said, 'Well, what did you expect?'

She shrugged. 'Nothing, I guess. But I'm just dropping the hint that you need to go find a general store or something.'

'Me?' He raised his eyebrows and sighed.

'You're the guy with the wheels. Remember?'

'Don't you have a driving licence?'

She turned away from the cupboards, lounged back against the work-tops and asked, 'Would you really trust me to drive the love of your life?'

He leaned a hand on the doorframe. 'I take it you *can* drive?'

'Sure! I drove plenty in Boston. And I remembered to take out an international licence before coming over here.'

'Then feel free to take the Land Rover. Any time.' He dropped his car keys on top of the kitchen units.

'I'll need you to show me how. You can do that this afternoon.'

'Are you hinting I should go out right now and push a trolley round a supermarket?'

'You won't find a supermarket here,' she said. 'But you can go get the shopping in from *somewhere* while I pop the kettle on to boil.'

'I see you're opting for the easy job.' He gave a mock sigh and picked up the keys again. 'All right. I get the message.'

'You're a truly liberated man!' She flashed him a mocking smile.

After a quick lunch, they drove into the town they'd passed through earlier. Richard said he'd like a look round the bookshops, so they arranged to meet back at the car park later on. Amy found the local studies library, and began her search on microfilm for a report of Kip's accident.

It was an easy search. The toppling of a sixteen-ton army trailer into a local river and the loss of the American servicemen had made front page headlines. Amy relived the nightmare Kip must have experienced as she read through the newspapers; it must have been horrific, she realized. Making photocopies of the relevant facts made her feel like a ghoul. Wouldn't it be better, she wondered, to let the whole episode rest? But she forced herself to carry on when she remembered how Kate had pleaded with her to find Kitty. There was no way of tracing the girl other than by raking up all this heartache, she knew.

She found as she scanned the screen that many local people had been interviewed for the newspaper, especially those who worked for the emergency services that had been rushed to the scene of the tragedy. There were ordinary souls too, who had turned out to try and help – farmers with tractors, mechanics from a nearby engineering works with heavy lifting gear, fishermen who knew well the currents of the fast-flowing river and could advise on where the hapless soldiers might be washed ashore.

As she read what had been printed Amy began to feel physically drained of emotion. And when she'd finished she sat with her head in her hands and finally came to terms with Kip's death. In the silence of the hushed library she realized that in coming to this place she had finally laid his ghost for ever. There were no tears left to shed; those had all been spent two years ago. It was a trite and often incongruous cliché, but life really did go on.

She'd never forget Kip. She knew that implicitly. But the relationship had always been one-sided; Kip had loved only Kitty! Amy knew that *she* herself had never figured romantically in his life at all.

She replaced the roll of film in its drawer, and gathered together all the photocopies relating to the accident. When she met Richard back at the car park she was composed. He took one look at the wad of papers under her arm and gently took them away from her.

'I'll put these on the back seat. You look as though you could do with a cup of tea.'

She nodded. 'I have a lot of names to contact.' She was subdued, she knew. Not at all her usual bubbly self.

'Okay,' he said, 'but not today. They can wait until you've had a good night's sleep.'

It was nice to have someone take charge of her, to sit her down in a quiet little café and to order a pot of tea and hot buttered toast for her without even asking what she wanted. Ordinarily, she would have picked up the menu and read it avidly. Today she knew she needed pampering a bit.

When the tea came, he poured it out and said, 'Do you want to tell me about it?'

She relaxed. It was easy to do that in his company. He made no demands on her emotionally. He was like no other man she'd ever met. Her eyes met his across the silver and the china and the sparkling white tablecloth, and a smile touched her lips. His forehead was drawn into tight

184

lines, making his dark liquid gaze both touching and stern at the same time. He was concerned for her, she could see.

'Don't look so damn worried,' she said, leaning forward and picking up her cup with both hands.

'You don't need this sort of hassle,' he replied. The censure he felt for Kate Weldon was there in his voice, but there was also compassion mingled with a need to understand why she'd undertaken this task for the American woman who had adopted her.

His hands were clenched together on the table-top. She took a sip of the hot tea, then replaced her cup in its saucer. Then she reached over and touched his hands. 'Kate took the place of my mother,' she explained. 'She and Marty gave my life meaning when my childhood world had crashed. Don't you see? I have to do this one last thing for them because they're not here and they can't do it for themselves. It would be too hurtful for Kate and Marty to do what I've done today. Kip was, after all, their only son. To me he was just my adopted brother . . .'

His jaw tightened. 'You know damn well that's not true. You were in love with him. You can't tell me it's been easy reading all that horror stuff about his death today.'

'No.' She looked down at the table, then once again her gaze flitted up to rest on his face. 'But I'm not in love with him now, Richard,' she said simply. She withdrew her hand from his, and picked up a piece of toast. 'Eat up,' she suggested with a wry grin. 'Come on, Richard, this might be the only decent meal you get for the rest of the day. Cooking's not really my speciality.'

'We're eating out later,' he said, reaching for his own cup of tea.

'We are?' Again she experienced the delight of being looked after. And it wasn't like her at all, she realized.

185

Normally she was the most independent of people, the kind who liked to organize her own life, in her own time and in her own way. Somehow it was unnerving having another person making all the arrangements whilst she fell in with them. But what was really starting to worry her was the fact that she was beginning to *like* being looked after.

CHAPTER 13

In her London flat, not a ten-minute walk from the *Diary* offices, Catherine Blake scooped up the last bit of apricot and semolina pudding from the Postman Pat dish and said, 'Open wide now. This one's for the pussycat.'

'Pusca!' The toddler banged her hands on the baby chair's plastic table in front of her, but obligingly opened her mouth, showing off several tiny pearly white teeth and screwing up her eyes.

'Good girl! Look, what a clean dish!'

'Mum-mum-mum.'

There was a buzz from the doorbell and Catherine looked up from the table and said, 'Who on earth . . .?'

'Erf,' the baby said, repeating the last word. 'Erf. Mum-mum-mum.'

'You, my girl, are getting too big for your baby-boots,' Catherine said as she got up from the kitchen table and walked across the sitting room to the door. She peeped through the spyhole, then muttered, 'Oh, no!'

The bell buzzed again – impatiently, Catherine thought, now knowing who the caller was. In the few days she'd known him at the Hawkwood Arms in Derbyshire, he hadn't been noted for his tolerance. She opened the door. At least he had the grace to look slightly apologetic.

'Hi!' He was untidy as ever, but the shirt was clean – if crumpled. Why he insisted on always wearing that hideous checked jacket, though, she couldn't imagine. Maybe it was to make a point. Or perhaps he just couldn't be bothered to find anything else in his wardrobe – if he possessed anything so mundane as a wardrobe! Today the jacket looked worse than ever because he was wearing an ugly kind of rucksack on his back.

'Hi, to you,' she said. 'How did you find me?'

'If I said the telephone directory, would you believe me?' She could almost persuade herself that the lilting Scottish brogue had been turned on especially for her benefit.

She shook her head. 'Not a chance. I'm ex-directory.'

'I don't want to get anybody into trouble.' He looked down at his shoes, then back at her.

That naughty-little-boy look did nothing for her. Where men were concerned, Catherine was wary. 'You've been to the office,' she said. 'You've been talking to that new kid, I bet. You've probably turned that spoilt-brat look on her and she's taken pity on you.'

'She was so impressed with the spoilt-brat look that she offered me a cup of coffee before giving me your address.' He gave her a lazy smile. Mark Powell, she realized, never did anything in a hurry – not even smiling.

'You'd better come in.'

'That's very kind of you,' he said in a mocking voice, stepping over the threshold as she moved to one side.

'I don't like wise-guys.' She closed the door firmly and put the chain on.

'Neither do I. You're very wise to avoid wise-guys.'

She'd had a busy day. 'Look,' she said, 'I'm going to have an early night, so come in, get to the point of this visit and then push off, will you?'

From the kitchen came a loud wail. 'Mem-mee-meee.'

He looked startled. 'I'm allergic to cats. They bring me out in spots.'

'It's not a cat, idiot. It's a baby.'

'Ye Gods! You're not married or anything, are you?'

'Why? Aren't your intentions honourable?'

'God! I can't stand women with a sense of humour.'

'Probably because you don't have one yourself.' She turned and marched back to the kitchen where she whisked the baby out of the highchair and then turned to face him. 'This is Kimberley – Kim for short,' she said.

He came over to her, looked the baby in the eye, took hold of her tiny hand and said solemnly, 'I'm Mark, Kimberley – and your mummy doesn't like me very much, even though I've brought her some very nice pictures.'

Startled, Catherine said, '*Diary* hasn't approached you for any stills recently – unless . . . Oh, no, it's not that new girl Tracey again, is it? She hasn't gone and . . .?'

'No, no, no,' he said, shaking his head. 'Don't go blaming the new kid for everything. Don't you remember? In Derbyshire I said I'd let you have some of the pictures I took of Wydale Hall.'

'So you did. But I thought you were just being polite.'

'I'm never polite.'

'I didn't like to say that, but I agree with you all the same. It was exceedingly *impolite* the way you turned all surly and non-communicative when I actually got you into Wydale.' She hitched the baby more firmly in her arms, then said, 'Look, let's go back into the sitting room. This little one begins to feel like a ton weight when you've held her for more than a few minutes.'

189

She led the way back into the tidy and fashionable sitting room.

'You have a nice place here,' he said, slipping the rucksack off his shoulders and letting it slide down to the ground.

'Take your coat off,' she invited, more because she couldn't stand the sight of the garish checks than because she wanted him to stay.

'Thanks. It's warm in here.'

'I keep it like that for the baby.'

'She's a cute little girl.'

'I think so too.'

'How old?'

'Just had her second birthday.'

'And Daddy?'

He didn't pull any punches, she thought. 'No daddy. He died.'

'I'm sorry.'

She smiled grimly. 'So am I.'

She sat down with the baby on her knee. He knelt on the floor and pulled the rucksack open, delved inside and brought out a handful of ten by eights.

He passed them over to her. 'Can you use them for the feature on Wydale Hall? And before you ask, I don't want any payment. Consider this a friendly gesture on my behalf and feel honoured – because I don't very often make friendly gestures.'

She placed them on the couch beside her then gently lowered the toddler onto the floor. The child stood with one thumb in her mouth, watching what Mark Powell was doing.

Catherine went through the pictures. They were good – much better than the ones she'd taken herself when she

190

was in Derbyshire. She laughed up into his face. 'These are great. I love this one of the ruin – and those of the winter garden. Old Mr Weldon showed me round on the second day I was there. It must have been a lovely place at one time.'

'Yes,' he said. 'Now, though, it needs a great deal of money spending on it to make it anything worthwhile.'

'I really ought to pay you for these . . .'

'No,' he insisted. 'They're yours.'

'But . . .'

'I'm not strapped for cash, Catherine.'

'No, but – oh, Mark, you're so very young. You have a living to earn like the rest of us. All the time we've been using your photo-library, I've imagined you to be quite middle-aged.' She laughed. 'It was a shock actually meeting you in Derbyshire.'

'Maybe you should do a feature on me in your magazine,' he suggested.

'Hey, don't tempt me. It would make good copy – telling our readers how you've achieved all that you have done in so short a time.'

His face hardened a fraction. 'That would take all of two sentences,' he said. 'One – I had a mother to support; two – I left school at sixteen without qualifications but with a passionate interest in photography and an art teacher who saw my potential.'

Baby Kim lost interest in the conversation, and Catherine watched as her daughter trotted over to a wicker basket full of toys in a corner of the room, where she sat down and started flinging things around.

'Would you let me interview you?' Catherine's interest had been aroused.

He shrugged. 'Maybe. One day.'

191

'I mean it, Mark. Yours sounds a fascinating story.'

'As I said – perhaps one day. At the moment there are people who could be hurt by what I might say.'

'*Diary* doesn't go in for lurid personal details,' she said. 'You would be in charge at all times.'

Lazily he said, 'But I might just *want* to hurt somebody by telling the truth. What would *Diary* think about that?'

She stared at him, perplexed. 'You're a strange man,' she said. 'I never know quite how to take you.'

'That was said very graciously – and not in your usual men-are-all-shits manner,' he said. 'But I guess you really see me as one big ego-tripper. Most women do. I've never yet met one who understands me – except my mother, of course.'

Catherine began to relax a little. She leaned back against the cushions of the couch and said, 'Just *why* did you want to get into Wydale? You seemed very intense about it at the time. Couldn't you just have telephoned and asked permission to take pictures? Or walked up to the front door for that matter?'

'I like to be a little more subtle.'

'That doesn't answer my question.'

'You should be with MI5 – not *Diary*,' he said. 'I bet you terrorize everybody you interview, Ms Blake.'

'It's all part of my charm,' she said drily.

He glanced over at the baby, playing happily in the corner of the room, and said, 'I quite fancied you in Derbyshire, you know.'

'But not any more!'

'Kids aren't my scene. If I let myself fancy you now I'd have to start being all fatherly to young Kimberley, and I can't face that.'

'If it's any help – you're too young for me.'

'You can't count age in years – and up here – ' he tapped his forehead ' – I'm more ancient than you'd believe. But enough of me. Tell me – how do you cope with a toddler? I mean, you're a working girl.'

'*Diary* has it's own crèche. I also have a very obliging elder sister who shares this flat with me.'

'Oh! We're likely to be interrupted at any minute, then?' He looked round interestedly.

'We can't be interrupted if we're not doing anything, can we?' She laughed.

'We are doing something. We're talking. Socializing. I was just about to ask you a very important question.'

'Sorry! I'm busy most nights. I don't get much time with my baby if I go out.'

'How did you know I was going to ask you out?'

'In my job, you get to know the answers to the questions before you fire them. People are very predictable.'

'Come up to Scotland and meet my mother one week-end,' he said. 'We can take Kim with us. Mum's not like me – she actually adores kids.'

'Wha–at?'

'That caught you out, didn't it?' For the first time ever, she heard him laugh with genuine amusement. She liked the sound.

'You don't know me.'

'You did me a favour – so I owe you one. And short of propositioning you, a weekend with my mother is the next best thing.'

'Oh?'

'You gave me a ticket into Wydale. I feel I can drop in there again now. That housekeeper made me a pot of really lousy tea.'

193

She looked at him sharply. 'Just what is your interest in the place?' she asked.

'Ah! That would be telling,' he said. 'But maybe if you hang around me long enough you'll find out – when I give you that interview.'

'I won't be hanging around, Mark,' she said sharply. 'I'm twenty-six, an unmarried mother and I don't "hang around" men.'

'I'm twenty-two. Make a note of that for when I give you that interview. Twenty-two and a millionaire – well, almost.'

Catherine raised her eyebrows. 'I still won't be hanging around – not even if you're a millionaire ten times over. You should be chatting up younger girls. Girls like the one at Wydale. She's nearer your age than I am.'

'Amy Weldon! God forbid!'

'You said that as if you didn't hit it off with her.'

'She's okay.'

'What have I said?' Catherine frowned 'I thought she was nice.'

'You hardly saw her.' His head jerked up. His eyes narrowed. 'What's *your* interest in her?' he asked.

'Nothing.' It was said quickly. Too quickly, she knew. She looked away from him, at the baby playing in the corner.

'There *is* something. I've rattled you, haven't I?'

'I don't know what you mean.' She sprang to her feet.

'You brought her name up deliberately just now. Do you have an interest in the Weldon family – other than using them for the magazine feature?'

'Mr Powell, I have to get Kim off to bed. It's been a long day.'

'Okay. I can take a hint ' He got up from the floor and picked up the rucksack and jacket.

'Look – I didn't mean to be rude. It was good of you to bring me the pictures . . .'

'Are you going back to Wydale?' He shot the question at her with a directness that startled her and almost made her think he knew the real reason she'd gone there in the first place.

Her cheeks flamed. 'I thought I'd take the magazine proofs up to Derbyshire. Just to get the old man's okay on them.'

'Don't you usually do that kind of business by post?'

'Sometimes,' she hedged, feeling decidedly uncomfortable. He was like a dog with a bone. Somehow he'd latched onto the idea that her interest in the big house in Derbyshire was more than the professional kind.

'It's that girl, isn't it?' he said. 'You just had to get a mention of her into the conversation, didn't you? Now, why was that, I wonder?'

Catherine sat down again, her hands clenched in her lap. He came and knelt in front of her. Flinging away his jacket and bag, he sat back on his heels and studied her face.

'Hey, what is it? You seem really worried about her.'

Very slowly and very precisely, she said, 'Amy Weldon advertised in several newspapers to try and find me.'

'She *advertised*?' he said in obvious disbelief.

Catherine nodded. 'That's why I did the story on Wydale. I needed to find out what she was after, but I drew a blank.'

'You're losing me along the way,' he said.

'Yes.' She stared at him, then nodded again. 'Yes, I suppose I am, but it's a long story.'

'I have all the time in the world,' he said, raising himself up to sit beside her on the couch. 'All the time in the world – and you look like you need somebody to talk to.'

CHAPTER 14

Amy loved her bedroom overlooking the reclaimed marshland, and the high shingle bank of a beach that only just allowed a glimpse of the sea. Richard had deliberately chosen the second bedroom for himself, the one with hardly any view at all except for the winter-bare garden belonging to number three, The Lane, and the gardens of its neighbours – numbers one, five, seven and nine.

As they washed up the breakfast things in the sparsely furnished kitchen he asked, 'What time is your first meeting? The one with – who is it, now? The fire-chief who was called out to the accident involving Kip Weldon?'

She nodded and said, 'Yes. His name's Rupert Bonney. It's not until two this afternoon, and then at three-thirty there's that retired schoolmistress who lived nearby and ran out to see if she could help when she heard the crash.'

'And this evening?'

She turned away from the work-top she'd been wiping down and frowned. 'A girl who worked in a bar – apparently at a pub that Kip and the boys frequented. She was mentioned only briefly in the newspaper articles as a 'bystander' – though what that means, I don't know. You wouldn't really think there'd be any 'bystanders'

196

hanging around in a cold and wet country lane at midnight, would you?'

'Seems funny.' Richard slung the damp cloth he'd been drying crockery with over his shoulder and said, 'Is that it? Have we finished? I never realized boiled eggs and toast could make such an amount of washing up.'

'All done.' She tweaked the drying cloth off him and hung it up beside the window on a hook put there for the purpose.

'What do you want to do this morning, then?' He leaned against the fitted units and folded his arms.

'I want to walk on an English beach.' She was already striding towards the door that linked the living room with the kitchen.

'I'll go along with that. There's nothing I like better – though it's a while since I was at the seaside. Especially with a bitter March wind buffeting up for a gale like it is today.'

'Do you mind it being so cold?' She hesitated at the door and halfturned back to him.

He gave a short bark of a laugh. 'What? When I work outdoors in the freezing depths of winter in darkest Derbyshire? Amy, being here is pure heaven when I think of all that choking limestone dust and the lorries churning up mud and grit whatever the weather. Here, I don't have to use ear protectors against the noise of the blasting; I don't have to wear a hard orange hat either, or goggles . . .'

'Okay!' Her easy laughter rang out. 'I get the message loud and clear. We'll walk on an English beach all morning, shall we? Just so you can get some fresh air into your lungs – poor old hardworking man!'

'Less of the "old",' he growled. 'You'll find I don't need a zimmer frame yet.'

197

She ran lightly up the stairs to get her jacket and scarf, and heard Richard opening a wardrobe door in his own room. When she was ready, she poked her head round his door. 'Will I do?'

He grinned at her as he pulled on his leather jacket and zipped it up. 'What would you do without that yellow scarf?' He shook his head and his eyes crinkled with merriment at the corners. 'I love that yellow scarf.'

'I like yellow.' She lifted her shoulders in an impatient shrug. 'Come on, slowcoach.' She pushed her hands into her pockets and brought out her gloves.

'Not yellow?' he asked, coming across the room, and, when they were both out on the landing, closing the door firmly.

'Yellow gloves would be a bit much, wouldn't they?' She pulled them on as they went downstairs. 'Lizzie knitted them for me.' At the bottom of the stairs she held out her hands, palms downwards. 'Black. It's serviceable – so Lizzie said. But I made her put these little orange flowers on the back, just to liven them up. Do you like them?'

'I like anything on you.' His voice was light.

'Don't start anything,' she warned. 'We're here on a mission. I don't want any hanky-panky – and that, by the way, is another of Lizzie Abercrombie's sayings. Hanky-panky – I like it, don't you?'

'I've led a sheltered life,' he teased. 'I don't think I'd know hanky-panky if it kicked me in the teeth.'

Outside the wind hit them hard as they set off down The Lane towards the beach. It all but took Amy's breath away, surging as it did off the north sea and then up and over the steep shingle bank. The Lane gave way to coarse flattened grass and ridged uneven ground. By the time

198

they'd climbed to the top of the shingle her hair was snarled and matted against her face.

'Hell's bells.' She turned to him, laughing again. 'I should've fastened my hair back. You're not wearing a tie or anything that I could borrow, are you?'

'I'm on holiday,' he said. 'I don't wear a tie on holiday on principle.'

'Guess I'll just have to get used to having my eyes beaten out by all this hair, then.' She pushed her hair away and held it tightly at the back of her neck as she swung from him to look at the sea. The beach on the other side of the shingle bank was patterned with rows of wooden spikes, she saw. She jerked her head towards him as he came up to her. 'Those sea defences look real mean.' She nodded in the direction of the spikes.

'You can't walk around with your hands behind your head all morning,' he said, and, shoving one hand into a deep pocket of his jacket, brought out a tattered old fabric tape measure. 'Here! Will this help hold your hair back? It's one I used for measuring Gabriel when I was working on him in the old chapel back home.'

'Hey! That's great, Richard.' She reached out to him and the wind gusted again and snatched up her hair. She was blown almost off her feet and reeled away from him, squeaking, 'Heck! This is some wind.'

He laughed and caught up with her as she stumbled down the beach. 'Hang onto your hair,' he ordered as they came face to face again. 'Hang onto it just where you want it anchoring, and I'll tie it back for you.'

'Okay!' Specks of sand whipped up from between the shingle stung her eyes, and her cheeks would be glowing, she knew, because she could see the tip of her nose if she squinted slightly, and that was red. 'Gee! I must look a sight.'

'A sight for sore eyes,' he said softly against her ear as he turned her round with her back to him while he fastened up her hair with the tape measure – doubled to make it more easy to handle.

She felt a prickling right down her spine as his fingers touched the back of her neck. It would be so easy to lean back and let those gentle giant's arms go right round her. Easy, too, to forget all about Kitty and Kip – *and* her promise to Kate Weldon. What wouldn't be easy, though, was coming to terms with her conscience if she did all of those things. She wasn't a girl to go back on her word.

She steeled herself to resist the longings he aroused in her, and when he'd finished tying the tape into a bow, she faced him and said brightly, 'Thanks for the tape measure, but not for the compliment. A sight for sore eyes, indeed. Richard, this trip is not intended as a prelude to anything romantic.'

'I understand that perfectly,' he said, in as solemn a voice as she'd ever heard from him.

'You are not being serious, Mr Boden.' She tossed her head and marched away from him, down to the sea that was crashing in great plumes of spray onto the beach.

He didn't follow, and when she looked to see what he was doing she saw he'd got a pair of binoculars up to his eyes and was scanning the heaving ocean.

'Hey! Can I have a look?' she called out.

He held the binoculars out towards her. 'Be my guest.'

She raced back up the beach. 'What were you looking at?'

'The other side of the Wash.'

'This great chunk of water's the Wash? I didn't realize.'

He pointed westwards. 'Over on that side is Lincolnshire. You can just make out buildings and things in the mist on the far shore.'

She lifted the binoculars to her eyes and focused them. 'So you can. I didn't realize there was anything out there except water.'

'Water is all there is if you look straight out.' He got hold of her shoulders and made her face round to the right a bit. 'Now look again. You might see boats – though with a tide like this, *I* wouldn't like to be out there.'

'No. There's just water. And storm clouds.' She sighed and handed the binoculars back to him. 'Come on. Let's walk. It's too freezing cold to stand still.'

'Old lady,' he mocked. 'You're not up to this – an English mad March day.'

'We have far worse winters in Boston,' she told him as they began to walk slightly below the ridge, where the wind wasn't so keen.

'This, my dear girl, is an English *spring*, not winter,' he said, laughing.

'I have an odd sort of feeling, Richard. About this woman I'm supposed to be meeting tonight,' she confessed as they went along.

'Want me to come along? You've arranged to meet in a bar somewhere, haven't you?'

She looked up at him. 'Maybe she won't talk if there's two of us.'

He shrugged his big shoulders and said, 'Well, you can always go in alone, then I'll follow and sit at a table somewhere near.'

'It's being a bit devious, isn't it?'

'If it makes you feel easier, what does it matter?'

'I'm just being stupid, I guess. Yet I feel kind of . . . excited. D'you know what I mean?'

'I know one thing,' he said as they tramped along in the shingle. 'I know you're getting over the infatuation you had for Kip Weldon, Amy.'

She stopped walking, and, a little breathless from the effort of keeping upright in the wind on the uneven ground, faced him. She considered his words for some minutes, then said, 'Guess that's what it was really. Infatuation. Not love. You need something more than hero-worship for a love affair to blossom, don't you?'

'I guess so,' he drawled.

'You're mocking me.' She stood, head on one side. 'Apologize,' she said. 'You have no right to mock my American accent, Mr Boden.'

'I love your American accent, Miss Weldon,' he replied.

'Richard! Don't!' She felt very self-conscious and the tone of his voice was making her heart race. She was beginning to feel she ought to have come down to Norfolk by herself. Proximity with this gorgeous man was not to be recommended – not when there was work to be done, a hefty problem to be solved. Romance was definitely not something she was good at. She just had to take herself in hand and be firm – and dedicated to the task in hand, she realized.

He was staring beyond her now, though, along the shingle ridge to where two kids were kicking a colourful plastic ball around. The wind was playing havoc with it and carrying it high and wide each time they kicked it. They were screeching and yelling and racing after it one way, only for the wind to catch it again and toss it in the opposite direction.

Amy's attention drifted away from the children and back again to Richard. His face had softened as he watched the two playmates. She wondered if he was

202

thinking of what might have been had Grace and the baby lived. She couldn't bear to see the raw hunger on his face. Life wasn't fair, she silently raged; if anyone deserved happiness it was Richard.

She turned again to watch the children – a boy and a girl with not much more than a couple of years separating them in age. They must be brother and sister, Amy thought. The boy managed to kick the ball again and it came bouncing along the ridge. Then the wind caught it again and carried it down to the sea. The children raced after it.

'Heck! Those bloody sea defences.' Richard set off at a run towards the kids, and they stopped their headlong flight when they saw him, and backed away from him.

'It's okay,' she heard him shout above the roar of the sea and the whistling whisper of the wind swishing through the coarse grass that grew along the ridge. 'But be careful of these spikes. They're sharp, see? If you were to fall on them . . .'

'Our ball's in the sea, Mister,' the little girl piped up.

Amy sauntered towards them and heard Richard say, 'Stay here. I'll get it for you.' And he loped off down the beach just as a huge wave flung the ball back out of the water at his feet.

He caught it easily and threw it back to the children, then he walked back to Amy as the pair raced away again.

'Play on the other side of the ridge,' he yelled after them.

The little girl turned and waved to him, and they disappeared over the ridge to safer ground.

'Kids!' he said, smiling, as she came up to him. 'They don't see danger anywhere, do they?'

'You love them, don't you?' She faced him now and continued gently, 'You ought to have kids of your own. You'd make a great father.'

203

The smile vanished from his face. 'No,' he said. 'I'll never have children, Amy. I've told you that before.'

'Where's the snag?'

'The snag's in the getting of them. I wouldn't mind if they were delivered by the postman – or Santa Claus – but I'd never willingly put a woman through the hell of childbearing.'

'Maybe it's not the hell you think it is.'

'I lost Grace that way. Remember?'

'I think *you're* the one letting sacrifice turn your heart to stone,' she said guardedly. 'Not me.'

Pain made his face look drawn – the pain of remembering, she guessed, not actual physical pain. 'Oh, Amy,' he said, and suddenly his shoulders sagged and his eyes lost their usual light.

'I'm sorry, Richard. It had to be said. I think we know each other well enough to talk about such things, don't you?'

He turned his face to the sea and his thick, dark hair was lifted and tousled by the wind. She could see flecks of grey in it now. She wanted to reach out her hand and touch it. But there was this huge chasm between them, she realized. She was attracted to him. Yes. She knew she was. But the things she wanted and the things he wanted weren't the same things. And for either of them to give way was too big a compromise. It wasn't something she could talk him out of, she realized. Talk couldn't sweep away a fear so great as the one he carried around with him.

'Do you still love her?' she asked. 'Do you still love Grace?'

He made an angry movement with his hands. 'What kind of question is that?' he wanted to know.

'It's an easy question,' she said. 'But maybe you should

204

search your heart a bit more before you answer. Questions are never difficult – answers often are, though.'

She turned and walked away from him, and headed back to the house.

Amy's meeting with the fire-chief didn't turn up any more information than what she had already gathered at the records library the previous day. She was disappointed. All he could tell her were cold, stark facts.

The weather had been atrocious on the night of the accident, he said. The US Army had often used that road. The soldiers were familiar with it. Traces of a heavy engine oil had been found on it that might have been a factor in making the sixteen-tonner skid as it approached the road bridge. They'd never know for certain, though, whether it had been the heavy rain, oil on the road, human error or an act of God that had turned a simple skid into a full-scale tragedy.

'Has anybody ever talked to you about Kip Weldon?' Amy asked. 'Kip Weldon – the man whose body was never recovered from the river?'

He shook his head. 'Not that I recall,' he said.

'You'd remember if they had? A girl, maybe? A girl called Kitty?'

Again, the answer was negative. 'Never heard the name,' he replied.

The retired schoolteacher wasn't much help either. She was a nice old lady, very formal, very precise. When asked the same question by Amy, she pursed her lips and said, 'There *was* a woman there. I remember her very well.'

'Tell me . . .' Amy was eager.

'A very common young woman, my dear. Nobody you'd want to be associated with, I'm sure. She said she worked at the Bricklayers Arms near Skegness. She was a long way out from *that* area, though. It makes you wonder just why she was alone on a dark, deserted road on a night like that, doesn't it?'

Amy returned to the house and Richard in the late afternoon, parking the Land Rover neatly at the side of the little lane outside number three. He came to the front door and watched as she jumped down from the driver's seat. 'Did you manage the Land Rover okay?' he called out.

'Fine. No problem. I didn't realize until you showed me that it's just like driving an ordinary car. I guess the gears foxed me a bit.'

He laughed. 'But you don't need ten forward speeds for normal running. I use it in rough country, remember. And you don't get much rougher country than a limestone quarry.'

'Richard, I'm starving. What have we got to eat?' She passed him in the doorway, then wrinkled her nose up in delight at the aroma coming from the direction of the kitchen.

'Just get your coat off and go and sit down at the kitchen table,' he said. 'I've been slaving over a hot stove all afternoon – and as I'm a man who usually dives into the freezer for his main meal every night, heaven only knows what this sausage casserole's going to turn out like.'

'You've made a sausage casserole?' She stripped off her coat and left it in the front living room, then dived for the kitchen.

He followed her. 'Well, I'd bought sausages yesterday. They were still in the fridge, and in a cupboard I found a packet of casserole mix. It looked like gravy when I'd stirred some water into it, but I followed the instructions and it seems okay.'

'Have you done vegetables with it?'

'Roast potatoes. They were easy.'

'Sounds great to me.' She slid into her seat and looked up at him expectantly.

'Do I have to dish it up as well?'

She nodded, but said nothing.

'Pour the tea, then – and tell me about your afternoon.' He went over to the stove and she poured out two mugs of steaming hot tea that he must have brewed when he heard the Land Rover pulling up outside the house.

Over the meal, she told him of her wasted journey.

'Maybe the girl you're meeting tonight will have more to say.'

She sighed, and glanced across the table at him. 'I hope so. She can't be any worse than the man who slammed the phone down on me yesterday, I suppose.'

'That was the one called Roger Claybourne, wasn't it?'

'Mmm. Wonder what he has to hide. He was really rude to me when I telephoned him. Said I should let sleeping dogs lie, and it wasn't decent to go raking up the past.'

'Sounds a bit of a crank. Did you explain what you were after?'

She nodded. 'I asked him if he knew anything about a girl called Kitty, and he told me to go to hell.'

'Well, that's one to cross of your list of possibles, then,' Richard said.

'I guess so. I don't want to ruffle anybody's feathers.'

Jane Weaver was a tart, and knew it. At forty, she doubted she'd ever change, even though she was comfortably off now. She liked and got on well with men. Her lifestyle suited her and she didn't regret a thing she'd ever done. Men had been good to her, she reasoned. They had paid for a decent home, a good standard of living, so why should she complain? They got what they paid for, and she waved them goodbye without regret.

She saw the girl walk into the crowded bar and look round the place with interest. She was a good looker. Not classically beautiful, perhaps – that nose was too sharp and her hair needed a few highlights to get rid of that rural-cornfield look – but she was leggy and confident, in sleek, tight trousers and a swingy little black jacket. As the girl's gaze came to rest on her Jane lifted a hand in greeting. She'd commandeered the only quiet corner in the place, tucked away beside the inglenook fireplace where a roaring log fire blazed.

'You're Miss Weaver?' The accent was unmistakably the one she'd heard on the other end of the phone yesterday.

Jane nodded and smiled. 'Sit down, honey. Or somebody will whip that chair away. This place is crowded. Too crowded for a comfy tête-a-tête, I think. Maybe we should move.'

Amy sat down. 'It's nice and warm in here.' She slipped the chic little jacket off. Underneath it she was wearing a bronze silk blouse.

Jane's red lips twisted in a complimentary grimace. 'Not many women could wear black and brown and make it look as good as you do, Amy Weldon.'

Amy said, 'Can I get you a drink?'

Jane Weaver only had to flick a look at the barman and give a nod before one of the girls came over to take their order. 'This one's on me. Okay?'

Amy said, 'Straight orange. I'm driving.'

The older woman gave the order. 'Make that two.'

'You're driving too?' Amy shot the question.

'Not me!' Jane threw her dark head back and laughed. 'I live here, honey. I own the place.'

She saw Amy Weldon's eyes widen with surprise. She always liked it when people did that. It made them sit up and take notice of her. Probably it made them think they'd been mistaken in their first opinion of her. But she never tried to be something she wasn't. First and foremost, she was a tart. Tarting had set her up for life. But now, at forty, with striking looks and a figure any twenty-year-old would envy, she could afford to take things easy.

'Is it always this popular?' Amy was looking around at the well-dressed couples, the beams and gleaming copper, and obviously noting that the adjoining restaurant through a wide archway had no vacant tables.

Jane stubbed out her cigarette in the ashtray. 'Most of the time. At first they used to come to see *me*. Now they know they get good value for money and excellent cuisine. It's the best place around these parts.'

'I don't know Norfolk at all.'

The drinks arrived. Jane Weaver said, 'That's why you need me, I suppose. I won't beat around the bush any more. You want to know what happened that night two years ago.'

The girl opposite her sat forward in her seat. 'Yes. I need very much to know what happened. I have to find somebody, you see. Somebody connected with one of the men who died.'

'Kip Weldon! Yes – you said on the phone.'

'Did you know him?'

'Oh, yes. I knew Kip. More serious than the other young Americans, he was. But he knew how to have a good time.'

209

The girl looked down at the drink in her hands. 'Do you know exactly what happened that night?' She tilted her head back as she drank deeply of the fruit juice.

'Yes. I was there.'

The girl didn't speak.

Jane met her silent gaze. 'I was in the transporter and I shouldn't have been. Nobody knows this except you. I rely on you to keep quiet about it. Those lads all died. I wouldn't want their folks to have to face up to the fact that they were breaking army regulations by having a passenger that night.'

'You – you were their passenger?'

Jane swirled the juice round in her glass, then drank it down. 'In a manner of speaking I was a passenger. That's all you need know, honey.'

'You were with one of the men.'

Jane gave a brittle little laugh. 'Dead right. I was with one of the men – but it wasn't Kip Weldon. Kip wasn't that sort of guy. He was strictly the one-woman sort. He didn't play around.'

'You don't have to spare my feelings.'

'I'm not doing that. I'm telling you the truth. There was nobody Kip cared about except his Kitty.' Jane looked long and hard at the girl. Her face was pale, but she was composed.

Amy said, 'Tell me all there is to know.'

'Not much to tell.' Jane's shoulders lifted in a shrug. 'We hit oil or something on the road. The lads were all laughing and joking. Matt, the one I was with, said – ' She broke off, wondering how to make the next bit more palatable, wondering, too, if it was really necessary.

'Tell me. Please. I want to know everything about those last moments.'

'As we went into the skid Matt said he hoped the next ride he got that night would be just as thrilling . . . Look, kid, I'm not proud about what I did, but . . .'

'It doesn't matter. Really. I'm not judge and jury, Miss Weaver. I just care about Kip – and the girl he called Kitty.'

'I don't know her full name. I wasn't interested in Kip – see? He was just one of the lads, but not the sort to waste his money on women like me.'

'Just on Kitty, huh?' The girl managed a sort of smile.

Jane Weaver leaned forward. 'They were going to be married, I think – Kip and Kitty. He showed me a photo of her that night. She looked nice. Decent. Tall. Dark-haired. She had a nice face – soft-like, and rounded. Not fleshy. I don't mean she carried a lot of weight. She was sort of comfortable-like, but, as I said, very tall.'

'Heck!' The girl suddenly seemed to crumple. She leaned her elbows on the table and rested her forehead in her hands.

Jane had just been about to pick up her handbag and give her the photo to look at – the photo Kip Weldon had handed her seconds before the transporter slewed over the road and all hell had been let loose.

'Hey. I've upset you.' The photograph was forgotten. Jane half rose to her feet.

The girl looked up, rubbed a hand across her eyes to get rid of a tear. 'Heck, I'm sorry. I'm embarrassing you.'

'No, honey. You have a good cry if you want to. Nobody can see you here in this corner.'

'I'm not going to pieces, honestly. It's just so good to be talking to somebody who was with Kip. I only wish you'd asked him what Kitty's other name was. I just want to locate her.'

'It wasn't straightforward, see? Kip's friendship with Kitty.'

The blonde head shot up. 'What do you mean?'

'Kitty had already been engaged to somebody else.'

'No!' The girl sat bolt-upright.

''Fraid so. I think that's why nobody knew her name. Kip said she was scared of her ex even though it had been over with him for some months when she met Kip. She was real scared of this other guy. He'd given her a beating at some time or other – that's when she broke off the engagement. He only narrowly escaped a jail sentence. It didn't put him off, though – he was always pestering her.'

'So that's why Kip kept quiet about who she was? So the man wouldn't find out she was seeing somebody else and cause even more trouble?'

'Seems like it.' Jane Weaver took out an exquisitely engraved cigarette case and opened it. 'Smoke?'

Amy shook her head, then said, 'I keep coming up against brick walls when I try to find out her name.'

'Well – there is a way, I suppose.'

'A way to find out who Kitty is? Was?'

'Oh, yes, honey. What I *do* know is the name of the guy she was engaged to. The guy who was terrorizing her.'

'You know? His name?'

'I'd go careful if I were you, though. Don't say I didn't warn you. I think this man could be very dangerous.' She took out a cigarette, tapped it thoughtfully, then closed the gold case with a snap.

'But I have to know, Miss Weaver. Please – tell me his name. I'll move heaven and earth to find Kitty.'

'Okay, then. But remember – approach him with care, girl. And don't go meeting him on a dark night in some bar like you did with me. Some of you Americans are too trusting altogether. Kip Weldon was like that – and look what trouble that caused.'

'Just tell me the name of the man Kitty was engaged go. Please . . .'

'Okay. Okay. I'll give it you straight. Can you remember it or do you want to write it down? I can give you his name and his address too. He's a market gardener, see? He grows cabbages – fields and fields full of cabbages. Acres upon acres of cabbages. And he lives not twenty miles from here.'

'I'll remember it. Tell me.' Amy had half risen to her feet, and her hands grasped the edge of the table till her knuckles turned white. 'Tell me,' she pleaded. 'For God's sake, tell me his name . . .'

Jane Weaver's eyes narrowed through a haze of smoke as she lit up the cigarette. 'Okay. You asked for it,' she said. 'His name's Claybourne – Roger Claybourne. And he lives at a place called Halfpenny End.'

CHAPTER 15

It was just after ten when Amy arrived back at the cottage.

'You need a drink,' Richard said. 'You look frozen through. Sit by the fire while I make some coffee.'

'Do you have any whisky? I sure feel like I need a stiff drink.' She shrugged herself out of the little black jacket and laid it on a chair, then went over to the cumbersome and chintzy sofa and sank into it.

'Whisky's not something I carry around with me,' he said. 'And unfortunately, unlike hotels, cottages don't have a hospitality tray in the bedroom.'

She smiled weakly. 'Just kidding, Richard. I don't really like the stuff. I just feel absolutely whacked. It must be this sea air.'

'You've taken on a mammoth task,' he said gently, coming across the room to crouch down in front of her. His eyes were dark with concern. 'Amy – slow down a bit, will you? We have all the time in the world – well, until Saturday anyway. That gives us another three days.'

'Jane Weaver told me that Roger Claybourne – the man who was so rude to me on the phone – and Kitty were once engaged to be married,' she said.

'Heck, no!' He gazed at her, dismayed. 'So where did Kip Weldon come into it?'

She patted the seat beside her. 'Sit down,' she said. 'The coffee can wait. I want to tell you everything I learned from Jane Weaver.'

He joined her on the sofa; it was cramped with the two of them on it because the cushions were so fat. He sat partly sideways and rested his arm along the back of it, behind her head. That way he could see her face as she recounted what Jane Weaver had told her.

When she'd finished, he said, 'What was she like? This Weaver girl?'

'Five feet two-ish, forty-something, dark hair, good-looking, smartly dressed . . .'

'No! That wasn't what I meant. Was she telling the truth, do you think? About being in the transporter with those lads? And all the rest of it – Kitty and Roger Claybourne, etcetera?'

'There's no doubt in my mind, Richard. She *was* telling the truth.'

'She was that kind of lady, huh?'

She sighed. 'Richard! She was a hooker! But I believed her; that's all that matters.'

'A hooker? A prostitute? Heck, Amy, I should have gone with you. It's not right – you going off to that sort of place alone.'

In a firm voice she said, 'It wasn't "that sort of place"! It was a bar, okay? It was respectable – and even if it hadn't been, I wouldn't have needed a chaperon. Stop treating me like a kid, will you?'

'Okay!' He held up a hand.

'I don't need a nursemaid.' She scowled at him.

'I'm sorry.'

She was sorry too, when she saw that look of hurt surprise in his eyes. He was only being protective, she

guessed, but what he didn't realize was that she didn't
need a bodyguard. She'd never had time for the knight-in-
shining-armour sort of men.

In the States, at college, it had all been so different.
She'd been one of the guys. Equality – like sex and drugs –
was a fact of life. Maybe she'd been one of the lucky ones
who had grown up able to differentiate between the good
and the bad. Kate and Marty had a liberated attitude
towards kids, and had brought her up with their own
standards. At the moment Richard was making her feel
hemmed-in with his over-considerate attitude.

She pushed herself up from the sofa. Those comfy
cushions were stifling her, just as Richard's regard was
stifling her. And sitting there, so close to him, was doing
her no good either, she reasoned. She was attracted to the
darn man. Couldn't he see that? She didn't want him just
sitting beside her, his arm across the back of the cushions
but not touching her. She wanted that arm around her.
She didn't want to be treated like a kid. She'd never felt
less like a kid and more like a woman in her life before
now.

Suddenly she needed to get out of the house – away from
him. She jumped to her feet, snatched up her jacket, thrust
her arms into it and buttoned it up to its high neck. 'I'm
going out,' she said, making for the door.

'You're crazy! It's half past ten,' he said, not moving
from the sofa. 'You can't go looking for Roger Claybourne
at this time of night. Anyway, like the woman said, he's
dangerous, and I'm not going to let you meet *him* alone in
some sleazy club – or anywhere else for that matter.'

'Richard Boden, don't talk to me as if you own me,' she
flared, facing him and inwardly seething. 'Do you think I
have no sense at all?' she asked. 'Would I really go

waltzing off to look for a maniac at this time of night? No! I'm merely going for a walk. Richard, I'm so full of energy I feel like a power station ready to explode.'

'Do you want me to come with you?' He'd turned his head away from her. He was looking into the leaping flames of the fire.

She knew she'd hurt him, but hardened her heart still further. 'No!' she said. 'I want to be alone to work out what I'm going to do next. You stay here – or else go to bed if you're tired.'

With an angry exclamation he was on his feet and facing her. 'You don't like being patronized yourself,' he flung at her, 'so don't do it to me, Amy. What the hell's the matter with you?'

She gave a short bark of laughter. 'We're getting too cosy,' she said. 'Don't you feel it yourself? Heck, Richard, before Christmas you were treating me like a woman – a real woman. Now I'm the kid-sister all of a sudden, who has to be wrapped in cotton wool so she won't get hurt.'

'You're the one calling the tune,' he reminded her. 'I wanted to give you time to get to know me. Amy – ' he held out a hand to her ' – I want to marry you. I've never made any secret of that. But we've only known each other for a couple of months, and I'm not the sort of man who'd pressurize a girl – don't you know that, for God's sake?'

'We don't know each other at all,' she said, for no reason feeling like bursting into tears. 'Underneath all the camaraderie we're still strangers.' She flung up her hands despairingly. 'Richard – what are we doing here together? It's not helping our relationship, is it? Living in the same house . . .'

'It would have been better in a hotel,' he said. 'But it was impossible to get rooms; you know that.'

'Yes.' Her voice was flat. 'At least we wouldn't have been thrown together quite so much, would we?'

'And being thrown together,' he said quietly, 'we each of us instantly back off when we feel we're getting too close. Is that what you're getting at?'

Shakily she said, 'I didn't realize you'd noticed what was happening.'

He thumped his head with his hand and said, 'God, Amy! I'm not entirely without feelings. I'm not made of bloody stone. Of course I can see how things are.'

'But we never talk . . . We never get close . . .'

'No,' he said, his voice infinitely kind, 'but that's something we can remedy when the time and the place are right.'

'Like on our wedding night?' she flared.

'Would that be so terrible?'

She stared at him as if he'd lost his senses. 'Nobody waits that long nowadays.'

'Couldn't you marry me without knowing what I'm like in bed?'

She felt the colour rushing to her cheeks. She hadn't expected him to be quite so direct.

She pulled the door open and a gust of icy air rushed in. 'Go to hell,' she said, and promptly marched out into the night.

Breakfast next morning was a slightly strained affair. Amy had got up early and cooked it, so when Richard came down she was just at the egg-cracking stage, just before popping them into the pan and frying them.

He poured out two mugs of steaming tea, then joined her over by the stove. 'I've used your phone again,' she said, thinking perhaps it would be best if last night could be put behind them and forgotten. 'I hope you don't mind.

I tried to call Roger Claybourne but there was no reply.'

'You know you don't have to ask. Of course you can use it. You can call Timbuctoo if you want to.' He sounded irritable and out of patience, which wasn't like him at all.

'I don't know the code for Timbuctoo!' She used a spatula to lift out the eggs, one after the other, and place them beside sausages and grilled tomatoes on two plates.

'Very funny!' He didn't even smile.

'Okay. It was corny. So eat up your breakfast.' She gave him one of the plates and took the other to her side of the table.

'Are we having our first row?' he wanted to know.

'No. We had that last night.'

He sighed. 'How about forgetting it and starting all over again?'

She'd spent a wretched night, tossing and turning and thinking about Kip Weldon, and worrying that Richard might just want to pack up and go home this morning.

'We don't have a single thing in common,' she said as she began eating her breakfast. 'So what's the point in saying we're going to start all over again?'

'In some ways we were getting on pretty well.' He gave her a fleeting glance across the table. 'Until last night.'

'Until I went out and talked to a hooker. Then you came down on me like a ton of bricks and started issuing orders about who I can and can't see on my own.'

'I did not,' he said quietly. 'But there's no way you're going to see Roger Claybourne on your own. Can't I voice concern about you once in a while?'

She put down her knife and fork, picked up her mug of tea and took a long, steadying drink of it, before saying, 'If I'd had my own damn car, I would've been here on my own. There'd be nobody to "voice concern" about me then, would there? You'd have been busy at your quarry, and maybe you would have given me a fleeting thought now and then, but you wouldn't be forever looking over my shoulder – or giving me orders.'

He seemed to be thinking over her words for a while, then he said, 'You have a point there.'

'Well, thank you. I'm also sitting here wondering how long it's going to be before you ask me where I went when I slammed out of the house last night.'

'I have no intention of asking you that,' he said.

Feeling a little subdued, she said, 'I went for a walk on the beach.'

His mouth twitched as he tried not to smile. She saw it.

'Okay,' she said, 'you've proved me wrong. I almost expected you to be waiting at the door when I came back. But you weren't – thank God!'

'Would you have hit me, if I had been there?'

'Probably,' she said, finishing off her breakfast and pushing her plate away. 'Though I'm not usually a violent person.' She sat looking at him for several moments, and when he said nothing she went on, 'And that's something else . . .'

'What is?'

'You! You used to be a prize fighter, didn't you? You told me you once killed a man in the ring. Yet I've never seen you behaving violently – not even remotely so.'

He grinned at her. 'Most of the fighters I knew in those days were just big softies at heart – especially where women were concerned. They'd fight tooth and nail to win a bout in a boxing ring, but, like me, they preferred their domestic lives to run smoothly.'

'Did life run smoothly with Grace?'

A shadow passed over his face, but he didn't hesitate in

his answer. 'Yes,' he said. 'We were happy, I think. At least, I was – and I always assumed Grace was too. We got along well – liked the same kind of things. Good music – bicycle rides in the country – a run into Hatton to the cinema. All those boring little things couples do together.'

She leaned her arms on the table. 'I hate being stuck at Wydale so much. That's why I need wheels. I really shall have to get myself a car, Richard.' They were on a better footing now, she decided. The row seemed to have cleared the air a little. It was better, she supposed, to have things as they had been between them – boring though that was – than to be at each other's throats all the time. 'How much would I have to pay for a little car, do you think? It wouldn't have to be brand new, of course, and I guess I could pick up something reasonably economical to run. Would you help me find one?'

He smiled at her. 'Yes, Amy. I'll help you get a car. But, in the meantime, how about me bringing Grace's bicycle over to Wydale for you? You wouldn't feel such a prisoner if you could get out of Lizzie's clutches once in a while, would you? And one or two bike rides together – you and me – might be just what we need to get to know each other better.'

They were getting back on the old friendly footing, she realized, and she was glad. Last night's blow-out of her temper had been completely out of character, and, after she'd cooled down with a stiff walk along the dark beach, she'd realized she'd been more than a little hasty. Richard had been good to her. There was no getting away from that. But nearly three months had passed since she'd first met him, and it seemed sometimes that their friendship was going nowhere.

And Wydale needed putting on its feet again!

221

If Uncle Gif wanted Richard to invest money in the old place before it was too late, marriage seemed the only way it could be achieved. It wasn't fair to expect Richard to save the old house without some sort of collateral – she knew that – and of course his security was *her* – or, to be more precise, her inheritance!

She'd had time to think of what marriage to Richard Boden would mean. She liked him, but was liking enough? She was attracted to him too; he was a good-looking man with a pleasing personality. But she'd always assumed that when – and if – she got down to marrying somebody, she'd first want to know that he and she were sexually compatible. She wasn't promiscuous. She hadn't slept around. She'd always reasoned, though, that when she met the right man she wouldn't necessarily have to wait for marriage in order to make love. Well, nobody did, did they? Not in this day and age, she decided.

'Would you mind me having Grace's bicycle?' she asked him, getting up to clear the table.

'Why should I mind? It's only gathering rust in an outhouse at the moment.'

'Then I'd like to have it, Richard.'

He gathered up the two mugs and brought them over to the washing up bowl. 'That's settled, then. I don't know why I didn't think of it before.'

She nodded, and splashed hot water onto the crockery in front of her.

'Amy?'

'Hmm?' She twisted her head round to look at him.

He had a worried expression on his face. 'We need to talk – seriously,' he said. 'We need to get things sorted about Wydale, and . . . things. Hell! This is difficult.'

'You've changed your mind?' she asked, her heart suddenly

222

seeming to grow cold. 'You don't want marriage after all?'

She was losing him. At least that was how it looked to her. He was trying to let her down gently. And it was all because of that silly argument which had started last night and had then continued this morning. There was a downward spiralling of her spirits as she looked at him, and life, she knew, was going to be bleak and lonely without him.

'I don't want – ' His phone, which usually accompanied him everywhere and was at that moment on one of the working surfaces, suddenly started to bleep. 'Damn!' he said, and hurried over to pick it up.

Amy felt numb. She hadn't, until then, realized just how much she had come to depend on him. Hadn't realized either just how much it was hurting, knowing he didn't want her –, for that was surely what he had been just about to say when they'd been interrupted.

'It's Lizzie Abercrombie.' He held out the phone to her. 'She wants a word with you.'

She took the phone and moved away from him and over to the window with it. 'Hi, Lizzie! How're things at Wydale?'

'In a pretty pickle! Gif Weldon's in a right old state.'

'Why? What's wrong?'

'I didn't want to phone you, but I thought you ought to know – he's doing too darn much for that Duncan Ward. Running himself into the ground, he is – up and down, up and down to the cottage. And in this weather it's just too much for him to cope with. It's been raining cats and dogs for the last two days, the river's in flood and Gif's coming back here soaking wet two or three times a day. Enough's enough, I keep telling him. But you know what he's like . . .'

'Do you want me to come home, Lizzie?' Amy could tell the housekeeper was really worried.

223

'No, no, child. I just wondered if you'd phone him and have a word with him. Maybe he'll take more notice of you than he does me. But apparently Duncan's had a slight stroke, and, of course, knowing how things are between them – ' Lizzie broke off, seeming somewhat agitated.

'Lizzie – I'll come back. We can be packed and away from here in half an hour. If Uncle Gif's so worried about Duncan's illness, it's only right I should be there.'

'No, don't do that. Just talk to him, will you? He said he'd be back around lunchtime, so if you could give him a call then. Make him see sense – or ask Richard Boden to talk to him. That might be best anyway . . . But, Miss Amy, I've had that creepy dream again – you know, the one I told you about where you were on one side of the river and your uncle on the other. And I can't get it out of my mind.'

'Oh, Lizzie, don't worry about it. Look, I'll ring Uncle Gif about two this afternoon. Will that be okay?'

'Sure it will, lovey. I'm just a silly old woman – panicking like this. Are you okay down there in Norfolk?'

'Yes. We're fine, Lizzie. Now, promise me you'll ring me straight away if you get worried again?'

'Yes. I'll do that. And I'll pretend to be ever so surprised when you phone up to talk to your uncle.'

Amy laughed softly. 'Yes. You do that, Lizzie.'

She walked back across the kitchen and handed the phone to Richard. 'Lizzie's worried. Duncan Ward's had a slight stroke.'

'Yes, I got the gist of it. Gif's taking it hard, I suppose?'

'Seems like it. Lizzie wants me to have a word with him – tell him to slow down a bit, I think.'

Richard put the phone down, then turned to her. 'Amy – you do know about those two, don't you?'

'Those two? Lizzie and Uncle Gif?' she asked, starting

224

to laugh. 'Oh, Richard, surely you don't mean what I think you mean?'

'Not Lizzie,' he said. 'I'm not talking about Lizzie. I'm talking about the lawyer.'

'Duncan? What about him?'

'Oh, God! You don't know, do you?' He replaced the phone on the work-top, then sighed. 'I thought – I *hoped* perhaps Lizzie might have said something, but obviously not.'

'What *are* you getting at? All I know is that Lizzie can't stand Duncan. I've only met him a couple of times myself – and that was a long time ago. He never comes up to the Hall – and you'd think he would, wouldn't you? He and Uncle Gif have always been such good friends.'

She moved as if to start washing the dishes again, but Richard shot out a hand and fastened it on her shoulder. 'Come here,' he said. 'There's something you've got to know. You should never have been kept in the dark about what was going on in the first place.'

'Richard! What's the matter? You look as if . . . Oh, heck! It's not that Uncle Gif's got something terrible the matter with him, is it? I know he's not been well, but – '

'Will you be quiet for a minute?' Richard rarely raised his voice, but he did now.

She clamped her lips shut and glared at him.

'Right. Now, listen. There's no easy way of saying this, so I'll come straight out with it – your uncle and Duncan Ward are lovers.'

Before she realized what she was doing, her hand came up and delivered a hefty slap across his cheek. 'You bastard!' she flared. 'How dare you insinuate – ?'

'I'm stating a fact,' he said, grabbing hold of both her hands and forcing them down to her sides before she could attack him again. 'It's true,' he said. 'But take it easy, will

225

you? Gif and Duncan Ward didn't invent homosexuality, for God's sake, so calm down!'

She stared at him, utterly speechless, and knew he was speaking the truth. Richard wouldn't lie to her. She knew that implicitly.

'Haven't you ever wondered why he sent you to America?' he asked, still hanging onto her hands.

Of necessity he was standing very close to her. He had to do that in order to stop her lashing out again. Now, however, she didn't want to lash out. Things began to make sense at last – things she'd never understood before. Like the way Gif Weldon spent most of his time down at Duncan Ward's cottage, and the way Lizzie had stopped *her* going down there to meet him that day – and, of course, as Richard had just pointed out, Gif Weldon's lifestyle must have played a great part in her being brought up in America, instead of at Wydale with him.

She sucked in a great breath of air and said despondently, 'Wow! Have I been a dumbo?'

'You would have discovered the truth eventually,' he said calmly. 'With your capacity for finding things out, you'd have – '

'Poked my nose in where it wasn't wanted,' she said, nodding. 'Yes. I get your point, Richard. You can let go my arms now, by the way. I'm not going to bash you again.'

He released her, but still stood where he was. 'You've had a shock,' he said. 'It was insensitive of me, blurting it out like that.'

'Did I hurt you?' She looked up into his face. There was a bright red weal across one cheek. 'Heck! I'm sorry, Richard.' She reached up a hand and touched it. 'God! Did I do that?' Her eyes flicked up to his, then both her hands were touching his face, holding it, her thumb

226

stroking the red mark she'd inflicted.

'I think I shall survive the slap,' he said softly, and his eyes crinkled at the corners in the way she loved them to.

Her hands fell away from him as she remembered that before the phone had rung she'd been absolutely sure he was going to say he didn't want to marry her. She'd been sure of that. Now, though, it was obvious he didn't even remember the conversation they'd been having. She moved away from him and finished putting the things back into cupboards, then busied herself wiping down the table and the work-tops. She felt his eyes on her, watching her wherever she walked, whatever she did.

When she'd finished tidying up, she said, 'I think I'll try and ring Roger Claybourne now. The sooner I can get this business cleared up, the sooner we can get back to Wydale.'

'Yes,' he said. 'You must be worried about your uncle. I'll go and lay a fire in the living room while you arrange a meeting with this Claybourne fellow. But I meant what I said, Amy – I'm coming with you. No argument.'

She watched him walk away from her, wanting to call him back, needing to know where she stood with him and desperate to ask him so many questions. But what was the point, she reasoned. It was all too obvious that he'd had second thoughts about investing his money in Wydale. And who could blame him?

She leaned heavily against the cupboard units as she dialled Roger Claybourne's number again. And, as before, though she waited and waited for a reply there was none. She made up her mind then to go over into Lincolnshire and wait for him to return to his smallholding. He couldn't avoid her for ever, she decided, and all too soon it would be time for her and Richard to make tracks for home.

CHAPTER 16

'It's crazy – going all that way into Lincolnshire when you can't even get a reply to your phone calls.' Richard was keeping his cool with difficulty, and beginning to realize she was the most maddening creature he'd ever known. And this mood she was in was new to him – all quiet and with a hurt look in her eyes.

He tried to analyze it, and came to the conclusion that she hadn't been the same since talking to Lizzie Abercrombie half an hour ago. And she hadn't attempted to pick up the threads of their former conversation – not that he could remember now exactly where it had broken off. The phone ringing had put paid to any talk about their own future, and he could understand her not wanting to talk about marriage – and Wydale – and all *that* entailed now. She'd had a shock – finding out about her Uncle Gif.

He was sorry now that he'd been the one who'd had to break *that* piece of news to her. She'd gone off into this quiet mood since then, and he sensed it was more because she felt she'd been hoodwinked by the old man than because of the fact that Gif Weldon was gay!

'Well – what do you suggest, then?' There wasn't the usual thrust to her obstinate jaw as she turned away from the window to look at him

He fought down the urge to stride across the cosy little living room and sweep her into his arms, and said instead, 'I suggest we have lunch around twelve o'clock, then you can ring the damned man again and see if he's returned to his cabbage patch.'

A smile seemed to be tugging at her mouth as she replied, 'Jane Weaver said Roger Claybourne owned fields and fields full of cabbages – not just a "patch", for heaven's sake.'

'Well, he must have to go home some time if he has a business like that to run! He can't ignore the phone for ever.'

'So what do we do until lunchtime?' Her gaze went slowly around the room. 'Everything's spick and span in here, and the fire is blazing away.'

'A walk,' he said. 'A walk will blow the cobwebs away. Why not take your video camera onto the beach today?' He kept his voice deliberately light. 'Lizzie's bound to want to know what this place is like – '

'You forget,' she broke in. 'There's nothing to play a video film *on* at Wydale.'

He grinned. 'Bring her over to my house, then. I've always wanted to be one of those people who bore their friends silly with holiday pictures, haven't you?'

'Oh, Richard . . .' For a second the old dancing light was back in her eyes again, then they dulled over and she shrugged and said, 'Okay! Let's go on the beach.'

The wind was blowing off the land, sweeping in a south-easterly direction across the Wash from Lincolnshire. It was still very cold. Amy had taken film of the little house from the outside, and then some of the other cottages and a couple of pretty caravan holiday homes. Now, as they climbed the shingle ridge, she aimed the camera at Richard, and, laughing when he saw her doing that, he strode over to her and said, 'Let's see how you like being on the receiving end for once, shall we?'

She handed him the camera. 'Have you used one of these things before?' Her head was tilted towards him, her eyes teasing. She'd tied her hair back with a thin navy blue ribbon before leaving the house, and the faithful yellow wool scarf was wound several times round her neck.

His heart was thundering as if it would burst. God! Did she know the effect she had on him when she looked at him like that? he wondered. With difficulty he concentrated on the video camera's viewfinder and said, 'Of course I have. We're not all living in the Dark Ages in Derbyshire, you know.' He looked up from filming her to say, 'Well, do something. Lizzie will be disappointed if you just stand there grinning.'

'You want entertainment too?'

He nodded, and returned to the viewfinder.

'A handstand, maybe?' Again she tipped her head on one side. 'Or running on the spot?' This she started to do, slowly, with the sea behind her.'

'Great stuff, this,' he said. 'I'm glad you're not doing an audition for an action movie – ' Hell!

Suddenly he lost her from the picture, and, looking up, saw that she'd dashed off down to the edge of the sea.

'Do you mind?' he called after her. 'I was just getting good at the focus.'

'Richard!' She was waving to him and yelling. 'Richard! Come here! Richard, it's those kids again.' Then she started running back towards him, grabbed hold of his arm and tugged him down the shingle bank, slipping and slithering to avoid the spiky sea defence posts. 'Oh, God,

Richard, they've got a dinghy or something – and with the wind behind them they're being swept out to sea . . .'

He looked where she was pointing. 'Hell,' he muttered, and pushed the camera into her hands. 'Here! Take this.' Then he delved one hand into his pocket and thrust his phone at her too. 'Call the coastguard,' he ordered. 'Call nine-nine-nine! I'm going to see what I can do.'

'Richard . . .' He heard her scream as he raced away from her towards the children, who were now starting to panic as they realized they were a good way off the shore and in no position to get back to it.

As he ran he tore off his jacket. Then, hopping from one foot to the other, he divested himself of shoes and socks. Next came his thick sweater, then his jeans. Each item of clothing littered the beach until, clad only in boxer shorts, he was level with the terrified children in the dinghy, which was out fifty yards or more into the North Sea – and drifting further out with each second that passed. He plunged into the sea without further thought, and the ice-cold shock of it took his breath away as it crept up to waist-height.

'Hold on!' he yelled, waving both arms at the children. 'Don't panic.' He gasped as he felt his muscles contracting with the cold. God! Not cramp! he prayed.

Somewhere behind him he heard Amy screaming his name. 'Richard! Richard!' He couldn't turn round and shout that he was all right because that would waste precious seconds. He hoped she'd called the coastguard, though, because at that moment he doubted his own ability to keep a clear head when all his body was turning to ice and a dreadful numbness was creeping over him.

As he waded towards the dinghy the beach suddenly fell away beneath his feet, and he went under the water completely. When he fought his way to the surface, he was disorientated. He trod water and kept afloat while his anxious gaze sought and found the children again. He was nearer to them now. The tide must have carried him some distance when he was submerged, he realized.

He was glad now that he'd kept up his weekly visits to the indoor pool at Hatton after Grace died. His best and strongest stroke was the crawl. Determination drove him cleanly through the water, and, after what seemed like hours but could only have been minutes, he managed to snatch at a rope that was trailing in the water from the drifting dinghy.

The children were both fully clothed. He realized how dangerous it would be for them if they went into the water like that. And they were standing up now, screeching and waving at him. And the dinghy was tossing and pitching, and trying to buffet him under the waves again.

He reared up above the side of the rubber vessel, hanging grimly on to it and steadying it as he yelled, 'Sit down! Lie down! Just keep still!'

The little girl was sobbing and shrieking, 'I want my mummy . . .'

'Get down!' His voice was harsh. The child just had to be made to understand and obey.

He knew his only chance now lay in towing the dinghy back to the shore. There was no way he could manage two panicking youngsters actually *in* the water. They were togged up against the cold in padded anoraks and – his heart sank – Wellington boots, of all things, which would fill with water and anchor them to the ocean floor if they went overboard.

He hung onto the side of the dinghy, breathless and freezing. 'Down!' he yelled. 'Both of you! Do as I say. Get down! And pull those boots off.'

The boy grabbed hold of his sister and flung her into the bottom of the boat, then joined her there, one arm across her, holding her still while he wriggled the boots off her feet with his other hand.

'Good lad,' Richard muttered, though he could still hear the little girl having hysterics as he slid down into the water again and turned his head towards the shore.

God! It was a long way back. Amy must be that little black speck standing out against the shingle bank that was behind her. Yes. He saw a flash of yellow. Her scarf! Seeing that made him rustle up all his reserves of strength and strike out again, towing the dinghy behind him.

Several times he went under the waves. The wind was against him, pitting its strength against his, howling down onto the waves, lifting them and forcing him back with them, out to sea. The pain in his lungs was agonizing, but he kept his eyes focused on the yellow scarf. And then his head started to spin and he could see double figures, then three, then four.

He screwed his eyes up tightly and shook water from his hair. All he could think about was getting the children back safely to shore. He heard the wail of a siren, then shouts, and knew he must be getting nearer the land now that sound was carrying to him. Then figures were wading out, splashing around him, manhandling the boat, and he knew he could let go of the rope.

He lay back in the water, no longer caring about the cold and the numbness creeping over him. Hands dragged at him as he looked up at an ashen sky – and then something woolly, wet and sodden hit him in the face. There was a flash of yellow – that damned scarf of hers! He tried to laugh but his teeth were chattering with the cold.

Her face, her dear little pinched and frightened face, was

unfamiliar without its usual bright self-assured expression on it. The grey eyes were stricken, not dancing and teasing as they normally were. He'd never seen her like this before, she was so pale, so ghostly – and what on earth had she done to her hair? It was hanging damp and bedraggled down the sides of her cheeks. She was hauling on his shoulders, keeping his head above water as the stronger, bulkier figures got him safely onto the beach.

Amy was pushed aside then, and an ambulance crew half-smothered him in a red blanket. But he flatly refused to go to hospital.

She led him into the little house on The Lane with him still clutching the red blanket round his shoulders. Somebody else brought inside his clothing – which had been gathered up off the beach. And then they were alone.

'I feel an idiot dressed like this.'

He stood on the hearthrug, warmed through now from the heat of the fire.

She hadn't uttered a word – not in the water as, half-submerged herself, she'd supported his head, not on the beach, and neither had she spoken in the ambulance that had brought him the short distance from the shingle ridge to the house in The Lane. He'd been checked over by the paramedics and given the okay, and now he was feeling fine – but a little foolish without his outdoor clothes.

'Are you all right, Amy?'

She was still standing beside the door which she'd closed quietly when the paramedics had gone. He looked across at her. She nodded her head and whispered, 'Yes.'

'Hey, I'm the one supposed to be in shock,' he teased her gently.

234

'Richard!' she said. 'Oh, Richard.'

He forced a smile, hitched the blanket around him with one hand and held out the other to her. 'Don't look so tragic,' he said. 'The kids are okay. Once out of the water they looked on it all as a great adventure.'

'You could have been killed.' Her face was still white and stricken. 'I saw you go under . . .'

'I came back up, though.'

'Don't joke about it.' She suddenly seemed to come to life. 'For God's sake, Richard . . .' Her voice rose on a note of hysteria.

'Hey! Come here.' His hand was still stretched out towards her.

She ran to him, still in her sea-soaked duffle coat and clinging, wet scarf. She wrapped her arms around him and held him tightly on top of the red blanket. He could feel her body trembling from top to toe. He rested his lips on the top of the lank blonde hair and murmured softly, 'Amy . . . Amy.'

And suddenly he realized why she was so tormented. Kip Weldon had drowned, and this morning's accident must have brought the whole ghastly business back to her. He shut his eyes and held her close to him until her shivering was under control. Even then, though, her head still rested against his shoulder and she made no effort to move away from him.

Carefully, so as not to disturb her, he unwound the yellow scarf from round her neck and allowed it to fall onto the floor. 'You're wet,' he said. 'You shouldn't have gone into the sea.'

'I had to. *You* were there.' Her head moved slightly and she looked up into his face.

He managed to unfasten her coat and ease it off. It

235

joined the scarf at her feet. 'You'll get pneumonia in these things. You're like a drowned rat.'

Her laugh was tremulous. 'You say the nicest things.'

'Come on. Take them off.'

Her eyes searched his face. 'I don't want to let go of you.'

'It's natural,' he said. 'I expect it brought it all back to you?'

'Brought what back to me?' She looked puzzled.

Huskily he said, 'Kip Weldon's death.'

She stared at him, disbelief slowly dawning in her eyes, swiftly followed by a red-hot anger. 'You just *have* to be joking,' she flared.

'Amy – I understand what you must have gone through.'

'You *understand*?' She spat out the words and then pushed him away. Her face was a mask of fury as she backed away from him towards the door that led to the stairs where she choked out, 'You don't have a clue. You really don't have a clue, do you?'

'Amy – come back. Don't go. I don't want you to be on your own – not with the memories my dunking must have rekindled.'

'I never gave him a damn thought!' she cried. 'Kip Weldon was the last thing on my mind out there. It was *you*, Richard. You! Don't you understand?'

'Amy . . .' He shook his head, baffled by her reaction.

She tore the door open and, holding it so, yelled across the room at him, 'I thought I was losing you. You disappeared under the water so many times . . . And if you'd gone – what would have been left for me?' Tears started trickling down her cheeks. She seemed not to notice them. She stared at him, then shook her head and said brokenly, 'I love you, Richard Boden. But you

236

don't care, do you? You see me as security for a bloody loan to rebuild Wydale, and that's all I mean to you.'

'Amy – no,' he croaked, thinking that he had in fact died out there and gone to heaven – because she'd said she loved him.

A flash of her old spirit surfaced. Her chin came up in a defiant gesture that only the tears belied. 'Okay!' she said in a proud voice. 'I'll be your security. I'll marry you. Any time – anywhere. Name the day. You just go see my uncle Gif and arrange things, huh? That's what you want, isn't it? And it's the only way open to you if you want to ever own Wydale!' Her laugh was bitter. 'A heap of stones,' she jeered. 'A heap of stones for a *man* of stone.'

'Amy . . . Amy . . .' He couldn't believe his ears. Couldn't believe that she might actually care for him in any way except as a friend. He searched his heart for the right thing to say, but before words could form he heard her give a great sob.

And then she was out of the room with the door slammed shut behind her, and he heard her footsteps on the stairs as she raced to her bedroom. Another door slammed, vibrating throughout the little house.

He stood dazed and wondering for several minutes, then he threw the red blanket down onto the fat-cushioned sofa and bent and picked up his jeans. Slowly he looked down at them, then his head came up and he stared at the ceiling, imagining her up there, alone in her bedroom, shedding tears because she'd been afraid of losing him. He held the jeans in his hand for only a moment, then he turned and hurled them at the nearest wall.

The time for hesitation was past, he decided. He strode across the room, pulled open the door and raced up the stairs after her.

CHAPTER 17

She was on a low padded stool in front of her dressing table mirror, and she jerked her head round as he burst into the room.

He'd half expected to see her in floods of tears, still shivering in her damp jeans maybe – not sitting there in bra and panties, tissuing her make-up off, with her jeans, sweater, socks and shoes strewn all over the floor.

'Go away,' she said in a hard voice. 'I have to make myself look decent, for God's sake.' She eyed him up and down. 'Speaking of which, maybe you should do the same thing, huh? Boxer shorts are okay for lovers, but when it's a marriage of convenience we're talking about . . .'

'Amy! Let's not start all that again.'

Her eyebrows shot up. 'Isn't that what you've come up here for? To start another argument?'

'No.'

She aimed the tissue at a wastebin beside the dressing table, then looked at him again. 'Why, then?' she asked. 'Why are you here? *Your* bedroom is across the landing. I suggest you turn right round and go find it – *Mr* Boden.'

'I thought you were upset.' He held out a hand placatingly. 'That's why I followed you . . . At least – that was one reason.'

'Let's hope the second reason is more believable than the first,' she replied, picking up and snapping open a tiny gold powder compact and gazing into it. 'Wow! Do I look a fright?' She continued staring at her reflection, obviously waiting for him either to leave the room or give her some good reason for staying there.

He walked over to her and stood behind her so he could see her expression in the large dressing table mirror. 'You said you loved me.' He kept his voice on an even keel with much difficulty. It would have been easier to have opened wide the window and shouted it for all the world to hear – which was what he wanted to do right at that moment.

She glanced at him in the mirror and scowled. There were still traces of tears left. Her eyes were watery and her nose an angry red.

'I hate to see you like this,' he said.

'Do you think *I* like to see me like this?' She slammed the compact down on the dressing table top, and glared at him in the mirror. 'Some girls,' she said, 'can reach a man's heart by shedding tears. Me? I just get puffy eyes and a sore nose!'

'I guess I'd better ditch you, then,' he said on a note of resignation. 'It's either that or make damn sure I don't ever upset you again, because I don't think I could eat my breakfast across the table from you if you had puffy eyes and a sore nose too often.'

'Very funny!' she said, in a voice laden with sarcasm.

Serious now, he said, 'I hate to think I could do that to you.'

'Do what?' She began attacking her hair with a fine-bristle brush.

'Upset you so much.'

The brush stopped in mid-air and she wagged it at him

239

in the mirror. 'Look,' she said, 'I want Wydale rebuilt – or whatever – and you want some security. Okay, you've got it. I said I'd marry you and I don't go back on my word. Snap me up while you've got the chance, Richard. We pass this way but once – if you get my meaning.'

He folded his arms and looked down on her shining gold hair. 'I get your meaning,' he said quietly. 'You're not going to offer yourself up on a plate again, are you?'

'Definitely not. There'll be other takers if you don't want me.'

'I want you.' He was very still. He stood watching for her reaction. She just carried on brushing her hair, and while she did that said coldly, 'Prove it, Bodie.'

'Prove that I want you?'

'Uh-huh!'

His eyes narrowed. What was she up to? 'The only way I can prove it is by telling you.'

'Or showing me.' She put the brush down and swivelled round to face him.

He kept his eyes on her face and away from the scrap of lacy satin covering her breasts. He couldn't ignore those luscious shoulders, though, or the deep tempting hollow of her throat. Fully clothed and with that damned yellow scarf on she was forever getting him aroused – let alone like this. Didn't she realize she was playing with fire?

'Put something on,' he growled. 'For God's sake . . .' He swung round away from her, his eyes searching for something, anything, to make her less attractive. There was a wrap of sorts lying across the bed. He snatched it up and thrust it in front of her. 'Here! Cover up.'

She ignored the outstretched hand and stood up right there in front of him – all legs and leanness. She turned slowly till her back was towards him, then she said, 'Put it on for me – if my near-nakedness bothers you.'

'It bothers me!' he snapped.

She held her arms out and he slipped the garment onto them, then hitched it up to her shoulders. But before he could move his hands away from her she'd whipped herself round to face him again, moving close up against him in the circle his arms made.

'Amy! No!' he said.

'Hold me.'

'I am holding you for God's sake . . .' And against his will he was doing just that. His hands were sliding over the silky fabric of the wrap – over her shoulders, then gliding down to her waist.

'I want you underneath the kimono.' She got hold of his hands and pulled them to the bare skin of her midriff.

'Kimono?' he said, struggling with his conscience and more than that – his body too, which was on fire with wanting her.

'It sounds a darn sight sexier than "dressing gown" don't you think?' She placed her own hands on his shoulders. 'Hey – I'm attempting to seduce you, but you're sure making it difficult to do that.

'It won't work.' He held himself tense and away from her. 'Heck, Amy . . .' His voice was soft with desire, yet adamant with resolve. 'This isn't what we came here for. I can't – I won't take advantage of you.' He looked down into her eyes, raw hunger in his own, and saw only mockery staring back at him.

'You want me,' she said.

'Yes. I want you – and I also want to marry you.'

'So try before you buy,' she mocked.

'Don't cheapen this,' he said. 'Don't, Amy.'

241

She leaned up on tiptoe and put her lips to his. 'You still haven't convinced me that you really *do* want me,' she said.

It took an effort of will, but he pushed her away, muttering, 'You said downstairs that you loved me, Amy. But this isn't love. You're making a mockery of what I feel for you.'

A light sprang to her eyes. 'What you feel for me?'

'I love and respect you. Isn't that enough for you?'

Slowly she brought the edges of the kimono together and covered herself. Then she tied the narrow sash at the waist and moved away from him to the window.

He knew he'd been a fool to refuse all she'd offered. And he was sorry he'd been so brutally honest with her. He went across the room to her and stood behind her – so close he could smell the scent of the sea in her hair, and the will-o'-the-wisp teasing perfume she always wore. She was as old and wise as the ocean waves; she was as young and fresh as the morning. She was his day, his night, his sun, his moon; she filled his thoughts and his heart with her laughter – and her hard-headed practicality.

He laid his hands on her shoulders and felt the tension go out of her. She leaned her head back so her hair touched his fingers, and he moved up closer against her. She reached up and took hold of one of his hands and brought it round to her breast, threading it through the loose neckline of the kimono so he could touch her flesh. Her skin was more like silk than the garment she wore; he felt it pulling taut as she strained against his hand, and the nipple grew into a tight little ball of hardened desire.

He thrust his head down to nuzzle against the hollow behind her ear while his lips savoured the warm flesh of her neck, her throat and then – as he slowly turned her round to face him – the firm sweet promise of her warm and generous mouth.

For long minutes they remained locked in a liquid silence – a silence that he knew would have to be broken.

'This is where it ends, my Amy,' he whispered. 'For today anyway.'

'No,' she murmured. 'This is the beginning, Richard. We can't go back now.'

Somehow he found the strength to pull his hand away from her breast; he felt her shudder as its warmth was removed. Her upturned face was framed by the golden sheen of her hair and her grey eyes burned into his with a ferocity like that of a tigress pursuing its prey. 'Why?' she wanted to know. 'Why don't you *want* me?'

He took her face between his hands. 'Do I have to spell it out?' he muttered. 'It would be too risky. We could start a new life inside you here, my love.'

'A baby?' Her eyes grew soft and dove-like.

He nodded. 'I won't take the risk, Amy. I can't.'

'You came away with me and you didn't think to bring . . . anything with you?' A shadow of a smile touched her face.

'Heck! No! I never intended . . .'

'At college – back in the States – they told us never to leave things to chance.'

He laughed softly. 'I never went to college.'

'I never left things to chance. I always carried the damn things in my bag – like they told us to – but I never got the chance to use them.'

'Amy . . . what are you saying?'

'I never took them out and threw them away, Richard. And my bag's over by the bed.'

★ ★ ★

243

She had her back to him, curled up against his nakedness. His arm circled her waist and the flat of his hand was resting against her bare thigh. This was how it should always be, she thought sleepily. This was how it *had* to be when somebody loved you.

And he loved her.

That fact was slowly sinking into her brain as she lay locked in the warmth and comfort of the big double bed. He loved her.

Slowly she slid over onto her back, being as quiet as she knew how. He must be asleep – he'd been lying so still since the storm of passion that had engulfed them.

He wasn't asleep. He was half-lying, half-leaning on the pillow beside her own. He was gazing down at her face.

'Make love to me again,' she murmured. 'That sure was something special, Mr Boden.'

'No,' he said, but his eyes were crinkling at the corners and his mouth was smiling. He bent over and touched her lips with his, gently and feather-soft.

'No?' she asked against his mouth. 'Wasn't it good for you, then?' Her eyes were teasing. She was in no doubt about what his answer would be.

His face became serious. 'It was a pure and precious thing we did,' he said. 'But Amy – my darling girl – you should have warned me . . .'

'If I had,' she said solemnly, 'you wouldn't have touched me before we were married, would you?' She reached up a hand and brushed her fingertips along his lips. 'It's no big deal, you know.'

'Virginity's no big deal?'

'The kids I was with in college would have given me hell if they'd known I was so inexperienced. You have to put on a brash face so they think you're like all the rest. That was why I carried those rubbers around.'

'You fooled me.'

'But it was good, huh, Richard?' Her smile was wide and inviting.

'It was good. Take my word for it.'

'So! Make love to me again.'

'Let's talk weddings first.'

'How long does it take here in England?' she wanted to know.

'For decency's sake – or otherwise?'

'Otherwise. I want to be married to you. I like what you do to me.'

He groaned softly. 'Don't,' he said. 'For heaven's sake, don't make this more difficult than it is.'

'I got scared when you never mentioned love.'

'Was that why you changed towards me? Why all of a sudden we became strangers?'

'It was just before Lizzie telephoned,' she said, needing to clear up any misunderstanding. 'We were talking – you and me – about Wydale, and I thought you were just about to tell me we were through.'

'Good heavens, girl. What made you think that?'

'I asked you if you'd changed your mind, and you replied, "I don't want . . ." – and then the phone rang and we never got back to sorting anything out at all.'

'And you really believed I didn't want *you*?' He sat up straight and pushed the pillows back against the headboard of the bed. 'God, Amy! How could you think that?'

'But you did say . . .'

Patiently he explained, 'I'd been worried about you when you'd gone out to see Jane Weaver last night. I knew I shouldn't do it, but I did lay the law down a bit about you going alone. This morning I regretted it. I wanted to apologize. I wanted to tell you I didn't intend backing you into a corner – didn't want to turn you into the kind of wife who has to ask permission from her husband for everything she does. Amy – my darling girl – I love you for what you are now, not for what I can turn you into. Does that make sense?'

'So you weren't going to say you didn't want me?'

'Hell! No!' He swivelled round to face her again. 'Amy! Stay the way you are. Fight with me. Argue with me. But don't, for God's sake, ever leave me.'

'I have no intention of leaving you.' She scrambled up alongside him and wrapped her arms round him, hugged him. 'We have to make a move, though.' She braced her hands on his shoulders and pushed herself away from him to look deeply into his eyes.

'Why? Where are we going?'

She leaned over to the bedside table and picked up her travel alarm clock. 'It's one-thirty,' she said. 'I promised Lizzie I'd ring Uncle Gif, remember?'

'Heck! I forgot all about the old man.' Richard dropped back against the pillows.

'Can I tell him we're going to be married?'

'Sure!' He grinned at her. 'It might take his mind off his own worries.'

'Then can we go and find Roger Claybourne?' She eased herself off the bed and stood looking down at him.

'How can I refuse you anything when you look so bloody gorgeous with nothing on but skin?'

She sat beside him in the Land Rover with rain pouring down in torrents and the windscreen wipers having to work overtime to disperse it from the glass in front of them.

'I suppose this is what makes Roger Claybourne's cabbages grow,' he grumbled.

'I wish he'd answer his phone.' She peered out into the gathering gloom of the wet afternoon.

'I'm getting the feeling he probably knows you're after him,' Richard said.

'But why should he avoid me? What's he possibly got to hide? All I want to do is find Kitty.'

'There's a possibility you haven't thought of,' he said. 'Kitty could have turned back to him, I suppose, after Kip died. Perhaps she married him and he doesn't want his wedded bliss turned upside down by an inquisitive little gal from America.'

Quick as a flash she came back at him, 'Well, if Kitty *is* married to him, why doesn't *she* answer his blessed phone?'

'You have a point,' he said. 'Let's hope we find somebody at home when we get there.'

'Halfpenny End. It's a strange-sounding place.' She studied the map on her knee. 'We turn off at the next road left.'

'Yes,' he said, 'I memorized it. I knew I'd get no peace until you'd been to the place – Roger Claybourne or no Roger Claybourne.'

'You talk about me like I'm a real pest.'

'I'd rather have you home and talking wedding plans than driving round damp and dreary cabbage fields.'

'We're coming to the fork in the road that's marked on the map.'

'Yes, love. I know.'

Halfpenny End was no more than a single track road, leading, it seemed, to nowhere. Half a mile on, however, between acres of spring cabbage plants, Amy saw a lone farmhouse.

'I think we've found your man,' Richard said, slowing the Land Rover, which was already going at nothing more than a crawl. 'There.' He pointed to the building which at this distance looked remote and hemmed in by flat fields; there wasn't even a tree to break the monotony of its surroundings.

'What a cheerless place.' Amy shivered. 'Thank goodness I didn't come by myself.'

'All this rain and the grey sky doesn't help, does it?' He glanced at her, and she looked at him and smiled.

'I hope he's at home.'

Richard turned the Land Rover onto a rutted path that was obviously the only way to get to the house. 'There are no lights on in the place.'

'Heck! It's real creepy countryside around here.'

The four-wheel drive made light work of the uneven ground, and soon they were drawing up outside the house, which was even more daunting close up than it had looked at a distance. Some of the upstairs windows were shuttered. An outhouse, which was really no more than a lean-to, had a door that was hanging off one of its hinges. Mud had solidified to make a kind of yard where other outbuildings were built in a half-rectangle. There was no sign of life.

'I'm going up to the front door.' She turned to Richard. 'I won't go inside – I promise.'

'I'll come with you.'

For once, she didn't argue.

She jumped down from the Land Rover, pulling her waterproof jacket collar up round her neck as she ran over to the house. There was no garden, just a sea of mud and weeds, but as she reached a path made up of half a dozen cracked and broken slabs she halted, and waited for Richard to catch up with her.

'What is it?' he said, as she seemed unwilling to go any further.

'Look,' she said, pointing. 'A rose bush beside the door. In all this wilderness a tiny, stunted rose bush.'

'It'll never survive. Not in the middle of all these weeds.'

She went forward, tentatively. A dismal little tag hung from the bare branches of the bush. She bent down and took hold of it. On it was a faded picture of a white rose but the name of it had weathered away. For some unknown reason, a cold chill prickled down her spine. She sprang to her feet and ran up to the front door, which was sadly in need of a coat of paint.

She hammered on it loudly, and Richard came up and said, 'Hey! You'll frighten the poor guy away if he's in there.'

'I don't care. I hate it here. I just want to talk to him and be gone.'

'There's nobody here, Amy.'

She banged hard on the door again, becoming agitated. 'What's he up to? Why won't he talk to me?' She clenched her fists and beat on the door again.

They stood in silence then, under the weathered and creaking porch that was doing little to protect them from the blustery wet weather. All around them the sky was darkening. The stillness was profound.

And then Richard's telephone started to bleep and the sound made her shriek. 'What the hell . . .?'

'It's okay.' He pulled the phone out of his back pocket as she pressed her hands to her face and gazed wide-eyed at him. She wished now she hadn't insisted on coming here.

Richard was talking on the phone. It was Lizzie Abercrombie on the other end of the line, she realized. He looked disturbed as he listened.

'What is it?' Amy whispered.

He held a hand up for her to be quiet. 'It's difficult to hear you, Lizzie,' he was saying. 'We're out in the wilds – I can't get a good signal.'

The phone was crackling, Amy could hear, but Lizzie had raised her voice and suddenly the words came through, loud and clear. 'Gif . . . heart-attack . . .'

'Oh, no!'

'We're coming home, Lizzie.' Richard was speaking again to Gif Weldon's housekeeper. 'Just do as the doctor says. We'll be back before midnight.'

Amy stared at him as he put the phone away. 'Uncle Gif . . . he's not . . .'

'Gif's had a heart-attack.' Richard reached out and took hold of her hand and ran back with her to the Land Rover. 'Duncan Ward died an hour ago. Your uncle was with him. Lizzie said he was past consoling. His heart couldn't take the strain of his grief.'

'Oh, Richard . . . And I was just talking to him before – telling him about the wedding and everything.'

'Come on, love. Get inside.' He held the door open for her and waited till she was settled before going round to the driver's side of the vehicle.

'Hold on a minute,' she cried as he started up the Land Rover. She'd had an idea. She reached for her bag and fumbled inside it.

He let the engine idle while he watched her frantically scribbling a note on the back of an envelope she'd found. 'A good idea,' he said. 'Leaving Roger Claybourne a note means he'll have to read it when he does eventually come home. He can't ignore it.'

She hopped out of the vehicle, ran up to the front door and pushed the envelope through the letter box, knowing she couldn't do anything more for the moment.

Roger Claybourne was forgotten then in the dash back to the cottage, the packing of her weekend case and the cleaning out of cupboards and refrigerator. 'We can't leave anything perishable,' she said as Richard came into the kitchen after taking all their belongings out to the Land Rover and stowing them away. 'And what about the keys to this place?'

'I've just spoken to the owner on the phone and explained why we have to leave,' he said. 'He told me his sister lives at number nine – just a few doors away. I can leave the keys with her.'

Sick with worry, she said, 'I just want to get back to Wydale, Richard.'

He nodded. 'I know, Amy.' He looked at his wristwatch. 'It's nearly six o'clock,' he said. 'We should be home before ten. Lizzie won't have to spend a night on her own in that great barn of a place if I can help it.'

CHAPTER 18

The next few days were hectic. There was Duncan's funeral to arrange and Gif to visit in hospital. The heart-attack hadn't been too severe, but her uncle, Amy found, had aged considerably since she'd last seen him. He desperately wanted to be discharged from Hatton General Hospital, and the doctor there told her that it might be best if he did go home to Wydale as he was just pining away where he was.

Amy had accompanied John Graham in the car to fetch Gif home. As they turned off the main road and drove past Duncan Ward's cottage her uncle broke down and sobbed into his handkerchief. Amy felt tears welling up in her own eyes. She was distraught because she didn't know how to handle the situation. Awkwardly she placed her hand on Gif Weldon's coat-sleeve and said, 'I'm sorry, Uncle Gif.'

He wiped his face with the handkerchief and said, 'He was my friend.'

Knowing what she knew now about Gif and Duncan Ward, Amy could find no appropriate words of comfort. He'd kept the true details of his relationship with Duncan from her, and she didn't dare risk embarrassing him now by letting him know she'd found out the truth. Always there had been an unseen barrier between herself and her uncle, but only since Duncan's death had it become clear why she'd been sent away from Wydale all those years ago. Now she could understand him better, and she wondered if Kate and Marty had known how things were when they'd adopted her.

Gif insisted on going to Duncan's cremation. They all went with him – Amy and Richard, Lizzie and John Graham. They were all the family Duncan had, Gif said.

A week after the funeral, Amy felt as if things were returning to normal, and she began to take an interest in Richard's plans for an August wedding. Neither of them wanted a long delay. Wydale Hall was crying out for restoration and time was not standing still; it was still taking its toll of the old house. And Amy, with Barbara Weldon's portrait gazing down on her in the great hall, and with bright spring sunshine pouring through the windows, saw signs of deterioration all around her – cracked and crazed paving, gaps round the window frames, splintering timbers high up in the roof.

'I've neglected the old place.'

She turned to find her uncle standing beside her. 'I suppose it's easily done, Uncle Gif. We don't always notice what's going on around us, do we?'

'Tactfully put, child.' He gave her a grim smile. 'The truth is, though, I've just not cared enough about Wydale in the past, and now it's getting its own back on me.'

'Richard will make sure everything's done properly.' She looked up at the portrait over the fireplace, wanting to ask him about Barbara but not daring to bring up old memories that might upset him.

'*She* did the right thing.' His words were abrupt and to the point. '*She* got out while the going was good.'

Amy said gently, 'I wonder what happened to her.'

'I don't know and I couldn't care less. I was glad to be rid of her.'

'So you divorced her?' Amy twisted her head round to look at the bowed old man beside her.

He nodded and said, 'For desertion. She had no right to go off like she did. It made me look a fool.'

She was shocked at the bitterness in his tone, and more so because of his condemnation of Barbara. There was no hint of suffering in the words he uttered, no mention of being heartbroken when his wife had left him. It was almost as if he'd never loved her. And where did Duncan come into all this? she wondered. For surely Gif Weldon would not have married Barbara if he'd been in a relationship with the other man at that time?

'Wouldn't it be better not to have the portrait there? Still reminding you of her?' she asked.

'The portrait stays where it is.' He fixed it with a baleful stare, then abruptly swung round to face her again. 'You don't have to marry Richard Boden, you know, Amy. Maybe I was wrong to push you into his arms as I did.'

His words hit her like a shower of cold water, and anger was her first reaction. Did he really think he could blow hot and cold like this? she wondered. Was he so insensitive that he believed she was marrying Richard for his money after all? She quickly brought her hot temper under control and said calmly, 'I *want* to marry Richard. I love him.'

'It's not just for Wydale you're doing this?' His pale eyes were remote, cold.

'No. Not entirely. I admit, though, at first . . .'

A spark of light glittered in the pale eyes. 'There *are* other fish in the sea.'

Sarcasm came easily to her lips. 'But it's a *gold* fish you wanted for me, Uncle Gif. And there aren't so many of those around, are there?'

He made an uneasy little movement with his hands. 'I don't know what you mean, Amy, dear. But now you've fixed a date for the wedding – well, I don't know if it's the right thing for you.'

She laughed shortly. 'You want me to back out? To let Richard down? I thought you were his friend.'

'Amy! You're taking all this the wrong way. All I'm saying is perhaps you'd be better off with somebody nearer your own age. A younger man.'

'Richard's thirteen years older than me. Heck, he's hardly antique.'

'I don't know. I really don't know . . .' He shook his head slowly, and seemed to be considering something deeply.

'Uncle Gif. I've told you – I love Richard.' She held out a hand to him. 'Believe me,' she pleaded. 'I know what I'm doing, and I'm not marrying Richard merely because he can put Wydale to rights. I couldn't marry somebody I didn't care for, and I really do care for Richard. The date is set for our wedding and Kate and Marty are coming over from America – and they're happy with my choice even though they've never met him. Kate said in her last letter that I'd told her so much about Richard she felt she knew him already.'

'All right, child. All right.' He sounded impatient with her, and made as if to walk off down the corridor to his study adjacent to the kitchen. But he hesitated just once more, to turn and face her and say, 'Amy – I'm asking you – put the wedding off for a while. For me. Please, my dear.'

255

'No!' She was aghast.

'Amy – I don't feel it's the right thing to do.'

Standing straight and tall, and facing him directly, she said, 'That's your problem, Uncle Gif. I'm not calling off the wedding.'

'Then I won't take a damned penny more of his money!' The old man glared at her, then swung away from her and hurried off to his study.

It was a cool, sunny day in London, but Catherine Blake had found a sheltered spot in St James's Park for little Kim to feed the ducks. Catherine was crouching beside her daughter at the water's edge, and from time to time she looked up and across the green swathe of grass towards the Mall. He was late, but she was accustomed to that.

To Mark Powell time meant nothing. If he was engrossed in a photo session nothing else mattered to him, and it *had* been the middle of last week when he'd rung up and they'd arranged today's meeting. He could have forgotten all about it, she reasoned, but it didn't worry her unduly. She was determined she wasn't going to let herself get involved again. And anyway, the age difference between her and Mark bothered her. He was twenty-two and she four years older. Added to that, she had a daughter. She was a one-parent family, and she liked it that way.

Mark Powell had latched onto her, though. Since that night when he'd come to her flat with the photographs of Wydale Hall she'd seen him several times – usually with Kim, but on one occasion her sister had babysat and she and Mark had gone to the theatre. She liked him. He was good company. He knew how to talk, and he was interested in her work.

She heard Big Ben striking twelve. He wouldn't be

coming now. He'd said he would meet her around eleven-fifteen.

Kim turned away from the water, her baby-hands reaching out for more crumbs to throw to the ducks. 'More, Mummee.'

'None left, darling.' She bent towards the toddler to scoop her up and put her back in the baby buggy.

'You didn't save me any bread to throw to the ducks?'

The voice was one she'd just convinced herself she wasn't going to hear that day. She looked up at him. 'I was just about to give up and go home.'

'Aw. Don't do that. You know me, Kit, darling – I just can't keep track of the time.'

'I'm not your "Kit, darling"! You make me sound like a soldier's bag.'

'Will it help if I say I'm sorry?'

She loved the rich Scottish burr of his voice, but today she wasn't going to be seduced by it. 'You can cut the canny brogue,' she told him. 'You're one guy who knows how to turn on the charm when you want to – but with me it doesn't work.'

'But I have the rest of the day to do with as I want.'

'Unfortunately, *I* don't.' She placed the baby in the buggy, wrapped a blanket over the little girl's legs and fastened the harness securely before standing up and facing him. 'Kim wants her lunch. And so do I,' she said.

'There *are* places where they provide highchairs at tables,' he pleaded.

'Kim's cold.'

'And Kit-Kat's in a bad mood,' he said, laughing softly at her.

'Don't call me that.' Her mouth grew hard. 'I've told you before – I don't like being known as anything but Catherine.'

257

'But *he* called you Kitty. You told me he did.'

Her head jerked up. 'Kip called me Kitty because he loved me. He called me Kitty because it sounded right with Kip. Kip and Kitty! Kip and Catherine just didn't have the same ring to it – or so he said.' She laughed softly as she remembered, then glanced at him and said, 'And now it's Kim and Kitty – and right now there's no room for a man in my life. Okay?'

He allowed the heavy photographic bag to slide down from his shoulder onto the ground and held out a hand to her. 'Hey! Forgive me, will you? Though I don't know what I've done to upset you.'

'You've been late,' she stated. 'Three times in a row you've been late, and I'm getting a bit tired of standing around waiting for you.'

'It's my work . . .'

'I work too,' she reminded him. 'And my one day off a week is precious to me.'

'You haven't been back to Derbyshire by any chance, have you?'

She stared at him. 'Why do you ask that?'

He shrugged. 'Because you weren't at home last weekend when I called you.'

'I went to see my aunt at the coast. Not that it's got anything to do with you.'

'I think I might just go back there. To Derbyshire. How d'you feel about a weekend at the Hawkwood Arms again?'

'Why?' she asked.

He laughed – a little guiltily, she thought. 'No reason. I'm just curious, that's all.'

'Why should I want to go there again?'

'There's the girl,' he said. 'The girl who advertised all over Lincolnshire and Norfolk for you.'

258

'I can guess what she wanted. She's out to find Kip's child; I'm sure of that. They've set her up – Kip's parents in America – to find me. And I can't risk them knowing they've got a grandchild. They might try to take Kim away from me.'

A frown cut deeply into his brow. 'Don't they have a right to even *know* about Kim?'

'They have no rights whatever,' she snapped. 'So keep your mouth shut, Mark. I don't want any trouble.'

'She seemed a nice kid, I thought – the Weldon girl.'

'Yes. Not so much a "kid", though. I hear she's getting married in a couple of months' time. I sent some proofs of the article to old Mr Weldon, and rang him to let him know they were on the way. That housekeeper spoke to me and you know how she goes on and on – well, she told me all about the wedding. Apparently old Mr Weldon's had some sort of heart-attack too, but he's over it now.'

The eyes of the man in front of her became guarded as he asked, 'Heart-attack, eh?'

'Mmm. Look, Mark, I really do have to go. I have a hair appointment at three.'

'I can't persuade you to come to Derbyshire next weekend, then?'

She shook her head. 'No. Not on your life. I'm not taking any chances. And Mark . . .'

'Yes?' He was bending down to pick up his gear. He looked up at the strained note in her voice.

'No mention of me if you see the girl. Promise me that. I told you the truth that night because I trusted you.'

'It's forgotten,' he said. 'I won't breathe a word about your past. But when shall I see you again?'

'You've got my number,' she said. 'Phone me!'

* * *

259

Mark Powell watched her as she walked away, pushing the baby-buggy across the grass between the trees. Then, slowly, he pulled the crumpled letter out of his pocket and stared down at it, wondering why he hadn't told her that old man Weldon had written to him. The letter had been sent on to him from the Hawkwood Arms and he didn't have to read it again to remind himself of its content.

'It's a matter of some importance . . .' Gifford Weldon had written.

But he could ignore that urgent message, Mark supposed. What good would raking up the past do at this late stage? But wasn't this what he'd wanted all along? he mused. Wasn't this the reason he'd gone to Wydale in the first place? To find Weldon and make him pay for what he'd done in the past – both to himself and to his mother?

Thinking of his mother, snug now in Scotland in her neat little bungalow, and financially secure for the rest of her life, he wondered if perhaps it was time to let go of the past – and, more to the point, time to forgive. He was curious, though. Gif Weldon's letter had stirred something inside him. The man was, after all, his father.

Talking to Catherine just now, he'd asked her if the Weldons in America didn't have a right to know about their grandchild. So wasn't it just being hypocritical on his part to keep Gif Weldon in the dark over the fact that he had a son?

Weldon obviously suspected something. And Mark knew that he had no choice but to go and face him – whatever the outcome of their meeting might be.

CHAPTER 19

'Lizzie Abercrombie! You're in a right old sulk. What's the matter with you, for God's sake?'

When Lizzie wasn't to be found in the kitchen that morning, Amy had gone looking for the housekeeper, and had finally found her in the winter garden.

'Nothing's the matter with *me*!' Lizzie kept her face averted and jabbed viciously at a smoking bonfire with a long spike of lopped off hawthorn.

'Well, talk to me.' Amy threw up her hands in despair.

'I have been talking to you.'

'Oh, yeah! When I yelled, Good Morning, Lizzie, you answered me – just. But when I tried all the usual stuff like, Are you okay? and Isn't this sunshine glorious for late April? you scowled and muttered and gave me black looks. What have I done? For God's sake tell me.'

'Stop saying "God's sake", Miss Amy. If I've told you once, I've told you ten thousand times. Gif Weldon don't like to hear that sort of talk.'

'Uncle Gif's not here. He seems to have disappeared off the face of Wydale this morning. Have you two had words again? Is that why you're sulking?'

Lizzie flung the hawthorn stick onto the top of the bonfire, then swung round with her hands on her hips.

261

'Words! Well, yes, you could say we've had "words" – that's if you're being polite. Words were what I said to him. Insults were what I got back.'

'Insults!' At once Amy was concerned. 'Oh, surely not, Lizzie.' She walked slowly up to Lizzie and said, 'Come on, Lizzie. Tell me. If Uncle Gif's being unkind to you . . .'

'Unkind! Huh!' Lizzie tossed her head and would have turned away again had not Amy put a restraining hand on her arm.

'Lizzie. Tell me. I know he's not been easy to live with. In fact, he and I are always having "words". It seems that after planning all my future for me with Richard, he now wants me to call the wedding off.'

'What?' Lizzie just stood and gaped at her.

'That's right, Lizzie. So tell me, just what's going on around here? Suddenly nothing makes sense any more.'

'You're telling me. This morning – to my face – he tells me I'm nothing more than a meddling old woman. And what's more – he told me I should keep my nose out of his business because I'm only a servant and servants, so he said, can easily be replaced.'

'Lizzie! No!'

'Yes, Miss Amy. That's what he said.' Lizzie fumbled in her pinafore pocket and produced a large white handkerchief. She proceeded to blow her nose loudly, then dabbed at the corner of one eye. 'A bit of smoke from the bonfire in my eye, I expect.' She tried to smile, but looked comical and woebegone, and extremely bewildered.

'Hey! Come over here and sit down on the garden seat. Let's have a chat, huh?'

'Chats aren't going to help any.' Lizzie shoved the hanky away again, but followed Amy nevertheless.

262

They sat facing each other, one on either end of the half-moon-shaped bench. 'Why was Uncle Gif so nasty to you?' Amy wanted to know. 'What brought it on, Lizzie?'

Lizzie sniffed. 'He's seeing somebody this morning. Has he mentioned it to you?'

Amy frowned. 'No. He hasn't mentioned anyone to me.'

'It's that creepy young fellow with the camera. The one who was always flying over the house in his helicopter.' Lizzie nodded at Amy's look of amazement, and said, 'Yes. It's true. And you know my feelings about him. Down-right rude he was last time he came here with that nice Catherine Blake. Don't you remember how he just lounged about the place looking all smug and self-impor-tant? I watched him from a window upstairs, giving the place the once-over just as if he owned it. I reckon he might be a burglar – come to joint the case. That's what they say, isn't it?'

Amy tried not to smile. 'Case the joint, I think is what you mean, Lizzie. But I don't think he's a gangster or anything like that.'

'He was a right scruffy one, though, was that Mark Powell.'

'He wore designer clothes,' Amy pointed out. 'Though I must admit I hated that red-checked jacket.'

'I hated him full-stop.' Lizzie looked glum.

'But why is he coming here? Did Uncle Gif say? And why all the secrecy? Surely there was no point in keeping it from me?

'That man's a law unto himself.' Lizzie glowered. 'Since Duncan Ward died, Gif seems to have inherited some of his friend's personality traits. Duncan was always a cunning and wily old devil. Always had to have his own way in everything.'

'But they were two of a kind, Lizzie. Uncle Gif always wants his own way too – and he too can be awkward.'

'They deserved each other. That's all I can say – ' Lizzie stopped herself suddenly, realizing she might have said too much.

'It's okay, Lizzie. Richard told me about Uncle Gif and Duncan. But I wish I'd known the truth from the start.'

'I didn't want you to ever find out, girl. Didn't know how you'd take it.'

'I was shocked at first, but we can't choose who we love, Lizzie. It just happens. I hate it when the truth's covered up, though – pushed under the carpet like a heap of dirt.'

Lizzie shook her grey frizzed head. 'I'll never understand them two – Duncan and Gif – as long as I live.'

'It's over now,' Amy said gently. 'Try and be patient with Uncle Gif. He must be missing Duncan dreadfully. I suppose we ought to be pleased he's taking an interest in things again – even if Mark Powell is a man both you and I detest, Lizzie.'

'You can say that again, girl.'

'Perhaps Uncle Gif wants some more photographs of the Hall. There has to be some simple explanation for Mark Powell coming here today. Look – what time is he due? Maybe I'll be there to meet him.'

'Oh, he's not actually coming *here* – not at first, anyway. Gif says the lad's staying down at the Hawkwood Arms again. He told me they wouldn't want any lunch, that John Graham's taking him down to Hawkwood in the car and then they're lunching out up Derbyshire somewhere. That's when I got on my high horse and told him he wasn't giving me much notice if he expected me to make up a meal later on today when they came back.'

'And that's when Uncle Gif said . . .'

'I was a meddling old so and so and to watch my step 'cause I was only a servant – lowest of the low, he said.'

'Oh, Lizzie.' Amy slid along the seat and took hold of the housekeeper's hands in her own. 'Lizzie – he flies off the handle for no reason these days. Try not to take any notice of him.'

'It's all right for you. You're soon going to be out of his clutches. You'll marry Richard Boden and go off to live at Hatton-in-the Dale – and then what's to become of me?'

'Uncle Gif will still need you,' Amy reassured her. 'Don't let him see he's upset you. Okay?'

'If you say so.' Lizzie managed a grin at last, and together they started back towards the house.

In the great hall at Wydale, Gif Weldon pulled on his overcoat and gloves, then glanced up at the portrait of Barbara. 'He's your son, all right! Who could mistake those eyes,' he sneered, and with a burning hatred in his eyes he hurried across the hall to the outside door. He was breathless by the time he got there, but he managed to turn and look at the portrait again. 'I have still to be convinced, however, that there's any part of *me* in him!' His right hand clenched tightly into a fist, and if he'd been a less rational sort of man, he knew he would have shaken it at her.

John Graham drove them – the old man and the young photographer – to an inn on the moors above Blackthorn Pass, where they lunched, talked together for a couple of hours, then returned to Wydale Hall.

Amy was in the courtyard just setting off somewhere on her bicycle as the black car drew up against the front door. Mark Powell saw her hesitate, bringing the bike to a slithering halt as John Graham slid out of the driver's seat and walked round to open the back door for Gif Weldon. Mark opened his own door and got out. It irked him when he saw Weldon smugly expecting to be waited on hand and foot. The man was capable of opening a car door for himself, surely!

Mark raised a hand to Amy and called out, 'Hi!'

She managed a sort of smile and acknowledged him. 'Nice to see you again, Mr Powell.'

He walked round the car and across the courtyard to her. 'You're not running away, surely? Not just as I arrive?'

Her face was strained. 'I didn't know you'd be coming back here. Lizzie just told me that you and Uncle Gif were lunching together somewhere.'

'I'd like to talk to you before I go back to London.'

'I expect I'll be around.' She tossed her head.

'Going somewhere nice?' He wished he could go with her – somewhere nice or otherwise. He was bored to tears with the old man and his ramblings this morning.

'Just a ride. I told Richard I might go over and have a look at his quarry.

'Wow! That's what I call devotion to duty.' There was no malice in the words. He didn't want to alienate her. He knew why he'd been summoned to Wydale. Gif Weldon suspected something, he was sure. He'd made several veiled references to his former wife that morning – and to Amy and her inheritance.

'It's no "duty"! I'm interested.' She forced a bright grin and mounted the bicycle again.

Mark Powell turned on every bit of charm he possessed. His voice, he knew, was his greatest asset, and his dark eyes, too, could be used to advantage. 'I really need to see you. Properly, if you know what I mean. We didn't hit it off too well when I was here before, did we?'

She looked at him as if she were searching his very soul, and he couldn't help feeling a tiny bit uncomfortable. 'Mr Powell,' she said, obviously ignoring the pleading in his eyes, 'I don't think you and I have anything more to say to each other, do you?'

A more straightforward and honest girl he'd never met. Inside he was squirming, for only he knew what angry intentions had brought him here. Suddenly he wasn't liking himself.

He thought quickly. Liquid looks and a pleading voice would get him precisely nowhere with this girl. 'Okay,' he said. 'We hate each other's guts. I'll give you that. But I guess we're two of a kind in many ways.'

'I don't think so.' Her voice was like ice.

She pushed off on the bicycle and left him before the conversation could go any further, and behind him Gif Weldon's thin voice called out, 'Mr Powell. I think we should go inside.'

He whirled round and joined the old man.

'Why did you bring the camera?' Weldon asked as they walked into the main hall.

Mark shrugged. 'Habit, I suppose. I rarely go anywhere without it.'

'We'll go to my study. Then I'll ring for Lizzie Abercrombie to bring some tea.'

It grated on Mark again – the way Weldon treated his servants. 'Not for me, thanks. I'll need to be getting back to the pub and packing my bag soon.' He followed the old man down the passage all the same, and accepted a seat beside the window in the somewhat dark little study that afforded a limited view of the lawned rose garden.

'This would make a great picture . . .' Mark turned and admired the diamond paned leaded glass, then twisted his head to look at Weldon, ensconced behind his desk now. 'In the summer – when the roses are out . . .' He got to his feet and walked into the middle of the room, then faced the window again.

'D'ye see what I mean?' He framed the window with his hands. 'With the window open, and the merest glimpse of the flowers framed between these gaunt stone walls and the heavy window frame and all that leaded stuff it would be from darkness to light – a good caption for a picture, don't you think?'

Weldon sat back in his chair and smiled grimly. 'I'm afraid I don't see much beauty in anything at my age,' he said. 'But you have the gift of artistry, my boy. Those photographs you took of the Hall in winter were very good.'

'Very good' was putting it mildly, Mark knew. The pictures had been excellent. In the depths of winter he had seen a mysticism and a beauty in the old stones that had torn at his heart. He'd loved the old house from his first sight of it – which had been from the skies above Wydale. It was only down on the ground, however, that he'd discovered the house had a heart – and people who loved it. And that was when his plans had started to fall apart.

He couldn't settle or give his mind to anything in the austere little room. He wanted to be out there in the garden, aiming the lens, adjusting the focus, capturing on film the budding greenness of those spring-green leaves, the sharp needle points of thorns and the tight embryo buds of the roses.

'Sit down. I want to talk to you.' Weldon's voice held a touch of irascibility.

Mark returned to the green leather armchair beside the window and sank into it. 'I get carried away when I see something worthwhile,' he said.

Weldon grimaced. 'You think my roses are worthwhile?'

'Every time I come here I see something new – something I want to take away with me.' Mark spread his hands helplessly. 'Can I help it if I find Wydale so captivating?'

Gif Weldon stared broodingly at the photographer's hands. 'You have the hands of an artist,' he said, and he held out his own. 'You have the hands *I* once had – before arthritis turned them into these misshapen, useless things.'

'You were a surgeon. It must have been hard giving up a career like that.'

'How do you know that I was a surgeon?' Weldon's head jerked up. 'I never told you.'

The time for play-acting was past, Mark knew. All morning they'd played a kind of hide and seek with words. Old man Weldon had asked him about his background in a roundabout sort of way and Mark had retaliated by bringing the subject of Amy into the conversation whenever he could. But Gif Weldon had fended off all questions about his own past, being only interested, it seemed, in that of the young photographer.

'My mother told me about you,' Mark said, timing his bombshell beautifully.

The old man was breathing shallowly. '*Anybody* around here could have told you,' he muttered, letting his hands drop onto the desk in front of him. '*Amy* probably told you the last time you were here. Or that reporter woman – though I was careful what I did tell her.'

'My mother told me,' Mark said again, slowly and distinctly. 'My mother was your wife, Mr Weldon. Let's not beat about the bush any longer. You know in your heart why you asked me to come here today.'

Hoarsely, Gif Weldon said, 'You still call me "Mr Weldon", however – not . . .'

'Don't *ever* expect me to call you Father!' Mark managed a brusque little laugh. 'It would be hypocritical, wouldn't it? A father is somebody who cares for his children. A father is somebody a son can look up to and admire.'

Gif Weldon seemed to shrink into his great leather chair as he said, 'And you can't do that, it seems?'

'I can't respect you. I couldn't respect anybody who allowed my mother to live the kind of life she did after you divorced her.'

Almost inaudibly, Weldon muttered, 'I didn't know about *you*, though. I didn't know she was pregnant when she left Wydale.'

Several seconds elapsed before Mark spoke again. When he did, he had to force out the words. 'Why did my mother leave you? What could you possibly have done to her to make her so bitter that she never even told me about you until I was old enough to leave home?'

Weldon shook his head slowly. 'I – I can't tell you that . . .'

Powell half rose to his feet. 'You *have* to tell me,' he ground out, on his feet now and striding across to Weldon's desk. 'How can I begin to understand your rejection if I don't know what happened?'

'You are best not knowing.' Gif Weldon closed his eyes wearily and laid his head against the back of his chair.

Mark thumped the desk. 'Tell me,' he insisted. 'I have to know.'

A flicker of a smile touched the old man's lips, 'No. All

you need to know is that I'm convinced now that you are my son.'

Slowly, Mark pushed himself away from the desk. 'What do you mean by that, you old devil?' He stood straight and tall, glaring down at the old man.

Weldon opened his eyes again. 'I'll have to talk to Barbara, but I don't ever want to see or meet her again.'

Mark nodded in agreement. 'She wouldn't want to see you. I do know that. Do you know what kind of life she had with Derek Powell – the man she married after she was left on her own with a baby – *me* – to bring up alone in the seventies? It wasn't easy, you know, twenty-odd years ago. It wasn't the benevolent society we have today.'

'She brought it on herself. She could have stayed at Wydale.'

Mark shook his head. 'Oh, no,' he said with a catch in his voice. 'There was something here that frightened her – something here that she couldn't face. She preferred life with a drunken slob of a man who beat her and kept her short of money till the day he died to the life she could have had here with you.' His eyes narrowed. 'I *will* find out,' he promised. 'I'll move heaven and earth to discover what you did to her – what kind of a monster you were.'

Weldon sighed. 'I was no monster, but if you want to know what happened you'll have to ask her. I certainly won't tell you. And you would be best not knowing what went on between Barbara and me – I can promise you that.'

Mark thrust his hands into the pockets of his jeans and turned away in exasperation. 'Two stupid people,' he muttered. 'That's what I'm beginning to think you two were.' He swung back to the man he now knew was his father. 'An argument? Was it some petty row that went wrong? Some silly disagreement where neither of you would back down? Because if that's the case . . .'

'No!' Weldon rose wearily to his feet. 'No!' he said. 'It was nothing so simple. But I refuse to be interrogated by you about it. It was something that could never be reconciled, so believe me and put it from your mind.' He hung onto the edge of the desk, swaying a little, then he lifted a grey face to look into the eyes of his son. 'Only one thing needs sorting out now – and that's the future of Wydale. You know, of course, that I've made a will leaving everything to Amy?'

Mark swallowed uneasily. This wasn't going to be easy. 'Yes.'

'After all these years I can't just tell her she's going to get nothing.'

Mark sucked in a deep breath. 'I realize that . . .'

'But I owe it to your mother – and to you – to put things right.'

Mark would have butted in there, but the old man held up a hand and said, 'Let me finish. You came here with a purpose. It wasn't just coincidence that you arrived that day with Catherine Blake, was it?'

'No,' Mark admitted. 'I'd been hanging around Wydale in the helicopter for a long time – you know that.'

Weldon nodded.

'It was the only way. I had to see for myself what was at stake.'

'So you wormed yourself in by the back door. With Catherine Blake's help. Does she know?'

'Know?'

'Does she know you're my son? Did you confide in her? Did you boast about it?' There was impatience in Weldon's voice.

272

'Catherine knows nothing about my real interest in Wydale.'

'God knows why, but I believe you.' Weldon sighed and walked round the desk and over to the door. 'I'm going to have to ask you to leave now.' He shook his grey head worriedly. 'I have to be alone to think about my next move. You understand?'

Mark didn't follow him. 'There's nothing you can do now,' he insisted. 'Surely you do realize that, don't you? You can't disinherit Amy – especially now she's marrying that quarrying bloke in order to put the old house to rights again.'

'You have money!' The old man's lip curled maliciously. 'You could put the place to rights yourself.'

Mark was appalled at the lack of feeling Gif Weldon was showing towards Amy. His temper rose. 'You can't just order people to do this and do that,' he exploded. 'People have feelings. Amy has come all the way from America to care for you. You can't treat her like just another servant.'

'Wydale Hall is my property to do with as I wish.' The words were coldly calculating. 'If I want to change my will, I shall do it.'

'Oh, no . . . I don't go along with that . . .'

'You have no choice, my boy. I don't care a toss for what you might think. As my son, you are the one with a claim to Wydale.'

'But what about Amy?' Mark stood his ground.

'If you feel so strongly about Amy, why don't you do what any red-blooded man would do?'

Mark stared at him, perplexed. 'I don't know what you're getting at.'

'It's a simple solution. Marry the girl. That way you'd both have Wydale.'

CHAPTER 20

Amy was happy as she cycled back from the quarry at Hatton-in-the-Dale. Richard had given her a quick tour round the dusty limestone outcrops and she'd met most of the workmen there. Her heart had been touched as she'd heard the pride in his voice as he'd introduced her as 'the girl who's going to be my wife'. Back at the little pre-fabricated building that served as an office she'd laughingly refused his offer of a lift back to Wydale in the Land Rover in half an hour's time.

'I can be back there in twenty minutes now I have wheels of my own,' she'd told him.

'It serves me right, I suppose, for supplying the bicycle,' he'd grumbled. 'But, Amy, I'll come over there, shall I? Right after I've closed up the quarry for the night.'

'Mmm. That'd be great. I'll tell Lizzie to put something nice on for tea when I get back.'

'So long as you're there, I don't care what I eat.' He'd leaned over and kissed her on the forehead.

As she pedalled slowly up the drive to Wydale now, past Duncan Ward's little cottage, with its small garden just coming to life with clumps of lupins and white mossy flowers in the rocky borders, she wondered what was going to happen to it. Uncle Gif hadn't said anything about reletting the place, but maybe it was too soon yet to expect him to make any decisions like that. All the same, she thought, it would bring in a little money to supplement all that Richard was thinking of laying out on Wydale if a tenant could be found or the property sold.

The line of trees alongside the winding lane had branches that met and twined together overhead, and there was a tracing of green above her through which the cool spring sunshine dappled the road. Amy breathed in the pure clean air and tried not to think of how angry Uncle Gif had been a few days ago when he'd tried yet again to make her put off her wedding to Richard.

These days she couldn't understand him, but she tried to make allowances for his moods. Duncan Ward's death had been a tremendous blow to him, she knew. Perhaps he was feeling low – and lonely – and thinking she would be leaving him very soon to be Richard's wife. But there was Lizzie at Wydale to look after him, and John Graham to drive him around in the car. And it wasn't as if she was going away to the other end of the earth, she reasoned within herself. Hatton-in-the-Dale was no more than a ten-minute drive away from Wydale.

A ten-minute drive! Heavens, she thought, Richard would be catching her up if she dawdled much longer. She'd taken enough time cycling back from the quarry already. There had been so much to stop for along the way – fresh green hedgerows, a blackbird singing its heart out and lambs grazing on a steep hillside. Her video camera, now neatly fastened away inside the leather bag on the back of the bike, had been in prominence for much of the afternoon. The batteries would need charging up again tonight, and she'd have to ask Richard if she could go over to his house once more in order to transfer the film onto a video cassette so she could send it to Kate and Marty in America.

As she approached the pack-horse bridge over the Eston Amy looked over towards the clump of trees that half hid the old chapel from the road. Richard had set men to work rebuilding it some weeks ago, and it was coming along nicely. She decided she'd just have time for a quick look at how it was progressing before pushing the bike up the steep incline to the Hall. Leaving it leaning against a tree on the far side of the pack-horse bridge – knowing Richard would see it there if he came by in the Land Rover – she ran lightly down the grassy slope towards the chapel.

It was deserted today. The men, she knew, worked on it mainly at weekends, when Richard could be there to advise on what needed doing. It was still a mere shell of a building, but the rubbish had all been carted away and the site was already acquiring a neat and tidy appearance again. Much of the wallwork had been rebuilt with the original stones – cleaned up, of course – and the place was once more taking on the appearance of a chapel, with mitred holes left in the walls for the window frames whenever they should be needed.

Inside the building, she picked her way carefully around boxes of floor tiles and pallets of roof slates, huge lengths of planed timber and several heavy oak doors that were sealed in clear plastic. She looked up above the nave at the sturdy oak beams that had survived the fire. Waterproofed and bituminized felt had been securely fixed over the purlins and subsidiary rafters of the roof to keep out the weather, and there wasn't a lot of light managing to get inside the place at the moment.

Suddenly, though, there was a flash of brightness. She blinked and whirled round. 'Who's there?' she yelled.

There was a scuffling up above her in the far corner of the chapel, over where the altar had once stood and where now the organ loft was in the first stages of renewal.

'Amy? Is that you?'

'Oh, heck!' It was a voice that, once heard, was immediately recognizable. Who could mistake those soft Scottish tones for anyone else but Mark Powell?

'Mr Powell? Mark? What are you doing?' She started walking towards the front of the chapel, then stopped as two legs appeared through a trapdoor above the organ loft – two legs clad in black denim, with leather boots on the end of each one of them.

He wriggled his way through the hole, which was no more than six or seven feet off the ground, and then dropped down in front of her. His camera was slung round his neck on a leather strap and bounced against his chest as he landed.

'What's wrong with the stairs?' she asked, knowing she sounded crotchety and out of sorts – but she hadn't expected seeing *him* here.

'The stairs might look rigid, but they're not. They're just leaning up there waiting to be properly fixed. There's nothing holding them at all. That's why I hauled myself up through the trapdoor. It's the same all over the place – bits and pieces left unfinished. You should be careful where you walk and what you touch. The workmen you've got in here need careful supervision, if you ask me . . .'

'Nobody's asking you, Mr Powell,' she replied primly. 'But if you insist on peeking and prying into things that don't concern you – well, you can't complain if you get hurt, can you?'

'I wouldn't want anybody to get hurt,' he said. 'That's why I'm warning you. Okay?'

277

'Did Uncle Gif say you could come down here?'

'He indicated I could have a wander around and take some pictures before I leave for London tonight.'

She brightened. 'You're leaving? So soon?'

'That doesn't do my ego much good – you sounding so damn cheerful about me going,' he said, brushing sawdust from his sweatshirt and trousers, then checking that the camera was still in one piece.

She shrugged. 'Why should I care what you do?'

'Why, indeed?'

'Have you finished your business with my uncle?' she asked.

He stood and looked at her, tilting his dark head on one side as he said, 'Unfortunately – no.'

'Oh?'

'Amy! It's not easy . . .'

'You don't have to tell me why you came,' she said flippantly. 'If Uncle Gif wants to have his little secrets that's okay by me.'

'It's hardly a "little secret"!'

'Look – I'm late. I have to go.' She didn't want to stand here talking to him. And even though she *was* curious as to why Uncle Gif might be taking an interest in him, she had a sudden niggling feeling at the back of her mind that it might turn out to be something she didn't want to hear.

Was Mark being targeted as Duncan's replacement? she wondered. The thought left her with a slightly hollow feeling in the pit of her stomach that she instantly interpreted as hunger. She didn't want it to be anything else. She had no reason to judge, she told herself. People had a right to their own preferences when it came down to relationships. She'd always managed to keep an open mind about homosexuality before; now, though, when it

278

was so close to home, she was having to rethink a lot of her principles.

He caught up with her as she walked towards the back of the chapel, and laid hold of her arm, swinging her round to face him. She became aware of the seasoned smell of wood, the dry-as-dust atmosphere now that the chapel was no longer doused with damp and rotting debris. His fingers tightened round her arm. 'Hey, what's the matter?' he asked. 'Why are you running away from me?'

'I'm not.' She tried to shake his hand away from her. 'Just let go of me, will you?'

Immediately his hand fell away from her. 'Amy,' he said, 'I really need to talk to you. There's something you ought to know, you see.' His brow furrowed and he raked one hand impatiently through his thick dark hair. 'God, this is difficult,' he said. 'I just don't know how to tell you, but – '

'Don't try,' she said. 'It's perfectly obvious what's going on. I suppose you're going to tell me you're moving into Duncan Ward's cottage any day now.'

'Duncan Ward? Who the hell is Duncan Ward?' He looked thoroughly perplexed.

'Oh, come on,' she said. 'Don't try kidding me you don't know.'

'I've never heard of the guy,' he said, shaking his head in amazement.

'You surprise me.' She whirled round and broke into a run. She felt she had to get away from him. She couldn't bear to hear the truth.

He caught up with her, grabbed at her again and pulled her round to face him. 'What the hell's the matter with you?' he said softly.

'With me?' She began to laugh, but the sound was feeble and without mirth even to her own ears.

279

'Just listen to me, will you?' he said. 'Just listen for two minutes.'

All the fight went out of her. 'Okay,' she said. 'I'm listening. But don't expect me to understand. I may be broad-minded, but – '

'*Your* uncle is *my* father,' he said.

Her mouth fell open in a little 'Oh!' of shock. She made no other sound. She just stared at him.

'I'm sorry,' he said, letting go of her. 'I knew it wouldn't be easy. But there's worse to come.'

She couldn't run away from him; her feet were glued to the floor. She heard him saying, 'The old devil wants me to marry you. Can you believe it? He's scared of telling you that I'm his heir and he doesn't want to hurt you. So his way out of this sorry mess is to marry us off to each other so we'll both inherit Wydale.'

She stood transfixed, taking in his words but still not believing she'd actually heard them uttered. They were so very different from what she'd been expecting to hear.

'Well, say something. For God's sake, say something.'

'How?' she croaked at last. 'How can he be your father? He couldn't make love to a woman, surely?'

'A woman?' His forehead was a mass of lines as his eyebrows shot up and an expression of horror filled his face. 'What the hell are you getting at?' he wanted to know.

'Uncle Gif! And Duncan Ward,' she muttered awkwardly. 'They were . . .' She stopped, unable to continue, regretting now that she'd said anything at all. But it had all happened so quickly she'd spoken before thinking.

'Hell! No!' He closed his eyes and leaned his head back. 'No! No!' he said.

'Mark – please – don't be upset. If you stop and think about it logically – '

'Logically!' He opened his eyes and his head fell forward again. He was deathly pale. 'He's my father,' he ground out. 'For God's sake – you're telling me he's gay, aren't you?'

Dumbly she nodded.

A minute ticked by in silence, then he said in a low voice. 'And before you thought – you actually thought that I might be . . .'

She nodded again.

'You bitch! You bloody bitch!'

'Mark – no!' She put up her hands to ward him off, but it was too late.

'I'll show you,' he snarled, but his voice didn't rise beyond a whisper. 'I'll show you I'm not what you thought me to be.' His hands shot out and grasped her shoulders. He dragged her up close and his lips descended on hers in a fierce and brutal kiss.

She struggled and kicked and twisted, screamed at him to let her go, but he was stronger than he looked and she was powerless.

And then she heard a noise resembling that of a bull in full charge, and Mark Powell's grasp on her loosened as he was jerked away from her as easily as if he'd been a rag doll.

She was flung aside, landing on a pile of the long planed timber, which suddenly gave way and collapsed all around her. When she eventually managed to take stock of what was going on around her she saw that Richard and Mark were locked together, fighting, with Richard's superior weight giving him the advantage over the slimmer, more lightweight man.

She screamed at them to stop, but they either couldn't or wouldn't hear her – so she scrambled out of the wood pile and flung herself between them, trying her hardest to prise them apart.

Mark Powell overbalanced and went staggering backwards. Richard got hold of her shoulders fiercely and propelled her over to a wall. 'Stay there,' he ordered. 'And don't move until I say – '

The sentence was cut short as Mark came up behind him, grappled with him again and then, as Richard turned round, caught him with a hooked right under the chin.

Richard spun across the chapel floor. Until then, Amy realized, Richard hadn't actually landed a single punch on the younger man. As Mark moved in on him again, however, Richard lurched to his feet and swung a clenched fist at him.

Mark went down. Richard dragged him up again by his sweatshirt. Neither man had been wearing a coat or jacket so they were unhampered by heavy clothing.

Amy, breathless, leaned back against the wall and looked up as the sounds of their scuffling and grunting echoed all around the place. In a high recess she saw that Angel Gabriel had been mounted in a prominent position, sideways on to where the altar would eventually be positioned. It must have been one of the last jobs the builders had done, hauling Gabriel up there, she realized, for a ladder was still there, the topmost rungs propped against the alabaster angel, keeping it in place.

She groaned as she saw the two fighting figures rolling on the floor and getting precariously close to the finely balanced ladder. She rushed forward yelling, 'Be careful . . . the ladder . . .'

But both men were beyond hearing her now; both were obsessed with beating the living daylights out of each other. She glanced round for something – anything – to break up the fight. They'd moved away from the ladder now. She turned her back on them, saw a hard-bristled broom leaning against the wall and snatched it up. She turned back to the men. If she could thrust it between them, trip them both up, perhaps . . .

Mark caught Richard with another right hook. Richard staggered backwards, blood streaming from his nose and forehead – and went right into the ladder.

The rungs bounced. The bottom of it skidded sideways and the top of it crashed into Gabriel. Gabriel rocked back and forth, back and forth as the ladder slid down the wall and careered across the floor.

Richard looked up. Gabriel was toppling. Amy screamed. And Mark Powell threw himself sideways in an effort to knock his opponent out of the way.

But Richard's weight withstood the younger man's lunge at him, and Amy saw the angel crash right down on top of the man she was planning to marry.

Amy sat beside Richard's head, her lightweight jacket making a pad with which she tried the stanch the blood which was flowing freely from a deep wound. Mark Powell was keeping pressure on a gash across Richard's shoulder, where a dagger-like piece of alabaster was sticking out from between skin and bone. They both heard the wail of a siren at the same time and looked up at each other across the unconscious man.

'Don't move,' she said. 'They'll find us. I gave them detailed directions.'

'Thank God his mobile phone still worked.' Mark's face was deathly pale and bloodstained. Bruises were already beginning to show and his knuckles were red raw.

In seconds, paramedics were on the scene and taking over from Amy and Mark.

'What happened?' the female driver asked.

Amy looked at Mark and said, 'The chapel's being renovated. A ladder wasn't positioned properly and it slipped and knocked the angel from up there.' She glanced up towards the roof and the now empty alcove.

'We were fighting,' Mark Powell said quietly. 'It was all my fault.'

'He's losing a lot of blood.' The man tending Richard gave his companion a meaningful look.

'I'll radio through to A and E – warn them we'll need blood.'

'He's O positive.' Amy slipped a hand inside one of Richard's pockets and produced a small card. 'He always carries this. He's written his blood group on it.'

The woman read it quickly. 'A donor card.'

'How did you know he carried that?' Mark Powell asked huskily.

Amy shot him a glance that was full of meaning. 'I'm going to marry him. Remember?' Her voice was tense. 'I know all I need to know about him. I love him.'

Mark was on his knees beside Richard. He looked stricken. As Amy's accusing eyes fixed themselves on him he staggered to his feet and stumbled away to the side of the chapel.

'Maybe you should go to him?' The woman in the green uniform smiled at her. 'There's nothing more you can do here at the moment. Be ready to come with us in the ambulance, though.'

'He will be all right?' Amy glanced from one to the other of the two people she was depending on to pull Richard through this nightmare.

284

'He'll get the best possible treatment. And we were on hand pretty quickly.'

'But his head . . .' Amy gulped back tears that were threatening to overflow again.

'Try not to worry.' The woman touched her hand.

There was nothing more she could do to help, she knew, so she walked across to Mark Powell, who had his arm leaning on the wall and his head bent onto it.

'Richard wouldn't have wanted you to say you and he had been fighting,' she said in a dull voice. 'And it won't do you any good, you know.'

Slowly he raised his head and looked at her. 'What you mean is, it won't do me any good if he dies, don't you?'

'Don't say that.' Tears were running unashamedly down her cheeks now, but suddenly she couldn't find it in her heart to hate Mark Powell. He had at least tried to save Richard when he'd seen the angel heading towards him, she realized.

'I'm sorry . . . God that sounds so trite.' His voice broke and his lips began to tremble.

She laid her hand on his shoulder. At that moment he looked as old and vulnerable as her uncle Gif had looked when Duncan had died. And, seeing him so, Amy was in no doubt that he really was Gif Weldon's son. The resemblance, once the haughty mask was down, was uncanny.

'I can't bear to think of life without Richard,' she said. 'Oh, Mark – what am I going to do?'

CHAPTER 21

They were a sorry little group in the hospital relatives' room – Amy, Lizzie Abercrombie, John Graham and Mark. To Amy every second was an eternity as they waited for news of Richard. She sat, dry-eyed now, with Lizzie beside her holding her hand. The others tried to make conversation, but every time footsteps were heard in the corridor outside a breath-held silence descended on them all.

Mark Powell was restless, and kept jumping up and pacing to the window and back again. Eventually John Graham suggested he and Mark should go outside for a while and walk round the hospital's grounds. It was a cool spring evening and still light outside, even though it was nearly eight o'clock.

'A good idea,' Lizzie said, shooting Mark a malevolent look, and when they'd gone she said to Amy, 'I don't know why *he's* here at all, that photographer fellow. If it hadn't been for him . . .'

'Don't, Lizzie. Don't blame Mark. I think in a funny kind of way both he and Richard were enjoying the scrap – until Gabriel fell. Mark did try to push Richard out of the way, but . . .' Her voice tailed off miserably, and she drew her hand out of Lizzie's, fumbled for a handkerchief and blew her nose hard.

'That damned angel! And after all the work he put into it.'

Amy, to her horror, found herself smiling weakly as tears welled up again. How like Lizzie it was, she thought, to try so hard to make sense of what had happened that she could imagine Gabriel bearing a grudge of some sort and actually leaping down onto Richard because of it.

'Gabriel was probably trying to stop the two of them fighting over me,' she whispered brokenly.

Lizzie sat sideways on the low settee and looked at her for several seconds without speaking. Amy blew her nose again.

'You really do care about him, don't you?'

Amy's head came up. She looked long and hard at Lizzie. 'Did you ever doubt it?' she asked.

'I thought maybe you'd just fallen in with the old man's plans. After all, there's no other way to save Wydale, is there? Richard's money is needed – and badly.'

'Perhaps it was like that in the beginning. I know I joked about it to you that first day I found out about Richard's and Uncle Gif's crazy plan, didn't I?'

'Yes, Miss Amy, you did.' Lizzie shook her grey frizzed head. 'I never even considered you might really think of marrying him, though. But then it just seemed to come natural-like – this friendship with Richard Boden. You didn't set out to hate him from the start like some girls would have done. I mean – well, it was pretty stupid of Gif, thinking he could force you into an arranged marriage in this day and age, wasn't it?'

'I think I fell in love with Richard the first moment I met him – down in that little room at the back of the chapel. Oh, Lizzie, he's the kindest, most wonderful man I've ever known – ' She broke off on a sob, then sprang to

287

her feet. 'Lizzie – I can't stand this waiting. I've just got to know what's happening.'

She ran over to the door, whipped it open and raced blindly out into the passage. She saw a blur of white just as she hit it, and two arms took hold of her and stopped her going any further. She looked up and recognized the doctor who had first examined Richard when he was admitted.

'Richard . . . where is he?' she blurted out. 'We've been waiting here for hours and hours, and nobody's told us anything.'

'He's fine. Now, let's just get back into the relatives' room and I'll tell you all I know myself.'

'You're lying. He's not "fine", is he?' She beat her clenched fists against his shoulders. 'You're just telling me anything to keep me quiet, aren't you?'

Lizzie's voice behind her said, 'Doctor! For God's sake let her see him. She's going out of her mind with worry.'

'Okay! Come with me. He's very groggy, though. He can't remember what happened, but that should right itself eventually. We're going to have to keep him in for a day or two, however.'

'He's conscious?' Amy felt the room spinning round her.

Lizzie grabbed hold of her and steadied her. 'Hey! You just take care.'

Amy's hand flew to her head. 'I'm all right, Lizzie. I've had one or two giddy turns this past week. I thought I might be going down with a bug or something.'

Lizzie looked sceptical, but Amy's face was wreathed in smiles. 'I'm going to see him.' She glanced at the doctor again. 'I *can* go see him, can't I? You weren't kidding me?'

'No! I'm not kidding.' The man half turned to go back the way he'd come. 'I'll show you I'm not kidding if you come with me.'

Lizzie accompanied them to the door of the recovery room. 'There's no lasting damage,' the doctor said. 'But a vein that was almost severed in Mr Boden's shoulder caused us some concern. He's had an emergency op to tidy that up, however. That's what's taken so long. He's quite weak through blood loss, but we're making that up now. Tomorrow should see him looking a lot better. It's fortunate he's a very fit man.'

'I'll go back and wait for you,' Lizzie said as Amy turned to her. 'You go and see him. Put your mind at rest so you can get a good night's sleep, lovey. John Graham will run us all back to Wydale then. Goodness knows what your Uncle Gif's thinking – us being away all this time.'

As the clock struck ten, Gif Weldon was not pleased. He'd seen no reason for all of them to go rushing off to hospital just because Richard had been unfortunate enough to fall against a ladder. At least, that was the tale Lizzie had spun, but, knowing her aptitude for making mountains out of molehills, he doubted Richard had suffered much more than a bump on the head, no matter how serious they all imagined it to be.

He was waiting for them in the lamplit great hall when they arrived home. He was hungry – and he was angry.

'Do you know what time it is?' He pointed meaningfully at the grandfather clock. John Graham, he noted, had had the good sense to keep out of his way. He'd be putting the car away by now, but he'd not escape his wrath, Gif promised himself. He'd be having serious words with the chauffeur tomorrow!

Lizzie said to Amy, 'Go up to bed, child. I'll deal with him. I'm used to him in this kind of mood.'

The housekeeper's words enraged him even more. 'She

can stay!' he bellowed, pointing an accusing finger at Amy. 'And you'd better have a good excuse for this,' he ranted on. 'I've had nothing to eat or drink since I went out with that photographer fellow this morning – and it's not good enough, I tell you. It just isn't good enough.'

Lizzie sighed and slipped out of her coat, draping it over her arm as she made for the kitchen. 'I'll get you a sandwich and some cocoa,' she said.

'A man needs a meal. A proper meal.'

'Well, you're not getting one,' Lizzie said. 'You'll make do with a sandwich or nothing at all. This has been one day I could well have done without.'

Amy went over to her uncle. 'Richard had a nasty accident, Uncle Gif.' She tried to placate him.

'A bump on the head? Some accident. Where have you been? That's what I want to know,' he sulked.

'We've been at the hospital.'

'Pshaw!' He pushed her out of the way and she stumbled and almost fell.

'Hey! That's enough.' Lizzie came between them and shook a warning finger at him. 'You leave the girl alone. She's been through a worrying time.'

But Gif Weldon had spent long hours brooding because all his staff – and Amy as well – had left him to his own devices without giving him a single thought.

'You're in this together,' he bellowed. 'This is some excuse you've all thought up so you can go out and enjoy yourselves.'

'Uncle Gif. Didn't you see the ambulance?' Amy cried.

'I saw nothing! Nothing!'

'Well, didn't you hear its siren?'

Amy was almost crying, he saw, but he didn't care. They'd all be crying before much longer, because he was

290

determined he was not going to put up with such treatment. They were turning the tables on him – questioning him like this. This was *his* house, he reasoned, and they had no right to question him. They'd had no right to go and leave him either. 'I might have wanted the car,' he said sulkily. 'And then where would I have been? Hunting all over the estate for John Graham – that's what I'd have been doing. Hunting for a man who was gallivanting around the country with you pair. Enjoying yourselves, were you?'

'Uncle Gif! Oh, Uncle Gif – no. How could you think such a thing?'

Tears were pouring down the girl's cheeks. Well, it served her right, Gif Weldon thought sourly. He rounded on Lizzie Abercrombie, who was striding out towards Amy and then putting her arm round the girl's shoulders. 'It's *me* who needs attention,' he shouted, stabbing at his chest with his fist. 'Me, woman. You're the servant – remember? You're the one who takes orders. And don't you forget it.'

'Old man,' Lizzie snarled, hurrying the girl away towards the stairs, 'get out of my way.'

'You're fired!' he yelled. 'Get out of my house, Lizzie Abercrombie.'

'It'll be a pleasure!' Lizzie yelled back at him. 'Just give me five minutes to pack my belongings.'

In Amy's bedroom, Lizzie sat her down on the bed, then turned back to the door and drew the bolt across. 'That's just for good measure – to keep the old bear out. I'm fed up with him. I tell you, Miss Amy, I've just had my fill of his moods, and as soon as you're married I'll be looking for another position.'

Pale-faced, Amy watched as Lizzie came back across the room to her. 'Lizzie – I've never seen him like this before.'

'I told you what he was like the other day, didn't I?' Lizzie's grey head bobbed up and down as she nodded. 'Well, he's getting worse. Now he's starting on you, and I just won't have it. I've been accustomed to his funny little ways for years, but there's no reason for you to put up with him.'

'Perhaps we ought to have told him the truth about Richard and Mark fighting in the chapel.'

'No. That would have confused him even more. And at the moment that Mark Powell is the blue-eyed boy in Gif Weldon's world.'

'Lizzie – sit down. I want to tell you what Mark said to me earlier today. I don't want you to hear it from anyone else – it would be too much of a shock.'

Lizzie sat on the edge of the bed facing her. 'So? Go on. Nothing I hear in this house can shock me, I can promise you that.'

'I think this will, Lizzie. Mark Powell is Uncle Gif's son.'

She'd barely had time to relate all she knew to Lizzie before there came a banging on the bedroom door.

'Amy! Amy!'

'Oh, no! It's Uncle Gif again.' For some reason Amy felt a wave of weakness washing over her. This she could well do without. Today's happenings had been traumatic, and she felt she couldn't cope with anything else. It was beginning to worry her, this woozy light-headedness, the feeling of being swept up into a tide of weariness she couldn't bring under control.

'Go away,' Lizzie called out.

'I just want to tell my goddaughter something. Do I have to ask your permission for that, woman?' He banged on the door again.

Amy got to her feet and went across the room. 'Leave him be,' Lizzie warned. 'He'll only start all over again.'

'He'll probably keep it up all night anyway.' Amy let out a deep sigh and drew back the bolt on her door. She opened it then, and said, 'Well, Uncle, what is it?'

'Forgot to tell you before,' he muttered a little self-consciously. 'Phone call. Around seven tonight, I think it was.'

'Kate and Marty?' she asked.

'No!' For a moment he stared blankly at her, then said, 'A man. Robert somebody or other.'

Patiently she said, 'I don't know anybody called Robert.'

'I wrote it down.' He fumbled in his pocket and pulled out a scrap of paper. 'A name and a number for you to return the call. Surly-sounding fellow. Said he wouldn't ring again. That if you wanted him, you'd have to call him yourself.' He handed her the paper, then abruptly turned and walked away from her back down the corridor, and she heard his footsteps clumping on the stairs.

She closed the door and looked at the paper he'd handed to her; it was crumpled. She smoothed it out as she walked back towards Lizzie. Under the bright electric light hanging over her bed she read the name 'Roger Claybourne', and underneath it was a number. But the room was spinning again, and her head felt as if it would burst.

A ringing in her ears grew louder and then blackness blotted everything out.

CHAPTER 22

'Miss Amy – if I didn't know you better . . .' Lizzie was suspicious, that much was obvious.

'Don't fuss, Lizzie. I'm tired, that's all.'

'You promise me you'll see a doctor – then perhaps I'll stop worrying.'

'I've seen doctors aplenty today.' Amy managed a weak grin.

'Don't get saucy with me, my girl. You've been taking too much on yourself while you've been here. And the old man doesn't help – going on like that.'

'There's nothing wrong with me.' Amy wanted to be left alone. 'Look, Lizzie,' she said, 'if this dizziness doesn't clear up by the weekend, I promise I'll go see somebody about it. Okay?'

'What's written on that piece of paper? Has somebody been bothering you?'

'No.' With a shock, Amy found she was still clutching in her hand the note with Roger Claybourne's telephone number on it. 'It's just somebody I was trying to trace in Lincolnshire when we went down there – Richard and I. I left a message for him to contact me and now he's done just that.'

'Welll I hope you're not thinking of dashing off down

there again. Richard Boden won't be up to travelling far for a long time yet, you know.'

'I wouldn't dream of dragging Richard all that way again,' Amy said. 'For heaven's sake, Lizzie, what do you take me for? A prize idiot or something?'

'We–ell!' Lizzie looked solemnly at her. 'I suppose a good night's sleep might put some roses back in your cheeks, so I'd better leave you be – that's if you're sure you're okay.'

'Lizzie! You're only in the next room, for God's sake. I can always knock on the wall if I feel funny again.'

Lizzie snorted. 'There was nothing "funny" about you fainting like that.'

'It wasn't a real faint. I came to quickly enough, when you hauled me onto that chair and made me put my head down on my knees. Please, Lizzie, don't fuss over me so much. I'm okay – really I am. And I promise I'll call you if I feel the teeniest bit ill.'

'I'll go and make you a nice cup of tea. That'll steady your nerves a bit, huh?'

At the thought of Lizzie's tea, Amy felt her stomach starting to heave. 'No, thanks.' She forced a smile. 'I just need some sleep.' She stifled a yawn with the back of her hand.

Lizzie shook her head. 'Okay, then.' She walked over to the door, then turned and lifted a hand, one finger at the ready to lay down the law. 'Now, promise me – '

'I promise!'

At last she was alone. And when Amy was sure Lizzie had gone to her own room, she pushed herself very carefully to her feet again. All this rushing around was doing her no good, she realized, for already she suspected not what was *wrong* with her, but what was delightfully, deliriously *right*!

She went over to the desk and ran her fingers over the alabaster bookends that Richard had carved for her when she'd first come to Wydale. She smiled down at the angelic faces so beautifully worked into the smooth marble-like material. Standing between the bookends were three volumes – her diary, the poetry book Richard had given her and a dictionary. There was no choice tonight. She pulled out the diary, opened it on the desktop and started counting off the days since the time she'd been at the cottage in Norfolk.

With a smile on her lips she came to the present day. 'Richard Boden,' she murmured softly, 'you sure are going to have one hell of a shock when you come home.'

There was one thing she had to do before she went out that morning, and that was to telephone the number Gif Weldon had handed her the night before. It was a surprise when a masculine voice answered on the second ring with the clipped words, 'Roger Claybourne here. Can I help you?' She'd grown so used to nobody answering when she rang his number that for a moment she was lost for words.

She recovered herself quickly, however, and explained who she was and what she wanted.

He said, 'I was abrupt with you the last time you spoke to me, Miss Weldon. I apologize for telling you to go to hell. I had a lot on my mind. I was just about to go into hospital, where I've been ever since. That's why you found nobody here at the farmhouse when you called and left your note.'

'I really do need to talk to you, Mr Claybourne.'

'You'll have to come to Lincolnshire. Some things can't be talked about at a distance.'

'Oh – I was hoping you might be able to tell me over the telephone. Lincolnshire's a long way for me to come just at the moment . . .'

Her mind was buzzing with the things she had to do today. First of all there was the foreman to see at Richard's quarry, then she had to pick up some things Richard would be needing from his house. Later today, too, she wanted to spend some time with Lizzie. Lizzie was getting in a right old tizz about Uncle Gif, Amy realized. Some things would need sorting out at Wydale, because if Lizzie carried out her threat and gave up her job there things would be thrown into chaos. Roger Claybourne suggesting a meeting in Lincolnshire was one thing she hadn't expected. She'd hoped a quick phone call to him might shed some light on the Kitty mystery

She said, 'Couldn't you just tell me the name of the girl you were engaged to?'

'It's here or nowhere I'll talk to you, Miss Weldon. Take it or leave it.' He was brusque and to the point, and she knew he could just as easily slam the phone down again now, as he had done that other time, if she upset him enough.

'I'll come,' she said. 'When would it suit you to see me?'

Without a moment's hesitation, he said, 'Tomorrow. I'll expect you tomorrow. And come alone. I won't talk to you if you bring anyone else with you. Do you understand?'

Uneasy, she tried to reason with him. 'Tomorrow is a bit short notice.'

'Tomorrow or not at all. I don't have time to haggle over this. Yes or no, Miss Weldon. I need an answer now.'

'We–ell . . .'

'Five seconds. Yes or no. Five – four – three – '

'Yes! I'll come.'

'I'll be here all day. Waiting for you. Goodbye, Miss Weldon.' The phone went dead.

As she drove over to Hatton-in-the-Dale she tried to stop her mind going over and over the horrific events of the previous day, but it was hard to wipe out the thought of Richard – Richard who was usually so strong and full of life – lying helpless and unconscious on the floor of the chapel.

She was glad when she got to the quarry, where she hurried over to the hut known affectionately by Richard as 'the office' to tell the foreman, George Shipstone, what had happened.

George was an unflappable little man nearing retirement age who Richard depended on utterly. He quickly assured her that he could cope until things were back to normal. 'Give my regards – and those of the lads – to the boss, will yer, Miss Weldon?'

Happy that there was nothing that George couldn't attend to, she went back and climbed into the Land Rover, but before closing its door she called out, 'I'll do that, Mr Shipstone.'

At the hospital last night she'd realized that Richard would need some things from home, like pyjamas, shaver and toothbrush, so she drove down from the quarry and into the valley, and within minutes was drawing up outside the grey brick house where he lived. Looking at her watch, she saw it was only ten minutes to ten as she walked up the steps to the front door.

It felt strange letting herself into the place with Richard's keys. On the occasions she'd been here before it had always been as a visitor, though Richard had told her innumerable times to treat the place as her own. Now, it seemed, she was going to have to do just that. Today she wasn't here just to transfer her film cassettes onto video, though many hours had been spent in the past few months doing just that, she recalled.

She checked the rooms as she came to them – the dining room on the right, the small cloakroom and then the front sitting room on the opposite side of the hall to the dining room. This was a large but comfortable room, with its huge bay window overlooking the quiet street and plush mossy green velvet curtains hanging in luxurious drapes from ceiling to floor. This was her favourite room in Richard's house, and she stood in the doorway with a tiny smile tugging at her lips as she saw the half-dozen videos she'd made stacked on one end of the high Victorian mantelpiece.

She'd asked Richard if she could leave them there because without any means of playing them at Wydale there hadn't seemed much point in taking them back. Into those little boxes were crammed all her first impressions of England, and on a sudden impulse she walked across the room, slipped one video from its casing and, bending down, placed it in the machine. She knew which bit of film she wanted to see, and in the space of a few seconds Blackthorn Edge appeared on the television screen.

She sank to her knees in front of the television set, down onto the thick wool carpet with its muted mixture of jewel-like colours which she loved. The rest of the room was furnished plainly, but with taste. Most of the furniture was very old and heavy, and she remembered the cold winter evenings she'd spent here with Richard, when a huge coal fire had blazed in the grate adding an aura of cosiness to the warmth that was given off from ample central heating radiators all around the house.

She watched the screen as the camera panned round the steep-sided Blackthorn Valley on that day they'd started out on the drive down to Norfolk, Richard and her. Then came a close-up of the little pack-horse bridge in the very bottom of the gorge. The sheer stark beauty of the place made her catch her breath as she saw again the rugged road, twisting and turning along the knife-edge drop, until the little car park that had been her vantage point was reached.

For a few seconds the camera focused on Richard as he leaned on the dry stone wall and turned his head momentarily towards her, laughing. His words came clearly to her: 'I hope this bit is going to be edited out.' But she hadn't been able to do that – to deliberately blot him out of the picture.

And as she gazed now at his dear, dear face, and heard his voice, a lump came to her throat. She bit down hard on her bottom lip, trying without success to forget what might so easily have happened yesterday at the old chapel. The thought chilled her – Richard could so easily have been killed! And, if he had been, these images of him, imprinted on film, would have been all she had left of him. A few minutes of him laughing at her and saying, 'I hope this bit is going to be edited out . . .' and a few more scenes on the beach in Norfolk . . .

Tears sprang to her eyes. She blinked them away, telling herself not to be so morbid. But terror had clutched at her heart. He had so nearly been taken away from her. She clicked off the machine with the remote control that was gripped so tightly in her hand it was hurting. She turned and walked quickly out of the room then, forcing herself not to dwell on what might have been.

Upstairs in his bedroom, though, his presence still

lingered as she rummaged through a chest of drawers for things to take to the hospital, and the bittersweet scent of his aftershave hit her as she opened the door that led into the adjoining bathroom. Swiftly she collected what was necessary, reminded all the time of him and missing him so much.

She ran lightly down the stairs and checked the kitchen – it was cool in there; it didn't catch the sun like the rest of the house. This room and a small study overlooked the garden at the rear. Through the window she saw apple trees heavy with blossom in the small orchard at the far end of it, and the grass was dotted with yellow primroses.

She had an overwhelming longing to have him here with her. This was where she belonged. Never before had she experienced such a feeling of peace as she did in this house. A clock somewhere near struck the half-hour. She glanced at her watch again. 'Half past ten,' she muttered. They'd told her she could go and see him at any time, but after eleven the doctors would have done their rounds. She smiled to herself, picked up all the things she'd come for, and made her way to the front of the house again.

Apart from a slight paleness, Richard looked his usual self as she greeted him with a platonic hug and a kiss in the deserted dayroom of the hospital.

'I'll need to get a private room if I'm in here much longer,' he grumbled from his chair, where he was anchored to a saline drip on a cumbersome wheeled frame. 'I can't even get a proper kiss out of you.'

'It's all this glass,' she said. 'It's like living in a square goldfish tank. No privacy at all.

'And hot enough for tropical fish too.' He laughed and hung onto her hand. He was dressed in his own clothes –

shoes and socks and trousers – but with a hospital pyjama top for a shirt. 'You've no idea how ridiculous I feel dressed like this,' he said. 'If I stand up there's "Derbyshire Health Service" stencilled on the back of this thing, but they told me my shirt was almost ripped off me by Angel Gabriel.'

She perched on a small table next to him and gently touched the scar at his hairline, which had small, angry-looking stitches inserted across it. 'Your poor head,' she murmured.

'I have more embroidery over my heart.' He grimaced. 'Gabriel sure had it in for me yesterday, Amy.'

'Gabriel assisted most ably by Mark Powell,' she corrected softly.

'You haven't told the poor guy that all this is his fault, have you? It wasn't, you know.' His eyes suddenly turned bleak. 'I vowed I'd never hit anyone ever again, but when I saw him trying to kiss you . . . God, Amy, I went wild. I could see you struggling and kicking and yelling at him – and my mind snapped.'

'He wasn't hurting me,' she said. 'It's a long story, though, Richard.'

'Then sit down and tell me,' he said gently. 'For I can see from your face that something's troubling you.'

She pulled a chair up near to him and sat down, then told him all that she knew herself – that Mark Powell was Gif Weldon's son, and about Gif wanting her and Mark to be married to each other so they'd both inherit Wydale.

'And that was why he tried to rape you?'

She smiled and leaned forward to take hold of Richard's hand. 'Mark wasn't trying to rape me. Unfortunately, I mistook what he was trying to tell me. I thought Mark was destined to be Duncan Ward's replacement. Now can you

302

understand why Mark went mad at me when he knew what I was thinking?'

Richard gave a long, low whistle. 'I certainly can. He had no right to touch you, though. I can't stand the thought of any man touching you.'

'He's gone now,' she said. 'Gone back to Scotland. He said he had to go and face his mother, who, for all these years, had refused to tell Mark anything at all about his real father except his name.'

Understanding began to dawn on Richard's face. 'You told me once that his face seemed familiar, didn't you? Now I realize why that was. It was because of Barbara Weldon's portrait hanging in the hall at Wydale. He's very like his mother – especially around the eyes. I suppose Barbara didn't know how to tell the lad that his father was gay.'

Amy nodded. 'That's the conclusion I came to. Goodness knows how Barbara did become pregnant with Mark, though, because Uncle Gif's relationship with Duncan Ward goes back in time even further than his marriage to Barbara.'

'It's something we'll never know, Amy.' His eyes crinkled into a smile. 'Even if Gif was gay from the word go, I suppose there must have been some attraction between him and Barbara – or else why did he marry her?'

'I've been thinking about that.' Amy let go his hand and sat back in the chair facing him.

'And what conclusion did you come to?' he asked.

'Well, you know what a stickler for protocol Uncle Gif is – everything has to be just so. I'd think that in his younger days there'd have been his career to consider. Just remember in the nineteen-sixties and seventies if he'd been suspected of having a relationship with another man his reputation would have been lost. There would have been disgrace and discredit. He might even have been ruined financially.'

'So what you're saying is a wife gave him respectability?'

'Yes.'

'But what woman would go along with a marriage like that?'

'Perhaps Barbara didn't find out until it was too late.'

Richard looked thoughtful. 'You could be right.'

'I have a feeling I am. My guess is that Barbara just managed to get what she wanted out of the marriage – a baby – and when she knew she was pregnant she just up and left Uncle Gif.'

'And married somebody else after he divorced her.'

Sadly she said, 'I don't think the second marriage was happy either. From what Mark told me, his stepfather was unkind to him and his mother.'

'Are we likely to get any more repercussions from your Uncle Gif's flamboyant past?' Richard wanted to know.

'Heck! I hope not.' She laughed softly and leaned towards him again.

'There are no more secrets, then?' His eyes searched her face.

A little bit too quickly she answered, 'None you need worry yourself about just at the moment.'

He frowned. 'What does that mean, Amy? Is there anything else you're not telling me? Is something worrying you?'

'Hey,' she said, 'the doctor here said I was to cheer you up – not bog you down with troubles.'

'You haven't answered my question, though.'

She thought swiftly. 'Of course there are worries,' she said, knowing a denial would only make him suspect

304

something. 'There are little niggling worries about our own wedding, Richard.'

'What kind of worries – ?'

She broke in impatiently, 'Worries about whether you'll be okay. Worries about Kate and Marty coming over from America – I really want Marty beside me on my wedding day.'

'And is that a problem?'

A little white lie wouldn't hurt, she thought desperately. And it would allay any suspicion that all was not well. After leaving Richard today, she planned to drive straight to Lincolnshire – but she couldn't tell him that. If things went according to plan – her overnight stay in a hotel was already booked, and she should see Roger Claybourne first thing in the morning – she knew she could be back visiting Richard in hospital by late afternoon tomorrow and he'd never suspect a thing.

'Marty's work's important,' she said. 'It might be difficult – him coming over here at such short notice. That's my biggest worry.'

'Amy! Darling, darling Amy!' He held out a hand to her. 'Come here, and let me kiss you. You shouldn't have to carry the weight of this wedding on your shoulders. Heck, love, if Marty can't get over then we'll change the date. There's no problem!'

She pushed herself out of her chair, went over to him and wrapped her arms round him – careful, though, not to hurt his shoulder. 'I love you,' she whispered as she bent and kissed his upturned face. 'Richard Boden, I love you so very, very much.'

Lizzie Abercrombie stared at her in open-mouthed horror. 'You're doing what?'

'I'm driving into Lincolnshire. It's not far, for God's sake.'

'It's more than a hundred miles, girl. Are you out of your mind? And what does Richard say about it?'

'He doesn't know and he's not going to know.' Amy dropped her overnight suitcase on the floor at the bottom of the stairs and faced the wrath of her uncle's housekeeper without letting any hint of the trepidation she was feeling herself show in her face.

Lizzie's angular arms stuck out as she planted her hands on her hips and said, 'I'm not going to let you go. You're crazy, girl. Plain crazy. This bug to find Kip Weldon's kid is turning your brain. You know that, don't you?'

Steadily, Amy said, 'Look here, Lizzie, Kate and Marty are coming over from the States for my wedding. I owe it to them to give them some news of Kitty. This man – this Roger Claybourne – he knows her real name. He was once engaged to be married to her. Can't you understand? I've just got to go and talk to him.'

'Oh, yeah! If it's only talk you're interested in, why didn't you talk on the telephone?'

'He wouldn't. He said I had to go there – and, Lizzie, I've got to go. I promised Kate I'd find Kitty, and this is the only way I can do it. Hell's bells, don't you think I feel bad enough – getting married to Richard and not going back to the States to live? I promised Kate when I left Boston that I'd go back. I never imagined I'd finish up staying over here. The least I can do now is put her in touch with Kitty – Kitty and the baby – if there *is* a baby – a little grandchild for Kate and Marty.'

'I don't like it. There's something fishy! Why wouldn't he talk to you on the phone? Why do you have to go all that way?'

Amy sighed, walked over to Lizzie and got hold of her belligerent arms and shook her hard. 'Lizzie Abercrombie – you ask too many questions that I don't know the answers to. All I know is I've got to see Roger Claybourne. I've booked myself a room at Lynn – that's the nearest big place to Claybourne's farm at Halfpenny End. Tomorrow morning I'll go see him, bright and early. That way I can be back here by around two in the afternoon, and Richard won't need to know a thing about it.'

'But *I* know – and it worries me! I could come with you, I suppose . . .'

'No. This Claybourne guy said I had to go alone.'

Lizzie shuddered. 'Creepy!'

'It'll be broad daylight when I go to see him. And I've got Richard's mobile phone with me.' She let go of Lizzie and patted the back pocket of her jeans.

Lizzie said, 'What'll I tell your Uncle Gif?'

'He won't even notice I'm missing. There's no need to tell anybody anything.'

'And if Richard phones from the hospital?'

'Lizzie! Use your imagination.' Amy was impatient to get on her way. She didn't want all these questions. She was more than a little apprehensive about meeting Roger Claybourne, and Lizzie wasn't helping matters by her concern.

'Tell him a lie, you mean.'

'No. Not exactly. Look – the sooner I get off, the sooner I'll be back.' She stared in a deliberate manner at her wristwatch. 'And it's nearly half past three now.'

'Phone me when you get there.' Lizzie's gaunt features were puckered into lines of anxiety.

Amy smiled and immediately regretted her stand

against the housekeeper. Lizzie was, she knew, only concerned for her.

'Of course I will, Lizzie,' she promised. 'And I'll be back before you even notice I'm gone.'

CHAPTER 23

Mark Powell replaced the handset of his mother's telephone and sat staring grimly into space until he felt a hand on his shoulder and looked up.

'Is the man all right, son?'

He nodded. 'Yes. I talked to the housekeeper at Wydale. It's obvious she blames me for what happened. I was a fool, Mum. I shouldn't have fought with him . . .'

'If it's anybody's fault it's mine.' Barbara Powell – once Weldon – gave a great sigh and limped away to stare out of the window of her small bungalow.

He got to his feet wearily. 'Don't say that. Of course it isn't your fault. You weren't to know I was intent on finding out who my real dad was.'

She turned back to him. 'You couldn't be blamed for wanting to know – neither of us have any fond memories of Derek Powell, do we?'

'No, Mum. You didn't deserve the life he led you.'

'I ought to have realized, though, that you'd one day want to know more about Gif Weldon.' She lifted her hands in a passive kind of gesture. 'But I was too embarrassed to talk to you about him. Y'do understand that, don't you, Mark?'

'Aye, Mum. I do now. Nobody would want to admit to

309

being taken in by the scoundrel the way you were.'

She shook her head. 'No! It wasn't that. I behaved no better than a whore, son. I wanted a baby so bad. And I felt cheated. But now you know the truth. And people have been hurt because of me . . .'

'Not people, Mum. One man.' He slapped one hard hand against his forehead. 'God knows what came over me. But when that girl . . .'

'Amy Weldon?'

He nodded. 'When she started hinting that I might be taking the place of the old man's lover . . .' He swallowed painfully. 'Mum! I felt sickened by everything at Wydale. None of it mattered to me any more and yet when I first went there I was determined to get it all for you – the house *and* the old man's money. Except that I found out there was none of that to get. Amy's marrying that Boden fellow because he can put the old Hall to rights again. Mum, I can't stand it – seeing the way Gif Weldon's manipulating all those people.'

'He manipulated me too, Mark. Don't forget that, will you?'

'I don't forget it. I'll never forget it – or forgive him.'

'I think you should. Amy Weldon sounds a nice girl. I think she would want you to. She must have had just as great a shock as you did when she found out the truth about her uncle – *and* about you being his son,' she said with emphasis.

'Maybe so.'

'So what's worrying you?'

'Something that damned housekeeper said. Something about Amy going to Lincolnshire.'

'For a holiday?' Barbara Weldon made her way slowly over to the table and sat down with a grimace of pain.

310

'Mum – is that arthritis bad again?'

'No more than usual.' She managed a smile. 'Put the kettle on, will you, love?'

He went through to the kitchen and did as she asked, bringing two blue pottery mugs back with him, and balancing a jug of milk as well. He placed them on the table and said, 'I put two spoons of tea in the teapot through there, is that okay?'

'Aye,' she said, 'that's fine. It won't take the kettle long to come to the boil.'

He looked down on the woman and said, 'It wasn't greed that made me go and find Gif Weldon, you know.'

'Oh, I know that.' She nodded and glanced up at him.

He crouched down in front of her and took hold of her hands. 'Wydale is rightfully mine. Mine and yours. More yours than mine, actually.'

She chuckled softly. 'You're getting in a right old pickle, aren't you? What would I do with a barn of a place like that?'

'Sell it,' he snapped. 'That's all its good for. And he owes it to you to make some sort of amends.'

'No, lad.' She shook her head. 'Gif Weldon owes me nothing. He threw me a lifeline when my folks died and I was left destitute, so I can't hate him completely. I just wish he'd been honest with me. I'd have gone to Wydale, but not as his wife. He wanted a housekeeper but felt obliged to offer me marriage. He's not really a bad man, Mark.'

'He's selfish and tyrannical. He married you because he thought it would give him respectability to have a wife.'

'But there's some good in him. No man is completely bad.'

'He uses people . . .'

311

'Oh, is that all?' She gave a high little laugh. 'Haven't we all at some time *used* somebody?'

He scowled and stood up. 'Mum, I have to make a phone call.'

'Go ahead, son. You're the one who pays the bills around here. You don't have to ask my permission.'

'It's to London. To Catherine.'

'I like the sound of your Catherine. Bring her to see me one day.' Barbara Weldon heard the sound of the kettle boiling in the next room and struggled to her feet again.

'Mum – I can do that . . .'

She waved him aside. 'You stay here and speak to Catherine,' she said. 'I'm perfectly capable of making a cup of tea.'

Catherine Blake's concern was genuine. 'Amy Weldon *can't* have gone looking for Roger Claybourne,' she said. 'Just tell me, Mark. What exactly did Mrs Abercrombie say to you?'

'Well, I rang to speak to Amy – to ask her how her fiancé was feeling now he's out of danger at the hospital. The housekeeper said Amy had set off this afternoon for Lincolnshire – on her own.'

'But it might not mean anything. Surely she can't know about Roger and me?'

'Why else would she go there? Catherine, I've done enough damage to that girl. I wouldn't like to think she's walking into trouble – and from what you told me about Roger Claybourne she could well be doing that.'

'He's evil.' Catherine felt a cold chill creeping over her even as she spoke. 'He tried to kill me, Mark.'

'Perhaps Amy Weldon won't try to find out about you from him.'

'You're saying that, but you think otherwise, don't you? That's why you've rung me, isn't it?'

'Hell! I don't know. There's nothing we can do, is there? But she's such a determined brat. Once she gets a bee in her bonnet there's no stopping her.'

'So what do you suggest?' Catherine asked.

'We could follow her.'

'Talk sense, Mark. You're in Scotland – I'm in London. And Amy Weldon must be halfway to Lincolnshire by now.'

'We can't just sit back and wait for him to beat her up the way he did you.'

'He beat me up because I'd broken off our engagement. He doesn't have any reason to harm Amy,' Catherine said in a practical tone.

'You're right, of course. Maybe we should just do nothing.'

'Yes. I think that would be best.' Catherine's mind, however, was working overtime. She knew from experience what Roger Claybourne was capable of. That was why she'd moved away from the area where he lived. Oh, he could be charming, she knew. But that charm was all an act.

Mark Powell was speaking again. 'I'll tell you what I'll do, Catherine. I'll telephone the housekeeper at Wydale again tomorrow. She said she was expecting Amy back by mid-afternoon then. If Amy *is* home, then we have nothing to worry about. But if not . . .'

'Yes,' Catherine said absently, 'if she's not back, that's the time to start worrying.'

When Mark had rung off, she sat back in her chair and watched Kim playing with a set of building bricks on the rug in front of her. Her words to Mark had been designed

313

to put his mind at rest and keep him safely in Scotland. But in her heart she knew she couldn't ignore the facts herself.

Amy Weldon had advertised high and low for 'Kitty' to contact her. And 'Kitty' – up till now – had ignored her pleas. Now, however, Catherine knew she had to act – and fast. Amy could be in deep trouble if she didn't, she realized. Just the mention of Kip Weldon's name had at one time been enough to unleash all the demons of hell in Roger Claybourne's mind.

Catherine heard a key being turned in the lock of the flat, and sprang to her feet. Her sister was home. There was no time to be lost. Sue could always be relied upon to do a spot of babysitting!

The day was perfect for driving, and a complete contrast, Amy thought, to the last time she'd been in Lincolnshire, when it had rained all the way home. It was early evening and the sun was low in the western sky behind her now. Hedgerows were snowy white with May blossom, and the air was heavily scented with it. It would be nice, she mused, to be married to Richard right at this moment and be driving off on honeymoon with him to some secluded spot.

But August wasn't far off, and for Kate and Marty to be at her wedding had meant giving them fair warning to come all that way across the Atlantic. It would be worth the wait, she reasoned, if it gave her that little extra time she needed in order to trace the elusive Kitty. And she knew now that she was on the right track. Kitty had been Roger Claybourne's girlfriend – his fiancée. And now Roger Claybourne had had some miraculous change of heart and had agreed to talk to her. Amy felt her spirits lifting. And in two or three days' time Richard would be out of hospital. Everything, she decided, was going her way – at last!

She arrived at the hotel around half past seven, rang Lizzie and told her she'd arrived safely, and by nine she was in bed.

Tomorrow was going to be hectic.

At Wydale the phone rang again, just as Lizzie was going up to her bedroom.

She hurried across the hall, muttering, 'Who on earth can that be?' And the grandfather clock struck ten as she picked up the receiver.

'Hello, Lizzie. Is Amy there?'

Lizzie's legs all but buckled beneath her. 'Richard Boden?'

'Of course. Don't you recognize my voice tonight?'

'She's not here.' Lizzie's mind started working over-time. He'd want to know where Amy was. So why had she gone and said that. Why hadn't she told him the girl was asleep in bed?

'Not there?'

Lizzie cleared her throat, playing for time while she tried to think up a lie that wasn't exactly a lie. 'Nope, 'fraid not. You're out of luck. How're you feeling, Richard? Better, I hope. Have they been giving you a rough time in there?'

'Stop stalling, Lizzie. What's going on? Where's Amy?'

'Er . . . out!'

'Out?'

'Yes.'

'Is it too much to ask where?'

'Er . . . some hotel. Probably having a meal by now.'

315

'Alone?'

'That I don't know.' Lizzie beamed into the phone. At least that wasn't a lie.

She heard him sigh on the other end of the line. 'Oh, well, I'll have to leave her a message, then.'

'Yes. That might be a good idea.' Lizzie began to breathe normally again.

'Will you tell her I'm being let out of here tomorrow and can she come and fetch me? They've had some sort of rush on tonight and they need the bed. They don't have any emergency ones left, and as I'm more or less back to normal now they're chucking me out.'

Faintly, Lizzie croaked, 'Out? Out of hospital?'

'Ten o'clock in the morning. And I can't wait to get home. You'll pass the message on, will you, Lizzie?'

'Oh, yeah! I'll pass it on – no problem there.'

'Thanks, Lizzie.' He sounded vaguely worried. 'You're sure Amy's okay? It is getting rather late for her to be out.'

'Sure. She's okay.' Lizzie was beginning to panic inwardly. All she wanted was for him to get off the phone so she could ring Amy and give her the news that in other circumstances the girl would have been delighted to hear.

When he'd rung off, she stood for several minutes just listening to the grandfather clock ticking away in the corner. Then, with a huge sigh, she began dialling the number of Richard's mobile telephone.

Amy woke with a start as soon as the phone bleeped, and continued bleeping. She shot up in bed and snatched it up from the bedside cabinet, her heart beginning to race. Surely no one would be ringing her from Wydale at this time of night unless it were an emergency. 'Richard . . . Oh, Richard . . . Please don't let it be bad news about

Richard,' she babbled almost incoherently as, all thumbs, she tried in the dark to get the phone the right way up.

'Lizzie!' She almost shrieked the woman's name as she heard the all too familiar voice coming over to her.

'Hey. Just listen here, will you? He's coming home tomorrow. Just phoned me and I had to lie – yes, *lie* madam – for you. What the heck could I tell him? I ask you – would you do the same for me, I wonder? And now it's landed us all in a mess. And all because you took it into your head to do a midnight flit to God knows where. Are you listening? 'Cause you should be. You can just get right back here and do your own explaining, girl, because *I* am definitely not going to be around at ten o'clock tomorrow morning. Count me out. O – U – T! Understand?'

'Lizzie! What are you going on about?'

'Richard Boden, that's what I'm going on about. I knew no good would come of you going off like that. You know the old quote, "O, what a tangled web we weave, When first we practise to deceive . . ."? Well, I'm through with covering up for you. You just get back here before morning, that's all I have to say to you, girl.'

'I can't, Lizzie – not now I'm so near to learning the truth about Kitty.'

'*Can't!*' Lizzie screamed into the phone.

'Calm down. Now, tell me, why is Richard being discharged early from hospital?'

'Some emergency. No beds.'

'Okay. Now, keep calm and listen to me.' Amy's mind was working on a solution. 'Get John Graham to fetch Richard from the hospital, Lizzie.'

'And what do I tell Richard, Eh, girl? Tell me that, will you?'

'I'll ring him at home. What time did you say he's due out?'

'Ten!' Lizzie's reply was surly. Amy could imagine a belligerent hand being stuck on her hip and her elbow sticking out at an angle.

'Look – I'd ring Richard tonight, except it's too late now. But don't worry, Lizzie. I'll phone him at ten-thirty sharp at home tomorrow morning, I promise. Just get John Graham to have him home by then. You won't have any explaining to do – honest you won't.'

'*You'll* have explaining aplenty to do, madam!' Lizzie snapped.

Amy grinned. 'I'll take my chances. Richard will understand. He won't be angry.'

'He'll be wild. If he knew where you were now, he'd be out of his mind with worry – just like I am.'

'I'm a big girl, Lizzie. I crossed the Atlantic all by myself. Remember?'

'I don't want none of your lip, my girl. I'm going to bed. And you – well, you just get yourself home as quick as you can. Understand?'

'Yes, Lizzie,' Amy replied meekly, and then said, 'Goodnight!'

The phone went dead and Amy replaced it on the bedside cabinet again, smiling to herself in the darkness. Richard was coming home. And in less than twenty-four hours she'd have him all to herself again. Everything was starting to work out just the way it should. She snuggled down in bed and yawned. It had been a long day. But tomorrow was going to be a *good* day – of that she was convinced!

318

CHAPTER 24

Halfpenny End didn't look quite so bad as it had done in pouring rain the last time she'd seen it, Amy thought as she crawled the Land Rover round the winding one-track lane between the fields of cabbages. The house still looked abandoned, though; there was no sign of life as she approached it – not even a wisp of smoke escaped from its tall chimneys.

She turned off onto the even narrower track that led up to the house and pulled the Land Rover up near the front door. As she slid out of the driver's seat and down onto to the ground she saw that the little rose bush had been neatly pruned and some of the weeds had been cleared out from around it. It still looked deprived of nourishment, however, and as if it were struggling to survive in the patch of hard ground up close to the foundations of the house.

She stood looking down at it and hitched her leather shoulder-bag into a more comfortable position. A watery sun was coming up from the east directly behind the house. It was early – not yet nine o'clock – and she hoped Roger Claybourne was up and about and not still in bed. She ought to have telephoned him first, she supposed, especially as he'd told her on the phone that he'd been ill. But he *had* said he'd be there all day – waiting for her.

She shivered slightly as a cool breeze swept across the wide open never-ending landscape that was inhabited only by cabbage plants. How could anyone exist in this wilderness? she wondered. With just cabbages for company. She turned round and looked back in the direction she'd come. About a mile away across the fields she could just glimpse the odd car travelling along the one major road that led from West Norfolk to Lincolnshire.

That breeze was getting stronger, she realized, and she began to feel the cold on her bare arms. When she'd left the hotel in Lynn it had been a warm, balmy morning, and she'd just pulled on an easy-fitting short-sleeved shirt with her jeans and pushed her heavier sweater into her overnight bag. Well, it might be warmer inside the house. She swung round to it again, then took the few steps needed to reach the front door under the still creaking porch. She knocked hard on the flaking paintwork, and after a few seconds had elapsed heard a shuffling inside the house. She held her breath and listened, eager now to meet Roger Claybourne and finally clear up the mystery of Kitty. The door opened a few inches as somebody peeped out, then it opened wider and she was instantly shocked at how ill the man looked.

His drab brown shirt hung on him as if originally it had been made for a much larger man. Over the top of it he wore an equally big grey cardigan. His trousers were baggy and his feet were encased in grimy carpet slippers. He was tall, but stooped, and his eyes were grey and lifeless. At least, she thought, he must have been telling the truth when he'd said he'd spent some time in hospital. To her mind, he ought to be still there.

'Mr Claybourne?' she asked. 'I'm Amy Weldon. I hope I haven't arrived too early.'

He pulled the wool cardigan more closely around his thin skeleton of a body and said in a whining kind of voice, 'No. No. You're not too early. I get up at six every morning. Habit, I suppose, from the days when I was active and managed all this –' one arm swept a wide semi-circle, taking in the cabbage fields ' – on my own. But come along in. I can't stand the cold.'

He pulled the door wide and she saw he was shivering. She couldn't imagine any harm befalling her from such a broken, pathetic creature as he was, so she stepped inside the house and followed his shuffling footsteps down a narrow, dusty corridor, past two or three depressingly dirty doors and to a kitchen at the far end.

The heat in there was intense. It came from a small electric fire standing on a raised red quarry tiled hearth. All three bars of the fire were switched on and the odour of sour milk, rancid cooking fat and staleness hit her as soon as she walked through the door.

Queasiness had, in the last few days, become a way of life for her. Even Lizzie's tea brewing in the pot every morning had more than once had her turning round and racing back upstairs when she'd been on her way down to breakfast. In her bedroom she'd had to steady herself, then throw open the window and take several deep gulps of fresh air before venturing down to the kitchen again. She'd heard a lot about morning sickness in pregnancy, but had never before believed how debilitating it could be. She couldn't even face some of her favourite foods these days, let alone the permeating stench of Roger Claybourne's kitchen.

Her stomach was churning. He seemed not to notice her discomfort, however, and motioned her to sit down in a chair near the fire. She shook her head and made for a

corner near the door, which was farthest away from the
heat and the scraps of unappetizing food still left on the
table. He must have been having his breakfast when she'd
arrived, she thought, for a plate on the table held greasy
bacon rind and a mess of runny egg and fried bread. A
haze of smoke still hovered above a gas cooker beside the
window, and a blackened frying pan told its own tale.

'I'll sit here, if you don't mind. I'm not used to such a
warm room.'

'Warm?' His pale face screwed up as if in pain. 'I don't
find it warm. I shall be glad when summer's here again.
That bloody fire costs the earth to run.'

She managed a smile of sorts. 'I don't want to take up
much of your time, Mr Claybourne – '

He broke in impatiently, 'You're not thinking of running away as soon as you arrive, are you? I thought you
wanted a good long talk. That's why you've come all this
way to see me, isn't it?'

Uneasily she nodded. 'I do have to get back rather
quickly. My fiancé has had an accident, you see, and – '

'Why do you want to know about Kitty?' He'd
shuffled round in front of her and was staring intently
at her as he hugged the grey cardigan to his emaciated
body again.

Honesty was the best way round a tricky situation, she
decided. 'Kitty was a friend of my brother,' she said. 'He
sent letters home to America telling us about her, but all
we knew was the name Kitty.'

'How touching,' he sneered.

'Mr Claybourne – you were there on the night Kip
Weldon died, weren't you?' She looked up at him and
suddenly felt sorry for him. It couldn't be easy, her
rubbing salt in his wounds, however old they were

322

now. He had once cared deeply for Kitty, she reasoned, and now she was raking up the past and obviously bringing back all the hurt for him.

His eyes narrowed. He said, 'I heard on a local news bulletin that an army vehicle had gone into the river. I took the tractor to see if I could help, but it was too late by the time I got there. They'd recovered all the bodies but one. I never dreamed *he* was the one who was missing.'

'How could you have been expected to know?' she said softly.

'I could have got her back if it hadn't been for him. Kitty thought I didn't know what was going on, but I'm not a fool.'

His eyes burned fiercely in the white face, giving him a slightly vampirish look. He must have been quite good-looking at one time, Amy thought, for he had a good strong jawline, a high forehead and widely spaced eyes. His dark hair was now lank and thinning, but if those things he was wearing had at one time been a good fit, he'd have had much the same kind of physique as Richard – tall, wide-shouldered, with narrow hips and a tremendous strength in his arms and legs.

He gave a long sigh, then walked over to a dresser at the back of the room, which she'd scarcely noticed before. On its surface was a framed and faded black and white photograph of two elderly people – a man and a wo-man. As he moved slightly she saw a dusty white artificial rose lying in front of the picture. Her mind clicked into action. A rose bush beside the front door and a white plastic rose in front of a photograph. It was eerie.

He pulled open a drawer and took out a shabby photo-graph album and carried it to the table. Pushing aside his

323

breakfast things, he opened it and began looking for something. The album was upside down to Amy, so she couldn't see the small pictures easily at all.

'Ah! This is it.' He slipped one photograph out from its page, where it had been held down by four corner pieces. He came back across the room to her and held it out to her. 'This is me five years ago. I didn't look like I do now.' His mouth tilted down at its corners as she took the photograph from him and stared at it.

As she'd imagined, he'd been good-looking – handsome, even. The coloured photo showed him standing on a beach in swimming trunks. His tanned and healthy body had been one to be envied, she saw. There was laughter in his eyes, but a haughty expression marred the features. Yes. He'd been a good-looker – and he'd known it.

'Nice,' she said, handing it back to him.

'Kitty took the snap,' he said. 'It was when we were together. Before *he* came on the scene.'

'He?' she asked pointedly, knowing full well who he meant.

'Kip Weldon! The man who ruined my life.'

'I'm sorry you were hurt.' It seemed a contrite and silly thing to say, really, but she'd seen the pain flare in his eyes and remembered the heartache she herself had suffered when Kip had been reported missing. She knew what it was like to lose somebody.

He stared at her for several seconds before saying, 'I'm sorry he was your brother. You seem too nice to be anything like him.'

'Kip was nice too,' she said, springing to the defence of Kip, who was unable to defend himself now.

'He ruined my life. But I think I just told you that, didn't I?' He went back to the table and slipped the

324

photograph back into the album, which he then closed and carried back to the dresser.

'Do you have a photograph of Kitty?' she asked eagerly, rising from her seat and almost leaping across to the dresser. Without thinking, she flung out a hand and rested it on the album he was holding. 'Could I have a look, do you think?' Her eyes flew up to meet his. 'I – I like looking at old photos,' she finished lamely.

'She's not in here.' He shrugged her hand off the book and put it away in the drawer again. As he closed the drawer, his gaze fell on the black and white framed photo on the dresser. 'This is old,' he said, picking it up and giving it to her. 'It's my mother and father before they died.'

She stared at the picture. 'You're very like your father,' she said, handing it back to him.

He shook his head as he replaced it on the dresser. 'No,' he said, 'I'm nothing like him.'

'In looks, I meant.' She tilted her head on one side to try and read the expression on his face as he stared down at the photograph, but it was unfathomable. He picked up the white plastic rose, looked at it, shook some of the dust off it and said, 'He was an undertaker. He had this thing about white roses.'

'Oh?' Amy felt as if cold water was trickling down her spine. She didn't think she wanted to ask why Roger Claybourne's father had had a 'thing' about white roses.

He was going to tell her anyway. There was a slightly devilish twinkle in his eyes as he turned to her again. 'That was my job,' he said.

'Your . . . job?' she asked faintly.

'Putting the white rose on the breast of the corpse in the coffin when the grieving relatives were coming to pay their last respects.'

Amy's stomach gave another lurch.

He looked amused at her discomfort, which must have shown in her face. 'I must only have been five or six years old when I started helping Daddy in the funeral parlour,' he said. 'That was when I was put in charge of the white rose.'

She sat down again. He was trying to shock her; that much was obvious. She couldn't think of anything to say so she kept quiet.

'We only had one white rose, and this is it. The very rose that has rested next to hundreds of hearts that have stopped their beating.'

Weakly she asked, 'Did Kitty know about the rose?'

His laugh was high. 'I used to tease her with it. I once pushed it into her hair – her gorgeous, silky soft brown hair.'

Keeping her voice as even as she knew how, Amy said, 'That was a rotten thing to do to somebody you professed to love.'

'It was a rotten thing they did to me – making a kid of that age look at dead bodies day after day.'

Amy began to wish she had never come. 'Do you intend telling me Kitty's name?' she asked sharply. 'Because, if not, I see no reason for me staying any longer.' She got to her feet again and faced him.

He toyed with the rose a moment longer, then flung it back onto the dresser. 'It became a habit,' he said, 'placing a rose beside a dead person. Mother and Father were cremated, though, so all I have is the photo – not a grave.'

'You should have burned the rose,' she said. 'It's only served to lumber you with unhappy memories.'

'That's all I have left anyway. Unhappy memories.' He walked away from her and sat down beside the electric fire.

326

He looked across the room at her then, and said, 'And there's nothing else for me now. Just memories.'

'I'm sorry.' She stood stiffly against the door, watching him – and not trusting him an inch. There was more to come, she was sure. He had a captive audience and he was making the most of it. She began to feel just a tiny bit afraid of him.

'I only have a few months to live,' he said.

The room suddenly whirled around her. 'God!' she muttered, and sat down again, her hands flying to her head and her shoulder-bag slipping down onto the floor at her feet. When the spinning had stopped, she saw he was watching her.

'Are you okay?' he asked.

She nodded. 'I'm okay. You gave me a shock.'

'I have cancer,' he said. 'That's why I wasn't here when you called before.' His voice was uncannily matter-of-fact, considering the enormity of the news he'd just imparted. She had the feeling he accepted his condition without question. Welcomed it, almost, as if it were something he had a right to – cancer!

'I'm sorry . . .' The heat from the fire was getting too much for her. She felt sick and dizzy. She wanted to get away from here. She'd learned nothing – but the thought had crossed her mind that she might be holed up here with a psychopath, and that worried her.

'Liver and lungs,' he said, almost as if he were making casual conversation. 'They say I drank too much and smoked too much, and now I'm paying the price.'

Again she muttered, 'I'm sorry – I really am sorry.'

'You don't care,' he said. 'So don't pretend.'

'Maybe we should talk about something else.'

'Kitty?' he asked in amusement.

'Yes. That is, after all, why I came here.'

'What are you going to do when you know her name?'

'I'd like to meet her.'

He shot one word at her. 'Why?'

'Because I'd like to meet the girl my brother was going to marry,' she replied.

'I nearly killed her once, you know,' he said.

In a flash, she remembered Jane Weaver telling her that Roger Claybourne had attacked Kitty, that he had only narrowly escaped a prison sentence. She closed her eyes and cursed herself for not having the sense to do what she'd done before – check out local newspapers, local records. It would have been so easy, and it might have avoided this meeting with Claybourne in person.

At the time, though, there had been other things on her mind, she remembered. Richard had rescued those children from the sea, and afterwards . . . This wasn't the time to start thinking along those lines, though, she thought, with a rush of colour staining her cheeks. And then there had been the phone call from Lizzie to say that Uncle Gif had suffered a heart-attack. Really, it was no wonder she'd forgotten that one little snippet of information from Jane Weaver which could have saved so much trouble.

But it wasn't too late, she told herself. There was still time to go to the local records library – even today, before she returned home, if she hurried. Roger Claybourne was playing a game of cat and mouse with her, she realized. She doubted whether he had ever intended giving her Kitty's name. She grabbed for her bag and stood up quickly, and the room starting swaying again. 'I have to go,' she said. 'I'm sorry for taking up your time, Mr Claybourne, but I can't stay any longer.'

'No!' He was up out of his chair and across the room

328

before she knew what was happening. He planted himself between her and the door to the long corridor that led to the front door. There was another door, though, one leading to the outside from the kitchen, and she ran to the opposite side of the room and snatched at the handle.

She heard a soft laugh behind her. 'It's locked,' he said.

She spun round to him. 'Open it,' she demanded. 'You can't keep me here against my will.'

'You wouldn't be the first,' he said. 'Kitty knows what it's like.'

She leaned back against the door, feeling incredibly ill and cursing herself again – this time for coming here in the throes of morning sickness.

'I don't know what you're getting at,' she said, 'but I'd advise you to unlock this door, Mr Claybourne.'

'The last one locked in here never regained consciousness.' His voice was silkily sweet. 'A pity, that. I wanted to make him suffer.'

Her mind whirled. 'Him?' she asked, with weakness blanketing her mind.

'You might as well know. It was Kip Weldon,' he said. 'I found him that night – face-down in the river, two miles from the spot where he went in. I dragged him out with a tree branch. Brought him here.'

'Kip?' Her heart leapt. 'Kip? Here?' She stared at him, wide-eyed and terrified.

He nodded slowly, then began to laugh, softly at first, then the tone rose higher and higher until the sound chilled her soul. Her hopes had been raised, but now reason began to take over. Kip couldn't be here. There was nowhere he *could* be. If he were upstairs there'd have been some sound – especially if Kip had heard her voice. There were the outbuildings, of course, but she ruled them out instantly. They were ramshackle buildings with no windows and broken doors.

Then she remembered what Roger Claybourne had said – 'The last one locked in here never regained consciousness . . .' And for some reason she thought of the stunted white rose bush planted against the front door, struggling for survival, a pitiful thing, half-dead.

'Kip . . .' she whimpered, suddenly not wanting to know what had in fact happened in this house two long years ago, and regretting the impulse that had driven her to put her own life in danger by coming here.

'It's no use calling for Kip,' Roger Claybourne said, moving away from the door, obviously knowing she wasn't going to run anywhere now. 'Kip's dead.'

Her head shot up. 'You murdered him.'

'He wasn't worth murdering. There was hardly any life left in him. All I had to do was wait.'

She was crying helplessly now, and in the absence of a chair to support her sank down onto the floor, her head in her hands.

'I was scared they'd find out at first,' she heard him say. 'But it really doesn't matter any more. I won't be around to face the consequences, you see. I'll be dead before they can bring me to trial. Not that there'll be a trial. I told you, all I had to do was wait for him to die, and that's what he did – a couple of hours after I brought him here.'

'You monster . . .' she sobbed.

He walked back to the fire and sat down with his back to her. 'You wanted to know Kitty's name,' he said.

'I can find out without your help.' She jerked her head up again and stared at the back of his head. He was rocking backwards and forwards slowly on the chair.

'I might as well save you the trouble,' he said. 'Her name wasn't really Kitty – that was just what she liked to be called. Catherine was her real name. Catherine Blake! Are you satisfied now, Miss Amy Weldon?'

CHAPTER 25

Catherine Blake's face held grim determination as she headed off the Al and out towards Peterborough, skirting the large town at its early morning rush hour and then veering off towards Spalding. It was a road she knew well, having lived in the area for most of her life until the last two years.

She'd have been living there still, she supposed, if it hadn't been for Roger Claybourne and his overwhelming obsession with her. After the attack he'd made on her, however, she'd realized she would never be safe so long as she was within reach of him. And after Kim was born she'd moved down to London with her sister, and Sue had found a niche for her at *Diary*.

This flat, fertile country, however, would always be home to her. And she was glad she still had Aunt Mary and the cousins to come back to now and then, even if only to let little Kim know she had some roots – a family who cared about her. London might be their home now – hers and Kim's, and her sister Sue's too – but Catherine loved the space and the freedom that Lincolnshire offered. It was natural, she knew, to think longingly about the place where she'd been born and brought up, but while ever Roger Claybourne was there she realized she could never return permanently, no matter how much she'd have liked to.

The signpost pointed to Halfpenny End, but she had no need of road signs. She knew the place too well. The twisting, turning little road up to the farmhouse held no terrors for her, despite there being a wide and deep water dyke on one side of it and a rutted cabbage field on the other. The house, when she saw it, didn't look any different from how it had when she'd seen it last. As she drew nearer she saw that its woodwork still needed a coat of paint, and the brickwork hadn't been repaired in years. She pulled up alongside the only other vehicle outside the house.

'Wow!' she breathed. 'A nice new Discovery – just what I'd like to lay *my* hands on.' Roger must be doing well out of his cabbages, she mused, never dreaming for a moment that the Land Rover could belong to anybody else.

She'd set out deliberately early in order to arrive at Halfpenny End before Amy did. She looked at her watch. It was just after ten. She wondered how long she'd have to wait, because not for anybody or anything was she going to get out of her car until the other girl arrived. Roger Claybourne wasn't going to get the chance to start knocking her about again, of that she was determined.

She sat and waited, gazing round the place and noting its air of decay and dilapidation, thinking vaguely that something was different. But what? She twisted round in her seat and looked at the outhouses, frowning at them. They were as they'd always been, so it must be the house that had changed in some way. She stared hard at the front door and its rickety porch. Her eyes swept up to the roof and the chimneys, then down again, examining each window, the door again, the hatch to the cellar . . .

She drew in her breath. 'The wooden hatch! Gone!' But it had always been there, just above ground level under the left-hand side window. She peered closely at the brick-work. It wasn't new. The mortar between the bricks did look cleaner than the rest, though. He'd bricked up the old cellar and used old chipped bricks so it wouldn't be obvious. She wondered why he'd done it. The cellar had been used to store coal and apples, and wood for the fires. The hatch had been the only way into it – though there had been a boarded-up door that had once allowed access from the pantry . . .

And then she saw the tiny stunted rose bush and a cry broke from her lips. 'No!' It would be white. She knew it would be white, even though there wasn't even a bud showing yet. Roger hated flowers. There was no way on earth he would plant flowers outside his front door, unless . . . 'Oh, God, no. Not the girl. Not Amy Weldon.'

Fear leapt in her throat. From this distance she couldn't see if the soil had been disturbed recently or not – and she didn't dare get out of the car to find out. She started up the engine, reversed quickly and shot off down the lane. There must be a telephone box somewhere – and yet she couldn't remember seeing one. This time Roger had gone too far. Murder was something she couldn't turn her back on.

She wished now she hadn't let him off the hook for the beating he'd given her – wished in vain that she'd agreed to give evidence against him. But she'd been scared of his temper and his threats. And the case had been dropped.

She drove as if the devil were after her, swerving all over the little lane in her hurry to get to a call box and ring the police. In her haste, she shot out onto the main road whilst still twisting round to look behind her. A screeching of brakes had her sobbing under her breath and hanging onto the wheel of her car as her own brakes locked and slithered her sideways across the road.

The other car was large and white. It mounted the grass verge and came to a halt halfway up a grassy bank. Her own car was stationary now, and she pulled the handbrake on, then wrenched at the door handle. She ran back across the road to the other car. Two uniformed figures were getting out – a man and a woman. She saw then that the car had a red stripe down its side and a 'POLICE' sign on top.

Amy's tears had dried when he brought her a cup of tea and sat down facing her on the floor, holding it out to her.

'Drink it,' he said. 'You've had one hell of a shock.'

'You can't keep me here,' she said, looking at him and ignoring the outstretched hand.

'I've no intention of keeping you here. You're free to go any time you wish.'

'Like right now?'

'If that's what you want. Yes.'

'You do realize I'll go straight to the police?'

He nodded, and smiled a tight little smile. 'I'll be glad to get it all out in the open. At least my conscience will be clear.'

'Where is he?' she asked. 'Where is Kip?'

'You know where he is,' he said. 'You don't need to ask, do you?'

'You buried him? Under the rose bush?' All emotion was drained from her now. In a strange kind of way it was a relief, knowing what had happened to Kip. Always at the back of her mind had been the hope that he would turn up alive and well somewhere. And she hadn't been able to let go of him until she knew for certain he was dead.

He shook his head. 'Not exactly. He's in the cellar

behind the rose bush. It was the nearest I could get the damn thing to him.'

'And he died? He really died? You didn't kill him?'

'I told you – I found him face-down in the river and I fished him out. At first I thought he was dead. Then I felt a faint pulse. I must have been crazy, bringing him here on the tractor. It was only when I dragged him into the house that I realized he was beyond help.'

'How do you know that?' she cried. 'He might have been saved if you'd got him to a hospital.'

'I've got a good knowledge of first aid. I tried to resuscitate him – even gave him the kiss of life. I wanted him alive, you see. I don't know what I intended doing with him, but I couldn't bear the thought of him having her while I spent the rest of my life without her.'

'You're mad,' she said.

He shrugged, and held the cup of tea out to her. 'You must think what you like,' he said. 'All I can say is, I'm not a killer.'

'You beat up your girlfriend,' she accused him.

'Yes. Catherine was my one weakness. I couldn't see any point in life without her when she told me she wasn't going to marry me.'

She suddenly remembered Richard, and looked at her watch. It was half past ten. 'I have to make a phone call,' she said, reaching into her back pocket. 'Do you mind?'

He shook his head and grimaced. 'Call the cops,' he said. 'I shan't put up a fight.'

'It's not the police I want to ring. It's the man I'm going to marry. He doesn't know I'm here.'

'I'll be upstairs,' he said, and placed the cup and saucer on the floor beside her. Then he got up and left the room.

* * *

They dug up the rose tree and threw it to one side. Then they removed all the soil and broke down the wall that had taken the place of the wooden hatch. Inside the house, banging and hammering could be heard from the team that had been hastily summoned from police headquarters. They were in the pantry, trying to get into the cellar that way. The front of the house was swarming with cars. Stakes had been driven into the ground and tape stretched between them.

Somewhere inside, Roger Claybourne was talking to police officers. Amy and Catherine Blake sat in the Land Rover, waiting and watching.

When the covered stretcher came out through the front door Catherine's head fell forward into her hands. Amy got out of the LandRover and forced her legs to carry her over to the men who were carrying Kip. She steeled herself to ask in an unsteady voice, 'Do you want me to identify him?'

The officer in charge said gently, 'That won't be necessary, Miss Weldon. He's been down there for two years. We'll need to check dental records before we can be sure he's the right man, but I don't think there's any doubt. He had an identity tag on him – and Army papers.'

Amy was very calm now. 'I see,' she said. 'What's going to happen to Roger Claybourne now?'

'It depends,' the man said. 'After an autopsy we'll find out if there's any evidence of Keith Weldon being murdered or if he died of natural causes. At the moment, I'd say it was the latter.'

'It's strange hearing him called Keith,' she said. 'He hated the name. He was always known as Kip.' They were taking the body away now, putting it in an unmarked police van. 'Is there any objection to us going back inside the house?' she wanted to know. 'Catherine's in a state of shock. She's shaking all over.'

'She thought she'd seen a ghost when you came out of the house – it was you we expected to find in the cellar, you see, not this young man who we believed had drowned two years ago.'

'I'll go get her. It's nice and warm in the kitchen. I've been there for the past hour and a half talking to Roger Claybourne.'

'He didn't attempt to harm you?'

She managed a smile. 'No. Why should he?'

She kept her arm round Catherine as she led her into the house, though if the truth were known she was in need of support herself. 'It's crazy us sitting outside,' she said. 'But the police want us to hang on here for a while.'

'How can I look him in the face?' Catherine cried. 'It really was all over between him and me – long before I met Kip.'

'Maybe we won't have to face him. They'll probably have him in one of the other rooms.'

'You said he was ill.' Catherine hesitated in the long corridor leading to the kitchen.

'He's dying, Catherine. He has cancer.'

'He's paying for what he did to Kip, then.' The other girl's voice was without pity.

'He told me he didn't kill Kip and I think I believe him,' Amy said quietly.

A door opened and Amy caught a glimpse of Roger Claybourne's bowed figure at the kitchen table. He didn't look up. Catherine reeled away and muttered, 'God! I feel sick.'

Amy accompanied her up the stairs to the bathroom.

'I'll wait here outside the door for you,' she said, feeling wretched herself. This morning's nausea was beginning to assert itself again. She felt herself going light-headed, but Catherine had disappeared into the bathroom and there was no one to hold onto.

She staggered across the landing and pushed open a door. There was a bed inside the room and she lowered herself down on it, sitting with her head in her hands until the dizziness had passed. When it had, she took stock of her surroundings – Roger Claybourne's own bedroom – and her eyes began to slowly fill with tears.

Catherine came looking for her, pushing open the door and saying, 'I thought you'd gone back downstairs.'

Amy said nothing, merely pointed to the far wall. Over and around a chest of drawers a kind of shrine had been set up, with what must have amounted to a hundred different photographs of Catherine. Round a small electric lamp on top of the chest, photographs in frames were arranged. There were silver frames, brass ones, wooden ones, heart-shaped ones, and on the wall it was the same. Catherine stood transfixed.

Amy said, 'He must have put the lamp on at night and lain here looking at you for all these years.'

A sob shuddered through the other girl, then she turned and walked out of the room and down the stairs.

Amy followed her into the kitchen. Roger Claybourne was standing up between two police officers who were about to take him away. He looked ill and in pain, but he made no complaint.

Catherine walked up to him and Amy pressed her fingers to her lips, afraid for a moment that Catherine was going to hit him. She didn't. She just stood and looked at him, then said, 'Did you kill him? I want the truth.'

Very quietly he said, 'No. I didn't kill him. They'll find out I didn't when they do the autopsy.'

Catherine held out her arms to him and both police officers stepped aside, though still kept a wary eye on him.

When Amy left the room Catherine and Roger Claybourne were locked together in each other's arms.

CHAPTER 26

Richard was angrier than she'd ever seen him before. 'You should never have gone there alone,' he raged as she faced him at home in his large and airy sitting room where he'd sat all day waiting for her.

It was six in the evening and she was tired. It had been a bad day, and she hadn't felt up to driving all the way back to Derbyshire after what had happened at Roger Claybourne's house that morning. Knowing Richard would be worried, however, she'd forced herself to drink gallons of sweet tea, to stop tiredness overtaking her, and had made the journey in a little over three hours.

'A fine way to greet me,' she grumbled. 'I was thinking of you all the way back and then you start yelling at me the minute I walk in the door.'

'You didn't stop to think of me *before* you went off on your hare-brained errand, though, did you? Didn't it ever occur to you, Amy, that I'd be going out of my mind with worry when you didn't turn up at the hospital this morning?'

She flung her hands out towards him as she stood in the doorway. 'Richard – I didn't know you were coming home until late last night. What did you expect me to do? Turn right round the minute I'd got there and drive back there and then?'

'Of course not. But you knew Roger Claybourne had a reputation for violence. You shouldn't have gone alone.'

'He wasn't violent towards me,' she stated. 'He's a sick man, Richard. He's terminally ill. And anyway, are you going to stop yelling long enough to let me tell you what happened today?'

'I expect it was a wild-goose chase.' He looked sulky. 'You didn't give much away when you rang me this morning. You just said you'd see me later today. What the hell was I supposed to think, Amy? You go jetting off on your own – '

'Richard! Stop it!' She ran across the room to him, fell on her knees in front of him and wrapped her arms round his waist. Laying her head gently against his shirt, she said brokenly, 'Richard, it was awful – what happened today. They found Kip's body. For God's sake don't shout at me any more.'

He held her close then, and his bad mood melted away like snow in summer. 'Amy – Amy, my darling girl,' he whispered. 'What are you saying?'

In a subdued voice, she recounted the events of the day, calmly and quietly. She didn't break down. Tears wouldn't help anybody now. When she'd finished her mind was clear, and she felt free of Kip Weldon's ghost for the first time in years.

Richard stroked her hair and said gently, 'Amy – can you ever forgive me. I didn't give you a chance to explain, did I?'

She tilted her head and looked up at him. 'I knew you'd be mad as hell,' she said. 'I was expecting the worst and I sure got it.'

'If only I'd known . . .'

She moved away from him, afraid that her weight might

be too much pressure on his shoulder, but he pulled her close again and kissed her lips in a warm and tender way. 'I'll go make us a drink, shall I?' she asked. 'I don't expect you've eaten all day.'

'Lizzie Abercrombie's in the kitchen,' he said against her mouth. 'She's been killing me with kindness and drooling over that little house across the road that's still for sale. When I saw you pulling the Land Rover up outside I sent her to make a pot of her infamous tea.'

She groaned. 'No! Not more tea. I've consumed gallons of the stuff since this morning – still, if I can take it in the mornings, I suppose I won't bring it all back up at this time of day.'

He looked at her strangely. 'What on earth is all that waffle supposed to mean?' he asked.

Realizing only then what she'd said, her hand flew to her lips. 'Nothing,' she replied huskily. 'I'm just not thinking straight.'

'Lizzie told me you'd been a bit queasy this past week.'

'Uh-huh . . .' She cast her eyes downwards, unable to meet his gaze.

'Amy – you're not . . .?'

Her eyes flew up to meet his. 'I'm not going to lie to you. Yes, I'm pregnant. And before you ask, I don't know how it happened – I mean, we took precautions, didn't we? But nothing's a hundred percent safe is it?' Her head drooped a little and she looked down at the carpet, dismayed with herself for letting her secret out in the wrong way at the wrong time. She hadn't planned to tell him like this. She'd been waiting for a suitable moment. But, she wondered, how did you know which was a suitable one and which wasn't?

She raised her head again and looked straight at him. 'You're going to be real cussed about this, aren't you? But

343

I wouldn't have you angry or upset for the world, Richard. I know what your feelings are on this subject – and you know mine.'

He started to laugh softly and said, 'The best-laid plans . . . etcetera, etcetera. Maybe sometimes it's better to keep your options open, huh?'

'Is this your way of saying you don't mind?' She tipped her head on one side and considered him shrewdly.

'I'm not wildly excited about the prospect of you going through nine months with a ballooning waistline and then hours of exhaustion giving birth,' he said, sobering instantly. 'But what's done is done. It's nobody's fault. We were in this together.' His eyes softened and he lifted one hand and stroked her hair. 'Remember how we were together?' he asked gently.

'Oh, Richard.' She clung to him and muttered, 'I've been going bananas – not knowing how to tell you. I thought you were so dead set against me having kids that you'd want me to have an abortion.'

Pain flared in his eyes. 'I'm haunted by the fact that I killed a man accidentally,' he said. 'Do you think I would *deliberately* take the life of my own child?' His hands fastened on her shoulders as he looked directly into her eyes. 'Amy, don't ever be scared to confide in me; I'm only human, for God's sake. And one thing's certain, my love, even if we make this same mistake a dozen times over, I'll never ask you to get rid of a baby.'

She felt overwhelmed with emotion and shrugged herself away from him, fumbling in her jeans pocket and producing a handkerchief to mop at her eyes. When she'd recovered a bit, she leaned back on her heels and said, 'You were so adamant we shouldn't have children, Richard. Now, though, you don't seem to mind.'

344

'I'm scared,' he admitted. 'I never thought I'd find love again, you see. I'd led a bachelor existence since Grace died, and I didn't like it. When I first met you, I wanted you . . .'

'In the chapel at Wydale?' Her eyes widened.

A smile spread slowly across his face. 'Even then. I'd never met anybody like you in my life before, but I wanted you. And, as I grew out of just wanting and into loving you, I didn't dare even consider the thought of losing you. I remembered how my world had ended for a while after Grace had gone, and I realized that one way I could prevent that happening again was not to get you pregnant.'

'I could get run over by a bus,' she said steadily.

'If that thought had crossed my mind, I'd probably have started a campaign to ban buses on every road in the damned country by now,' he said, starting to laugh. 'But I get your point. I can't protect you twenty-four hours a day. I wouldn't want to anyway. I made the mistake of thinking Grace was an extension of myself when she married me. With you, I know you won't let me do that.'

'I was right, then, to go swanning off to Lincolnshire without you – is that what you're saying?' she teased.

He became serious. 'I was *very* wrong to yell at you like I did when you came back. It's your life, Amy. Even when we've been married for fifty years, I'll still be looking at you and wanting to wrap you in cotton wool – but I'll know better than to try it.'

'You'll make a super father, Richard, if you treat our kids that way too.'

'Let me get used to the idea before you say that. I'm still in shock from finding out I *am* going to be a father.'

She scrambled to her feet. 'Do you mind if I tell Lizzie?' she asked.

345

'Lizzie's not the problem,' he said, getting up from the chair and putting his arms round her. 'Gif Weldon is, though. How on earth are we going to break the news to him?'

'We won't,' she said in a determined manner. 'We're getting married in August. That's only another three months away – and, really, it's of no concern to Uncle Gif whether I'm pregnant or not. He washed his hands of me all those years ago when he sent me to Marty and Kate.'

'You're still smarting from that rejection, aren't you?' he said softly, holding her close to him.

'Am I?' She looked up at him candidly.

He nodded. 'I'll make damn sure you're never rejected again, though,' he promised.

She gave him a solemn kiss on the lips, then stood back and said, 'I brought the rose tree home with me, Richard. Do you mind if I plant it in a corner of the garden somewhere?'

'The rose tree?'

'The little bush that was planted against Roger Claybourne's front door. The police ripped everything out of the ground when they tried to get into the cellar.'

He smiled. 'And you felt sorry for the rose!'

She nodded and looked embarrassed. 'Look – I know I'm crazy, but I had to do it.'

'You're not crazy. You can give the little rose bush place of honour in the middle of the lawn if you want to.'

'No. It's a shy little rose. It hasn't even got a bud on it.'

'With your determination to save it, it soon will have.' He laughed.

'You don't mind?'

'I'm not jealous of a rose bush, sweetheart.'

'It was Kip's rose bush, though.'

'Kip's dead,' he said gently. 'And I think I know what's going through your mind.'

'It's the final curtain,' she said, knowing that she spoke the truth. 'The last reminder of a love that never was. I never felt for Kip what I feel for you, Richard. I never even started to know him as a man. Why, today, I could even feel it in my heart to be sorry for Roger Claybourne. I realized at last that he really had loved Catherine, and it was only when Kip appeared on the scene that *his* world started falling apart. Catherine knew it too, I think. She stayed with him, anyway, and went with him when the police took him away.'

Richard took hold of her hand. 'Come on,' he said. 'Let's go through to the kitchen and see what Lizzie's doing, shall we? And then, when we've had a bite to eat, we'll go and find a suitable spot in the garden for Kip Weldon's rose.'

Amy cycled over to Hatton-in-the-Dale every day to tend the rose. It soon took root, and by the end of June it was strong and healthy and was covered in shiny leaves. For Kate and Marty in America it was a sad time, though. The autopsy showed that Kip had died of hypothermia brought on by being in the freezing river for two hours that winter night. Nothing Roger Claybourne could have done would have saved him. Kip's remains were flown back to America for a proper funeral, and Amy and Richard went over to Boston for a few days, taking with them photographs of little Kimberley Blake.

It was arranged that Catherine would be at Amy and Richard's wedding in August, with her little girl so that she could meet her American grandparents, and Kate phoned regularly after Amy and Richard returned home to tell them of all the surprises she was bringing over for Kip's little daughter in August.

Catherine got in touch with Amy by letter and said she was moving back to Lincolnshire with Kim, so she'd be able to look after Roger in his last months. She would never love him, she said, but she understood a lot of his actions now.

In July the weather turned hot and sultry; there had been no rain for weeks. Amy still cycled regularly to Richard's house – sometimes in the morning, sometimes in the afternoon. She knew Richard didn't like her using the bike now she was nearly five months pregnant, but he hadn't forbidden her to ride it.

He'd kept his word. He never issued ultimatums. He accepted that she was responsible for her own actions. She loved him more and more for his tolerance. She wasn't going to take any chances with the baby, though, and she realized that the bike rides would soon have to stop. She felt remarkably well, however, especially now the morning sickness had gone.

All the same, today would be the last day, she vowed, that she would cycle over to Hatton-in-the-Dale. The wedding was only a week away. Her little rose would survive now, she knew.

It was hot in the garden. She went back into the kitchen, which was cool and sunless, and sat down near the open door in an old cushioned rocking chair that she and Richard had fallen in love with at an auction two weeks ago. She sipped at a glass of iced orange juice and looked out at the garden, which was ablaze with flowers. Tonight Richard was taking her into Hatton to the newly opened Arts Centre to see an amateur production of *Hobson's*

Choice, which had been given good reviews in the local papers. She was looking forward to it. Her life, she decided, seemed to be settling down at last.

She must have dozed after putting her empty glass down on the floor beside her, for she woke with a start when she heard a loud knocking on the front door. Slipping out of her chair, she went down the passageway to open it. Whoever was there seemed very persistent. The rat-tat-tatting of the doorknocker came again as she reached it. 'Okay!' she yelled. 'I'm here. Hold on a minute.'

John Graham whipped his flat chauffeur's hat off and mopped at his forehead. 'Thank goodness you're still here,' he said.

'Sorry, Mr Graham – I was having a doze in the rocking chair.' She grinned apologetically. 'Has Lizzie sent you to collect me?' She frowned, 'I'm sure I didn't ask her to. I was going to come back on the bike as usual.'

'Can I come in, Miss Weldon?'

'Sure!' She held the door wide open. 'Is this heat getting to you? Come and have a glass of orange juice. I can recommend it.'

He followed her into the kitchen.

'Sit down.' She waved a hand at the rocking chair and went over to the fridge.

'No, miss. *You* sit down. Mrs Abercrombie said I was to be sure to make you sit down.'

She whirled round to him. 'It's bad news, isn't it?' Her voice rose on a note of panic. 'Hey! What is this? God! You look awful. What's happened?'

'Sit down. Please, Miss Weldon.'

'Tell me!' she yelled. 'Has my uncle had another heart-attack? Is Lizzie ill?'

'No. No. Nothing like that . . .' He lifted both hands to ward off her questions. 'Please – sit down.'

'Tell me!' she shrieked. 'It's Richard, isn't it? Something's happened to him.' She was frantic. 'There's been an accident at the quarry and nobody dared come and tell me . . .'

'No! No!'

John Graham was shaking his head and trying to speak as she yelled at him again, 'Tell me! I can take it. Tell me . . .'

'It's the house, Miss Weldon.'

'The *house*!' She stared open-mouthed at him. 'The *house*?' she repeated again, and then started to laugh. 'What is all this? Is it some joke?'

'It's falling down, Miss Weldon.' John Graham was turning his hat round and round in his hands in the gesture of a man desperate to know what to do next.

'Falling down?' she echoed.

'It started with the western tower. It just went. There was a roar like – well, like nothing I'd ever heard before, then the whole hillside shook and the tower's foundations slid down towards the river, taking the whole west wing with it – and then the winter garden went as well.'

CHAPTER 27

Richard's Land Rover was the first thing Amy saw as they turned the last bend in the tree-lined road leading up to Wydale Hall. It had been left on the grassy bank of the river beside the pack-horse bridge, and John Graham pulled her uncle's car up alongside it and parked.

Horrified, she stared at the scene on the other side of the river. It was nothing short of a nightmare. The whole of Wydale's west wing had collapsed, she saw, and a mountain of stones and debris had careered down the hill, leaving a great swathe of earth looking as if somebody had swung a mighty scythe across it. Wydale's crumbling foundations were exposed on the northern and southern sides, and the courtyard had the appearance of a cake that had been neatly sliced through the middle.

John Graham seemed in shock. He just sat looking at the house and shaking his head, and made no attempt to get out of the car.

'Heartbreaking,' he sat there murmuring. 'Heartbreaking.'

Amy saw Richard detach himself from a group of yellow-hard-hatted men on the far bank of the river and come running across the pack-horse bridge. She scrambled out of the car and flew to meet him.

He held her tight as she came up to him beside the Land Rover, then they both stood and looked at the site of destruction opposite, where the yellow-hatted figures were now making their careful way up towards the house.

The winter garden had crashed down the hillside and wasn't recognizable as a garden any more. The ornamental lawn that had been situated right above it now clung perilously to the steep incline that was left, and little trickles of soil and rock kept dribbling down from it. Amy could see that it would only be a matter of time before thousands more tons of earth cascaded down towards the river.

A dam had been formed in a narrow part of the river by the fallen garden. Water was being forced to make a precipitous detour over rocks, stones and uprooted trees. She prayed it wouldn't rain heavily before the rubble could be cleared, for if it did the low-lying fields in the heart of the valley would be waterlogged if the river broke its banks.

'Where's Lizzie? And Uncle Gif?' Her head jerked up at Richard, and she felt guilty for not asking John Graham what had happened to her uncle and the housekeeper as he'd driven her to Wydale.

'They're both safe!' Richard's arm around her shoulders gave a protective and reassuring squeeze. 'John Graham took them down to Duncan Ward's old cottage.'

'They're not hurt any?' Her voice was sharp with concern.

'No. They're okay.'

'Who are the men? The ones you were talking to in the yellow hats.'

'They're from a engineering construction firm. I rang them immediately Lizzie let me know what had happened.'

Looking closely now, Amy saw there was a small white truck parked on the other side of the pack-horse bridge, near the old chapel.

'Is any more of the house likely to fall?' she asked, knowing full well what the answer would be.

Richard nodded. He looked pale and tense. 'Thank God you weren't there when it happened,' he said. 'I know how fond you were of the winter garden, and if you'd been . . . God! It doesn't bear thinking about.' His arm tightened around her shoulders even more, crushing her close to him.

'Hey! I'm okay,' she reassured him.

He smiled down into her upturned face. 'Why is your voice all wavy, then?' he wanted to know.

She was stopped from answering by a noise overhead and, tilting her head, she stared up into the warm July sunshine. She drew in her breath and muttered, 'Oh, no! Not him again. Not Mark Powell.'

'He couldn't know about this.' Richard frowned. 'It's barely a couple of hours since it happened. He couldn't possibly have heard.'

Amy saw the helicopter suddenly dip down low over Wydale. 'He didn't,' she said. 'Don't ask me how I know, but I get the feeling that Mark Powell's just had the shock of his life up there.'

As they watched the helicopter wheel away from the scene of devastation Richard said, 'I think you're right. I also think that Mark Powell will be joining us here before much longer.'

He was right. A couple of hours later, at Duncan Ward's little house at the bottom of the long winding drive that led up to Wydale, Mark Powell arrived.

'I saw smoke coming from the chimney and guessed

you'd all be here,' he said as Lizzie let him in.

The little living room was overcrowded already, with Gif Weldon, Lizzie, John Graham, herself and Richard in there, but it was only natural, Amy supposed, that once Mark had seen the catastrophe from his vantage point in the clouds, he would want to know what had happened. Tea was flowing freely – Lizzie saw to that.

The police had arrived and had cordoned off the whole of the Wydale estate from the main road, for many people must have heard about the fall of the great house on the local radio's news bulletins, and already a dozen or so sightseers had gathered out on the road in front of Duncan's cottage.

'I see you're back with the camera,' Amy said icily as Mark came up to her.

'I didn't know I was going to run into something like this,' he said. 'I couldn't believe my eyes when I looked down and saw all that mess. What happened?'

'The engineers seem to think it's because of all the rain that fell in December. It loosened the soil and worked its way right through to a fault in the clay that ran underneath the house. Part of the winter garden wall collapsed earlier this year, and Richard was concerned about it, but we never dreamed anything like this could happen.'

'It's a bad job.' Mark's face was serious. 'Expensive too. Especially if the rest of the house has to be taken down.'

She said nothing, but looked across the room to where Richard was talking to John Graham. Mark, she noted, had not bothered to ask if anyone had been hurt when the west wing collapsed. She'd tell him anyway, she decided. 'Nobody was hurt,' she said. 'We must be thankful for that, at least.'

She saw his face flush a dull red. 'Ouch!' he said. 'I

354

guess I should have asked that in the first place. Thanks for reminding me.'

She gave him a disdainful glance. 'You should get your priorities right, Mr Powell.' She turned away from him. 'Don't go.'

She felt his hand on her arm, and raised her eyebrows delicately at him. 'I have nothing to stay for,' she said. 'You and I will never see eye to eye.'

'Look – I'm sorry my first thought wasn't for anyone around at the time,' he said, 'but I could see you were all here – and not a scratch between the lot of you. There'd be more of a kerfuffle going on if anyone *had* been injured. I just took it for granted . . .'

'Okay,' she said, shrugging. 'But don't detain me. Uncle Gif's shaken up about this. I'm going to ask Lizzie if she can persuade him to have a lie-down.'

'He's *my* father,' Mark Powell said quietly. 'Maybe I should be the one to do that.'

She shook his hand off her arm. 'Okay,' she said, 'you do that. You seem mighty keen to take your place around here, so go ahead.'

'There's precious little inheritance left for either of us, is there?' he said with a grin.

'Is that what you think?' she asked.

'Well, the house looks as though it could be a big liability now, doesn't it?'

A hush crept over the room, and everybody turned to look at Mark Powell.

'Hey,' he said softly, '*I'm* not the villain of this piece.'

Richard came forward. 'It's hardly the time or the place to be talking of *anybody's* inheritance,' he said.

Gif Weldon spoke then. 'Leave him be, Richard. The lad's young. He doesn't realize what he's saying.'

Amy was angry that her uncle should be siding with Mark, for only she, Richard and Gif Weldon knew the truth. After a preliminary survey for subsidence a fortnight ago, Wydale and its land had been valued at well over two million pounds. Mark Powell could have found that out too, though, she realized. Gif could have told him. Perhaps that was why Mark had come back to Wydale – to make sure his father was prepared to accept him as his son.

Only one thing mattered to Amy. She wheeled away from Mark and her Uncle Gif in disgust and strode out of the room.

Richard found her in Duncan Ward's old English garden, looking down at a bed of roses in full bloom. The scent drifting up from them was heady. He came up behind her and placed both his hands on her shoulders.

'Richard!' She leaned back against him, feeling safe and not caring about Wydale any more. The house had held nothing but sadness and heartache for years, she realized, and now the past had finally caught up with them all. She had one fear and one fear only – though in her heart she knew it was irrational.

'Amy!' he said against her hair.

Slowly she turned round to face him. His hands still rested on her shoulders as she looked up at him. 'Richard – you've got the girl, but you do realize you're not going to get Wydale now, don't you? Uncle Gif's bound to make another will leaving everything to Mark now he knows he's his son.'

'Do you think that matters to me?' He gazed down at her.

'You've already put a lot of money into Wydale.'

His big shoulders lifted in a shrug. 'Some you win, some you don't.'

'But *I* went with the house – if you remember?'

'You were the only one who saw it that way, Amy. I never did.' His face creased into a smile, his eyes crinkling at the corners in the way she loved so much.

'You still want me, then?' she asked candidly.

'I love you,' he said. 'Who wants a house that size anyway?'

A discreet cough behind Richard had her peering round the side of him. Richard twisted his head too.

'I couldn't help but overhear.' Gif Weldon came slowly towards them in the gathering dusk of the warm July night.

'Uncle Gif. I'm sorry about the house.' His face was grey and lined. He looked a hundred years old, she thought.

'I can't go back on my word.' The old man stopped beside them, and glanced up meaningfully at Richard. 'A gentleman's agreement, you know. That's what we had.'

Richard's voice was kind but firm. 'We had no such thing, Gif. How could we? Arranged marriages just aren't in fashion any more.'

'All the same, you took her on with the house as your security, my boy.'

Amy's mouth fell open. She wanted to laugh out loud, but realized her uncle was deadly serious.

Richard held her tight and said, 'Amy's all I want. I release you from any agreement you thought we had, Gif.'

'I should think so too.' Amy grinned up at him.

But Gif Weldon was staring at them both and his mouth was set in a rigid, stern line. 'An agreement's an agreement,' he stormed. 'And I can't revoke the will I made leaving everything to Amy.'

'I don't want the house or the estate or anything – ' she began.

'I can't go back on a promise. And Wydale has always been intended for you, Amy,' her uncle said gruffly, swinging away from them and shambling back to the cottage door.

Amy looked up at Richard. 'It's plain crazy. He has a son. And I'm just a nobody.'

'And time's running out for the old man,' Richard said on a sigh. 'Yet his conscience won't let him do what he knows is right.'

'He's going to have to come to terms with his conscience,' she said. 'He can't seriously leave Wydale to me when he has a legitimate heir.'

'You really don't mind about losing everything, do you?' he said incredulously. 'You really don't care that you'll just be ending up with me?'

'I like your house,' she said, beginning to laugh. 'At least I can watch my videos there. You have an excellent electricity supply, Mr Boden.'

Lizzie and Gif stayed in Duncan's cottage and Amy went back to Hatton-in-the-Dale with Richard. Nobody asked or seemed to care where Mark Powell was staying. They all assumed he'd be at the Hawkwood Arms down in the village.

Lizzie caught the bus next day and went to Hatton-in-the-Dale to see Amy.

'Here!' Lizzie growled as they sat in the cool kitchen drinking coffee, with the sound of birds chirruping in the garden coming in to them through the open door. 'I got them construction fellas to bring out a few personal things – thought you'd want these especially.' She delved into her huge shopping bag on wheels and brought out the book-ends Richard had carved and Amy's diary and the volume

358

of poetry that Richard had also given her. 'And don't worry none. I didn't peek in the diary.'

Amy's eyes danced with laughter. 'Lizzie! I know you well enough to trust you with anything. Anyway, I don't have secrets – and if I did, I wouldn't write them down.'

'You can't trust nobody! Least of all crabby old men like Gif Weldon.'

Amy sat back in the rocker and said, 'Now what's he been up to?'

Lizzie sniffed and stuck her nose in the air. 'Only had to go rushing off down to Hawkwood last night, didn't he? To see that Mark Powell.'

'It's natural, Lizzie. I suppose it's kinda funny for Uncle Gif to find he's become a father at this late stage in his life.'

'I keep telling him, Miss Amy, he can't put the clock back. That Mark Powell needed a daddy when he was young – not now, when he's grown up and perfectly able to take care of himself. Only good thing about the lad is that he seems to have more sense about money than his father ever did. Well, he's got that helicopter for a start, hasn't he? And a motorbike I'd have sold my soul for when I was his age.'

'Lizzie!' Amy's laughter pealed out. 'Is this one of your well-kept secrets? Wanting a motorbike?'

Lizzie grimaced. 'A lot of the lads had bikes when I was young in the 1950s. Me? I didn't get lads easy, see? Not with my face and figure. So I got my heart set on a bike instead. Bikes didn't care what you looked like – and they were more reliable than a greasy-haired Teddy boy in drainpipe trousers.'

'Did you ever get the bike?'

'Nope! I had as much chance of an Ariel Roadster then

as I do now of getting that little house across the road from you. Your Richard laughed at me when I couldn't take my eyes off it last time I was here. Did he tell you?'

She nodded, and said, 'You'll need somewhere to live when Uncle Gif's not around any longer, Lizzie.'

'Yeah! Well, I was talking about Gif Weldon before I got sidetracked into telling you about my daydreams. I don't trust either him or that snoopy son of his – if he *is* Gif's son.'

'I don't think there's much doubt about that,' Amy said seriously.

Lizzie was silent for a few moments, then she said, 'There's something wrong with the old man . . .'

'Wrong?' Amy frowned and sat forward in her chair. 'Lizzie – he's not ill, is he?'

'Oh, no. Nothing like that. There's just something funny going on in his mind, if you ask me. He's been saying things.'

'What kind of things?' Amy was puzzled.

'Muttering all the time about letting folk down. And when I passed his bedroom door last night I heard him saying your name over and over again. I reckon he was asleep and dreaming. He sounded like he was in pain or something.'

'Maybe you should get him to see a doctor, Lizzie.'

Lizzie sighed and rolled her eyes at the ceiling. 'P'raps it's nothing. P'raps it's just because we're cooped up together in that little house that I'm noticing more things about him than usual. At Wydale we each had our rooms at opposite ends of that big house, lovey. Maybe he's *always* talked in his sleep. I don't know! Maybe it's the ghost of Duncan Ward haunting him – that poky little place sure gives *me* the creeps.'

360

'Oh, Lizzie – I don't know what to say. You could come here. Richard would welcome you with open arms, because I can't even boil an egg properly . . .'

'But what would happen to the old man then? He can't manage on his own, and he certainly won't leave Wydale or the cottage.'

'But you don't need to be there at night, Lizzie. You need your sleep. Why don't you let Richard fetch you over each evening? Uncle Gif doesn't need nursemaiding twenty-four hours a day.'

'I might take you up on that – especially if this talking in his sleep doesn't stop. I tell you, Miss Amy, it's getting me down – and I've not even had twenty-four hours of it yet.'

Amy was worried about Lizzie – and about Gif Weldon too. Wydale had been the pivot of their lives for so long, and after Lizzie had gone she began to wonder if the collapse of the house so soon after Duncan's death was just too much for her uncle to cope with.

CHAPTER 28

Lizzie's voice on the phone sounded worried. 'Look – I hate to ask this, less than a week before your wedding, girl, but can you come down here do you think? Gif Weldon's finally cracked.'

'Lizzie! What do you mean?'

'Oh, don't go getting yourself all worked up. He's impossible, you know. And now – the latest thing is he's had John Graham go up to the Hall and bring that ramshackle old car out of the stables.'

'What ramshackle old car? I didn't know there were any cars except the one John Graham usually drives.'

Lizzie gave a huge sigh. 'Don't you remember the little bottle-green one that Gif used to drive around in? You know – the open-top one?'

Amy laughed. 'Surely he doesn't still have that one? I was just a kid of twelve when he first took me driving in the Derby-shire hills in *that*, and it was ages old then.'

'He's hoarded it away all these years. It's been in one of the disused stables round the back of the house. Anyway, back to the problem. Your uncle's got some bee in his bonnet about taking up driving again. And I didn't know till this morning that he's had John Graham hard at it

362

oiling, cleaning and polishing the darn thing for the past week. John says it's still in good working order, and there's no real reason why it *shouldn't* be on the road again – but, Miss Amy, I don't trust Gif with it. He hasn't driven for years. So can you come and maybe talk some sense into him?'

'Sure, Lizzie! I'll get Richard to drop me off at the cottage this afternoon if that's okay. He's started coming home for lunch since I've been staying here, I guess he's getting a taste for my cooking – I don't think!' She pulled a rueful face, 'Though to tell the truth, I can actually knock up quite a good omelette now.'

She heard the relief in the housekeeper's voice as Lizzie said, 'Thank heavens somebody takes me seriously. That Mark Powell's been here again this morning, and he just laughs and says it's good that Gif's taking an interest in things again.'

'Well, perhaps it is, Lizzie.'

'No! Not this sort of thing!' Lizzie was adamant. 'If he took up watercolour painting or something safe, I wouldn't mind – but driving? No! I don't hold with that – not somebody who's been so morose and depressed just lately. Honestly, Miss Amy, he's up one minute and down in the depths the next. It just isn't right. And he flatly refuses to see the doctor . . .'

'I'll talk to him,' Amy promised. 'I really will come down there and see what I can do this afternoon, Lizzie.'

'Great!' Oh, and there're some of your belongings still here, you know – clothes and such like that've been brought down from the Hall. They eventually managed to shore up the roof in the kitchen and get into that cloakroom-cupboard place where you kept your winter duffle coat and boots.'

Amy smiled into the phone. 'In August, I don't think I'll be needing a duffle coat, Lizzie.'

Richard pulled the Land Rover up outside Duncan Ward's old cottage around two that afternoon, promising to pick her up again when he'd finished at the quarry at half past five. He whistled under his breath as he saw the neat little two-seater car standing in the lane beside the garden gate. 'Heck! That's a great little car, Amy. I never knew Gif had that.'

'Neither did I, until Lizzie told me this morning that Uncle had kept it hidden in the stables all these years.' Her smile was reminiscent as she said, 'When I first came to Wydale, he used to take me out all over Derbyshire in it. I remember him buying me a cute little camera so I could take pictures. It seems a long time ago now.'

'I'd like to take a look at it when I call back for you.'

'Why don't you come and say hello to Lizzie and Uncle Gif right now?'

He shook his head. 'Sorry, I can't. During blasting up at the quarry this morning we discovered a seam of alabaster that looks quite promising. It's quite a rarity now, so we're going to have a go at digging it out by hand so it won't get damaged.'

'Can't George Shipstone see to it?' she asked.

He laughed and ruffled her hair. 'You shouldn't encourage me to take time off from the quarry,' he said teasingly. 'Anyway, I want to be there to oversee it personally. We'll probably have to manhandle it onto a low-loader if we get it out in one piece – hence the pile of tough ropes in the back of the Land Rover.'

'Be careful.' A frown shadowed her forehead. 'You're not to take any risks, Richard. I'll never forgive Gabriel

364

for falling on you like he did.' She shuddered. 'Honestly, sometimes the very mention of alabaster gives me nightmares.'

'Don't worry,' he said. 'Gabriel taught me a couple of lessons – firstly not to get into a punch-up, and secondly to steer clear of alabster angels who jump down from church windows.'

Her eyes softened and she planted a kiss on his cheek and opened the door of the Land Rover.

'Take care yourself,' he said, when she stood on the ground to wave him off.

Lizzie came out of the cottage as Richard drove away and stood at the gate, her hands on her hips, elbows sticking out at an angle just as Amy had seen them hundreds of times in the past when Lizzie was concerned about something.

'Hi, Lizzie,' she called out, but Lizzie was scowling at the little green car outside the gate.

'A blooming Dinky toy,' she grumbled.

'Lizzie – it's lovely.' Amy ran her hands over the gleaming paintwork and admired the shining chrome of the headlamps and bumper. It must have been well protected in its stable, she decided, for even the cream leather seats were unmarked and looked like new.

'It's thanks to John Graham that it looks so good,' Lizzie admitted grudgingly. 'He says it goes like a bomb too!'

'Where's Uncle Gif?'

'Inside.' Lizzie jerked her head back at the house. 'Seems in quite a good mood for a change. But he's a dark horse – you never can tell what he's thinking – or what he's getting up to.'

'Lizzie! You're getting paranoid about him . . .'

'No, I'm not,' Lizzie insisted. 'He's strange. I don't care what you say, Miss Amy – he's strange just lately. Why, only yesterday he had John run him over to Hatton at a minute's notice. He just had to go – there and then – as if the very devil were on his tail.' Lizzie shrugged and let her hands fall to her sides. 'Came back hours later looking all smug and secretive, and wouldn't say where he'd been. John Graham said he didn't even tell *him* – he just made him drop him in the town centre and then pick him up again later.'

'Maybe he went shopping.'

'He didn't have no parcels when he came back.'

'Well, perhaps he was visiting an old friend or something.'

'Gif Weldon don't have any friends.' Lizzie's mouth clamped tightly shut, but after a few seconds she confided, 'He's up to something. I just know it. This morning he's been walking round the place humming. Humming all the blooming time so it fair got on my nerves. And when I asked him what he was humming for, he says, very mysterious like that I'll find out soon enough.'

'If he's humming he must be happy,' Amy said, pushing the gate open and going into the garden. 'I wouldn't worry if I were you, Lizzie.'

'I do worry. I've had that dream again – the one about you and him standing on opposite sides of the river and that little pack-horse bridge – and that blooming great angel . . .?'

'Oh, Lizzie – you mustn't harp on that so much. It's only a dream.'

'It's too near your wedding day for me *not* to take notice of it. I'm scared, Miss Amy – scared something will happen and spoil it for you. Or,' she added darkly, 'stop you getting married altogether.'

366

Amy felt a shiver run down her spine, despite the warm sun shining on her. 'Don't say things like that, Lizzie.'

'Hey! I'm a mean old woman! Take no notice of me.' Lizzie laid a friendly hand on her arm. 'But I *do* worry about you. And I can't help it. Everything's gone wrong this year. And I keep feeling the worst is still to come.'

Amy took hold of the housekeeper's hand and started walking towards the cottage. 'It's this place,' she said. 'I'm sure that's what it is, Lizzie. You must have it on your mind all the time that Uncle Gif and Duncan used to be here together.'

Lizzie pulled a hanky out of her apron pocket with her free hand and wiped her nose. She sniffed. 'You could be right. I hate the place.'

'What about that cottage across the road from Richard's house?'

'A pipedream, Miss Amy.' Lizzie's eyes were red-rimmed. 'Tom Abercrombie left me quite well off, but not *that* well off. I couldn't afford the asking price.'

'I'd like you to be near, Lizzie. After I'm married. And I'll need a friend when the baby arrives.'

Lizzie turned to her, tears welling up in her eyes. 'Miss Amy – I'd do anything for you. You know that. And there's nothing I'd like better than that little house, where I can keep an eye on you . . .'

'We talked about it – Richard and me. He'd buy it for you, you know.'

'No, girl.' Lizzie shook her head. 'I don't want to be beholden to anybody.'

'You wouldn't be.'

'Yes, I would.' A stubborn light in Lizzie's eyes chased the tears away. 'I don't want charity. I won't have it.'

They'd reached the door of the cottage. Amy turned to

367

the housekeeper. 'Lizzie – Uncle Gif's going to need more attention than you can give him before much longer.'

Lizzie looked down at the ground and muttered, 'Yes. I know. His mind's going – and fast. I see it every day. He gets a bit more absent-minded, a bit more cussed.'

A voice reached them from inside the house. 'Lizzie Abercrombie, where have you put my driving gloves?'

The two women looked at each other. Then Amy burst out laughing. 'Driving gloves? Am I hearing right, Lizzie?'

Lizzie nodded wearily. 'This morning he was asking me what time Duncan would be back from his walk.'

They went into the house. On the table, Amy saw her duffle coat, neatly folded, and the yellow scarf on top of it. Two pairs of her winter boots were under the table, tidily standing side by side.

'Your things.' Lizzie nodded at the table. 'I think the big house is almost cleared of stuff now.'

Gif Weldon's face lit up when he saw Amy. 'My dear girl. How nice to see you.'

'Hi, Uncle Gif.'

'Have you seen the car?' His eyes were bright as a blackbird's.

She smiled. 'I sure have, Uncle. It brings back memories of when I was a lot younger than I am now.'

'I remember that summer,' he said. 'I knew I'd only have you for about six months, and I wanted to give you something to remember England by. That's why I took you to all the beauty spots of Derbyshire.'

'I remember it too,' she said, smiling fondly at him.

He was more animated than she'd ever seen him in the months since her return to England. 'I remember the past far better than I do the present,' he said with a little grimace. 'Do you know, if it weren't for the morning newspaper, I wouldn't even know what day of the week it was?'

'Oh, Uncle Gif – I get just the same,' Amy said. 'It's not a privilege of old age to be absent-minded.'

'Come and see the car.' He whipped up her yellow scarf from the table and flung it at her. 'Come on. Bring the scarf. It can be cold up on the moors.'

'We're not going anywhere,' she said gently. 'And it's August, Uncle Gif. I wouldn't need a scarf in August – not even on the Derbyshire moors.'

She followed him outside, the scarf in her hand all the same. It seemed he couldn't wait to show off his car.

Lizzie called out, 'I'll make a pot of tea, so don't be long out there. Come back in when you hear the kettle whistling.'

Over her shoulder, Amy laughed at the housekeeper and shrugged.

'Go along,' Lizzie said. 'It'll make him happy if you take an interest. Even *I* had to go and sit in the front seat for ten minutes this morning while he showed me all the controls and everything.'

Outside in the sunshine, Gif Weldon turned eagerly to her and pulled open the passenger door of the little car. 'Sit inside, Amy. See – it's just the same as it was before. Nothing's rusted away.'

Obligingly she slid into the passenger seat. He closed her door then went round to the driver's side and got in beside her.

'The clock isn't showing the right time,' he said, peering closely at the dashboard as he closed his own door.

'I don't think it can be blamed for that,' she said, humouring him.

369

He pushed a key into the ignition. 'Maybe if I start the engine . . .'

'I guess the clock needs attention, Uncle Gif. John Graham might know what to do with it.' She leaned back in the seat and closed her eyes, letting the sun warm her face and the breeze ruffle her hair.

'You used to like going for a drive in the car,' he said at her side.

'Uh-huh. Guess I did.' She opened her eyes and smiled at him. He was sitting sideways, one arm resting along the back of the seat, looking at her with an unbelievably nostalgic expression on his face.

'I never wanted to send you away,' he said quietly. 'But Duncan said it was the right thing to do.'

All the half-submerged feelings of rejection surfaced again as she asked, 'Did you never consider saying no to Duncan?'

He shook his head. 'He was right, Amy. You were only a child, and I knew nothing about bringing up children.'

'Lizzie would have taken care of me,' she said, hardening her heart against him.

'But you had a good life in America, didn't you?'

She had to smile then. 'I had a great life there, Uncle Gif. Kate and Marty love me as if I were their own.'

'There you are, then. Duncan *was* right.'

'I suppose so.'

'Duncan was the one who persuaded me to make a will leaving everything to you. He said it would make up for sending you to America. Does it, Amy?' He tilted his head enquiringly.

'I wish I'd known the reason behind it all a long time ago,' she replied. 'It eats away at you when you get sent away and you don't know what you've done to deserve it.'

He nodded slowly and said, 'I never thought of it in that way.'

'It doesn't matter now, Uncle Gif.' She faced him, all bitterness slowly draining away from her. 'Things have a way of working out – and for me they certainly have done that.'

'Hmm.' He turned away from her and faced front again. 'That dratted clock annoys me,' he said, and with the words switched on the ignition.

She leaned forward. The hands on the clock were both on the number six. 'I think the mechanism must be broken,' she said.

He revved the engine, but the clock stayed at six-thirty.

'Damn!' He banged the dashboard with a clenched fist. 'I can't stand things that don't work properly.' He looked up and grinned at her, revved the engine again, and then, before she knew it, he'd slammed the car into gear and it was shooting off towards the main road.

'Heck!' She was jerked forward so her head very nearly hit the dashboard. 'Hey!' she cried. 'Put the brake on. Stop! We can't go out on the road; you don't have a tax disc.'

'Nonsense.' He laughed at her, exhilarated, it seemed, by the rush of air that was streaming straight at him over the low little windscreen. 'Of course it's taxed,' he yelled. 'I gave Duncan a cheque and he took it to the post office at Holborn.'

'Holborn!' She stared at him as he went straight out into the main road without even waiting to see if there was any traffic coming.

'This is London, my dear. Where else would I tax my car? I'm staying at the Bedford till Duncan moves into his new flat.'

'Uncle Gif!' she screamed as the car picked up speed and suddenly they were doing sixty along the little country road. 'Uncle Gif! Stop the car. I want to get out.'

He glanced across at her and frowned. 'Who the devil are you?'

'I'm Amy!' she cried. 'Uncle Gif – you're ill. You don't know what you're doing . . .'

'Amy . . .?' He looked at her again. 'Amy? Ah, yes. I must have been dreaming. For a moment I thought we were coming out of Russell Square.'

'We're in Derbyshire,' she gasped, hanging onto the door in her panic. Seat belts were fitted, but he was going so fast, she didn't dare let go of the door to try and locate hers.

She tried to think ahead, tried to remember if there were any traffic lights where he might have to stop or slow down. They were heading towards the town of Hatton. He'd have to stop there. He'd just have to stop if the lights were red.

He didn't. He just drove straight through them – all three sets of them – and car horns blared at him and pedestrians waved angrily.

Amy just held her breath and hung on as the speed never wavered.

But once out of Hatton, heading for the high moors, her worst fears were suddenly realized.

He was taking her towards the notorious Blackthorn Pass.

CHAPTER 29

Lizzie gazed in horror at the little green car speeding off towards the main road, then held her breath, her hand clutching at her throat as she realized it wasn't going to stop.

Her first inclination was to rush outside and yell at the top of her voice at Gif Weldon, but then she realized he wouldn't hear, with the noise of the engine and the wind rushing past like it was, making Amy's hair stream out behind her.

She waited just long enough to see which direction they would take – either right towards Hatton or left to Hawkwood. They turned right, and Lizzie wasted no more time. She ran from the living room into the tiny hall and snatched up the phone.

Richard would be at the quarry by now, and luckily Amy had jotted his mobile *and* his office and home numbers down in the address book they'd always kept lying on the table beside the phone at Wydale. Lizzie silently blessed the yellow-hats – as she called them – for thinking to bring the address book back from the Hall at the same time they brought Amy's winter coat and boots.

Richard answered at the first ring of his mobile, and Lizzie swiftly told him what had happened.

'Which way did they go?'

'Hatton,' she snapped. 'Get after them, Richard. God knows what the old man's up to now.'

'Phone the police, Lizzie.'

She nodded and said, 'Yes. I'd already decided to do that.'

'I'm on my way. They can't have got far.'

'No . . .' she sobbed, but he had already rung off.

Amy gritted her teeth and kept blinking her eyes to stop them watering in the wind that was making them sore. From time to time Gif Weldon looked at her. When he saw she was shivering, he shouted, 'Put the scarf round your neck. It will stop your hair blowing in your eyes.'

'Slow down, Uncle Gif. Please – slow down,' she pleaded.

To her surprise he did, dropping the speed from a steady sixty to around fifty as he said, 'Does that suit you?'

'Forty would be better. These roads are narrow.'

'It's a grand day, eh, Amy?'

She managed to slip her yellow scarf round her neck, hoping against hope that Lizzie had got a message to Richard. If Richard saw her scarf – even from a long way off – he'd know she was all right. And even though it was August, driving as they had been doing she'd become very cold. With a scared attempt at a laugh, she thought of the duffle coat on the table at Duncan Ward's cottage and wished she'd brought that too.

'You find something amusing, my dear?'

'Yeah!'

'Are you going to tell me?'

'I was wishing I'd brought my duffle coat.'

'Are you cold?'

'As death,' she said, then wished she hadn't said that.

374

She knew this road. Remembered it from when she'd last driven along it with Richard. In a few minutes' time they'd be able to see the steep, winding hill and the Blackthorn Ridge. At this speed he'd never make some of those bends, she thought, with a sick feeling in her stomach.

'You used to love the Blackthorn Pass,' he said, sparing a glance at her. 'When you were a little girl.'

She croaked, 'But I don't have my camera with me today, Uncle Gif. Couldn't we go back for it?'

She looked across at him and there was a twisted little smile playing around his lips. 'A good try,' he said in a cold voice. 'But it won't work, Amy.'

For a moment her heart stilled. It had been planned, she realized, this headlong flight towards the Blackthorn Pass. And now he'd made it through Hatton without being stopped he was getting complacent. That was why he'd slowed the speed. What she couldn't understand, however, was why he'd done this – lured her into the car, then driven off with her.

'Why are we going to Blackthorn?' she asked, trying to make it sound as if she hadn't got a care in the world.

'It's as good a spot as any,' he said as Blackthorn came into view.

'As good a spot as any for what?' she asked brightly. 'Are we going to have a picnic or something?'

'We did in the old days didn't we, Amy?'

She forced a smile. 'Yes.'

'I had to do something to make it up to you – for sending you away to live with Marty and that wife of his.'

'You've brought me up here today to make up for sending me away?'

'No. I didn't mean that. I meant I had to make a will leaving everything I owned to you.'

375

'You didn't have to . . .'

'Duncan said I must.'

'Good old Duncan,' she said under her breath, wishing at this moment that Duncan had kept his mouth shut. If he'd done that, this situation would never have arisen, she was sure.

The making of that fateful will seemed to be playing on Gif's mind for some reason. He turned to her again and said, 'I didn't know about Mark then, though. Nobody would have persuaded me to do anything I didn't want to do if I'd known about Mark.'

'You could still leave everything to Mark,' she said. 'If you turn round right now we could go into Hatton and find a lawyer . . .'

'I did that,' he said, picking up speed again. 'I did it yesterday.'

'So what's the problem?' she asked.

'I can't live with what I've done – and I couldn't face telling you . . .'

Her heart gave a lurch. 'Telling me what?' she asked in a faint voice.

They were climbing the winding road now, and the ground began falling away steadily beside her. She wondered if she could perhaps open the door and roll herself out, but at the speed they were travelling she knew she didn't dare risk it. If it had only been herself . . . But there was the baby to consider now. And that sheer drop down into the Blackthorn Valley could not be risked. She wouldn't stand a chance of surviving, she knew.

'I changed my will yesterday,' he said, then turned to her. The car veered to the left and onto the grass verge edging the chasm below her. She gave a little scream and flung herself at the steering wheel, her hand grasping it

376

and turning the car back onto the road.

He looked shaken and very white-faced. 'I wasn't going to tell you,' he said hoarsely. 'I didn't think I had the guts to tell you that I've left it all to Mark – with a small amount for Lizzie, of course.'

'If you weren't going to tell me – why did you bring me up here?' she asked uneasily.

'To take you with me. It will be easier that way.'

'Take me . . .'

'Over the edge,' he said in a very solemn voice. 'It will be all over in seconds, Amy, my dear.'

'No,' she said in a terrified whisper. 'Uncle Gif, no. There's no need for it.'

The car slowed again, for a particularly nasty hairpin bend. 'There's every need for it,' he said. 'I've let everybody down – you by building up your hopes that you'd one day inherit Wydale . . .'

'It doesn't matter,' she cried, tears streaming down her face. 'Uncle Gif – Wydale means nothing to me. I've got Richard and that's all I want.'

He seemed not to be listening to her. He continued in a flat voice. 'And Richard – I've let him down too. I bargained for his money to repair Wydale, and you were my bargaining power.'

'Richard doesn't care about the money he's thrown away on Wydale.' She turned to him, shouting to try and make him listen to her and to understand.

'And last of all I've let Lizzie Abercrombie down,' he said. 'Lizzie's cared for me and put up with my moods and depressions for years. I've let her down worst of all, I think, because Lizzie stuck by me when others would have walked out and told me to go to hell.'

They were rounding the tightest bend now. Amy hoped

no traffic would be coming the other way because they were still travelling far too fast for such a road. She turned round and looked behind her and caught a glimpse of a Land rover coming up fast behind them. It was too far away for her to see if it was Richard's, however, and the bend soon hid the vehicle from sight. But her spirits rose and she became determined to stall Gif Weldon for as long as she knew how.

But as they got round the bend and onto the long, almost vertical hill that led up to the vantage point where she and Richard had parked up on their way to Norfolk, right at its very summit, almost a mile away, she saw the blue flashing lights of two white police cars coming towards them.

Gif Weldon muttered, 'Lizzie Abercrombie! I might have known she'd do something like this. Why, oh, why can't that woman mind her own business?'

Amy, to her horror, saw him plunge his foot right down on the accelerator. 'Uncle Gif,' she screamed. 'Don't do this. You're not just killing me, you're killing my baby – Richard's baby . . .'

'A baby?' He glared at her in disbelief, but his foot lifted a fraction off the accelerator pedal and their speed slowed accordingly.

She nodded her head desperately. Tears poured down her cheeks. 'Don't kill my baby,' she whimpered. 'Please, Uncle Gif – don't kill my baby.'

He brought the car to a sudden, lurching stop. 'Get out,' he ordered. 'Get out of here, girl.'

She didn't stop to argue. She wrenched at the door-handle and staggered out onto the grass verge. Below her, only inches away, was a terrifying drop of two hundred feet or more. She felt herself swaying, heard the squeal of tyres on grass as the car leapt forward again. She whirled away from the edge of the precipice and saw Gif heading towards the grass verge again, fifty yards on from where he'd dropped her.

Oblivious, then, to the sound of a vehicle speeding up behind her, she began to run towards the little green open-top sports car which was bumping up and down on the grass now. She screamed at the top of her voice, 'Uncle Gif – no-o-o . . .' But it was already too late.

Wheels spinning, but with no ground to hold onto, the car went over the edge of the chasm. Blindly, Amy flung out her arms as she felt her ankle give way under her. She heard an anguished cry behind her.

'Amy . . .'

The ground dropped away and she was spinning dizzily down into the valley for a second or two, then she hit grass, and began rolling over and over, her eyes catching glimpses of a world in miniature below her – a tiny river, a pack-horse bridge, and a little green car that was whirling around in the air . . .

She clutched at grass, and when that came away in her fingers she grasped at twisted and windblown bushes that were scattered on the hillside. Cruel barbs of gorse scratched her arms and ripped at her hands as she fell. And then there was nothing but a sheer rockface rushing past her, until suddenly something knocked all the wind out of her and she found she'd stopped moving.

Gasping for breath, she was slowly able to take stock of what had broken her fall, and found it was a frail, stunted tree, growing out of a crevase in that bleak, black rock. It was a pitiful little tree, no more than a sapling, and it smelled strongly of elder. She knew then that it wouldn't hold her for long. And below, in the valley, as she carefully turned her head to look, she saw the wreckage of the little green car, smashed to pieces down by the pack-horse bridge. For some reason then, she remembered Lizzie's dream – the one of Gif Weldon standing on one side of the pack-horse bridge while she was marooned on the other.

She crouched across the little tree, one arm spread out against the rock, where her fingernails embedded themselves in a deep crack, while her other hand sought for and found the sturdiest of the tree's branches to curl itself round. She dragged her gaze away from the bottom of the valley and leaned her head sideways against the rockface, her cheek feeling the cold smoothness of it and her mind refusing to think beyond the moment.

If she once allowed herself to contemplate the hopelessness of her situation she knew she might just as well let go of her hold and allow fate to take its course. But she couldn't do that. She made herself think about Richard, and all the misery she would put him through if once she allowed panic to take over. She closed her eyes and in her mind walked with him again on a windswept shore, felt his arms around her and the warmth of his kisses as he held her close to him in the little house in Norfolk. And she knew that whatever happened now she'd known the true fulfilment of a deep and lasting love . . .

And then she heard a voice somewhere a long way above her – a voice calling her name.

'A – m – y . . .'

She tried to answer that anguished cry, but even as she drew breath to say his name the little tree creaked, and she felt a movement of its shallow roots against the face of the rock. She kept still and whimpered, only daring to move her head a little and look up to try and catch a glimpse of him.

There was no hope of that, she saw. A wide overhang of rock hid the road from her view, and she knew that the same overhang would prevent anyone up there from seeing her too.

The sound of terrible sobbing filtered down on the breeze to her, and she knew instinctively that it was Richard, who must have seen Gif's little green car down there and was now fearing the worst.

She tried again to call out to him, but her yellow wool scarf, still wrapped around her neck, muffled her voice. She heard a terrible cry above her again.

'A – m – y . . .'

'Richard . . .' she whispered – and the little tree creaked again. A long way off, she heard the wailing of a police siren, and then another sound echoed round the valley – a sound she knew well, one that had been familiar as the little helicopter had buzzed around Wydale all those weeks ago.

The helicopter came slowly up the valley, following the course of the little river. She watched as it hovered over the pack-horse bridge then wheeled away from the scene of disaster and came whirring towards her. To wave or make any sort of movement might tear the little elder tree out of the fragmented soil that held it, she knew. She could only hang on there and hope that he might see the bright speck of yellow as her scarf was ruffled by the wind stirred up by the helicopter's rotorblades. That same wind, though, she realized with horror, could so easily dislodge her from her perch.

As the cold stream of air stung her eyes she had to turn her head away towards the rockface again. Her hair fanned out around her head and the elder leaves rustled and shook against her hand. And then all was calm again as the helicopter veered swiftly away. She moved her head slowly to watch it soaring away up to the road. By its speed and the way it had expertly swung away from her, she knew he'd seen her.

Above her, she heard Richard's frantic voice shouting something, but she couldn't make out the words. Then the helicopter was back overhead, but so far up in the sky, hovering there, that not even the smallest draught of wind disturbed the little tree. He held the position, however, and she realized he was marking the spot where she was trapped for Richard.

The police car's siren was nearer now, but she knew that a police car wouldn't be equipped for such a rescue and that she might have some time to wait for a mountain rescue team to reach Blackthorn Pass. She tried to keep her eyes averted from the abyss below her, closing them as terror threatened to overcome her. Her hands were numb from clinging onto the rockface and the branch of the tree. Then something came hurtling through the air towards her and she screamed as the rope narrowly missed her.

She didn't dare reach out towards it. It was at least three feet away from her, hanging there, swaying backwards and forwards. It was a lifeline, but to lean over and try and grasp it might send her hurtling into oblivion, she knew.

She hung onto the tree, feeling cold now, and sick to her stomach. And then there was a noise just above her, where the overhang of rock had blocked her view of the road, and, carefully twisting her head, she saw the soles of a pair of boots, white with the dust of limestone ingrained in their ridges, scraping against the rock, scrambling for a foothold.

'Richard . . .' she breathed thankfully. 'Oh, Richard . . .'

'Hold on,' he said hoarsely as he braced his feet against the rock and then pushed himself off from it, so the rope that was holding him wouldn't chafe against the surface of it. And then he was hanging there beside her, grabbing hold of the first rope that had come down, looping it round her, under her arms, fastening it securely – and all in the space of a minute or less. He passed the ends of the rope round the one holding him and tied that too.

He spoke then, and there was a smile in his eyes now, replacing the intensely worried look that had been there all the time he'd been down there with her. 'If we go . . .' he glanced down into the valley '. . . we go together now, huh?'

'Heck!' she said shakily as she felt his arm go right round her and he eased her away from the tree. 'How are we going to get back?'

The siren was right above them now, and suddenly the ropes holding them began to sway alarmingly. A voice yelled down. 'Are you okay?'

Richard shouted, 'Get us up. We're okay!'

He used his body to take all the knocks from the sharp gritstone, wrapping himself around her and twisting his strong legs around hers as they were hauled with agonizing slowness up the face of the crag.

It seemed to take hours, but it couldn't have been much more than a few minutes before hands were hauling them onto the grass verge, and with Richard's help she stumbled to her feet as the ropes were loosened from about them both.

'We should get you to a doctor,' Richard said worriedly.

'I'm okay.' She leaned against him. 'I'm all right, Richard,' she said huskily.

'Lucky you had the Land Rover,' one of the police

383

officers said to Richard. 'But you shouldn't have gone over. We'd have got the mountain rescue team out – '

'It would have been too late,' Amy broke in. 'It was such a little tree that was holding me. But,' she whispered, 'what about Uncle Gif?'

'Nobody could have survived that fall – especially a frail old man like Gif Weldon,' Richard said gently.

Her hand flew to his face as they were left alone to walk back to the Land Rover. She tried to wipe away all trace of his tears, then decided instead to kiss them away. She clung to him, trembling as the realization of what had nearly happened hit her hard.

He lifted her into the Land Rover and then stood with his arms still locked round her, as if he couldn't bear to let go of her. 'Don't despise me,' he said, 'for crying like a baby when I thought I'd lost you.'

'It takes a real man to cry,' she said gently. 'And it takes love to make him do it.'

CHAPTER 30

Lizzie Abercrombie adjusted a fold of the green silk neckline of Amy's dress and carefully pinned on a small posy of flowers. 'There! That's perfect. I always loved hedgerow violets.'

'They seemed appropriate somehow, when I saw them nestling under the chapel wall at Wydale yesterday,' Amy said. 'Richard thought I was crazy, of course.'

'Richard still thinks you're crazy,' a voice said from the doorway of Amy's bedroom.

She whirled round to him and ran across the thickly carpeted floor, lifting her face for his kiss.

Lizzie grumbled, 'The groom shouldn't see the bride till they get to church, I'll have you know.'

'We're going in the same car together,' Amy said, turning to Lizzie. 'Richard could hardly keep his eyes shut all the way there, could he?'

'We – ll, I suppose not.'

Amy said, looking up at Richard, 'Anyway, you helped me choose the dress, didn't you?'

'It's perfect,' he said.

Lizzie gave a sigh. 'To you, anything would look perfect on her – even a yellow wool scarf,' she added, with meaning.

385

He laughed. 'You're right, Lizzie.' Then to Amy he said, 'There's somebody downstairs with a proposition for you.'

'A proposition?' She looked questioningly at him. 'On my wedding day?'

He lifted his eyes heavenwards and said, 'I suppose I'll have to get used to it – you being in demand all the time. Everybody's life seems to revolve around you, my girl.'

'Who is it?' Her eyes danced.

'Well, Catherine and Kim have just gone in the first car with Marty and Kate. Kate – as you've no doubt heard from the screeches and babytalk coming from the garden – has spent the last half-hour doting on her little grand-daughter. So, as Lizzie is still here with us, I'll leave it to your imagination who, of the wedding party, is left.'

She groaned. 'Mark! It has to be Mark.'

'At least I'll never be jealous of the man when that's the best welcome you can give him,' Richard said, laughing.

'What does he want?'

'Go down and see.'

'Richard! I don't want to. I want to get married.'

'We've got twenty minutes before the car comes.'

Lizzie cried triumphantly, 'Time for me to go across to my little house and measure up for curtains.'

'Oh, Lizzie!' Amy almost doubled up laughing. 'Can't you keep away? The people haven't moved out yet!'

With a hurt expression in her eyes, Lizzie said, 'They said I could pop in any time. And, anyway, they'll be gone in a fortnight – especially now they've got me as a cash buyer.'

'Thanks to Gif Weldon,' Richard said quietly.

Lizzie fumbled with a hanky and said, 'Yes. Who'd have

thought the old man would have left me fifty thousand pounds? Some of the money he inherited from that old skinflint Duncan Ward.'

'He told me he'd left you "a small amount",' Amy said.

'An understatement,' Lizzie murmured, screwing the hanky into a ball in her hand. 'It's a small fortune to me.'

'No tears today!' Richard ordered, and, giving him a watery smile, Lizzie shoved the hanky back into the pocket of her serviceable grey suit.

Amy said, 'Come down with me to Mark, Richard.'

'No.' He shook his head, suddenly solemn. 'It's you he wants.'

'Do you know why?' she asked, raising her eyebrows.

'He told me what he was going to suggest to you. He seemed to want my approval, but I told him you were a girl who'd make up her own mind.'

'This sounds very mysterious.' Amy frowned. 'Can't you give me a clue?'

'No. I'm not going to interfere in your life, my love.'

Lizzie snorted. 'You're not going to interfere? And you're going to be her husband? This I've got to see.'

Richard was patient with Lizzie. 'It's a pact I've made with myself,' he said, 'And Amy knows how I feel. After today she won't *just* be Mrs Richard Boden – she'll still be Amy, a girl with her own mind and with her own reasons for what she does with her life. We'll be man and wife but still two separate entities, with likes and dislikes that won't always run parallel.'

He held out his hand to Amy, and she placed her own in it and said, 'I'll shake on that, Richard.'

'Well!' Lizzie looked taken aback, then she quickly recovered herself to say, 'I shouldn't be surprised, I suppose – Miss Amy blew into Wydale like a breath of fresh air. She sure changed a lot of my ways of thinking; I know that.'

Amy squeezed Richard's hand. 'I'll go down and see Mark,' she said. 'But come and rescue me after five minutes, won't you?'

Mark Powell had come complete with camera. 'No!' she said as she marched across the lawn to him. 'This I do not believe. Can't you even come to a wedding without that damn camera?'

'You don't expect me to pay for those cosy-cosy snaps that your professional wedding guy will take of you, do you?' he asked, giving her a chance to see that too often hidden smile of his.

'What are you expecting?' she asked sweetly. 'Do you think I might pour a glass of champagne over the best man's head or something?'

'Hey! I'm the guy who saved your life, remember?' he said.

'You nearly blew me off the side of the mountain with your chopper blades.' Her laughter rang out, then her face softened. 'I never did get the chance to thank you, Mark . . .'

'Oh, hell. Don't go all sloppy on me,' he stormed. 'If we're going to hate each other's guts, let's make a good job of it, huh? Even if I did do you out of a couple of million pounds – ' he grinned ' – let's have no hard feelings?'

'Everything I want is here,' she said quietly, looking round the peaceful garden.

'But Wydale isn't within your grasp, is it?'

'Heck! What good is Wydale now?'

'It *can* be saved,' he said. 'That's what I want to talk to you about. I've had a team of surveyors up there. It's going to cost the earth, but I'm going ahead with it.

'You're mad.'

'Maybe, but look – let's go over and sit under that apple tree for a couple of minutes.' He walked over to a bench that Richard had told her he'd carved himself, many years ago, from the trunk of a fallen oak, sat down and waited for her to join him.

She walked slowly across the grass and sat beside him, halffacing him. 'Make it quick,' she said. 'I have a real pressing engagement in about fifteen minutes.'

'You look the part – a thoroughly modern bride. Nobody I know would have chosen that stunning shade of green to be married in.'

'I didn't want to look like a Christmas tree fairy, and I can't abide long frocks. I only ever had one – and I tripped up over it and broke my nose.'

'I'm not interested in your nose,' he said, with some impatience. 'I'm interested in your mind. Your brain. Your expertise.'

'My what?'

'Your expertise with a camera.'

'Hey! I don't possess any expertise with a camera.'

'Lizzie lent me a video film you'd left lying around at Wydale,' he said. 'You're a natural.'

'A natural for what, Powell?' she asked, looking at her watch.

'I'm going to turn Wydale into a museum and field centre,' he said. 'When the house is put to rights again, I'm handing it over to the new Arts Centre that has its headquarters in Hatton. And I want you to be in charge of it.'

She held up a hand. 'Hey – you're going too fast.'

'I have less than fifteen minutes to persuade you to come in on this,' he said. 'I've got to go fast.'

'What do I have to do?' she asked.

'Just be there. I want a photographic gallery up and running straight away – and not just stills. That's where you'll score – you're good at scene-setting, good with a video camera. I want to attract people to Wydale, and that means we have to have something visual to get the project off the ground.'

Interested, against her better judgement, Amy felt a sense of excitement rising in her.

'Are you with me? I tried to sound Richard out this morning, but he wouldn't commit himself until I'd talked with you.'

'Is it Richard you want for this venture – or me?' she asked sharply.

'You, of course.'

'Richard's good with alabaster – did you know that? What are you planning for the old chapel?'

He frowned. 'I hadn't got round to that,' he admitted. 'Any ideas?'

'Millions,' she said, getting to her feet and laughing down at him. 'Millions and millions, Mark.'

'You're with me in this, then?'

'So long as it doesn't take me away from my home, my husband and my family too much,' she said.

'Family, huh?'

She grinned at him as he rose from the bench and walked alongside her back to the house. Richard met them at the door.

'You two look pretty pleased with yourselves,' he said.

'Richard – I'm saying yes. Is that okay with you?'

'You know you don't have to ask,' he said, but his smile told her she'd done the right thing.

'I'll get off to the wedding, then,' Mark said. 'See you in church, people! I'm giving Lizzie a lift, so I'd best be off.'

When they were alone, Richard said, 'I've got something to show you.'

Surprised, she asked, 'What is it? Do we have time, Richard?'

'It'll only take a minute.' He began to walk to the far end of the garden, then turned and beckoned and said, 'Come on, slowcoach. That car will be here before we know it.'

She ran lightly across the grass and caught up with him, slipping her hand through his arm.

'This is very Mr and Mrs,' he said, dropping a kiss on her forehead as she looked up at him.

'What is?'

'Your hand through my arm.'

'What Mark would call a cosy-cosy picture.' She laughed.

He stopped at one of the flowerbeds and crouched down, pulling her down beside him.

'The rose,' he said, pointing.

She drew in her breath and said, 'It's flowered. Richard, it actually has a flower on it.'

'Kip Weldon's rose.' He turned his head and looked at her. 'I knew you'd be glad – but, like I told Lizzie a few minutes ago, no tears. Not today.'

She looked at the single white rose for several seconds, then stood up again, and he was beside her as she said, 'Lizzie once talked about time eating away at the stones of Wydale – she said it was sometimes best to let things be.'

'Lizzie's usually right,' he said.

391

They turned their backs on the little rose tree and walked back to the house. Lizzie and Mark Powell were walking down the long passage towards the front door and Lizzie turned round as she heard the footsteps behind them.

'We're off now!' Lizzie grinned. 'I sure am looking forward to this.'

Mark bent down and picked something up off the floor, then turned round too, and handed one of the two articles to Lizzie. 'You'll need this,' he said.

Amy's hand flew to her lips. 'Oh, no!'

Lizzie glared at her. 'What's wrong with you, missy?' she asked as she glanced in the hall mirror and stuck the bright blue crash helmet on her grey frizzy curls, then fastened the strap firmly, and with expert ease, under her chin.

'You're not going to my wedding on . . .'

Lizzie grinned. 'Mr Powell's kindly offered to give me a lift,' she said. 'And in the absence of that 1950s-style Ariel Roadster I always hankered after, I think his Harley Davidson will suit me just fine!'

THE EXCITING NEW NAME IN WOMEN'S FICTION!

PLEASE HELP ME TO HELP YOU!

Dear *Scarlet* Reader,

As Editor of *Scarlet* Books I want to make sure that the books I offer you every month are up to the high standards *Scarlet* readers expect. And to do that I need to know a little more about you and your reading likes and dislikes. So please spare a few minutes to fill in the short questionnaire on the following pages and send it to me. I'll send *you* a surprise gift as a thank you!

Looking forward to hearing from you,

Sally Cooper

Editor-in-Chief, *Scarlet*

P.S. Only one offer per household.

QUESTIONNAIRE

Please tick the appropriate boxes to indicate your answers

1 Where did you get this Scarlet title?

Bought in Supermarket ☐

Bought at W H Smith ☐

Bought at book exchange or second-hand shop ☐

Borrowed from a friend ☐

Other _____

2 Did you enjoy reading it?

A lot ☐   A little ☐   Not at all ☐

3 What did you particularly like about this book?

Believable characters ☐   Easy to read ☐

Good value for money ☐   Enjoyable locations ☐

Interesting story ☐   Modern setting ☐

Other _____

4 What did you particularly dislike about this book?

_____

5 Would you buy another Scarlet book?

Yes ☐   No ☐

6 What other kinds of book do you enjoy reading?

Horror ☐   Puzzle books ☐   Historical fiction ☐

General fiction ☐   Crime/Detective ☐   Cookery ☐

Other _____

7 Which magazines do you enjoy most?

Bella ☐   Best ☐   Woman's Weekly ☐

Woman and Home ☐   Hello ☐   Cosmopolitan ☐

Good Housekeeping ☐

Other _____

And now a little about you –

8 How old are you?
Under 25 ☐   25–34 ☐   35–44 ☐
45–54 ☐   55–64 ☐   over 65 ☐

9 What is your marital status?
Single ☐   Married/living with partner ☐
Widowed ☐   Separated/divorced ☐

10 What is your current occupation?
Employed full-time ☐   Employed part-time ☐
Student ☐   Housewife full-time ☐
Unemployed ☐   Retired ☐

11 Do you have children? If so, how many and how old are they?
_____
_____

12 What is your annual household income?
under £10,000 ☐   £10–20,000 ☐   £20–30,000 ☐
£30–40,000 ☐   over £40,000 ☐

Miss/Mrs/Ms _____
Address _____
_____
_____
_____

Thank you for completing this questionnaire. Now tear it out – put it in an envelope and send it before 31 March 1997, to:

Sally Cooper; Editor-in-Chief

SCARLET
FREEPOST LON 3335
LONDON W8 4BR
Please use block capitals for address.
No stamp is required!   MASOL/9/96

***Scarlet* titles coming next month:**

SUMMER OF FIRE – Jill Sheldon
When Noah Taylor and Annie Laverty meet again, they are instantly attracted to each other. Unfortunately, because of his insecure childhood, Noah doesn't believe in love, while Annie has trouble coming to terms with her terrifying past. It takes a 'summer of fire' to finally bring Annie and Noah together . . . forever.

DEVLIN'S DESIRE – Margaret Callaghan
Devlin Winter might *think* he can stroll back into Holly Scott's life and take up where he left off – but Holly has other ideas! No longer the fragile innocent Dev seduced with his charm and sexual expertise, Holly is a woman to be reckoned with. Dev, though, won't take 'no' for an answer, and he tells Holly: 'You're mine. You've always been mine and you'll always *be* mine!'

INTOXICATING LADY – Barbara Stewart
Happy in her work and determined never to fall in love, Danielle can't understand what Kingsley Hunter wants from her. One minute, he is trying to entice her into his bed . . . the next he seems to hate her! 'Revenge is sweet' they say . . . but Danielle, Kingsley's 'intoxicating lady', has to convince him that passionate love is even sweeter.

STARSTRUCK – Lianne Conway
'Even ice-cold with indifference, Fergus Hann's eyes demand attention' and they make Layne Denham realize an awful truth! To be starstruck as a film fan is fun . . . but to be starstruck in real life is asking for trouble . . with a capital 'T' for Temptation.